The Best American Mystery Stories 2019

The Best American Mystery Stories™ 2019

Edited and with an Introduction
by **Jonathan Lethem**

Otto Penzler, Series Editor

Mariner Books

HOUGHTON MIFFLIN HARCOURT

BOSTON • NEW YORK   2019

hmhbooks.com

ISSN 1094-8384 (print)   ISSN 2573-3907 (e-book)

ISBN 978-1-328-63609-6 (print)   ISBN 978-1-328-63611-9 (e-book)

Printed in the United States of America
DOC 10 9 8 7 6 5 4 3 2 1

"Coach O" by Robert Hinderliter. First published in *New Ohio Review*, no. 24. Copyright © 2018 by Robert Hinderliter. Reprinted by permission of Robert Hinderliter.

"The Keepers of All Sins" by Sharon Hunt. First published in *Alfred Hitchcock Mystery Magazine*, November/December 2018. Copyright © 2018 by Sharon Hunt. Reprinted by permission of Sharon Hunt.

"Open House" by Reed Johnson. First published in *Ellery Queen Mystery Magazine*, November/December 2018. Copyright © 2018 by Reed Johnson. Reprinted by permission of Reed Johnson.

"A Damn Fine Town" by Arthur Klepchukov. First published in *Down & Out: The Magazine*, vol. 1, no. 4. Copyright © 2018 by Arthur Klepchukov. Reprinted by permission of Arthur Klepchukov.

"The Walk-In" by Harley Jane Kozak. First published in *For the Sake of the Game*. Copyright © 2018 by Harley Jane Kozak. Reprinted by permission of the author.

"Top Ten Vacation Selfies of YouTube Stars" by Preston Lang. First published in *Deadlines: A Tribute to William E. Wallace*. Copyright © 2018 by Preston Lang. Reprinted by permission of Preston Lang.

Contents

Foreword

Plus ça change, plus c'est la meme chose. For *The Best American Mystery Stories* series, it's true: the more it changes, the more it stays the same.

When the series began in 1997, the guest editor was Robert B. Parker. I was the series editor. This year the guest editor is Jonathan Lethem. I'm still the series editor.

The mission back then was to try to read every mystery story published by an American or Canadian in 1996, and more than five hundred stories were examined in order to find the twenty best. For this edition, the mission remained precisely the same—but more than three thousand stories were examined.

A primary source for great crime fiction was the specialty magazines (*Ellery Queen Mystery Magazine* and *Alfred Hitchcock Mystery Magazine*), a handful of mystery anthologies, literary journals, and popular consumer magazines such as *The New Yorker* and *The Atlantic*. Today those publications are still a treasure trove of stories suitable for being collected in *The Best American Mystery Stories*, but other mystery magazines have been created (notably *The Strand* and the rebirth of *Black Mask*), the modest number of anthologies has mushroomed into scores, mostly from small publishers, and electronic magazines (e-zines), of which I was unaware in 1996, have drawn some highly talented authors to their sites.

The look of the books in this series remains largely unchanged twenty-three years later, but the hardcover editions have been abandoned to be replaced with electronic editions. Additionally, the original publisher was Houghton Mifflin and, after a merger, it is now Houghton Mifflin Harcourt. You (and I) would barely notice the difference in the books, because there is none.

Are these changes good or bad? Both, but mostly good. I lament the passing of the great Dr. Parker, as well as the loss of the next three guest editors: Sue Grafton, Evan Hunter (Ed McBain), and Donald E. Westlake. (Thankfully, the others appear to be in good health, still writing their popular and acclaimed books.) Examining literally thousands of stories is a huge challenge for Michele Slung, my invaluable colleague, who did all the preliminary reading then and still does; without her, this series could not exist, as I am such a slow reader that I practically move my lips when I read. The disappointment is that so many e-zines do not produce fully edited stories, some of which have unrealized potential.

There is, however, lots of good news, not least of which is that the distinguished publishing house of Houghton Mifflin Harcourt continues the series and supports it with outstanding attention to detail (I don't think I've ever seen a typo, to mention one element) and keeps most of the backlist in print.

The expanding numbers of small independent publishers can only be seen as a good thing. The optimism of starting a new business, particularly in an area that has minuscule profit margins, must be applauded.

Although the percentage of people in America who read books for pleasure remains below 50, more independent bookshops have opened than closed for six consecutive years, which warms the heart.

Enough! Time to get down to the reason you purchased this book. As seems to be true on an annual basis, this is a superb collection of original fiction about extremes of human behavior caused by despair, hate, greed, fear, envy, insanity, or love—sometimes in combination. Desperate people may be prone to desperate acts, a fertile ground for poor choices. Many of the authors in this cornucopia of crime have described how aberrant solutions to difficult situations may occur, and why perpetrators felt that their violent responses to conflicts seemed appropriate to them.

The psychology of crime has become the dominant form of mystery fiction in recent years, while the classic tale of observation and deduction has faded further into the background. Those tales of pure detection may be the most difficult mystery stories to write, as it has become increasingly difficult to find original motivations for murder, or a new murder method, or an original way to hide a vital clue until the detective unearths it. The working definition of a mystery story for this series is any work of fiction in which a crime, or the threat of a crime, is central to the theme or the plot. The detective story is merely one subgenre in the literary form known as the mystery, just as are romantic suspense, espionage, legal legerdemain, medical thriller, political duplicity, and stories told from the point of view of the villain.

As Michele reads the enormous number of submissions, she passes along those worthy of consideration, after which I select the fifty best (or at least those I liked best) to send to the guest editor, who selects the twenty that are then collected and reprinted, the other thirty being listed in an honor roll as "Other Distinguished Mystery Stories."

The guest editor this year is Jonathan Lethem, the outstanding author of *The Feral Detective*. His first novel, *Gun, with Occasional Music*, published twenty-five years ago, successfully combined elements of science fiction and detective fiction. After publishing three more science fiction novels, he published *Motherless Brooklyn*, a successful National Book Critics Circle Award winner. His next book, *The Fortress of Solitude*, became a *New York Times* bestseller. In 2005 he received a MacArthur Fellowship.

This is an appropriate time (it's *always* an appropriate time) to thank the previous guest editors, who have done so much to make this prestigious series such a resounding success: Robert B. Parker, Sue Grafton, Ed McBain, Donald E. Westlake, Lawrence Block, James Ellroy, Michael Connelly, Nelson DeMille, Joyce Carol Oates, Scott Turow, Carl Hiaasen, George Pelecanos, Jeffery Deaver, Lee Child, Harlan Coben, Robert Crais, Lisa Scottoline, Laura Lippman, James Patterson, Elizabeth George, John Sandford, and Louise Penny.

While I engage in a relentless quest to locate and read every mystery/crime/suspense story published, I live in terror that I will miss a worthy story, so if you are an author, editor, or publisher, or care about one, please feel free to send a book, magazine, or tearsheet to me c/o The Mysterious Bookshop, 58 Warren Street, New York, NY 10007. If the story first appeared electronically, you must submit a hard copy. It is vital to include the author's contact information. No unpublished material will be considered for what should be obvious reasons. No material will be returned. If you distrust the postal service, enclose a self-addressed, stamped postcard.

To be eligible, a story must have been written by an American or Canadian and first published in an American or Canadian publication in the calendar year 2019. The earlier in the year I receive the story, the more fondly I regard it. For reasons known only to the dunderheads who wait until Christmas week to submit a story published the previous spring, holding eligible stories for months before submitting them occurs every year, causing seething anger while I read a stack of stories while my friends are trimming the Christmas tree or otherwise celebrating the holiday season. It had better be a damned good story if you do this.

Because of the very tight production schedule for this book, the absolute firm deadline is December 31. If the story arrives one day later, it will not be read. This is neither an arrogant nor a whimsical deadline. The tight schedule was established twenty-three years ago and it's the only way to get the book published on time. I'm certain you understand.

                                                                           O.P.

Introduction

AS A KID, one who'd begun to want to write fiction by the time I was eleven or twelve, the first professional author I knew personally was Stanley Ellin, a master of the American crime short story. This was dumb luck for me—happenstance. Stan Ellin was one of the elders of the Brooklyn Friends Meeting—Quakers, as they're colloquially called—a religious institution to which my father began taking me for Sunday school around that time.

Stan was a native of Brooklyn, a former steelworker and shipyard worker and army veteran who'd self-educated as a writer by immersing himself in the storytelling classics like Robert Louis Stevenson, Guy de Maupassant, and Edgar Allan Poe. Among fellow writers he was celebrated for his subtlety and perfectionism, his measured craft. Never particularly famous in the wider culture, Stan was treasured in the field. He collected a few Edgars, was the president of the Mystery Writers of America, saw his works filmed a few times, and galvanized everyone who knew him personally with his integrity, fierce attentiveness, and droll charisma. When at some point in my teenage years I declared to Stan my intention to become a published writer, he encouraged me—barely. "Keep writing," he told me. Simple words.

Though he wrote remarkable and beguiling novels in a number of different modes—detective novels, urban noirs, Hitchcockian wide-screen chase thrillers—Stan's greatest accomplishment was in the art of the short story, and the yearly appearance of a new Ellin story in *Ellery Queen's Mystery Magazine* (he rarely managed more than one a year) was considered an event in the field. It took

me a long time to realize how lucky I was to read Stan's stories so
early on, since he was the writer in plain sight for me, my parents'
friend and a local fixture, the fellow who somewhat scandalized his
fellow Quakers with the darkness and sexuality in his late novels,
particularly *Mirror, Mirror on the Wall* and *Stronghold*.

Yet he was also, truly, a marvel. A wizard. Stan's story "The Question" remains one of the most acute and terrifying short stories I
know, a study in complicity and implication that permanently illu-
minated my sense not only of what fiction can do but of what wal-
lows in the recesses of the human psyche. "The Question" features
an unrepeatable twist, but that was Stan's signature: no two of his
stories make the same moves. Like those of his models, Stevenson
and Poe (and in some ways similar to those of international masters
like Julio Cortázar and Jorge Luis Borges), each of Stan Ellin's tales
is singular, a tour de force.

I realize I'm describing stories that don't appear in the anthology in your hands. You can seek out Stanley Ellin's fiction now,
or not. You can also skip this introduction, since that's one of the
main things introductions are for. I'll at least explain: when Otto
Penzler, who was Stan's great friend and supporter as well as editor
and publisher, asked me to consider selecting the stories for this
year's collection, the first thing I warned him of was that I'd want to
make the introduction a tribute to Stanley Ellin. Thankfully, Otto
didn't blink.

Stan helped make me the person who'd be invited into this remarkable situation—not only a lifetime of reading and writing
stories, of understanding how fiction can sustain a life and world-
view, but of being invited by Otto to delve into the riches of the
present version of the crime and mystery field and work with him
on putting together this roster of remarkable stories. I'm not ex-
clusively a crime writer (let alone a "mystery" writer, since I always
forget to put in clues), and some people might say that my sporadic
visitations to the role—three novels featuring detectives, in three
different decades—makes me a wonky choice for presiding over
this book.

I'm glad Otto didn't think so. One of the things I love most
about the present state of the crime field—or *genre*, that slippery
word—is how much its boundaries have expanded and shifted,
so that it has in certain ways engulfed and been engulfed by our
larger understanding of what stories and novels are and what they

can and should do. And yet (here's the paradoxical part), much like the cousin fields of SF and fantasy and romance, the crime and mystery field remains a splendid affiliation, a community of obsession—perhaps an example of what Kurt Vonnegut called a "karass." A family created by devotion.

Both sides of that coin are on view in the stories in this book: the strengths of a conversation within a self-defined community and the integration of its themes and motifs into literature—into the art of fiction—more widely. It's nice not to have to choose between these things! This recent editorial journey, this immersion in the present tense of the field, has caused me to discover just how vital and diverse and happily contradictory the variations within a so-called genre can be. An anthology, at its best, reproduces a fundamental condition of any field of art or literature: that it is, always, greater than the sum of its parts.

Crime and mystery are essential to storytelling not only because of the truism—a true truism—that every story that captivates your interest is at some level a mystery. Yes, mystery lurks in language, in narrative, just as it lurks in the human heart. But it's also the case that the specific do-wronging of one person or persons to another, and the impulse to explore or expose or make right the do-wronging, is the world we're born to, the life we live, however unnerving it is to dwell on it. Crime stories are deep species gossip. They're fundamentally stories of power, of its exercise both spontaneous and conspiratorial; stories of impulse and desire, and of the turning of tables. Crime stories allegorize the tensions in our self-civilizing, a process that's never finished. (If I were a biblical guy I'd say this has been true "since Cain and Abel," but since *Alice in Wonderland* is my bible I'll say "since the tarts were stolen and Tweedledum and Tweedledee strapped on their armor.") How can we not hang on their outcomes? Will injustice prevail? Might the oppressed outwit the powerful? Are we innocent ourselves, or complicit?

Turn these pages, and find out.

JONATHAN LETHEM

The Best American Mystery Stories 2019

ROBERT HINDERLITER

Coach O

FROM *New Ohio Review*

COACH OBERMAN WATCHED from his office window as a group of students prepared the bonfire by the south end zone. Two kids stacked tinder while another knelt beside a papier-mâché buffalo they would throw on the fire at the end of the pep rally. Oberman couldn't wait to watch it burn.

He'd just gotten off the phone with Mike Treadwell—coach of the Ashland Buffaloes—who'd called to wish him luck in tomorrow's game. Mike had been Oberman's assistant for three years before taking the job at Ashland High. And now, after back-to-back state titles in his first two years, he'd been offered the defensive coordinator position at Emporia State University. This would be the last time they'd face off.

"I'll miss seeing you across the field," Mike had said. "Although I sure won't miss trying to stop that Oberman offense."

This was pandering bullshit. In their two head-to-head contests, Mike's Buffaloes had routed Oberman's Hornets by at least four touchdowns.

"I just wanted to say thanks," Mike had said. "I couldn't have gotten this far without you."

He'd said it like he meant it, with no hint of sarcasm, but Oberman knew there was venom behind those words. In Mike's two years as assistant, Oberman had treated him badly. Mike had a good mind for the game, there was no denying that, but he was a scrawny wuss with thick glasses and a girlish laugh. He didn't belong on a football field. Oberman had banished him to working with the punter and made him the butt of jokes in front of the players. When Mike's brother-in-law became superintendent at Ashland and handed Mike the coaching job, Oberman had scoffed. And now Mike was moving on to a Division II college while Oberman was stuck muddling through another losing season with an eight-man team in Haskerville. He knew the irony wasn't lost on either of them.

Oberman picked up a playbook from his desk and flipped through it. In his seventeen years as head coach of the Hornets, the playbook hadn't changed much—mostly I-formation offense heavy on power runs and quick play-action passes. And in his first few years, those plays had been good enough to keep Haskerville near the top of the standings, even winning a couple regional titles.

After that, however, the program had gone downhill, bottoming out with a 2–8 record in '01 and hovering around .500 ever since. The plays weren't to blame. In a little Kansas town where cows nearly outnumbered people, he just didn't have enough decent athletes. He'd whipped his group of dimwitted farmer boys into shape as best he could, but it would still take a miracle to beat Ashland. He'd need to think of a genius game plan, something to put Mike in his place one last time.

Oberman dropped the playbook, grabbed his jacket, and stepped out of his office into the locker room. He took a deep breath of sweat, steam, and jockstraps, then made his way through the empty gym to the rear exit. Outside, a few of his players were milling around the field, either tossing a football or lounging on the bleachers watching the cheerleaders run through their routine. The pep rally would start soon. Oberman walked out to the sideline and stood there, hands on his hips, until a voice from the bleachers called his name.

"Coach O!"

It was his quarterback, Javi Esteban, sitting alone on the bottom row. He had a two-liter bottle of Pepsi gripped in one meaty hand and the other raised in a wave. Oberman stepped over.

"You sticking around for the fire, Coach?"

"Guess I am."

"Wanna throw a ball around?"

With his round cheeks and fleshy arms, Javi was built more like a trombonist than a quarterback. But he was nimble for his size, and strong. He could sidestep a charging defender and launch the ball fifty yards downfield with the flick of his wrist. When he was on his game, he had D-II talent, maybe even D-I. Oberman had already fielded a few calls from recruiters.

Javi was a quiet kid, with a sadness in his eyes even on the rare occasions he smiled. He didn't have much to smile about. His dad had lost both legs in Iraq, and his little sister had cerebral palsy. He worked weekends at the putt-putt course across from the cemetery. Football seemed to be the one bright spot in Javi's life, and he especially liked Oberman. After practice, he'd stay to help Oberman put away equipment. Sometimes they'd talk, but usually they just worked together in silence. It was at these times, Oberman thought, that Javi seemed most at peace. He liked the kid, but now he was in no mood to play catch.

"I've got to do some thinking, Javi. Save that arm for tomorrow."

"Okay, Coach. I'll be ready!"

As Oberman walked away down the sideline, he shook his head and cursed. Javi's eyes had been red, his gaze unsteady. That Pepsi bottle was probably a quarter full of vodka.

He'd been aware of Javi's drinking for two weeks now. Kids were kids, and he didn't begrudge them a few beers on the weekend, but one day Javi had looked wobbly in practice, a half-beat slow on all his reads, and Oberman had smelled liquor on his breath. He'd debated whether to say something, but the next day Javi was sharp, zipping the ball to his receivers, so Oberman held his tongue.

And then during last Friday's game, Javi threw three interceptions against the Willow Creek Muskrats—the winless, perpetually bottom-feeding Willow Creek Muskrats—including a first quarter pick-six that put the Hornets in an early hole. He looked dazed and sloppy. Oberman pulled him aside at halftime and asked him if he was fit to play. Javi insisted he was fine, and in the second half they came back and won, thanks mainly to their running game and defense, but the near-disaster cost Oberman a sleepless night mulling over what to do.

The following day, Saturday afternoon, he'd gone to Javi's house. He'd planned to talk with the family, make them aware of the situation so they could rein in the problem before it got worse. In the Estebans' living room, Javi's mom offered him store-bought cookies while Mr. Esteban sat scowling in his wheelchair, clearly drunk. Javi's little sister, Mia, sat on the floor watching a cartoon. She smiled up shyly at Oberman, skinny arms twisted across her chest. Javi, white-faced in the corner, looked at Oberman with such

panic and pleading in his eyes that Oberman couldn't bring himself to mention the alcohol. And the whole next week in practice,
Javi had been focused. Oberman had thought the problem was behind them. But now here was Javi tonight with the two-liter.

He'd have to say something. He couldn't afford another shaky
performance out of his quarterback, especially against Ashland.
There was too much on the line.

Earlier that day he'd been coldly reminded of how much was
on the line when the superintendent, Bob DiMarco, had called
him out to the district office for a chat. He'd lectured Oberman
about how a winning football team really brings the community together, lifts the spirits of the whole town. He was sure Oberman remembered what that felt like, all those years ago. It wasn't a threat,
exactly. Oberman had been the football coach and PE teacher at
Haskerville High for seventeen years now, and he doubted they'd
fire him even if he never won another game.

Still, it pissed him off that DiMarco thought he needed a pep
talk. The football team meant more to Oberman than anything.
His pride as a man, his sense of self-worth—it was all out there on
the field. Every day in practice he shouted himself hoarse, whipped
lazy blockers in the helmet with his whistle, and got down in the
mud with his players to show them proper technique. He didn't
need some bureaucratic prick telling him football was important.

The sun was falling behind the pine-tree shelterbelt surrounding the field. A faint clack and low hum sounded as the floodlights
came on and started to warm up. Oberman walked across the field,
cutting a wide arc around the cheerleaders. It had rained that
morning, and the grass was spongy under his feet. The field smelled
clean and earthy, and as he stopped at the 50-yard line and looked
from end zone to end zone, he thought of all the hours he'd spent
on football fields—all the joy, camaraderie, and lessons the sport
had given him over the years. He'd been playing or coaching since
he was eight years old. His happiest memories were all related to
football. He'd even been one of those clowns who proposed to his
girlfriend on the field. That had been his senior year at Fort Hays
State, when he ran up in the stands after the last home game of the
season, grabbed his girlfriend's hand, led her down to the sideline,
and knelt on one knee. Her name was Sandra, and they'd been
married now for eighteen years.

Remembering that moment—the giddiness he'd felt as he

loosened the tape from his ankle where he'd hidden the ring, the clamor of excitement through the crowd as they realized what was happening, Sandra's hand to her mouth, already sobbing and nodding before he could even say the words—remembering that moment made Oberman queasy. A great yawning cavity opened in his chest.

He'd found out last weekend that she'd been seeing Lonny Hinkle, the Haskerville High English teacher.

The past Saturday, after he'd come back from the Estebans' house, Sandra told him she wanted to have a girls' night with her old college roommate, Maisley. Maisley was living in Lawrence now, working in the provost's office at KU, and every few months Sandra would drive up to meet her for a movie and margaritas. She would crash on Maisley's couch and drive back to Haskerville the next day. Usually they'd plan their get-togethers a few weeks in advance, but Oberman knew Sandra had been stressed lately, dealing with her mom's dementia, so he told her to go ahead and have fun, and he would take care of Ruth.

Ruth had been living with them for three years since her diagnosis, but in the past few months she'd taken a sharp turn for the worse. She was always talking about trolls. They were everywhere, she said—their red eyes peeking out from air vents or under the couch. They wanted to tear her to pieces. Oberman and Sandra had to constantly reassure her that she was safe, that trolls weren't real. And so he'd understood Sandra's desire for a night away.

The following morning, before Sandra came home, Oberman got a call from his brother in Dodge City.

"Were you guys in Dodge last night?" his brother said. "I was dropping off Ashley at around one a.m., and I swear I saw Sandra coming out of that bar by the China Chow. But she was with this tall bald guy. It looked like he was wearing a scarf. You know anything about that?"

Oberman told his brother he was crazy, that Sandra had been home all night. And then he hung up, locked himself in the bedroom, and pulled out his hunting rifle from the back of the closet. Hands shaking, he took the gun from its case and laid it on the bed.

Could it be true? Was Sandra cheating on him? In the past year she'd started acting strange—trying a vegan diet, listening to New Age music, and reading books about spirituality and emotional detoxing. It'd left Oberman baffled and annoyed. At one point he'd told her that if he had to listen to one more second of that god-damn sitar, he'd throw the CD player out the window. He winked when he'd said it, but they'd been at odds since Ruth moved in, and maybe he'd been ignoring warning signs for a while. "I feel like I'm on the verge of a great transformation," she'd told him recently. At the time, Oberman had just rolled his eyes. Now, though, he wondered if her transformation involved Lonny Hinkle.

Hinkle had come to Haskerville two years ago from somewhere in the Northeast—Connecticut, maybe, or Vermont. He was in his mid-thirties, still single, and wore that red scarf nine months out of the year like a European dandy. Oberman had suspected he might be gay until a rumor came through the teachers' lounge that he'd moved to Kansas to escape a chaotic love triangle with the principal and home-ec teacher at his last school. In their few conversations, Hinkle had bored Oberman senseless with talk of animal welfare. He'd apparently adopted three rescue dogs and was trying to set up a regional ASPCA chapter. Sandra had recently started volunteering at the local animal shelter. That must've been where they'd met. Maybe, Oberman thought, they were in Dodge on some sort of humanitarian mission—saving a dog from an abusive home or scoping out a suspected exotic animal smuggler. Sandra had a big heart. He loved that about her, and he loved that ridiculous sweater she wore with a corgi on it, tighter than she realized. Made her look nineteen. And anyway, this wouldn't be the first time she'd forgotten to tell him about some volunteer activity. But as he stared at the rifle on his bed, his mind whirled with dark thoughts.

Oberman walked off the field, sat on the front row of the empty visitors' bleachers, and watched the stands on the home side slowly fill with people. All HHS teachers were expected to attend, but so far Hinkle hadn't showed. He wouldn't dare. Most of the other teachers had arrived, along with several dozen students and a few of the team's most ardent supporters. It wasn't like it used to be. Back when they were at the top of the league, half the town turned up for pep rallies, and game days brought out Hornets flags in every yard and motivational signs on every store window. These days no one could seem to muster much spirit. DiMarco was right.

When he'd gotten the call from DiMarco to come to the District Office, Oberman didn't think the meeting would be about football. In the aftermath of hearing about Sandra and Hinkle, he'd made a poor decision.

At least he hadn't shot anyone. In fact, by the time Sandra came home on Sunday, the rifle was back in the closet. He didn't say a thing. At practice and during games he was all snarling intensity, but off the field he couldn't stand conflict. In eighteen years of marriage, he'd never struck Sandra, never torn into her with hateful words, and never touched another woman. All Sunday he avoided her, sitting in the den with the Chiefs game on, thinking about what to do.

And then on Monday morning, when the teachers' lounge was empty, he put a bullet in Hinkle's mailbox on top of a sticky note that said END IT. But the janitor saw it first, and soon all the school employees were gathered in the lounge along with the police, who were saying that whoever put the bullet in the box could be charged with aggravated assault. Hinkle was white as a ghost, and no one would look at Oberman.

That's where things stood. So far the police hadn't talked to Oberman. That must mean Hinkle had played dumb when they questioned him. He wasn't ready to admit the affair. But that could change any moment if his fear began to outweigh his shame. And even if Hinkle kept his mouth shut, Oberman wasn't out of the woods. He'd written the note in blocky caps, but he hadn't thought to wipe the bullet before leaving it in the box.

There was also the question of how much other people knew. Had the other teachers really been avoiding Oberman's gaze when the police came, or was it just his imagination? The timing of Di-Marco's meeting had been suspicious, but the conversation hadn't strayed from football. Or was that in itself a sign that DiMarco was on to him? Wouldn't it be natural to bring up the big event from earlier in the week? Oberman's students were of course aware there'd been a major commotion on Monday, but their jokes and wild speculations made it clear they hadn't connected anything to him. So it was mainly DiMarco he'd been worried about, and possibly the other teachers, until the call today from Mike Treadwell.

It had only been a small comment at the end of their conversation. "By the way," Mike had said, "say hi to Sandra for me."

It could've been innocuous. Like everything else Mike had said, the tone had been friendly. But in his two years as assistant coach, he'd had only the briefest of interactions with Sandra. They might've exchanged a few pleasantries after a game or during a chance encounter at the grocery store, but certainly not enough to expect Oberman to pass on a greeting. Had a rumor reached Ashland? Had Mike heard about the affair, or maybe even seen Hinkle and Sandra together? There'd been a long pause on the phone before Oberman replied, "Sure thing," and quickly ended the call.

At the time he'd decided to give Mike the benefit of the doubt, convinced himself he was overthinking things. But now that he'd given the comment time to simmer, Oberman felt that Mike must know something. In fact, maybe that had been the whole point of the call—trying to psych Oberman out, or just rub it in. A little payback for the way Oberman had treated him. But to bring a man's wife into it over an old grudge—that was too far.

The pep rally had started now. On the field, four beefy linemen were performing a skit dressed in drag. They wore flowery dresses and long blond wigs, and as they sashayed around each other, bursts of laughter sounded from the stands. Out past the end zone to Oberman's right, the bonfire had been lit and was glowing weakly.

With all the activity across the field, Oberman suddenly realized how strange he must look sitting alone on the visitors' bleachers. As he stood up, he heard a sharp rustling sound from the shelterbelt behind him. He turned and peered into the dark tangle of trees but couldn't see anything. Probably a raccoon or a possum. But who knows—maybe Ruth was right and there was a hoard of trolls in the darkness just waiting to swarm out and tear the flesh from his bones. He gave a bitter laugh and then stepped away from the trees and headed back across the field. Although he took a wide angle around the skit, he still noticed several faces from the stands look away from the show and watch him.

Back on the home side of the field, Oberman stood next to the bleachers and watched his linemen wiggle their hips and address each other in falsetto. That was Sanders, Molovski, Banks, and Jackson. Four fat oafs with no talent. They were all going to get pancaked by the Ashland defensive line. The thought made him angry. If his team got steamrolled, he'd have to spend two hours watching Mike Treadwell grinning at him from across the field. Oberman could feel it already, as if it were happening right now.

It felt like the end of everything.

Javi was his only hope. When the kid was locked in, he gave their team a shot against anyone in the league, even Ashland. And there was Javi now, still sitting alone on the front row of the bleachers, a zoned-out look on his face even as everyone around him hooted at the drag show. The two-liter, almost empty, was squeezed between his knees.

Oberman approached the side of the bleachers and quietly called Javi's name. When Javi looked up, Oberman motioned for him to follow.

"What's up, Coach?" Javi said once they'd stepped away from the stands. He'd brought the two-liter with him. His face was flushed, eyes bleary.

"Let's go to my office," Oberman said. "We need to talk."

Javi frowned but followed his coach toward the gym. As they walked, Oberman grabbed the two-liter away from Javi. He unscrewed the bottle, sniffed it, took a swig, and grimaced.

"Come on, Coach," Javi said. "It's the pep rally."

"I don't know how you're still standing," Oberman said. They stepped inside the gym, and he tossed the bottle in a trash can by the door.

"It's the pep rally, Coach," Javi said again.

"And practice. And the Willow Creek game."

"Not the Willow Creek game."

"I sure hope the Willow Creek game. If that's how you play sober, we might as well flush the season down the toilet."

They passed through the darkened locker room and came to Oberman's office. He unlocked the door, and they stepped inside. The walls were covered with old team photos and clippings from newspapers announcing the team's regional titles. Next to his framed bachelor's degree was a poster of a football player in a three-point stance, two fingers taped together, face splattered with mud, gritting his teeth. Above the player were the words *When you win, nothing hurts. — Joe Namath.*

"Have a seat," Oberman said. When he looked across his desk at Javi, he felt sorry for the kid. At seventeen, Javi already seemed beaten down by the world. But Oberman admired his perseverance, the quiet courage that got him through each day. Seeing Javi sitting there staring down at his hands, his pudgy cheeks flushed and shoulders hunched forward, Oberman felt a sudden tenderness toward him.

"How are things at home, Javi?" he said.

"Ah, you know, Coach." He glanced up and then quickly back down. "Same old crap."

"How's your sister?"

"She's fine."

"And your dad?"

Javi shrugged.

"You're helping out your mom?"

"Yeah."

Oberman sighed and leaned back in his chair. He looked out the window. The bonfire was blazing now. As a precaution, a fire truck had pulled up twenty yards behind it. On the field, the cheerleaders were performing their routine as a pulsing dance song played from the loudspeakers.

They sat in silence for a minute, and then Javi raised his head.

"How are things with you, Coach?"

The question caught Oberman off guard. No one had asked him that in a while. He looked down at his desk. Next to the playbook, magazines, and grade sheets was a stuffed plush football that had been a birthday gift from Sandra back when they were dating.

"To tell you the truth, Javi, I've been better."

"What's going on?"

Oberman saw the concern in Javi's bloodshot eyes. He grabbed the stuffed football, squeezed it, and looked out the window again. Maybe he should tell Javi everything. He trusted him not to go blabbing. And who better to talk to about life's unfairness, about how the world can be absurd, and painful, and relentless?

The bonfire was raging. The cheerleaders formed a wobbling pyramid.

He'd tell him, Oberman decided. He'd get it all off his chest. He opened his mouth to speak.

And then Lonny Hinkle walked past the window. He was headed toward the bleachers, blowing into his hands, red scarf looped around his neck.

Oberman sucked in a breath. Unbelievable. What fucking nerve. Was he trying to prove a point, to show he wasn't rattled by the bullet in his box? As Oberman watched, Hinkle approached a group of teachers, grinning broadly. He gave one of them a jovial slap on the back. If he had the balls to come out tonight, Oberman thought, that meant he'd be there for the game tomorrow, smirking down from the bleachers as the Hornets got pummeled. Oberman dug his fingers into the stuffed football. His head felt like it would burst. He swung back to face Javi.

"What's wrong, Coach?" Javi said.

"What's wrong?" Oberman said. "What's wrong?" He leaned forward. "What's wrong is that you're trying to sabotage my team."

Javi frowned. He shook his head slowly.

"Listen carefully to me, son. I know things are fuzzy right now, but I want to make sure this gets through to you. Are you paying attention?"

Javi nodded, eyes wide.

"If you show up drunk tomorrow, I'll blow your fucking brains out."

Even as he said the words, he felt disgusted with himself. This hadn't been his plan. He'd meant to chastise Javi, sure, to tell him to get his act together. But not like this.

Maybe, he thought, Javi would take it as a joke. He watched him carefully, waiting for the slightest sign of humor. They could laugh this off, pretend Oberman hadn't been seething as he said it, pretend that when the words came out, they hadn't both believed them.

But Javi didn't laugh. He held Oberman's gaze and then slowly, as the weight of the words settled in, his eyes started to water. He blinked and looked down.

There was no going back now. A new reality had been established between them. They would both have to accept it and move forward.

"Are we clear?" Oberman said.

"Yes, Coach," Javi mumbled.

"Then get the hell out of my office."

Javi stood up unsteadily, gripping the back of his chair. He didn't look at Oberman as he left the office and shut the door softly behind him.

Oberman sat at his desk for a few minutes. He picked up the playbook and set it down again. He stared out the window at the fire. Finally he got up, grabbed the stuffed football, and stepped into the darkened locker room. Far at the back he could make out Javi slumped on a bench, shoulders shaking. Oberman locked his office door behind him and walked out into the gym. On his way to the exit, he tossed the football in the trash.

He'd already opened the back door, the cool air rushing in, when a thought occurred to him and he stopped and turned around. He came back to the trash can, peered inside, and reached down. He came up with Javi's two-liter. In four big chugs he drained the bottle and dropped it back in the can. Then he shoved the door open and stepped out into the night.

On the field, the cheerleaders were holding up huge cardboard letters while the crowd yelled "H-O-R-N-E-T-S . . . Gooooooo Hornets!" Oberman barely glanced at the stands as he made his way toward the bonfire. There were two students tending the fire, both freshman girls. After the last cheer had finished, the crowd would gather around the fire, and as the grand finale these two girls would throw the papier-mâché buffalo on the flames—glue bubbling, horns turning to ash, eyes bursting from their sockets.

Oberman stepped up to the girls. The alcohol hadn't hit him yet, but nevertheless he felt a giddy rush of energy. The girls looked at him nervously. "Hey, Coach," one of them said.

Now that he could see the buffalo up close, he could tell what a shoddy piece of work it was. It looked like a deformed dog with horns. He reached down and picked it up. It was so light, he thought. He almost laughed at how light it was. He stepped toward the bonfire and raised the buffalo above his head.

"Coach, hold on, it's not time yet!" one of the girls said.

"Coach O?" said the other, her voice concerned.

But Oberman wasn't listening. He was looking past the fire toward the shelterbelt. There in the darkness of the trees he could see them—dozens of red eyes glaring out at him. Above the crackling fire he could hear their gnashing teeth.

They watched him, unblinking. It was only a matter of time.

SHARON HUNT

The Keepers of All Sins

FROM *Alfred Hitchcock Mystery Magazine*

THE ALBRECHT MEN had a habit of being found floating on water.

The habit began with the grandfather, Carl, in Vienna in 1944. Alcohol was given as the reason he was floating lifeless in a turquoise-tiled pool, although the fact that he was swimming naked at the house of a man who had disappeared the previous day and that the man's wife had alerted police to Carl's demise, her face bearing signs of a fresh beating, gave pause to the idea that his death was simple misadventure. Still, money and the power of Albrecht's widow ensured that the death was quickly labeled as such. The woman who had alerted the police continued on in her house, draining the pool, then staying mostly in the kitchen, where she made a bed next to the gigantic stove that gave off a fierce heat, saturating the air with moisture. Fifty years later she was found curled up next to that stove, her hair wet and dripping.

The same year her body was discovered, Carl's son Caspar drowned in a lake on the opposite side of the world, in northern Ontario, where he owned a summer cottage that rose from the granite like a mountain, on land that was to have remained wild. The construction of the cottage had cost two men their lives after each fell, just days apart, onto the boulders below. Caspar's body had a softer landing in the water by the dock. Like his father, alcohol was mentioned, but in this case, the woman who found him was his own wife, who always wore long sleeves and never went in the water, although on that day the cuffs of her linen shirt were damp when the police arrived. She said she had tried to pull him out, but his body was too heavy, bloated from years of excess, so she tied his wrist to the dock and let him float until they arrived.

Christian, Caspar's only son, died in a lake in Switzerland twenty years after that. He had lost his grip on a ferry gate that came unlatched and from which he dangled until slipping into the cold water. There weren't many passengers left on the ferry at that point and all of them were below in the little room that smelled of oil. The crew heard nothing until the driver of a speedboat radioed that he'd found a body floating toward shore and scooped it up. There was no mention of alcohol, but Christian's girlfriend, Maud, had a hazy look, as if something toxic hadn't left her yet. Christian couldn't swim, but he liked the water well enough, she told the officer who came to investigate, having spent his summers at the family cottage in northern Ontario.

"Canada," she added, since the officer seemed confused.

He didn't look as if he traveled, rather like someone content to stay where he had been put, like Maud's grandmother Eleanor had been. She doubted her grandmother could have located Switzerland on a map any faster than this man would northern Ontario.

One of the reasons Maud had been so attracted to Christian in the beginning was how easily place-names fell from his lips, money having made travel as common to him as looking for bargains at the grocery store was to her. He had family still in London and Vienna. He would take her to Europe.

She doubted he thought he would die in Europe, but Christian never thought anything bad would happen—to him.

"Toronto," the officer said, pulling the name from somewhere in his head and smiling.

"Three hours north," she said, and he nodded as if a map had suddenly materialized on the desk between them and the location of the dead man's summers had been pinpointed.

Earlier in the summer, before Christian took Maud to Europe, he'd taken her to the cottage to meet his mother, whose skin was as white as the sweater and trousers she wore. The woman's black heels made a staccato sound along the granite floor before stopping in front of a sofa in the living room. She motioned for Maud to sit on a chair across from her and tea was brought out.

His mother's blond hair was a helmet that didn't move, but her red fingernails tapped the side of her cup at a pace that made it jump on its saucer. She stared at Maud, whose own fingers caught in her cup's handle, spilling tea into her lap.

"You're very pretty," the woman said, watching Maud press the napkin into the pool of milky tea.

"I'm studying history at university," Maud said, looking up from her lap and then staring at Christian. For once she wished he would interrupt her like he usually did and tell his mother that they met at a lecture and not some bar, which the woman obviously thought, but he stared out the window at the dock and the shining lake.

"We met at school, at a talk on Queen Anne that a professor from Oxford was giving. She had seventeen pregnancies, but no children survived her," Maud said, and heard Christian sigh.

"Queen Anne or the professor?"

This time Maud sighed. "Well, I mean Queen Anne."

His mother stood up. "Aristocratic blood gets so polluted with all that inbreeding. We should have a light lunch before you leave."

"I'm sorry," Maud said, focusing again on the officer's mouth. "What were we doing in Zurich? Like I told you, we were waiting for the evening train to Vienna. We were going to visit his uncle. Albrecht. He is a banker."

"Christopher Albrecht?" The officer suddenly straightened in his chair.

"Yes. Do you know him?"

He chuckled. "I know of him. They say he will become Austria's president in a few years."

Maud's shoulders heaved. She was still dehydrated, despite the water they'd given her at the police station. Neither she nor Christian drank much water all those hours on the ferry. He brought a single bottle with him, saying that since it was a tour boat there would be a canteen. Even when it turned out the boat was a ferry and there was no canteen, Maud had only a few sips of the water. By midafternoon, she told the officer, her head was so thick that she had to focus on every movement.

Right foot.

Left foot.

Walking had become as exacting as marching.

Everything felt so heavy, she said, and he nodded.

Now her feet fluttered up from the floor beneath her chair, although he couldn't see them from where he sat. Besides, he had returned to staring at the shiny red spot at the base of her throat, the size of a thumbprint, although he hadn't yet asked about it.

When she'd seen the spot this morning, it reminded her of a bull's-eye. The other marks, almost lacy on her collarbone, down across her breasts and the sides of her body, mapped out movements she was still trying to recall. Everything had been easily hidden by her sweater and jeans, but having thrown all her scarves in the garbage after seeing the marks on her wrists, she had nothing to cover up the bull's-eye. It bothered Christian to see it, and she was glad then that she hadn't made any effort to hide it.

The officer had said something again, she suspected, because he knit his fingers together the way he did every time he waited for an answer. They reminded her of that game her grandmother played at the kitchen table when Maud was eating her snack before bed.

This is the church, this is the steeple. Open the doors, there're all the people.

In another version, her grandmother kept all her fingers straight, as the officer did now, and asked, "Where're all the people?"

Maud would open her own church doors and wiggle her fingers. "There they are."

The two of them always laughed.

Now Maud's fingers were stretched out, quiet in her lap.

The officer looked at her with something that might be concern, but she understood now that people's expressions were as malleable as plasticine and as easily refashioned. Her own didn't betray the fear she felt, not that she would be blamed for Christian's death but that she was starting to remember what had happened to her, and once she did, no amount of water would wash that away.

Maud told the officer that by midafternoon the ferry had already stopped five times to let off people with bags of vegetables and books pressed against their chests and she and Christian realized that this was not a tour boat, as they'd been promised, but a ferry.

She didn't say that the sun pounded into them and the water, which from shore looked that beautiful teal blue, was black as she bent over the railing, waiting to throw up. For a moment she wondered how cold the water was and whether she was a strong enough swimmer to get to shore, any shore.

That thought left as quickly as it arrived, and leaning on the gate, Maud felt it give a little. She pulled back, but with another wave of nausea, she lurched forward and threw up what remained in her stomach, a sour-smelling liquid that formed an orange circle on the surface of the water.

When she looked at Christian again, he was watching her while drinking the last of the water, some of it running down his chin.

As she tucked herself back into what little shade the roof of the bridge provided, Christian closed his eyes.

A smell was coming off him, the smell he had when he was angry or excited, and it made her want to gag.

She had hoped for a lot of things on this trip, but mostly to feel secure in her choice of him and that he took their relationship seriously, but she realized, as she'd suspected after meeting his mother, that he took nothing seriously except his own wants. She could be easily replaced; she doubted he'd spend much time mourning her loss.

She closed her eyes for a few minutes, fighting back tears, although the hopelessness that had welled up in her as she stared out train windows had worn away. Things had festered for too long. Maud had learned, growing up, that there was a point of no return, when things or people couldn't be saved.

Her grandmother had raised her after her parents died in a car accident when she was seven, and although she was good to Maud, she made the girl traipse around the island they lived on to help care for the sick and dying.

Eleanor healed people, not with a laying-on of hands like a pseudo-Christ but with poultices and ointments, drafts and brews her father had taught her to make. Maud looked at wounds, with their murky gray infections and skin as fragile as tissue paper, and applied hot cloths that allowed the infections to flow out of the skin like undammed rivers. She lifted people's heads and forced liquid between their lips, and when she protested because of the rattling sounds and the stench, her grandmother's withering look was worse than anything confronting Maud in strange beds.

People who could not be saved whispered in Eleanor's ear, and, nodding, she patted a shoulder or an arm.

"I will keep them," she said of the sins they gave her to hold, and the dying fell back on their pillows, relaxing into death.

The people Eleanor would not save she still watched over until their bodies succumbed to the sickness that marched through their minds. Those people whispered their sins to her too, sweeping the filth from their souls into hers.

"Some people are diseased long before sickness takes hold of the flesh," she said. "With them, it's right to turn a blind eye."

When a body had been healed or was stilled by death, Eleanor stripped the bed and then swept the floor.

It was soothing to see everyday life continue after illness, trauma, or death.

"These too are part of life, but we pretend they won't happen until our luck runs out or fate takes hold."

Eleanor had been training Maud to take over healing, but Maud wasn't strong like her, she told her grandmother. She wanted to turn a blind eye to all of it.

"Sooner or later you won't be able to do that," Eleanor said, and didn't speak to Maud again until she whispered her own sins in her granddaughter's ear.

Maud sat forward in her chair.

"There was no place to sit in the little room downstairs, so we were stuck outside, on that bench. I told Christian we were going to miss the train to Vienna and he ignored me for hours after that."

There was a window in the room where Maud and the officer sat. Later she watched another officer at the front desk stand up and press at his hair when Christopher Albrecht arrived. She recognized him from a photograph in Christian's wallet. Albrecht's face was red, and for a moment she wondered if this man who talked about collapsing economies might be collapsing himself, but he strode forward in the way powerful people did, aware of and enjoying the fact that others watched them in a guarded, almost frightened way.

"There are some people it is best not to cross," Eleanor had said before she died.

Yes, Maud thought, watching Albrecht advance, *there are.*

He wore a pale gray suit, and when he got to the room, Maud noticed the teal-blue loafers on his feet. His fingernails shone. Although he extended his hand to the officer, he didn't take his eyes off Maud.

"What do we know?" he said, sitting in a chair, facing them.

Maud looked away, watching a cleaning woman sweep the hall floor. The sound of corn bristles along the wooden boards was soothing. She knew she should focus on the two men, but the way the woman's arms moved the broom, just enough to gather the dirt, back and forth, back and forth . . . she wanted to sleep, but

Christopher Albrecht tapped his fingers faster and faster on the table until she looked back at him.

The room that she and Christian had in Zurich was at the end of a hall with tattered blue carpeting. He liked the stark furnishings—a bed, table, and two straight-backed chairs—because they reminded him of boarding school in England, before his father had enough of Labour politics and emigrated to Canada. Even the lumpy mattress welcomed him to sleep when he was done with Maud, while she stayed awake, trying to tamp down the fear that threatened to choke her.

He had become obsessed with sex, relentless in pushing her to accept his advances at strange moments and in strange places. This trip had unleashed something in him, something that he seemed to keep harnessed at home, although there had been moments back there that the harness loosened and she felt herself shift from excitement to fear. The loosening of what had made him seem gentle and kind made her realize how badly she'd failed at judging him, and this frightened her more than anything.

In the room next to theirs was a man from Hamburg who introduced himself as Gerhardt. His breath was sour as he leaned close to Maud when he sat down next to her.

The waitress scowled, struggling to fit breakfast on the table, and Maud thought she saw Gerhardt's fingers brush against the woman's skirt before shaking Christian's hand.

"He used to make dirty movies," Christian said later, squeezing Maud's elbow as they headed out for the day. "Inviting girls back to his apartment and then going at it."

Maud pulled her arm away.

"It's only sex, for Christ's sake. If they all wanted to, what's the problem?"

"I can't see women wanting to, with him. He makes my skin crawl."

"Well, my uncle liked what he did well enough. He told me he used to get Gerhardt to make movies with him, before the Internet made it so easy to find whatever you wanted. You can see some of the movies online now, although he isn't too happy about that, since he became interested in politics."

Maud felt her stomach lurch.

"These dark places on the Internet keep all the sins now. They never disappear."

"Why is he here?" she said.

Christian smiled. "I guess to enjoy himself, like me."

Christopher Albrecht watched, waiting for a confession or at least an acknowledgment that she hadn't watched out for his nephew, who had brought her here and paid for everything.

Well, she had paid too, and that payment was becoming horribly clear as she pieced the fragments together: the sunset reflecting on something metal over by the window in their room, the sudden feeling that her legs would not hold her up any longer, plastic glasses on the bedside table, hands, too many hands, on her arms, fingers undoing the buttons of her sweater, sour breath.

She closed her eyes.

"What happened?" Christopher Albrecht repeated, and when she looked at him she wanted to shout, *You know what happened,* but instead said again, "He drowned in the lake."

"But how can that be all you know? Didn't you see him hanging on to the gate?"

"I had passed out," she said and was certain then, from the same eagerness in his eyes that she had seen in Christian's yesterday at breakfast, that he knew everything that had happened to her. He'd already seen it.

"Passed out," he said.

"Yes, passed out."

In the hall, the sweeping had stopped. The cleaning woman sank against the wall and sighed, although it might have been Maud herself sighing.

Her shoulders ached. She rubbed at the base of her throat, trying to erase the spot they couldn't stop looking at.

"It was a mistake," Christian had said before she got up off the bench to throw up.

"What was a mistake?" she asked, but he didn't answer.

"When I came to I had to piece together what happened," she said.

"And you have now pieced things together," Christopher Albrecht said.

"Yes, I have." Maud stroked the scratches on her hand. "I pieced things together," she said and stood up, looking at the officer. "I'd like to call my embassy now."

The officer nodded.

"This is not finished," Christopher Albrecht said, but uncertainty had crept into his voice.

Maud turned away.

In the hall, the cleaning woman took Maud's arm and drew her close, whispering in her ear.

Maud nodded and followed the officer down the hall.

The sweeping began again, drowning out Christian's whispering, his mouth so dry he could hardly speak, begging her for help as she'd loosened his fingers from the gate. By the time she picked up the phone to call the embassy, she couldn't hear him anymore. He'd quietly floated away.

REED JOHNSON

Open House

FROM *Ellery Queen Mystery Magazine*

TODAY HER FATHER'S name is Ismail, and he will be second
cousin to a Saudi prince. Her name, the one she picked out for herself earlier that morning at the breakfast table as they read over the
real-estate circulars, is Scheherazade. She likes the sound it makes.
Her real name is Nino, plain Nino, and she is twelve years old, dark-
haired, and wears flecked nail polish and low-top canvas sneakers
that she's decorated with a blue ballpoint pen.

The two of them, father and daughter, are on their way to
an open house across town. It's the first Saturday in March, the
weather warm for Massachusetts, and the sun dazzles through the
leafless trees. The smell of wet grass and pavement warms the air,
and overhead, swallows fly by them, their wings making the sound
of cards being shuffled.

"This one," her father says, stopping on the sidewalk.

The house, a brick-fronted Federal with a three-car garage, is
flanked by ornamental shrubs that are bound up in burlap for the
winter. Two balloons are tethered to the FOR SALE sign out front,
bumping and twirling in the spring breeze. As they turn up the
walk, Nino's father seems for a moment to consider taking her
hand, then doesn't. He's been more tentative than usual with her
lately, more uncertain of her likes and dislikes. He sees her only on
the weekends, and then not all of them, and she's grown this year
like a time-lapse seedling before his eyes. The days she is with him
seem to be a source of both anticipation and anxiety for him. Each
Saturday morning, he worries the events section of the local paper
like a Talmudic scholar, looking for activities to pass the time with

her, various fun things they can do together without spending any money, and this gives their time together a certain desperation, as if their only goal is to avoid becoming washed up on the shoals of late afternoon with the two of them sitting on the couch in his efficiency apartment, looking at each other with panicked blankness. It's not that father and daughter have nothing to say to each other. But these exchanges, when they occur, tend to have an excruciating artificiality, like the questioning of a prisoner by an awkward and unwilling interrogator. Fun activities are better; on this they are both agreed.

Inside the house, father and daughter are greeted by the real-estate agent, a large woman with black curly hair who wears a necklace made of flat gold links fitted together like vertebrae. She chats brightly as she shows them through the rooms—the sweep of living room, the Italian marble countertops of the kitchen, the "sol*ah*rium"—and Nino's father casually manages to drop a word or two about his cousins, the Saudi royals, with a sly look in Nino's direction. In actual fact he's from outside Tbilisi, capital of the Republic of Georgia, and most of his relatives are farmers and shopkeepers. But something about him makes the story believable: his accent, maybe, the soft-spoken schoolbook English he speaks, or the suit and tie he's wearing, his dark hair and skin and eyes, which are cupped in mournful circles. He emanates quiet respectability. He's in the market for a house, he tells the agent, where he can stay when he's visiting his daughter, Scheherazade, who will be attending a private school in Boston in the fall.

"Wonderful," the agent says, then turns to Nino. "Which school is it?"

Nino stares at her for a second or two, her mind empty. "Xavier's School for Gifted Youngsters," she says at last.

The agent makes an impressed sound. Which means she must never have had stepbrothers who kept her supplied with X-Men comic books, as Nino does, otherwise she'd know that Xavier's School for Gifted Youngsters is an institution for mutant superheroes. Nino feels pleased with her little lie. It gives her a guilty feeling of superiority, the thought that she is smarter for having deceived an adult.

But it's not deception, her father would tell her. It's pretending. Nobody is hurt by make-believe. He makes it seem like a lark, like they are going to these open houses for free entertainment, but

Nino understands that they fill some deeper need in him. Back in Tbilisi, before she was born, before he and her mother came to the U.S., he was a cardiologist, a respected man, someone to whom patients came for advice and treatment. Here he works weekday nights as a home nurse for an elderly Dominican woman named Elvira, whose son pays him in cash and doesn't ask for a Social Security number. All week long he attends to her wants and needs, and when the weekend comes, he wants someone to attend to his. He likes being courted by the real-estate agents, enjoys their hovering attentions.

The real-estate agent excuses herself to go and greet a young couple who have just come inside. Nino heads for the refreshment table, always the best part of these open houses. She peels back the cling wrap tented over the food trays and eyes the block of marble-veined blue cheese and browning apple slices. She helps herself to a gherkin. Her hunger has lately become bottomless. As she eats, she's listening to the conversation across the room between the agent and the young couple. The wife, mishearing the agent, wants to know what a Finnish basement is. Does it have a sauna? The man interrupts to ask about a sump pump. Nino doesn't know what a sump pump is, but she likes the sound of it. She tries it out in her mouth: *sump pump, sump pump.* One of those mechanical objects whose name is also the sound it makes while operating. What are some others? She's concentrating on coming up with more, and so she doesn't hear the lull in the conversation across the room, and that the real-estate agent is now addressing her. She wants to know if Nino and her father have signed the guest book. Nino looks around. Her father is nowhere in sight.

"Not yet," Nino answers, spotting the guest book on the table. She sticks a wedge of apple she's holding into her mouth—it's too big, and hurts the roof of her mouth when she bites down—and signs their made-up names in the book. Over the column marked ADDRESS, she pauses, pen hovering, then writes down the first address that comes into her mind, which is her father's. Where is he, anyway? She ducks into the living room. The husband of the couple is inspecting a closet. "Hollow-core doors," he says to himself, rapping on it with his knuckles in the confident manner of a male evaluating something outside his area of expertise.

Nino grabs another apple slice from the tray on her way through the dining room, then wanders upstairs to look for her father. She has this habit that she can't help, this way of moving soundlessly from one place to another. If she had any superpower, it would be this—the ability to creep up on people in total silence. It makes adults nervous. Shane, her stepfather, calls it skulking. But she doesn't mean to; it's just the way that she moves.

She finds her father in the master bedroom. He's standing in front of the mirror over the room's dresser.

"Hi," she says.

Her father jumps in surprise at her voice. There's a strange expression on his face, a flushing of his cheeks, as if she's caught him doing something he shouldn't be.

He opens his mouth to say something, but at this moment the real-estate agent comes into the room, out of breath from the stairs.

"Here you are," she says. "Have you seen the his-and-hers sinks?"

The following afternoon Nino is sitting in her father's galley kitchen and reading a Piers Anthony novel, her socked feet propped up on the hot radiator, when the doorbell rings. "Door," she says.

"What?" her father calls from the bathroom.

"Nothing, I'll get it," she says, getting up from her chair and unfastening the door chain. Standing in the spring sunshine outside are two police officers. One is an older white man with a graying mustache and heavy jowls, the other is a small and smooth-faced Latina with her hair pulled back into a bun.

"Is Mr. Gelashvili in?" the woman asks.

"He's in the bathroom," Nino says.

"Are you his daughter?" the older man asks her.

Nino nods. And because she doesn't know what else to do, and because the outside air is cold against her ankles, she opens the door wider and silently stands aside to let them in. The two officers stand awkwardly in the tiny kitchen, their boots leaking puddles on the yellowing linoleum, their jackets brushing against each other with a rustling sound.

"Did you say something, Nanuka?" her father calls from the hallway. He comes into the kitchen with shaving cream on his neck and stops short in the doorway.

"Can I help you?" he says to the officers.

"Mr. Gelashvili? Were you at an open house the other day?"

Her father doesn't move from the doorway. "Why?"

The woman officer explains. There was a theft during the open house. Some valuable personal items, including heirloom jewelry, were taken from the owners' bedroom during the day. The police are questioning everyone who was at the event. "We have a search warrant for your home," she says, unfolding a piece of paper and putting it on the counter.

"You are searching everyone's home?" her father asks.

The two officers shift uncomfortably.

"Mr. Gelashvili, would you mind telling us what you were doing at the open house?" the older officer says, looking around the kitchen, taking it all in: the ancient refrigerator chugging to itself in the corner, the contact paper on the countertops, the water stains on the ceiling. "Are you in the market for an eight-hundred-thousand-dollar home?"

"I'm studying for my real-estate license," he says.

"Then would you care to explain why you are in the guest book under a false name?"

Her father stares at the woman for a moment before speaking. His face is pale. Nino can tell he's afraid of the officers. Back in the Soviet Union you were afraid of the police, he's told her. But not here. Americans are honest people. This is why he left Tbilisi and came to this country.

"It was a game," he says, and then, when this seems insufficient, he tries to explain their Saturday-morning tradition. His voice is shaky, and nervousness makes his accent stronger. The story comes out sounding absurd; even her father seems to hear how improbable it all sounds, and his voice grows fainter and more halting. A police radio suddenly burbles, something about a child reported missing but now found. The older officer unclips the radio from his belt, still looking at her father, and turns down the volume. After a moment, the woman speaks.

"Mr. Gelashvili, have you been in touch with ICE?" she says. "Your visa expired some time ago."

Her father sags against the doorframe. "I am currently working with an immigration lawyer," he says in a voice that sounds as though he is reciting the words from an index card. "You may contact the offices of S. Ramachandran in Somerville, Massachusetts."

"Okay," the older officer says. "We're going to have to conduct a search. And get a record of your prints."

"The Saudi prince was a joke," her father says, visibly floundering. He looks to Nino, who is still standing near the outside door, for help.

"Your fingerprints," she says, in a voice hardly above a whisper.

The woman, Officer Laramie, tells her father to take a seat. When he does, she sets a briefcase on the kitchen table and takes out a photocopied form and an ink pad. The older officer snaps on a pair of blue latex gloves and starts opening cupboards and drawers. Her father watches him as Officer Laramie takes his hand and moves it from ink pad to paper and back again, one finger at a time, as if he were a child. He does not resist. When all fingers have been inked, he stares at the record of them on the paper with seeming disbelief, as if these marks could not have been made by his hands. He looks up at the officer.

"If the names in the book were false," he says, "then how did you know who I am? How did you know where I live?"

The policewoman puts the sheet of paper in the briefcase, then snaps the ink pad shut. "You wrote your address in the book," she says.

Nino, hovering uncertainly near the door, makes a sound in her throat. Her father looks up at her.

"Nanuka, go home," he says. "Go to your mother's." He turns to the police officer. "Can she?"

The officer waves to show she has no objection.

"Don't say anything to your mother, she will worry," her father says to her. "Everything will be all right. This is nothing," he says, waving his hand to show how little it all means.

Nino puts on her coat and boots. She looks back in the kitchen before she steps outside. The officer in the latex gloves is digging through the kitchen trash, while her father sits in his chair with his eyes closed. He's touched his forehead and left a smudged fingerprint above his left eyebrow, as if a gray moth has settled lightly on his forehead without him noticing.

"You're home early," Shane, her stepfather, says from the couch when she comes in from riding her bike home. He's got a towel around his shoulders and his dark hair is spiky from the shower.

"Yes," she says, unwinding the scarf from around her neck and taking off her jacket.

Shane tosses the running magazine he's reading onto the coffee table.

"How's your father?"

"Good," Nino says. Shane always asks her this when she gets home, and her answer is always the same. She knows he's asking only because he doesn't really care that much. Her father rarely asks anything about Shane—the name sounds like "Shame" when he says it—because he actually does care. Shane married her mother when Nino was six, which is how her mother got herself legalized in the U.S. Shane is the owner of three mall stores that sell nothing but vitamins, and drives a white Lincoln Navigator with THE VITAMAX EMPORIUM stenciled on the back window. In her conversations with her father, she tries never to mention Shane, but then she worries that he might notice that she never mentions her stepfather and decide that she is protecting his feelings by never bringing him up, which could then make her father think that she actually believes that he has something to feel bad about in regard to Shane, which he doesn't.

"Your mother's out shopping for dinner," he says. He stands up and cracks his back. He turns and sees her in the hallway, standing frozen at the door, and notices for the first time the look of distress on her face.

"Everything okay?" She looks at him, a feeling of panic hollowing her stomach. She wants to tell someone what she's done, but can't bring herself to open her mouth. He's good to her, Shane is, and even loves her in his Shane way, but he isn't her father.

"Yes," she says.

"Where are you going now?" he says, when he sees her putting on her coat again. "You just got in."

"Something I forgot to do," she says, and goes out.

But she doesn't go to her father's house. Instead she cuts through the park and heads toward the west end of town, where the open house was the previous day. She's going there because she already knows that her father took the things from the bureau in the upstairs bedroom. She also understands why he did it. She knows that he needs money to pay his debt to the immigration lawyer. He needs money to pay her child support to Shane and her mother, even though they told him it was okay if things were tight, they could wait. No, it was a matter of pride for him. Better to take something from someone wealthy, who didn't need the money. He didn't think he would get caught.

And maybe he wouldn't have, if she hadn't put down his address in the guest book.

Outside the house a group of boys are playing street hockey with a tennis ball. They pause to let a car pass by, then resume their game, not paying her any attention. The sun is setting through the trees, casting long shadows across the lawns, which are spongy and still matted down from last week's snow. She goes up the walk. Lights are on inside. She hesitates for a few seconds, then rings the bell.

The door is answered by a woman. She's trim, late forties, maybe, with variegated blond hair. "Yes?" she says, looking down at Nino with surprise. Nino's legs are shaking, and her voice breaks as she starts to explain: the police, her father, the fact that he would be sent away from her if they didn't do something to help. Hearing this, the woman's tanned face registers distress. "Come on inside," she tells Nino, ushering her through the door.

Inside, the house smells of fish sticks and baked potatoes. A dishwasher rumbles in the kitchen. The woman, who introduces herself as Jan, gets her a Diet Coke and pours it in a tall glass for her, and Nino sits at the bar stools at the stone counter. Jan's husband, a big man with a rosaceous bloom on his cheeks and a dark beard that looks somehow out of place on his face, comes into the kitchen and Nino tells the story all over again. "I was thinking that maybe if he returned everything and apologized, you would tell the police to stop," she tells Jan.

"Oh my," Jan says. She looks at her husband.

"What are you looking at me for?" her husband says.

"Come on, sweetie," Jan says to Nino, after a moment of strained silence. "I think you should call your father and tell him where you are, he's probably worried."

Nino doesn't dare ask if this means they have agreed to her plan. Instead she dials her father. He picks up on the fifth ring. She tells him she's at the open house. "Where?" her father says. She tells him again. "Oh, Nino," he says, but then, after making a muffled sound of cupping the phone with his hand, he tells her that he's on his way.

While they are waiting for Nino's father to come, Jan cracks and pours herself a can of Diet Coke and starts talking about the house, about the problems with trying to sell it in this market. Their property, Jan tells her, is underwater. For a moment Nino has an image of a wave engulfing the house and them all having to fight against the rush of water to get out, rise up to the surface. But now Jan is telling her all the details of their finances, speaking in a defensive tone that Nino doesn't understand. Until recently, Jan tells her, Richard — that's her husband, Richard — was the owner of a small business that designed and manufactured safety equipment for lacrosse players. The business went bust after a high schooler was injured wearing a helmet made by their company and they were sued by a personal-injuries lawyer. Richard has tried to start a new company, one that is now filing for bankruptcy protection, and Jan herself, who has a degree in sociology from Stetson University in Florida but has no professional experience, now has a job as a cashier at the Shaw's in neighboring Newton, where she's working for minimum wage under the keen-eyed supervision of her son's ex-girlfriend from high school, a young woman named Summer.

"I had a friend in first grade named Summer," Nino says, unsure of what she should say. "She was nice."

"Not this one," Jan says. "This one is a real piece of work."

The doorbell rings. Jan goes to get it. Nino's father comes into the kitchen. She sees his mournful face, his weary eyes, the shaving cream on his collar, and she feels such an intense surge of love, the feeling pressing against the inside of her chest like a balloon, that she starts shaking all over.

"Nino," he says. "What are you doing here? I told you to go to your mother's."

Nino gestures helplessly at the kitchen, the house. "I came here."

Her father nods to Richard, who is standing with a drink in his hand against the stove. "Well, now we can go," he says to Nino. "I'll walk you back. Thank you for calling," he says to Jan.

"Wait," Nino says. They can't go yet; now that she's gotten her father together with the owners of the house, they need to discuss what they can do. But first, she knows, her father has to tell them that he did it and ask them for forgiveness. That's how it works. "Don't you have something you want to say to them?" she says.

Her father looks at her. His eyes are meshed with capillaries. He is breathing through his nose.

"Yes, I do," he says. He turns to Richard. "Why do you leave jewelry lying around during an open house?"

Richard sets down his glass.

"Why did you write a fake name with a real address in our book?" he says.

Nino feels the situation slipping out of her grasp. In a moment, any hope of reconciliation will be gone. Richard's face is already brightening with anger. She knows that she has to act. She has no choice but to rescue this situation in any way that she can.

"I did it," she says. "I stole your things."

All three of them now turn to her.

Her father is the first to speak. "You?" he says.

She looks at him in confusion. There's unfeigned surprise in his voice, as if he actually might believe she's telling the truth. For a moment no one says anything. The ice in Richard's glass groans and cracks.

"No, you didn't," Jan says.

"Jan," her husband says.

"What? She didn't do it, so why is she telling us she did?" Jan says.

Now her father turns his bloodshot gaze to Jan. "How do you know?"

Jan glances away, looking out the window. The streetlights have just flickered on outside.

"I see," her father says.

"We are good people," Jan says.

"Maybe you should explain that to the police officers at my home," her father says, taking Nino's arm. "Or allow me to explain it to your insurance company. Can a person go to jail for this, writing a false claim?"

"Hold up there," Richard says. He moves quickly to stand between them and the exit.

Her father and Richard face each other in the narrow doorway of the kitchen. Nino can smell sweat and alcohol on the man's body. "Hey Jan, you see what you've done?" Richard says over their heads. "Any more great ideas?"

Jan uses the side of her finger to wipe mascara from her eyes. "Maybe they'll take money," she says, sniffing and then digging in her purse to pull out a checkbook.

"Of course," Richard says to his wife. "I thought you might say something like that." He turns to Nino and her father. "So you want a piece of the action?" It's an absurdly gangsterish thing to say, and he says it with all the awkwardness you might expect of a man in his late forties who has weathered two bankruptcies and fears losing his home.

Her father looks at Richard and says nothing, just holds the man's gaze for a drawn-out moment, jaw muscle pulsing. And then Richard turns to the side, waves his hand in the air, lets them through. "Go on then, screw it, whatever," he says. "What makes you think they'll believe you?"

Father and daughter go out. The neighborhood is quiet. When they reach the sidewalk, her father almost trips on something in the dusky light. A tennis ball. He bends down, picks it up. Then he turns around and hurls it with all his strength at the house, letting out a strangled sound. The tennis ball bounces off the brick facade, then rolls into the ornamental shrubs at the edge of the lawn.

"Come on," Nino says, and takes his hand, leading him along the sidewalk. They cross the street and continue on to the next intersection, heading for home.

Suddenly her father stops short. "Stupid, stupid," he says, hitting his head.

He sits down abruptly on the curb. Nino sits down beside him. "I should have taken the money."

The pavement still retains faint heat from the day's sun. Overhead, bats fly past, emitting faint cries. Her father hides his head in his hands.

Nino stands up and starts walking back to the house. It feels like a long way—somehow longer returning than going. She rings the doorbell, surprised how suddenly calm she's feeling, and when Jan opens the door, she tells her that she's come for the money.

Jan goes to get her checkbook while Nino waits silently in the kitchen. Returning, Jan fumbles the checkbook open, presses it flat against the counter, uncaps a pen; Nino observes that her hands are trembling, and she experiences an odd satisfaction in the woman's discomposure. "How much?" Jan says.

"Five hundred dollars," Nino says. It's a number that she plucks from the air, one that sounds large to her ears. She watches as Jan writes the amount, leaving the "pay to" field blank, then signs it and tears it out of the book. When she hands the check to Nino, the woman avoids making eye contact.

"Was that the doorbell?" Richard calls to his wife from the other room.

Nino goes out the door, holding the check in a damp hand. Her father won't want to take it from her at first, she knows, but he will eventually; what else can he do? It might be enough to cover the costs of the immigration lawyer.

She turns onto the sidewalk. A breeze stirs the tops of the trees. Transformers hum on telephone poles. A few stars shine dimly overhead. When was the last time she'd actually stared up at the night sky? She's remembering how her father had bought her a telescope for her tenth birthday, how impatient he'd been for darkness to try it out. He'd spent almost an hour getting it set up for her, slapping mosquitoes, making tiny adjustments of the lenses, while she'd read a book on the couch. *Come quick,* he'd said, running back into the apartment. So she'd followed him outside, into the narrow gravel lot at the rear of the building beside the trash bins. *Look,* he'd said: *Jupiter.* She bent down and put her eye to the lens but saw only darkness. In the time between them, the earth had kept turning, and the planet had fallen away from view. But she'd kept looking through the lens, imagining it hanging like an earring in the velvet of outer space. *Do you see it?* he'd asked. *I do,* she'd told him. *I see it.*

ARTHUR KLEPCHUKOV

A Damn Fine Town

FROM *Down & Out*

A LITTLE BOY in a red cape whooshes past me on the early-morning train. He's dead set on flying down this musty subway car headed for the airport. Kid Cape.

Heh, I must've had a costume like that for Halloween. Probably wore it too long too.

No one I scouted paid any attention to me thanks to this nondescript jacket in this indifferent pose with this vague stare. But this kid spins around, runs back, and eyeballs me. He's my daughter's age.

"POW!" Kid Cape says with a grimace and a tiny, hairless fist pointing at my nose. "I stopped you!"

I look around. The tourists are still asleep in the daze of the early train rocking us all from side to side. *Good.*

He wants a reaction like I used to. But I can't give him one. Another disappointed kid.

Go away, little man. This is cute, but I can't even smile. I need you to go away.

Kid Cape stares at me, not budging. His little fist trembles. The gray, uncorrupted eyes behind that cheap mask are intent on not being polite. *He knows what I am. We all know what I am.*

But I promise, I'll only do this as long as necessary. So just go.

I raise my hands, bow my head, and almost close my eyes.

"Whoosh!" The kid makes his own sound effects.

I glance up and Kid Cape's farther down the train car. He stops under one of those hanging hand straps—nooses for the nine-to-five crowd.

*

Kid Cape tries the same *pow* trick with a seated fella daydreaming in our car. A funny suitcase separates him from the hero. He smiles, and the kid takes off giddy, downright inspired.

Now I almost smile. It starts with the guy's well-traveled shoes. Terrible for giving chase. Mr. Suitcase is the right cocky, unsympathetic age. Flabby calves in shorts too cold for locals. That nonchalant reaction to Kid Cape? Couldn't imagine himself as a mark. He wears that goofy tourist grin. His eyes stare past the grimy train windows — this town's all new to him. The novelty has yet to fade, the real weather to spit on his days. A forgettable girlfriend naps on his shoulder. That bone propping up her eye socket? Cozy. My money says they won't make it past this year. Every other stop, he checks his well-worn Rolex.

But best of all? The bag. Dumpster chic. No luggage stickers. Outbound. Perfect.

My best scores came from ratty, inconspicuous luggage on this early-morning train bound for the airport. Never seen a fancy bag here that wasn't a knockoff full of things more at home at Goodwill than a pawn shop. People who travel with Louis Vuitton look-alikes live look-alike lives. But the slightly smarter set at least wrap the damn good in the quite ugly.

If you can afford this trip, you can afford to leave me a memento on my weekly round trip to nowhere.

Of all the police reports I once signed off on for precious bags, none ever itemized an engagement ring that woulda turned my ex, Cindy, into Cinderella. At least after that first score I afforded both alimony and our daughter's trip to space camp. At least her mind soared. That's worth losing a badge for. Most mornings.

Sitting always draws less attention than standing. So I do my seat rotations, staying clear of anyone who might notice or remember me. I study Mr. Suitcase through the reflections in the dirty windows each time the train departs. *What a goofy, unaware smile.*

Today I'll hit him three stops before the airport. Decent neighborhood with enough airport arrivals that if I turn two corners and walk slow, I'm an arriving local. Also the least-staffed station. And they hired that sap with the lazy eye for security. Worst case? Minimal resistance.

Hope that kid won't come back to see it. Don't feel like being someone else's excuse for bad behavior.

I exit the first door of the car and reenter from the second, wearing my baseball cap. We emerge from the last tunnel and morning light cracks into our car like a soft-boiled egg. I stand spitting distance from Mr. Suitcase, surfing the cheap waves of the train rocking forward. We pull into the stop.

He checks his watch, and when he rests his wrist back down on his chubby little thigh, it angles right up at me. *Wait. What kinda Rolex doesn't have hands?* No hours, no minutes, no seconds. I blink to make sure, staring longer than I should at an empty watch face. *I'm sure I pawned one exactly like that, except it told time. Did he remove the hands?*

The girlfriend jolts awake and sneezes on me. *Shit. Too close.*

But then she gawks at Mr. Suitcase.

"Oh, oh, I'm so sorry, sir." She brushes his shoulder.

He shrugs and smiles.

She dashes outta the open door. We're exactly three stops from the airport. I spot a guard napping in his glass cubicle. Mr. Suitcase is staring in the other direction, away from me. Doors of opportunity wide open.

What kinda man wears a watch that won't tell time?

The doors slide shut in my face. I let 'em. I take a seat. The disabled seat, facing Mr. Suitcase.

Kid Cape flies back down our car, picking up speed, aiming himself at Mr. Suitcase's bag. *Dammit, don't!* He runs up and lifts a bag that's bigger than him over his head like an ant. *Whoa.* The kid whispers that himself as he looks up at my score.

And the only other person awake enough to be shocked isn't. Mr. Suitcase stares up at his old bag with that same smile.

"Careful with that power," he says.

"Mikey! Mikey, where are you?" A mother's shrill voice plows into my ears.

Kid Cape wobbles, his secret identity exposed. He sets down the oversized bag. He examines his hands, the bag's owner, his hands again.

Mr. Suitcase raises a lone finger to his lips, agreeing to keep the hero's secret. Mikey smiles and dashes back past me toward his mother's squeaky voice.

I fixate on the bag. *What the hell's in there?*

*

We coast into the airport stop. End of the line. The incomprehensible announcements never wake anyone up—the final jolt of the car does the job. Passengers stand and check boarding passes, wristwatches, belongings. A series of paranoid pats. Mr. Suitcase's smile grows.

I make for the other door. He's the last person on the train. A fresh set of suitcases with peeling luggage stickers squeak onboard.

I exit. He doesn't.

The doors stay open. Soon after all the arrivals board, this train will turn around. I stand with one foot on the platform, the other still on the train, waiting for his move.

Mr. Suitcase steps off the train and I've got him in perfect profile.

His eyes close. He inhales and pushes the air out like an old steamer. And before I can make any sense of it, he turns around and drags his suitcase back onto the train. Mr. Suitcase pulls and grimaces like a kid didn't vault that bag over his head with ease. Its pipsqueak wheels yank my attention down as they cross the rumble strips. I favor the foot inside the train, lean in as the doors close.

Mr. Suitcase sits opposite of where he just was.

I lean on the handrail to his left.

His face has transformed—dimples gone, mouth relaxed, eyes sloping down in satisfied rest.

He raises his wrist and fiddles with the ring on the handless watch, rotating, rotating, perfect. *New time zone, of course.* He heaves the bag onto his lap and holds on to the zippers with both hands, like doorknobs he's not quite ready to twist.

Z-z-z-z-zip. The watch comes off his wrist and goes into a suitcase. An empty suitcase.

A grin tucks itself into my cheek. *I need a better way of picking targets. I should walk away, call this trip a wash, try again next week. Disappoint another kid in another cape by being a petty—*

"Do you need a suitcase?" Mr. Suitcase asks.

I glance around. He's staring at me. "Me? Why would I need a suitcase?"

"You seemed more interested in it than that kid was."

He made me. This is more humiliating than losing my badge.

"Are you in the market for one?" he asks.

"I don't need your suitcase, man." Bailing—the fastest way to seem guilty. Stay put.

"Maybe you can take it on a trip somewhere?"

He's seen me on this train before. He knows. "Me? A trip? Can't recall the last time I could afford a fancy trip."

"Well. You don't have to travel to travel," Mr. Suitcase says.

I slump into the seat across from him, nothing to add, no one to blame but myself. *I need a better way of picking targets, I do.* But I can't list my criteria. Can't decide which stop to take, where to go. I forget the map, stop profiling people, return to the same damn stations.

Third stop from the airport. An old woman yelps in German and something sends a jolt up my foot before tumbling down. The thief's on the ground with her purse and the guard's got a knee in his back before the doors close. *Did I . . . ?* I'm noticed and cheered and thanked with fancy chocolate. *Do they even know what I am?*

Mr. Suitcase isn't around to notice.

I remember asking my little girl why she wanted to go to space camp. *Duh! Because here is boring, Daddy.* I bob my head with the tracks like a little kid and stare, stare at the constantly shifting sky, finding the new in the familiar.

The Walk-In

FROM *For the Sake of the Game*

IT'S NOT EVERY day that you walk into your apartment and find that your cat has turned into a dog.

Okay, it was London, so it wasn't an apartment but a flat; and neither the flat nor the cat was mine, they were my brother Robbie's. But the dog was unequivocally a dog.

It was my second day in town, and because my brother's flat was new, and lacking pretty much everything—including my brother —I'd been out buying random moving-in things: toilet paper, dish drainer, red wine. I was in the hallway juggling these and trying to get his door open when I heard a clickety-clack on the wood floors on the other side of the door. Inside the flat.

Clickety-clack?

I glanced at the gilt number near the keyhole: 2B. Right flat, wrong sound. Touie, Robbie's annoying cat, padded around on silent paws. So who was this? Setting down my packages—parcels, as the Brits would say—I worked to get the door unlocked. At which point I was assaulted by the dog. A twenty-pound bulbous-bellied dog.

He—the gender was glaringly obvious—was corpulent, gunmetal gray, and so hair-free he appeared to have been skinned. His legs were stubby but his ears were large, and sticking straight up, rabbitlike. His face was all frowns and folds, a canine Winston Churchill digesting bad news. But he greeted me like I was a giant dog biscuit: when I bent to rescue my stuff from the floor, he launched himself at my chest, tangled himself in my crossbody bag, and slathered me with saliva. For a small dog, he had a lot of saliva.

I pushed the dog back into the flat and got the door closed behind us. "Robbie?" I called out, but my voice echoed through the bare rooms. No surprise. Robbie was my twin; I could feel his absence like a tangible thing.

I pushed aside thoughts of *Where's Robbie?* and made a grab for the dog's tag. "So who are you?" I asked him.

His collar looked just like the one Touie, the cat, wore: scarlet leather, the perimeter dotted with faux gems. One of Robbie's extravagances. Strange.

"Sit still, Dog. Let me read this." But when he did and I had, strange turned to bizarre.

The tag said "Touie" and the number on the tag was Robbie's cell phone.

My first thought was *WTF?* followed by *Where's Touie?* I wasn't her biggest fan, and she was definitely not mine, but I'd just spent five days relocating that cat from New York to London, a feat, on the misery meter, right up there with digging graves in winter. It just wasn't possible that she'd disappeared. I went through the flat, checking under the comforter where I'd last seen her, inside closets, and even the microwave, which Touie was too fat to fit into. There were limited hiding places. The only things Robbie had brought in, before disappearing, were five boxes of books and a bed, its toxic new-mattress smell wafting through the flat like bad air freshener.

The real Touie, like Robbie, was gone.

"Now what?" I asked, and the dog responded by sniffing around in a distinctive manner, suggesting a bladder situation. I unclipped the shoulder strap from my pink carry-on bag, fashioning a leash, and let the dog lead me outside. He had strong opinions about our route, one block to Baker Street and then a left, and another left, until I lost track of where we were.

The October day was murky with fog. And cold. I was wearing Robbie's red rain slicker, but it wasn't enough. How'd I gotten roped into doing this favor-turned-into-an-enigma-wrapped-in-a–*Twilight Zone* episode? Robbie had a lifetime of practice getting me to do stuff he didn't like doing—pet immigration in this case—but I'd had the same lifetime of practice saying no. Yet here I was, and minus the pet in question. How had it happened? *What* had happened? And why? And where was my damned brother? Seriously, what was I supposed to do? Call 911? Was the number even

911 in England? And then what? I wasn't one to chalk things up to supernatural forces, but it was a stretch to assume a criminal act. What self-respecting thief would want a plump, elderly cat? And why leave in her place this wheezing dog, straining at his makeshift leash, pulling me through London?

I'd been wrong about the dog's bladder: he was on a mission, and hardly paused to sniff, let alone pee. Oblivious to other pedestrians, he pushed onward like a horse heading for the barn at the end of a long day. Perhaps he lived around here? The thought gave me a glimmer of hope.

Oops. The dog came to a sudden squat and was now doing the unmentionable alongside an iron gate guarding a storefront. As I hadn't thought to bring along a plastic bag, I looked around guiltily, but no concerned citizens materialized to scold me. The storefront bore an ornate sign: THE RENOWNED MIRKO: PSYCHIC AND CARD READER. This was followed by a phone number, and then, in smaller font, WALK-INS — BOTH SORTS! — WELCOME. I was pondering that when I heard the tinkling of bells and looked up to see a man standing in the shop doorway.

We stared at each other. He frowned at me, his lips set in a horizontal line. He was tall and thin, the kind of thin that makes you think, for just a second, *stage four cancer,* but there was a kinetic energy about him, something in his gray eyes that nixed that impression. A high forehead, made higher by a receding hairline, made him look aristocratic, and strangely attractive, as did a three-piece suit more suited to a wedding than a psychic reading. I felt very American, and not in a good way.

"Unbelievable," he said.

"I'm sorry, Mr. —" I glanced again at the sign. "Mirko. I didn't bring a plastic bag — satchel — whatever you call them here — okay, never mind. If you have a paper towel or something, I'll happily clean this up for you."

"No."

"Okay, 'happily' might be overstating it," I admitted. "But I'm willing to — hey! Dog! Stop." The dog was greeting the Renowned Mirko like a long-lost lover and attempting to mate with his dress pants. I tugged on the leash.

"Go. Just go. Take yourself off," Mirko snapped, and then, to the dog, "Not now."

"Whoa. Hold up," I said. "Do you know this dog?"

"No."

"You do. You know this dog. This dog knows you."

"Nonsense," he said.

"It's not nonsense. He dragged me right to you."

"Leave."

"I'm not leaving," I said. "I'm walking in. A walk-in. Like the sign says. Both sorts!"

He gave me a curious look, but then glanced past me and said, "Bloody hell. Too late. Go in."

"What?" I looked over my shoulder.

"In, *in*, go inside, are you deaf? Quickly." The man took my arm and yanked me—he and the dog—through the open door.

The shop was warm, and musty with the odor of antiques and incense, the signature scents of psychics the world over. The decor was Victorian clutter. I got a fast impression of chintz, wallpaper, and books, books, books as Mirko herded me across the room to a kitchenette.

"Sit," Mirko said, and I thought he was talking to the dog until he pushed me into an armchair and scooped the dog into my lap. He then hauled over a rococo screen and arranged it in front of me, blocking my view of the room. He leaned in so close I could smell the damp wool of his suit. "Do not make a sound," he said. "Do not let the dog make a sound. This is critically important."

Before I could argue the point, the tinkling bell sounded again, signaling someone entering the shop. "If you value your brother's life, stay quiet," Mirko said, and walked away.

That shut me up.

The dog and I listened as Mirko said hello to someone. Actually, he said *zdravstvujtye*. A man responded in kind. In Russian. I knew a few words of Russian, but after the pleasantries, the newcomer told Mirko to wait. A second later came the sound of Barbra Streisand and Neil Diamond singing "You Don't Bring Me Flowers," a ballad Robbie once said made him want to cut off his ears. The music source was a cell phone, was my guess, and I wondered why we were listening to it, until I realized it masked conversation. I could pick out only random words now, during the song's lugubrious pauses, of which there were many. Then came the sound of a zipper zipping. The urge to peek around the screen was strong, but the dog began to struggle, wanting out of my arms and onto a small, narrow refrigerator next to us, on top of which sat a large frozen turkey, thawing, and a large ceramic Blessed Virgin Mary. As I thwarted his efforts to investigate the bird, the tinkling bell sounded again, and Streisand, Diamond, and Russian left the building.

"You may come out," Mirko said.

I came around the screen to find Mirko taking off his jacket and kicking off his shoes. Alongside him was a wheelie suitcase, fully zipped.

"So how do you know my brother?" I asked, and promptly took off my own jacket, the room being hellishly hot.

"I haven't time for this," he said.

"But you know where he is?"

"I do not." Now he had his vest off and was unbuttoning his dress shirt, as adroit as a stage actor doing a quick change. "I suggest you return to your flat, with the dog-who-is-not-your-dog, and sleep off the jet lag that you're trying to ignore. It's four in the morning Los Angeles time, and that red-eye you took did you no favors even with an exit row and a window seat. Nor does sleeping on floors agree with you."

My eyes must've widened. He smiled, before whipping off his shirt and giving me a view of his naked chest. Not a bad chest, if you don't mind skinny, which I don't, but I wasn't about to be distracted. "I don't know how you know the things you know," I said, "but all I care about is Robbie." The dog, perhaps reacting to my tone of voice, produced a sound that was less a bark and more the yowl of a human infant. "You tell him, Churchill," I said.

"Churchill? I'd have said Gladstone." Mirko walked to a bureau covered with tarot cards, opened a drawer, and took out a some clothes and a pair of Converse high-tops.

"Whoever that is."

"Victoria's prime minister, who more closely resembled a French bulldog." He pulled a T-shirt over his head, followed by a hoodie, a purple Grateful Dead relic from some bygone decade.

I stooped to let Gladstone wiggle out of my arms and over to Mirko, who was pulling on his sneakers, though not bothering to lace them up. "Fine," I said. "But you're pretty much the only person I know in London, not counting Pet Immigration, and I'm not leaving until—"

"Suit yourself." He stood up, ruffled his hair, and put on a pair of black-rimmed glasses. The transformation from aristocrat to geek was not just fast, it was total. From his pants pocket he withdrew a remote, which he aimed at the wall behind me.

A creaking sound like the opening of Dracula's coffin made me turn and see a wall-sized bookcase move.

Slowly, squeakily, so disorientingly I thought, *Earthquake?* the bookcase kept advancing into the room, as freaky as the Haunted Mansion at Disneyland. I fixed my eyes at random on one frayed book called *The Coming of the Fairies,* willing it to stay put, but nope. It moved. When I turned my attention back to Mirko, he stepped over his pile of clothes, grabbed the handle of the wheelie suitcase, and moved to a now-palpable gap between bookcase and wall.

Behind the gap was a door. Mirko opened the door and went through it.

I grabbed the dog and followed.

"What do you think you're doing?" he called out.

"Following you!" I called back. "What's it look like?"

It couldn't have looked like anything, because it was pitch-black except for the glow of Mirko's cell, bouncing along ahead of me. What it smelled like was a dank cellar, the scent intensifying as I followed Mirko down wooden stairs. When we reached the bottom, a light popped on.

We were in a long and narrow passageway, low-ceilinged, brick-floored, and lined with storage shelves. The kind of place that makes you think *bomb shelter* except that it was stuffed with . . . stuff. Furniture, art, armaments, and god knows what else, bubble-wrapped, crated up, or just scattered about. Mirko pushed aside a Roman helmet and heaved his wheelie suitcase onto a high shelf, showing an impressive set of muscles. He gave me a quick look, then took off down the passageway.

"Keep up," he called over his shoulder. "Unless you fancy being locked in."

I jogged after him, clutching the dog, until some three hundred feet later the tunnel ended in a second staircase. The lights went off behind me and in darkness I followed Mirko up the stairs, bumping into him at the top. "'S'cuse me," I mumbled, unsettled by his proximity, and his aftershave. Bay rum. Which I liked.

"This is where we go our separate ways," he said, working to unlock yet another door. A moment later we were out of the tunnel and in the back room of a supermarket.

It was a Tesco Metro, a British 7-Eleven. I followed Mirko through swinging doors onto the selling floor and the mundane world of Whiskas catfood and Wotsits Cheese Snacks.

Mirko marched through the Tesco with all the confidence of a store manager. I tried to match his gait and attitude, never mind that I was carrying an unattractive dog the size of a watermelon.

Once outside, he picked up the pace, his long legs at full stride, weaving his way through lunch-hour London, jammed with people. I caught up with him on the center island of some major intersection, waiting for the pedestrian signal. Before the light could turn green, Mirko stepped into the street, narrowly avoiding a speeding Volvo, and took off at a run. I said a prayer—a necessity, since the traffic was of course going the wrong way—and took off too, wincing at the horns honking at me. I followed him onto an escalator and down into London's Underground.

It was luck that I had a metro card—no, Oyster card, as they whimsically call it. I raced after him, dog squirming in my arms, through the turnstiles, over to some tube line or other, onto a platform, into a subway car, and out again at Liverpool Street, where we made our way to the train station. He made a beeline for a self-serve ticket machine and I found one too, as close as I could get to his. We bought tickets, me juggling credit card, dog, and purse. He then race-walked to a platform, and I hurried after, boarding a train labeled NORWICH. I walked the length of several cars, ignoring the stares of the presumably dog-averse until I found Mirko, at a table for four. As I approached, the train gave a lurch and I lost my balance for a moment, grabbing Mirko's shoulder to steady myself and ending up with a handful of shirt, at which point Gladstone scrambled out of my arms and into his lap.

Mirko accepted the dog but raised an eyebrow at me. "Took your time, didn't you?"

I plopped into the seat across from him, still panting. "Okay, where's Robbie? Also, who do you work for and what do you do, and also, what do I call you, because you're obviously not Mirko, and while we're at it, how do you know all those things about me, things not even Robbie knows? And don't say you're psychic, because you're as clairvoyant as a bagel."

He held my look. "One, that's what I intend to learn, but lower your voice, please, because I'm following someone and while he is three cars ahead of us, I imagine the entire train can hear you. Two, a small agency within the British government. Three, call me Kingsley. Four, observation. You're an American because of your accent. Someplace hot, because it's winter, yet you have a tan line near your clavicle from a sports bra, and another at your ankle, from your trainers, so not a vacation tan but a resident's. Your diction has no tinge of the American South, so not Florida, and the freckles on your left forearm suggest an inordinate amount of time spent on motorways with your arm resting on the window side, more likely in the ungodly traffic of California, than in Hawaii, and from the shade of your hair, Los Angeles. The lead on the dog is fashioned from a luggage strap and still bears the knot of elastic from an airline identification tag." He picked up the slack leash and proceeded to unknot the elastic. "Your neck is stiff," he continued, "suggesting someone who slept with her head against the window on the left side of an airplane. Front row, coach, standby, so last to board. With no seat in front of you to stow your bag, and by the time you boarded, there was no overhead space left, so the flight attendant checked your carry-on, which explains the tag." He set the leash down and Gladstone looked up at him. "You dozed —fitfully—on a floor last night, as evidenced by the bits of shag carpet in your hair."

"Is that supposed to impress me?" I asked.

"It does impress you," he said. "Your turn. How did you know which ticket to buy? You couldn't possibly see my touch screen."

"No," I said. "But I had a clear view of your forearm. I calculated the length of that, plus your fingers, factored in the fifty-five-degree angle your elbow was bent at, which told me where your fingers would land on the touch-screen keyboard, given the destination list from the drop-down menu."

That shut him up.

The train conductor approached. "Tickets, please," he said.

In unison, Kingsley pulled his out of his hoodie pocket and I pulled mine out of my jeans. We handed them over.

The conductor punched a hole in mine but frowned at Kingsley's. "Stansted Mountfitchet Station? You're on the wrong train, sir."

Kingsley blinked.

I gave the conductor my most charming smile. "I'm so sorry. My cousin is legally blind but refuses to ask for help. May I pay the difference for him?"

With a shake of the head, the conductor accepted the twenty-pound note I offered him, made change, and issued Kingsley a new ticket. "An assistance dog, is it?" he asked, directing the question at me.

"Gladstone? Yes," I said. "Years of training."

Once the conductor was out of earshot, Mirko said, "You nicked my ticket. Nicely done."

"I traded tickets," I corrected him. "Which is harder. Robbie and I played pickpocket as children."

"Not so good, though, at buying the proper ticket. You disappoint me."

"Same. Where'd I go wrong?"

"You assumed I used my index finger on the touch screen. I type with my thumb. A three-inch difference. Classic schoolgirl error," he said, but I could tell he was warming up to me. "When did you last talk to Robbie?"

"Five days ago," I said. "He texted me, saying would I please fly to New York, pick up his cat, Touie, and get her to London because his subtenant was threatening to drown her and he was stuck in England on a job. So I did. It was hell. Whatever lies ahead, let me tell you I survived Live Animal Border Inspection at Heathrow, which can make grown men cry, so your Russian mafia doesn't scare me."

His long fingers, on Gladstone's tall ears, stopped mid-pet. "Russian mafia?"

"The Streisand fan. At the shop. Some low-level operative, right? A smurf?"

"Beg your pardon?"

"Oh, please," I said. "You're obviously laundering money, you've got a tunnel filled with black market goods, a wheelie suitcase full of rubles—"

"What makes you think rubles?"

"Your Russian friend, during a sappy pause in 'You Don't Bring Me Flowers,' said *eight hundred million*. If that was pounds or dollars, you'd need a U-Haul to transport them. Rubles, on the other hand, come in denominations of five thousand, and yeah, you could stuff fifteen thousand of them into a suitcase. Which is around a million pounds, a million three in dollars." I wondered if, behind those gray eyes, he was checking my math. "Anyhow," I said. "My brother was part of this adventure. Whatever it is, it's got 'Robbie' written all over it, him being a Russian interpreter, as you of course know."

He studied me. "Have you told the police he's missing?"

"Yeah, they're gonna care that some random American won't answer his sister's texts. Or that his cat's been kidnapped and a dog has stolen her collar." The thief in question was now dozing, emitting fitful dog snores. "Nope. I'm gonna throw in my lot with you, Kingsley-if-that's-even-your-name."

"Not entirely your call," he said.

"I can be persuasive."

"Persuade me."

"I've got a gun in my purse," I said. "Once you catch up to your Russian friend, the one we're following to Norwich, it could come in handy."

An eyebrow went up. "Nicked that too, did you? From the tunnel?"

"Yeah. Which wasn't easy, given that I was in the dark, in a hurry, and hauling a dog."

"Is that it, then?"

"I've also got your wallet. You're flat broke."

The other eyebrow went up. "Pinch any bullets?" he asked, and held out his hand.

"You didn't give me much time." I passed him the wallet and our fingers touched.

He smiled. "Fair enough. Even a nonloaded weapon is a weapon."

The countryside out the train window raced by, deeply green, with hills so rolling they looked fake, accessorized by contented-looking sheep. To someone used to the parched fields of Southern California, it was downright exotic. Kingsley, in the seat opposite, had a view of coming attractions, while I watched what we were leaving behind.

Kingsley and I had steaming cups before us, thanks to the Greater Anglia Railway dining coach. Kingsley was a far cry from "Mirko"—unrecognizable, even—but even so, it took confidence to risk running into the guy he was tailing just for a cup of tea. Not that I was complaining; he'd brought me back a black coffee. I didn't ask how he knew my beverage preferences. Perhaps I had a speck of ground espresso on my earlobe.

"I'm a consultant," Kingsley said, stirring his milky tea. "I was hired to investigate the clandestine dealings going on at the shop of Mirko Rudenko. Having tapped his phone, I heard Mirko converse with a woman named Sarah Byrne, in a dialect called Surzhyk, a hybrid of the Russian and Ukrainian languages in which I am conversant but not fluent. So when Sarah Byrne made an appointment with Mirko, I rang up your brother to come eavesdrop with me."

I blinked. "Robbie's a spy? You guys are spies?"

"No, a consultant," he repeated. "Robbie, of course, knows Eastern European dialects the way a sommelier knows wine. I needed his expertise."

"Okay, whatever. Go on."

"We met outside the shop—'round the back—and listened through the flap of a dog door as Sarah Byrne and the Renowned Mirko had cream tea and a tarot card reading. All nonsense, of course, the tarot business, but then talk turned to gemstones." Kingsley's eyes lit up. "Mirko told Sarah he'd recently acquired a red diamond for a client. 'Come,' he said. 'I'll show you.' But when she stood, she was suddenly unwell. Mirko expressed concern. We heard the sound of creaking wood, people moving about, and then —silence."

"They'd gone into the tunnel."

"They had. If Mirko suspected foul play, he'd certainly avoid the front door. Robbie and I let ourselves in and found no one in the shop but a French bulldog. He was clawing at the bookcase so near the point of entry they may as well have posted a sign saying, PRESS HERE FOR SECRET PASSAGEWAY."

I glanced down at the snoring Gladstone.

"Although it did take me seven minutes to find my way in," he went on. "Embarrassingly slow. I left Robbie in the shop, as a safety measure. I've been locked in cellars once or twice and wasn't keen to do it again."

"And did you find Mirko and Sarah Byrne?" I asked.

"No, but I could hear them, at the far end. The woman was growing hysterical. I listened for their exit and then moved fast. Do you recall the tunnel's final meters, where the brick floor ended and the last bit was dirt?"

"No."

"Try to be more observant," Kingsley said crisply. "Fresh footprints, one of them a lady's spike heel, size four—six to you Americans—told me she was short, plump, vain, and increasingly unsteady on her feet. Mirko half carried, half dragged her those last meters and up the stairs, through Tesco's and onto the street. Which is where I found them. I helped them into a taxi, and in the process managed to acquire Mirko's mobile and the remote that opened the tunnel door. You're not alone in your pickpocketing skills. By this point Mirko was also feeling seriously ill, so I accompanied them to London City Hospital."

"Didn't they think that was odd?" I asked.

"Not once I saw who Sarah Byrne was. She wore an absurd black wig that fell off as we bundled her into the taxi, revealing her to be as blond as you are. I recognized her at once as Yaroslava Barinova. I had only to profess myself her greatest fan and beg the privilege of helping her. Frankly, they were both too sick to care."

Poison, I thought. "And who is, uh, Yaroslava—?"

Kingsley sighed. "The greatest mezzo-soprano since Frederica von Stade. I saw them to the hospital, got them admitted, and texted your brother with an update."

"And?"

He looked at me steadily. "I've heard nothing from Robbie since that day."

I stared at him.

"Breathe," Kingsley said, and I realized I'd stopped. "I found his mobile on Mirko's bookshelf, its battery dead. Not in itself a sign of trouble; your brother's careless about such things. I returned it to his flat, by the way." He frowned at me. "Stop leaping to dire conclusions. We haven't sufficient data, and you'll be no use to me in Norwich if your amygdala hijacks your cerebral cortex."

"That's an oversimplification of cognitive processes," I snapped.

"Don't quibble with me; I wrote a monograph on the subject."

I said, as casually as I could, "So what happened to Mirko and the mezzo-soprano?"

The pause scared me as much as the words that followed. "They were poisoned, of course," Kingsley said at last. "They'll be dead by the weekend."

Norwich, the end of the line, had an actual train station, old and stately. Kingsley and I strolled through it side by side, with Gladstone waddling between us. "Look relaxed," Kingsley said, "but prepare to move quickly. We'll soon need a taxi."

Our quarry was Igor, the Russian who'd come to the shop.

Igor had been the first call on Mirko's cell phone, after it was in Kingsley's pocket and Mirko off to the hospital. Kingsley could tell, from Igor's Russian and his use of the formal pronouns, that the man hadn't met Mirko. This gave Kingsley the confidence to impersonate the psychic when Igor offered to come round and collect a red diamond and hand off a suitcase of rubles.

"He had one moment of doubt," Kingsley said, "but I'm extraordinarily convincing as a gemologist."

"Old-school money laundering," I said.

"A refreshing change from offshore banking," Kingsley said.

"Delightful," I said. "But what's Igor got to do with my brother?"

"With luck, nothing. But we must eliminate the impossible."

While Gladstone and I had hidden behind the screen, Kingsley, in a feat of deduction involving Igor's footwear and clods of dirt —he'd apparently written a monograph on that too—had determined that Igor was bound for Norwich, and on either the 11:52 train or the 12:04. So here we were in a town with the kind of bucolic vibe I'd come to expect from watching *Masterpiece Theatre*. I had no trouble spotting Igor as the train crowd dispersed outside the station. He was a hulking figure, mostly bald but with a patch of red hair. Wearing a bright green windbreaker, he lumbered through the cobblestone streets with a bearlike gait.

We followed him to the town center, thick with boutiques and cafés. A large after-school crowd, noisy kids in plaid uniforms and their attendant adults mixing in with gen pop, meant that Kingsley and I didn't worry about being spotted. But Igor never looked back. He headed to an open-air marketplace, an Anglo-Saxon sort of souk in the shadow of a Gothic cathedral, with row upon row of vendors under striped awnings. We kept our distance now, and when Igor stopped at a kiosk we stopped too, twenty yards back, and Kingsley bought French fries served in newspaper. We then made our way up terraced stone steps overlooking the plaza.

"I assume Igor's getting his red diamond appraised," I said, nodding at a blue awning marked POPOV FINE JEWELRY, BOUGHT AND SOLD. WALK-INS WELCOME.

"Chips?" Kingsley pushed the French fries toward me, but as

they were covered in vinegar, I passed. Gladstone, however, helped himself. "And what will the appraiser tell him?" Kingsley asked me.

"He'll say, 'Igor, I hope you didn't pay more than thirty bucks for this because it's a third-rate garnet plucked from some dog or cat collar with a Swiss Army knife."

"Very good," Kinglsey said. "Not a garnet, though. Swarovski crystal."

I scratched Gladstone's neck, my fingers finding the empty setting where the crystal had been. "Where's the real diamond?"

He shrugged. "The tunnel, I imagine. Some government functionary will be months getting that place sorted."

"Wasn't it a risk, giving him a fake rock?"

"It shouldn't have been. But I fear I've miscalculated," Kingsley admitted. "I expected he'd go straight to his boss, at Finchlingly Manor, six kilometers down the road. Where government agents are waiting to take Igor into custody. That's where I planned to question him."

"But why *wouldn't* he authenticate the diamond?"

"Because Mirko was well trusted. The Cartier of money launderers. The De Beers of Marylebone. You don't survive in his trade by ripping off customers."

"Mirko isn't going to survive," I reminded him.

"And Igor has just reached the same conclusion regarding himself." Kingsley stood abruptly. "Off we go."

Igor lumbered along at a good clip now, leading us across a pedestrian overpass into a working-class neighborhood.

"Where's he off to then?" Kingsley asked. "If not to his employer, or the train station, or the airport—"

"Church," I said. "To pray for his immortal soul."

"Nonsense. If he were the churchy sort, Norwich Cathedral was right in front of him."

"But that's Anglican, right?" I asked. "He made the sign of the cross as he left the marketplace."

"That wasn't the sign of the cross, it was psoriasis. He's been scratching regularly. And in any case, Anglicans also cross themselves."

"But Anglicans cross left to right for the Holy Ghost part," I said. "Igor went right to left. What do you bet he goes to a Russian Orthodox church?"

"I'm not going to bet with you. Wouldn't be sporting. I've failed only four times in my entire career, and— *now* what's he doing?"

What Igor was doing was staring at his phone as he walked, twice doing a one-eighty, the sign of a man at the mercy of Google maps. Seven minutes later he reached a one-story brick building with all the charm and spaciousness of a vacuum cleaner store. A sign near the door read RUSSIAN ORTHODOX CHURCH. But the door was locked. Igor rattled it twice, then gave up and checked his phone.

"Let's go question him right now," I said.

"Have you never done a proper ambush?" Kingsley asked. "We need privacy. Pity that church is closed."

"Yes, pity that Russian Orthodox church is closed."

"Don't gloat," he said. "It's unattractive."

Minutes later Igor got his bearings and took off, with us following, until Gothic spires came into view, rising out of the drab suburbs.

"Cathedral of John the Baptist," Kingsley said. "Roman Catholic. He must've converted. And unless there's a mass in progress, that's where we'll make our move."

St. John's was what a cathedral should be, all white marble and stained glass resplendent in the dying light of late afternoon. A dramatic *Pietà* dominated the left half of the church, just past the transept, and that's where Igor stopped. He genuflected, crossed himself, and knelt.

Kingsley and I found a pew near the back. "It's weird to be in a church with a dog," I whispered. "And a gun. Why ambush him here?"

"We won't ambush," Kingsley answered. "We'll converse. Note his body language: he's dying to confess."

As if he heard us, Igor straightened his spine, turned, spotted us, and bolted.

Kingsley was after him in a flash, leaving me to grab Gladstone and follow, down the nave toward the altar, a left at the *Pietà*, around the back, and out the side door. Igor was faster than he looked, sprinting across a parking lot and into someone's backyard.

But it wasn't a backyard, it was an entrance to a park. We sped down a walkway, past a sign saying PAY HERE pointing to an "Honesty Box," through a vine-enclosed path and around a bend, into a glorious sunken garden.

The garden was rectangular, ending in a beautiful stone facade.

Igor headed that way, then peeled off to the right, scrambling with difficulty up a terraced wall and disappearing into a thick copse.

"Go left," Kingsley called over his shoulder. "The understory! I'll take the right!"

Having no idea what an understory was, I nevertheless scurried up a side stairway and into a thicket so dense that day became night. I set Gladstone down onto the forest floor and unclipped his leash so he wouldn't strangle himself, and made my way blindly forward, thinking I may as well have been back in the tunnel. I imagined Kingsley doing the same on the opposite side of the garden while our quarry waltzed back out and onto the street.

And then there he was, on the path in front of me.

Igor looked more startled than threatening. He stared at my hand, and I looked down too, to discover I'd drawn the gun from my purse.

Our eyes met. He was pale, and from the ears up bald. From the ears down he sported a fuzzy glob of red hair, a clown wig cut in half. It gave him a hapless air, Larry of the *Three Stooges*.

I tried to say "Stop" in Russian, but what came out was *zdravstvujtye,* which of course meant "good day," which was equally useless. Because Igor had already stopped and neither of us was having a good day.

"Where's my brother?" I blurted out, and then *"Gde moy brat?"* before realizing that this man would have no idea who I was, let alone my brother, in any language.

"You can shoot me," he responded, in very good English. "Please."

Maybe it was the influence of the Honesty Box at the entrance, but I said, "I'm sorry. My gun isn't loaded."

At that point Kingsley came crashing through the thicket behind Igor. He looked at my gun and between gasps of breath said, "Let's go down to the garden and find a nice bench, shall we?"

Kingsley was right about one thing: Igor was dying to unburden himself. Mopping his sweaty brow with his windbreaker sleeve, he said, "I was hired by—"

"Spartak Volkov," Kingsley said. "We know all that."

"Wait," I said. "*I* don't know all that. Who is Spartak Volkov?"

"Russian émigré," Kingsley said. "Tons of money, ties to both your government and mine. He hired Igor to assassinate—"

"Sarah Byrne," said Igor, nodding. "A simple job."

"For one with your skill set, yes. You're a poisoner by vocation and a baker by avocation. Your passion is pastry," Kingsley said, and then, noting Igor's surprise, "I saw it immediately."

"But how? You are not psychic!" Igor said.

"There are bits of calcified dough on your collar," Kingsley said. "Your fingers are stained from food coloring. Red Dye No. 3, which you must've brought from Moscow, as it's banned in England. Only an aficionado travels with his own food coloring."

"I use but a drop," Igor said, a tad defensive. "For my icings. Okay, and my jellies. Because Sarah Byrne, she loves to eat the English desserts. This I learn from Spartak Volkov. He makes my job easy. Sarah Byrne has been a long time from England, he tells me, and she visits now and wants her cakes. She will die for her cakes."

"Victoria sponge: arguable," Kingsley said. "But spotted dick?"

"Banoffee!" Igor said. "Figgy duff!"

"What on earth are you people talking about?" I asked.

"The remains of their cream tea," Kingsley said. "Masterfully done, Igor."

"I paid the chauffeur," Igor explained. "He tells me she goes on Thursday to a psychic. I set up my cart outside the shop. I wear my apron. My hat. She comes. She buys. Two of everything! She goes into the shop. I hear through the window: Mirko makes tea, they eat her cakes."

Little hairs on the back of my neck sprang to life, but I couldn't yet account for them.

"But when I report to Volkov, he grows mad! The woman, yes, the woman should die, he says. But Mirko? No. Because Mirko the Psychic, he tells me, is also Mirko the—the—" He waved his hands.

"Money launderer?" I offered.

"Fence?" Kingsley suggested. "Procurer? Black marketeer?"

"Yes! The whole world trades with Mirko! Everybody loves Mirko! Russian, Ukrainian, Bosnian, Herzogovinian—"

"Yes, yes," Kingsley said impatiently. "We get the drift. So you're in trouble. You call the number on the sign in front of the shop. I answer. You're relieved: Mirko is alive, you think. And Mr. Volkov is particularly relieved, as he has given Mirko a very large down payment on a very small rock. And now Mr. Volkov sends *you* with the balance, to collect his diamond. Like a common courier, but what choice do you have? Come, no need to look amazed, Igor. I happen to be a genius. But tell me: something made you suspect I was not Mirko. What was it? My accent?"

Igor shook his head. "It was the sign. 'Walk-ins welcome. Both kinds.' Do you remember? I say to you, 'I myself would like to be a walk-in. How does this work?' But you did not answer. At first I thought you don't *know* the answer. But then I thought. . . ." He shrugged. "We were there for business. For diamonds, not for spirits. We did not have all day."

"I don't have all day either," I said. "Can we get back on topic? So the two poisonees, Mirko and Sarah Byrne, went into the tunnel, thinking to get away from you, Igor, because they suspected what you'd done." I turned to Kingsley. "And you went into the tunnel after them. And my brother Robbie stayed behind in the shop. Not thinking 'poison,' just thinking 'hungry,' as he always is anytime he goes an hour without food." I turned back to Igor. "It's not just possible he'd be tempted by your sweets, Igor; it's virtually certain. But my brother's a picky eater. So what I need to know is, did you put polonium in every single thing you baked?"

A silence settled on us, so that I could hear the birds in the garden singing their twilight songs.

"How do you know my poison is polonium?" Igor asked quietly.

"Totally obvious," I said.

"*You* are a psychic!" he said, with awe.

"Nobody's a psychic!" I said. "You take pride in your work, and you like a challenge, and polonium takes talent," I said. "And experience. You probably trained in Moscow. Lab X. And also," I went on, "because everyone in this crazy story either *is* Russian or *knows* Russian, so everyone, upon feeling sick, thinks 'poison' and then they think about Alexander Litvinenko and his teapot of polonium and they're off to the ER, screaming 'radiation poisoning.' Including Robbie. Which is why he disappeared. So while I feel sorry for the psychic and the opera singer, I need to think about my brother now, so you need to tell me, Chef Boyardee, did you bake polonium into *everything?*"

"No, no," he said, shaking his head. "The flies' graveyard, yes, and the Garibaldi biscuit. But not the—wait!" He stared at me. "What opera singer?"

"Sarah Byrne," Kingsley told him, "was the alias used by Yaroslava Barinova whenever she was in London. She liked to go incognito. She also wore wigs."

If Igor had been pale before, he was now the color of toothpaste. The white kind. "Yaroslava Barinova?" he gasped. "I have killed Yaroslava Barinova? The greatest mezzo since Anne Sofie von Otter?" He clutched at his heart, scrunching his windbreaker in his big baker's hands.

I patted him on the back, but he was beyond comfort. "I deserve to die!" He pointed to Kingsley. "I give you rubles, you give me junk. Yes, I am stupid. I kill Mirko, the fence. Yes, I am sloppy. But now, now—" His voice rose to a scream. "Yaroslava—Barinova! —the pride of Perm!" His screams turned to coughing, and he reached into his windbreaker to pull out a tiny aspirin tin, from which he took a pill. He stuck it in his mouth, swallowing with a grimace. Then he began to cry. And cough. And cry.

"Oh, for God's sake," I said, and handed him my bottle of water. He knocked it back, drinking half, and wailed anew.

"Igor!" I yelled. "Toughen up. I'm sorry about your opera singer, but what about my brother?"

But Igor was done talking. A strangled sound emanated from him, an unearthly noise, like someone screaming with a closed mouth, or the braying of a donkey—his head reared back and then he fell forward. Kingsley and I, on either side of him, reached for him, but he dropped from the bench to his knees and into a kind of seizure, his mouth foaming. A dark calm settled over me as I held onto one arm and felt Kingsley holding onto his other, and Gladstone, one paw on the man's knee, howled. The four of us stayed like that for some moments, arms and legs entwined in a group hug there in the Plantation Garden, until the life drained out of one of us, and we were only three.

"Polonium for the customers," I said, "but old-school cyanide pill for himself. Poor Igor."

"Before you get all sentimental," Kingsley said, "consider this: Spartak Volkov had Yaroslava Barinova killed because she jilted him. A slow death, so she could think on her sins. That's what our Igor did. His life's work. Just eat your trail mix and try not to romanticize assassins." We were on the train back to London, side by side, now with Gladstone between us like a snoring armrest. Our adrenaline levels were returning to normal and our fingers and toes thawing.

If Igor's death was operatic, its aftermath was not. Kingsley had me help him remove Igor's green windbreaker, from which prints could be lifted.

"Theoretically," I said. "But practically speaking, unlikely."

"Don't argue. Leaving fingerprints scattered about is unprofessional."

It seemed to me that Igor looked lonely, lying there in a brown polo shirt that didn't cover his belly, and when Kingsley made a phone call to his mysterious government agency, I found Igor's iPhone in the grass, clicked on his iTunes, and set it on repeat so that "You Don't Bring Me Flowers" would accompany him to the afterlife.

But Kingsley plucked it from the grass on our way out. "Leave it here? Are you mad? A mobile is a font of information."

Once on the train, Kingston kept up a steady stream of conversation, clearly for my benefit. We tacitly avoided the subject of Robbie. "Shall I tell you what became of the cat?" he said suddenly.

"Touie," I replied, "is stuffed into Mirko's freezer. You had to remove a twenty-pound turkey to make room for her. I hope she was dead when you did it."

"She was. I stopped by Robbie's flat this morning to drop off the dog—my landlady, an excellent woman, claims she's grown allergic to him. I must've just missed you. You, on the other hand, did not even see a dead cat on your brother's bed."

"I saw her. It didn't occur to me to check her for signs of life."

"Ah. You see, but you do not observe."

"Why'd you give her collar to Gladstone?" I asked.

He looked at me, surprised. "Dogs need tags. She had no use for it anymore."

"Well, anyway," I said. "It was kind of you to spare me the ordeal of a dead cat."

"It was curiosity, not kindness. I'm interested in cause of death; I plan to test her for butane and benzene, for a monograph on mattress toxicity." He was quiet for a long moment, then said, "What *is* the other definition of a walk-in? Other than a client without an appointment?"

"It's a New Age term," I said. "It's someone who's tired of living, whose soul vacates their body so a more . . . *evolved* soul can move in. A spiritual celebrity."

"What nonsense."

I shrugged. "Some souls don't want to waste time with birth and childhood. They've been here before, and they've got work to do. But after the trade happens, the new souls generally forget they're walk-ins. Which means you—or I—could be some kind of historical figure and not even realize it. Da Vinci. Michelangelo. A dead Beatle."

"Right," he said. "That is the most ridiculous thing I've heard all day. And it's been a long day."

"Whatever," I said. "But next time you impersonate a psychic, you might want to notice the sign outside your shop."

"I saw the sign. All my senses are excellent. *Evolved*, even."

"You saw, but you did not observe," I said.

He raised an eyebrow. "I *observe* that you are picking out the sultanas in that trail mix I bought you. So you dislike sultanas. Does your twin share this aversion?"

I looked down at the small pile of dark, withered rejects, swept aside on the table in front of us. "What's a sultana?"

"A dried grape. Ingredient in sultana cakes, scones, Garibaldi biscuits, and the like."

"Ah—squashed flies?"

"Precisely."

"Oh, yeah. Robbie hates them. Raisins, currants, all dried fruit." Kingsley blinked. And a slow smile spread across his face.

As the train neared Liverpool station the *ping!* of an incoming text woke me. I'd dozed off, my head against Kingsley's shoulder. I looked at my phone.

> So long story short, I'm allergic to my new bed, thought it was something more serious and went to the ER and some idiot gave me penicillin, so THAT nearly killed me, but anyway, finally home, hope u weren't worried and btw, where are u? and where the f is my cat? xox

"What does that mean," Kingsley said, reading over my shoulder, "when you Americans sign *xox*? I understand *x*, but what's the *o*?"

I smiled at him. "I think I'll just show you."

PRESTON LANG

Top Ten Vacation Selfies of YouTube Stars

FROM *Deadlines*

THERE ARE NO professional hit men in America. That's not to say people don't take money in exchange for shooting a guy in the head. Some heavy kid gets a thousand bucks to whack another banger? Sure. But there's no suave pro who lives a normal life until he gets the call from his handler to take down your difficult mistress, your work rival, your wealthy uncle. And there's certainly no telephone number some suburban dad can call to order a fifteen-thousand-dollar hit on a Little League coach. It's a cool setup for a story, but I've been a reporter too long, covered too many murders—it can't really happen. Not only would a business like that get busted in a week, but there just isn't enough work out there to make it feasible.

Yet there I was, drinking with a man who told me that's exactly how he'd made his living. He called himself Brack. He had big, rough hands, but his voice was smooth and unexcitable.

"Another time I had to dress up like an emo kid to get into this club. You can laugh, but I put on the makeup and the skinny pants. Dosed the target's drink, then I hit that dance floor. Flopped around all moody. I even took home a girl with a fish skeleton on her backpack. The hit went down as an accidental overdose. A work of art, if I do say so myself."

His email had come to me out of the blue—*I've got a story to tell.* With nothing else going on, I decided to meet him. Then I almost walked out when he said he was a hit man. You can't write a legit article about a guy spreading bullshit in a bar, but in truth I'd been writing more and more trash lately.

I used to have a regular job with a real newspaper. Then I didn't. I used to do reporting. Next thing I knew I was putting out a lot of trend nonsense: *Why are the kids wearing their socks over their shoes?* Interview a few hip young things, generalize a bit, then get a clinical psychologist with a few bromides to put a button on it. I sold an article like that to the online arm of a national magazine. A few people read it. A lot of folks didn't read it but wrote salty comments underneath. Old friends probably thought, *Hey, Mike's doing pretty well for himself,* but when you factored in expenses that I never got reimbursed for, the piece netted me just over eight hundred bucks. It was my only income that month. My cousin works thirty hours a week at a frozen yogurt place. Last year she made more than I did, and she lives in a trailer with her mom, an EBT card, and a stack of really poorly written collection threats. I get just enough work that I still feel like a professional journalist but not enough to actually survive as a human being.

"Strangled this guy in a park one night with an ace bandage," Brack said. "Then I set him down on a bench. He sat there a day and a half before anyone thought to check if he was dead."

Body in a park, dead for more than twenty-four hours in public view? I'd look it up when I got home. We kept drinking and Brack kept right on talking. He once impersonated a Department of Agriculture agent, then shoved a rancher into his own decomp pit. He drowned a lady at the YWCA. He got a hunter with bear shot during pheasant season.

"But I haven't been in the field in years," he said. "I'm on the admin side now. It's a job like any other. Answering phones, managing personalities."

"How many people do you have working for you?"

"A few. It varies. Right now I'm a bit strapped for talent. They don't always last as long as you'd like them to."

I didn't think I'd been drinking that hard, but I started to feel pretty hammered. My tolerance had gone way down. I was a middle-aged, underemployed, burnt-out hack, but at least I'd avoided one cliché by giving up liquor as soon as I couldn't afford it. I spent my nights drinking Sanka, searching for paying venues that took unsolicited pitches.

"So you want to know why I'd even talk to you, right?" Brack asked.

"People enjoy my company."

"I looked you up: Michael Roth. I like the way you write. You don't try to show how smart you are all the time. You just tell us what's going on in regular English."

I'm a sucker for a compliment, and I was almost drunk enough to get into Mikey's 7 Rules of Unpretentious Journalism. Instead I smiled and nodded and let him continue.

"There's no one else within a hundred miles who could do a story like this."

Probably true.

"And you hate cops," he said. "Cops hate you, right?"

I wouldn't have put it that way, but he wasn't exactly wrong.

"You were writing about brutality before it was fashionable."

I wouldn't have said that either, but there was some truth to it.

"So you're not going to run and tell police about me. I know that."

"Okay. Say I write an article, and it gets a little attention," I said. "The police can pressure me to give you up."

"Don't we have a constitutional protection? An amendment? Something like that?"

I went on a bit about Judith Miller and Charles Manson and a few other pieces of legal pomp that came into my buzzing brain.

"What if it was a book?" he asked.

"Still tricky."

But maybe we could manage it. Offer up pretend facts as auto-biographical fiction. Or maybe we could go nonfiction and claim the source was a third party, or that I got my info from a man on his deathbed. It would probably all seem ridiculous in the morning, but I took the guy's phone number and stumbled out of the bar.

I wasn't looking forward to the trip home: a long wait, then a thirty-minute bus ride and a fifteen-minute walk. Out in the parking lot I considered the possibility that Brack had once been some local dirtbag who killed a guy for five hundred bucks, and now years later he'd invented this whole hit-man persona. Maybe one of the murders he'd told me about was real. If I could track him to it, that might be something. Or it might be nothing.

Along the shoulder of the road, I heard a single beep. Brack rolled down his window.

"What, you don't have a ride?"

I shook my head. It had come down to keeping the car or the Internet. In the twenty-first century the Web wins.

"Get in, man. I'll drive you home."

So I got in a car with a self-confessed mass murderer. At first we went the right way, but after about ten minutes he took a turn off the main road.

"No, stay straight another five miles," I said.

"I've got a different proposition for you."

My stomach tightened up just a bit.

"I've got a client. We're looking to get it done soon."

"Okay."

"I'll give you sixteen grand."

"For what?"

"If you'll do it. The hit."

"I'm a journalist."

"Hey, for six years I thought I was a glazier."

He took a thick wad of cash from the glove compartment and counted out six thousand dollars.

"That's for now. The other ten when you're done."

I shook my head and didn't take the money.

"Sudden. I know," he said, and kept driving, deeper into the hills. "There's this woman—nice lady. She marries Prince Charming. Wonderful, all wonderful. Eventually she meets his dad. Guy is really fucking creepy. You know how you sometimes get that off a guy? And when she talks to her husband's brother and sister, they don't come out and say it, but she thinks the old guy used to touch them."

"But they don't come out and say it?"

"Sometimes those people are like that. You know what I mean? Scarred. They just don't want to say it happened."

Yeah, I knew all about that. I'd done a series on adult victims of child molestation. It was the last good, honest journalism I'd done. I put in some real research and took the time to get the interviews right. I sold it as a three-parter to a big daily paper in one of our largest cities. Sober, intelligent people read my words and maybe learned a little something. I made about two dollars an hour on that job.

"But the husband—Prince Charming—seems to think his dad is a great guy. Fine, she'll just hold her breath and nod when she has to see the father-in-law twice a year. But three months back she had twins and the dad moved to town to be nearer his grandkids. The husband thinks it's great. Talks about letting old Gampy watch the kids while they go to the movies, have romantic steak dinners. That kind of thing. So far she's been able to put that off, and she watches Gampy like a hawk when he's in her house, but she's going back to work in a few weeks. Eventually he's going to be alone with those kids."

"She can't level with her husband?"

"Tell your husband his dad's a perv? How's he going to take that? But she also figures we're all better without this guy. Kids in the neighborhood? Maybe he's got a little chamber in the basement? Who knows? The guy is bad for the world. Take the money. It's yours."

He stopped the car in the parking lot of a convenience store and pulled a knapsack out of the back seat.

"In the bag you've got gloves, shoe covers, a key to the back door, and a Glock G29. You know how to use it?"

As it turned out, I did. I'd actually joined a club back when I was still at *The News*. I pretended it was so I could write a story. One of those *Hey, I'm a liberal guy trying to get into the mindset of all you redneck bastards who love guns*. But I have to admit it was a real kick to hold that little slayer in my hand. The Glock was exactly the kind I'd used.

"There's one bedroom upstairs. He'll be asleep. You put three or four in his head. Then you leave out the back. Same way you came in. You walk past the pond and into the woods. If you keep going about a mile, you'll come out on Rook Street. I'll pick you up, give you ten grand, and take you home."

I still hadn't touched anything he'd offered me, but when he handed me a photograph, I took it. It was the old guy—the pervert. Yeah, I could see it in his eyes. There's a few varieties of molesters. He was the type with the big, fake smile and the comfortable sweater. I'd seen plenty of them before. He did deserve to die, and I deserved sixteen grand.

There was a map showing me how to get from the convenience store to the house. The address would be clear on the mailbox. The neighbors weren't that close by. If all went well, they might not even hear the gunshot, and the body might not be discovered for a few days. As I neared the house, I saw all the lights were off. I approached the back door, but I didn't put in the key. I wasn't a killer. This was crazy. I had that one clean bolt of sobriety before I heard the snap of a shotgun blast. I ran and fell and another shot rang out. I was pinned between the side wall and the house. There were a few low shrubs about five feet away. I scuttled behind one of them.

"Get up. Then I'll put you down for good."

I could've made it to the wall, but he would've gotten a clear shot at my back. Or I could've run past the house, but then he'd have me at close range. Or I could've surrendered. *Please don't shoot.* But he'd already shot at me twice and threatened to kill me if I stood up. I heard him step off the porch and shoot again toward the bushes. There weren't too many places I could be hiding. He knew roughly where I was. As he drew closer, he came into view through a hole in the shrub. For a second I saw his face clearly, lit from behind by the porch light. I could see all the cunning, all the evil. I got him twice in the gut. Then I ran. Past the pond and into the woods like Brack had said. I made it out to Rook Street and walked along the dark road for fifteen minutes, but no one came to pick me up, so I ducked into the adjoining trail and stayed in there until morning, when I came out near the highway and found a bus stop some twenty miles from where I'd shot the pervert.

I was exhausted when I got home, and I fell asleep almost immediately. I woke up late that afternoon and checked the news online. There was a preliminary report of a murder up in the hills. Neighbors heard yelling and fighting from at least three people. Then gunshots. The old man died in the ambulance. I felt all right. I had the pulse of self-preservation, but the murder itself—those two shots to an old man's gut—wasn't really biting at me.

Maybe it was very stupid, but I went back to the bar where I'd met Brack and asked after him. I wanted my ten grand, and—though I'm a little embarrassed to say it—I wanted another job. I still wanted to believe there was a valid reason he hadn't met me on Rook Street or that his phone number was invalid. I saw this whole life of ease and leisure, punctuated by four or five hits a year. Maybe get my price up to an even twenty grand. But after four shots of bad whiskey, the image of me in a tailored suit, skulking in the shadows, sizing up victims, began to dissipate. I wouldn't be a hit man. I wouldn't get to call up Brack and say things like *The fly has been swatted.* I wouldn't even get my ten grand.

Six thousand bucks to kill a sixty-eight-year-old widower named Keith Pelfrey. The murder was a big local story. A friend of mine from New York even called to see if I was working on it and whether there was anything nationally interesting about an old guy shot on his back lawn. Pelfrey had worked as a financial adviser for forty years before retiring the previous May. He was one of those un-ostentatious rich guys: nice house, decent car, but nothing crazy. He'd lived at his current address for the past twenty-five years. All his money went to his only child, a daughter named Lana. There were no twin infants and no reason to believe Keith had ever molested a child.

A blogger called me one morning, a young guy who sometimes took me to lunch. He had some family money to keep him upright while he tried to take on local stories, and he liked to hear me talk about turn-of-the-century newsrooms— *We had to plug into a telephone jack to look at the Internet.*

"The police are basically nowhere," he told me over seafood. "A burglary gone wrong. Nothing left behind at the site. Really common weapon and ammo. They looked into a guy who robbed a few places with a handgun about ten years back, but that didn't go anywhere. There's even a theory that it was just a poor guy who took a wrong turn, went up to Pelfrey's place to ask directions, and the old man opened fire."

"Why would the old guy be so paranoid?"

"Old guys living alone? Once night falls, they're ready to shoot at anything that moves."

"So the cops have no one on the radar?"

"His daughter, of course. She's getting all the money, but they seemed close. She'd visit twice a year. They'd bike around the neighborhood with little helmets and kneepads. All very wholesome. And she was in Florida when it happened. Unless you think she hired a guy."

"That's pretty far-fetched."

"Maybe. But I have to say—and this is just raw hunch based on nothing—I have a feeling it's a professional job."

"How do you figure that? He didn't even get inside the house, Pelfrey got three shots at him before he fired back, then our pro gets the old man in the stomach and dashes off before he's even dead. Doesn't sound all that well put together." I ate more shrimp. I'd taken down nearly the entire plate while the kid had been talking. "I'd be wary about paying too much attention to *raw hunch*. Careful research and reasonable deductions are where the truth usually lies."

For the first time since I'd known him, he looked at me like I was an old buffoon who didn't realize his time was up.

"Maybe," he said. "But it's the wild ideas that get you clicks."

He ran with wild ideas for a while but ended up abandoning the story a few weeks later as his blog pivoted from local news to outrage pieces that fed a certain kind of political idiot.

Lana got her money without a hitch and moved to British Columbia, where six months later she married someone called Jonah Reed. Jonah was at least his third legal name. I tracked him back to a man named Lou Kovacs who'd managed a punk band in Georgia. Younger, prettier, but with those same rough, dangerous hands, it sure looked like Brack. Last I could tell, Lana and Jonah had sold all their Canadian property and flown to Amsterdam.

I thought I might feel the guilt eventually, but it hasn't come. Instead I feel an incredible sense of freedom, and for the first time in years I'm paying my bills with words. Last week my most widely read article was called "Top Ten Vacation Selfies of YouTube Stars." You might have seen it pop up on your screen, daring you to read it. If you do click on it—or any article like it—you can be sure that you're reading the work of a journalist who has abandoned any set of morals he may once have had. You can be sure that the writer has stolen from children, or gotten decent folks hooked on smack, or maybe even killed for money. And if you see a typo, an obvious inaccuracy, or a paragraph that seems spliced in from nowhere, don't tell me about it. I don't care. I'm making a living.

JARED LIPOF

Mastermind

FROM *Salamander*

IT WAS THE fall the NFL players went on strike, asking that their wage scale be calculated as a function of gross revenue—a demand the team owners recoiled from as if someone had upended a pitcher of urine across each vast mahogany desk. So my father had no Patriots game to watch on television, and he flipped on the *Wide World of Sports* to endure, in his words, "whatever arcane bullshit Jim McKay feels like blathering on about. It's probably gonna be cross-country skiing, or curling, or goddamn table tennis."

"Want to play Mastermind?" I said.

My father looked at me and then back to the TV, where coverage had relocated to a synchronized swimming competition, trying to figure out which option was less unbearable.

"Fine." But he left the TV on.

Invented by an Israeli postmaster, Mastermind was essentially a game of code-breaking where one player arranged four pegs of different colors behind a shield and the other player had twelve turns to guess the correct sequence. To make matters more difficult, there were six different peg colors and repetition was permitted, meaning there were 6^4 or 1,296 potential combinations. The code-breaker made his guess and then the code-maker would use even smaller black or white pegs to indicate how far off it was. A black peg meant correct color, correct position. A white peg meant correct color, incorrect position. No peg meant neither. The code-breaker used this information to make the next guess. Failed attempts generated cumulative data, applied in series. Games of this variety generally drove my father batshit, but my mother felt they fostered early cognitive development.

"I'll be code-maker," I said.

"Balls," said my father. He spun the board around to face him and chuckled, which seemed to make him cough. He glanced toward the TV again, as if the NFL strike might have been settled in the past few moments to spare him this tedium.

"Don't just put four of the same color," I said. "It's too easy."

"Don't tell me how to play. Now, look away while I do this."

He set four pegs behind the shield and awaited my first guess.

Across the street from our school lived a man with a broken face. He hadn't always lived there, but for the past three days, freed by the final bell, we'd walk past the yellow buses idling along the driveway and there he'd be, sitting in a window, an *X* of bandages across his nose, a gauze skullcap held in place by a chinstrap of medical tape. Just two eyes and some nose holes. A mummified king, silent and cryptic, scowling at everything beneath him.

Theories of his injury abounded.

"Race-car driver," said Benny Silver, my best friend. "Formula One would be my guess. And *that* is the result of one hell of a crash. Multiple flips, no doubt."

"What would a race-car driver be doing here," I said, "in that dump?"

The man smoked a cigarette in the third-floor window, two stories above Val's Barbershop and King Pizza, side-by-side establishments that shared the storefront at 1608 Chickering Road.

"He's in that dump," said Benny, "*convalescing.*"

Benny gathered and hoarded vocabulary words from his mother's grad school textbooks, words he planned to deploy in a courtroom one day, when he became a hotshot attorney.

"No, I mean, wouldn't a race-car driver rather *convalesce*," I said, letting Benny know he hadn't lost me, "in, like, an Italian villa, or a Back Bay brownstone, or a seaside mansion up in Newburyport? Those guys are loaded."

"The car *owners* are loaded," said Benny. "Drivers are like jockeys, hired help on the payroll."

"Maybe he's a boxer," said Mike Walden, with his bowl cut and wristbands.

"Maybe he is pilot of fighter jet," said Nader Al-Otabi, whose father had brought his family here from Saudi Arabia as part of some top-secret air force contract that Nader couldn't seem to shut up about. "Maybe seat ejects but cockpit remains closed."

"Again with the fighter pilots?" said Benny.

"Yeah, we get it, man," I said. "You know jets."

"And parachutes," whispered Nader.

The mummy's head swiveled toward us and we bolted like impalas spooked by a lion.

After school the next day Benny dragged me to Hanover Public Library. He'd seen something on the news the night before that demanded immediate follow-up. "I've had something of an *intuition*," he said.

"You sure it was on the news? Sounds like you've been watching *Dr. Who*."

"There's nothing wrong with *Dr. Who*."

"What's at the library?" I said.

"Shh." He put his finger to his lips. "Not until we get there."

Benny's sense of showmanship required a visual aid, and he said nothing further until we strode up the library's front steps and requested several rolls of microfilm from the librarian and commandeered a viewing machine. Even then I had to wait for him to shuttle back and forth across two of them before he finally pointed at the screen and said, "There."

The headline, dated July 22, 1982, read "Mickey Thutston Escapes from Walpole," above a pair of mug shots of the notorious bank robber himself.

"That was like three months ago," I said.

"Precisely," said Benny.

"Precisely what?"

"Oh, Oliver. Don't you see?"

I hated when he did this. We were in the same grade. We'd been friends since we were toddlers. But Benny was four months older than me, and whenever he found himself in the know he tended to treat me more like a nephew with a learning disability than a friend.

"See *what?*" I said, way too loud for the library's hushed confines. An oil painting of one of Hanover's founding fathers scowled at me from a gilt-edged frame. Any second the librarian's head would peek around the corner to reprimand me.

"Plastic surgery," whispered Benny.

I looked at the mug shot on the screen. Mickey Thurston was a handsome guy, there was no denying it. As in those old black-and-white photos of Paul Newman, Thurston's eyes looked chiseled from diamonds, the kind of eyes that made a woman's knees buckle. I'd heard stories about Mickey from both my father and my uncle Stan, who was a Hanover cop. Ladies' man. Folk hero. Blue-collar guys loved him in a Robin Hood kind of way. He only stole from banks, and everybody, even the cops, knew that the banks were the *real* criminals. According to the article, Mickey Thurston robbed over forty of them, never used a gun, and was arrested, convicted, and locked up in the early seventies. Then, back in July, he and four other Walpole inmates crawled out of a hole in the ground at the end of a two-hundred-foot tunnel and made a break for it. Three of them had been recaptured by lunchtime the next day. A fourth by sundown. And that left Mickey, out there somewhere. Presumably out of the country. There were more rumors about Mickey Thurston's whereabouts than theories about the broken man's face.

"Why would he hide here? We're only like fifty miles from Walpole," I said.

"Fifty-two, to be precise."

"Fine. I see you've done your research. Wouldn't *you* want to get farther away from the prison you'd escaped from?"

"Unless that's where everyone was looking for me. All I'm saying is that *nobody* would be looking for him this close to home."

Could this be the man in the window across the street from the school, wrapped in gauze? The eyes might have told me, but we hadn't gotten close enough.

"I don't know, Benny. Maybe."

"There's something else," he said. "They're offering a ten-thousand-dollar reward for any information leading to his capture."

That same fall, my mother began nursing school. The local community college offered a two-year RN program and she'd spent the summer reading anatomy and physiology textbooks in the same way my father read true crime and Stephen King in the living room recliner. Naturally, Benny considered her a medical expert worthy of consultation.

After she rubber-stamped Benny's extra place setting for dinner, we began our homework at the kitchen table. With half of our math problems completed, Benny locked eyes with me and jerked his head toward my mother, preparing food at the counter. This, evidently, was my cue.

"So, um, how does plastic surgery work?" I asked her.

"What?" she said.

All Benny required was an opening. "What Ollie means is *reconstructive* surgery."

I decided that I'd slap him in the mouth if he corrected me again.

She cocked an eyebrow. "Why?"

Though we hadn't discussed it, Benny was prepared. "You know Mark Hamill?" he said.

My mother spun around and put a hand on her hip. "I've heard the name once or twice."

"Well, between filming *Star Wars* and *The Empire Strikes Back,* Mark Hamill got in a car accident and needed reconstructive surgery. Hence, his altered appearance in *Empire.*"

"And this is why you're interested in plastic surgery?"

"In a manner of speaking," said Benny.

"Sorry, boys, but we're still on the respiratory system. Trachea to bronchi to lungs, then on to matters of the heart. Tell me what you want to know and I'll see if I can find it out."

I pretended to pull the question out of my ass. "How long, say, would someone have to wear bandages after having plastic surgery on their face?"

The sliding glass door flew open. "Smells good in here!"

My father worked at an electroplating shop. The chemical process, he explained to me, was a galvanic cell — in other words, a battery — in reverse, where the cathode of the circuit was the part to be plated and the anode was the metal to be plated upon it. Through the door he carried with him the odor of thousand-gallon vats of acid lining the plating shop floor beneath clouds of vapor that threatened all passersby with a fatal sickness. He crossed the kitchen and kissed my mother and opened the refrigerator to fetch a beer. Over a greedy first sip he surveyed Benny and me sitting there, pencils and graph paper and math textbooks scattered on the table. Which was when he noticed the fourth place setting.

"Whoa, hold on. Master Silver will be dining with us? You do realize," he said in his best old-money accent, "that we will be serving a mere *chicken* this evening. A most pedestrian bird, I'm afraid, but the butcher was plum out of pheasant, duck, and partridge."

One of my father's chief enjoyments in life was mocking Benny's improbably sophisticated adolescent palate, loudly and at great length. Over at the Silvers' apartment, Benny reveled in a paradise of exotic foods: cheeses pungent as gym socks; spicy brown mustards full of cracked seeds that stung your sinuses; venison and goose and even mutton on special occasions. My father threw a dishtowel over his forearm and pranced around in parody of a fancy restaurant's bow-tied waiter. "Mayhaps the master would like to see a dessert menu?"

"Moving on," said Benny, "the reason we're curious about facelift recovery periods is that Shoemaker's is selling a picture of Mark Hamill with his head wrapped in gauze, taken, they *claim*, in August of 1977, even though the accident occurred way back in January. If I can call the photo's date into dispute I might be able to haggle them down on the price."

Benny really *had* thought this through. Shoemaker's Hobby Shop was a killer toy-slash-comic bookstore where he and I spent pretty much all our allowance money. I couldn't be sure if this picture of Mark Hamill indeed existed, of what portion—if any —of Benny's story could be corroborated later by my mother or father, though it seemed unlikely that they would cross Shoemaker's threshold of their own volition.

Either way, Benny's deflection worked. At the mention of anything *Star Wars*–related my father's eyes glazed over. "I'm gonna go change out of these clothes." He left the kitchen, beer in hand, trailing fumes.

"I'll see what I can find out from my professor," said my mother.

Standing by the window of Ms. Hannum's English classroom and grinding a No. 2 pencil in the sharpener bolted to the sill gave you a clear view across Chickering Road to our fugitive's hideout. Benny and I spent the entire class breaking lead and alternating visits to the sharpener to see if he'd make an appearance. We'd each made three trips to the window and seen nobody, and I knew we were pushing our luck. The last time I got up Ms. Hannum said, "Mr. Zinn, you're not *carving* the words, merely inscribing them onto paper." I nodded and smiled, feigning embarrassment, knowing that the next time Benny or I got up she would lose her shit.

But then—the snap of graphite behind me.

"Yes, Mr. Al-Otabi?" said Ms. Hannum.

"My pencil has broken," said Nader. "I request permission to make pointed the tip."

"What sort of bargain-basement stationer is supplying you children with writing instruments?" she said. "Make it brief."

Nader tiptoed across the room and Ms. Hannum continued a lecture on Poe's "The Tell-Tale Heart" that had endured far too many interruptions already.

"The first word of this story is . . ."

Without raising his hand, Benny said, "True."

"Very good, Mr. Silver. What do you make of this? Someone else."

While she scanned the room, Benny whispered to Nader on his way past.

"Psst. While you're at the—"

At full volume Nader said, "Benjamin, you must not distract me from my errand!"

"That's it! That's *it*! *That's it!*" cried Ms. Hannum. "What in blazes is so interesting by the pencil sharpener?" She crossed the room to see for herself.

Benny shrugged and Nader held up his broken pencil.

She turned to me. "What about you, Mr. Zinn? Anything to say?"

"Well, you see, there's this—"

Benny cut me off again. "Ms. Hannum, as long as you're over there, you see that building across the street? The one with the pizza place and barbershop? Do you by any chance see somebody over there?"

If he finished another one of my sentences I would lay him out cold.

"*Mis*ter Silver, the town of Hanover does not pay me to conduct surveillance at the behest of my students. With your permission, I would like to finish with Mr. Poe's story."

Despite her reprimand, Ms. Hannum harbored a soft spot for Benny. Back on the first day of school he'd marched in the room and alerted her to the fact that his interest in law school demanded a comprehensive vocabulary and literary wherewithal, and he'd be damned if he'd settle for anything less than a straight A. I got the sense, ever since, that she considered him a scoundrel of the best possible sort, that if Benny were only thirty-five years older, she'd be all over his jock. On her way back to the chalk-

board, she said, "For your information, Mr. Silver, there is no one
in that building but a poor man recuperating from some grave injury, his head wrapped in gauze, smoking a cigarette in a lonely
third-floor window."

Benny turned to me, wide-eyed, and held up six fingers. If our
calculations were correct, the bandages would come off tomorrow.

One of my mother's professors had sketched a loose timeline for
us: bandages for a full week, face swollen for another two, the
bruised eye sockets of a raccoon for another month. On Saturday,
with the whole afternoon at our disposal, Benny and I sat on a
bench in front of the middle school, directly across the street from
the fugitive's apartment, shooting the shit. Benny owned Atari and
my parents had bought me Intellivision, and we argued about their
various merits and drawbacks. Benny conceded that Intellivision's
graphics boasted better resolution but maintained that the volume
of Atari's game cartridge library far outweighed the crisper picture.

"It's about having fun, Ollie, not simulating anything *real*."

"I guess."

"If we were after realism, then we might as well—"

Benny froze and clutched my knee. Across the street a city bus
pulled from the curb to reveal our fugitive, minus the bandages. I
slapped his hand away.

"Try to act cool," I said.

"So," Benny said, way too loud, "like I was saying . . ."

"Keep it together, man."

Benny shouted, "Graphics are a thing, but variety, I think, naturally is the thing . . ."

Unable to conduct surveillance while speaking cogently, Benny
tossed a word salad while our fugitive lit a cigarette and paced
in front of Val's and King Pizza. It was our guy, no doubt about
it. Bruises rimmed eyes that were like glittering gems, as if he'd
snatched the mask clean off the Cheeseburglar's face. He looked
up Chickering Road, awaiting something's arrival, and then he
flicked his cigarette butt into the street and went inside the building.

"You know what this means?" said Benny.

"This'll be good," I said. "And you can stop yelling. He can't
hear you anymore."

"Someone's coming to get him," he whispered. "If we're going to collect that reward, we need to act fast. He'll be in the wind before you know it."

"Maybe we should get Nader and Mike involved. We can cover more bases."

"Oliver, allow me to explain the concept of *division*," said Benny. "Ten thousand divided by two equals five thousand, correct?"

"Fine, then," I said. "If you're worried about your cut of the reward, then why get me involved? You could keep it all to yourself."

"Ollie, please. We're best friends."

It delighted me to hear him say this aloud. Within the dynamics of our quartet, I had always cast myself as Benny's right-hand man, the Chewbacca to his Han Solo, but there were times I wasn't so sure. Sometimes I'd catch wind of sleepovers I hadn't been invited to, and when we hung out the following week, I would find myself squinting with confusion at new terms that had entered the group's private lexicon in my absence, phrases like *douche chill*, inside jokes with me on the outside. Hearing him call me his best friend made my ribcage swell.

That is, until he continued, "Plus, we'll need to get your uncle involved."

Uncle Stan. My connection to the Hanover Police Department. That's all it was.

Uncle Stan lived on Beech Street, a couple of miles from our apartment complex. We decided to approach him at home the next day, while he was off-duty, instead of marching into Hanover PD and whipping the entire force into a lather and, as Benny put it, "gathering investors along the way." Every person we told, Benny said, would want in on the reward money.

"Not sure *investors* is accurate," I said.

"Irregardless," said Benny. "We only tell your uncle, and if he can slap cuffs on Thurston by himself, we're still talking thirty-three hundred apiece. Not too shabby."

We strolled beneath maples and sycamores and hemlocks in various stages of corduroy explosion, the sky gunmetal and threatening rain. I had managed to find out from my father, through a little code-making of my own, that Uncle Stan was off-duty on Sunday.

"How'd you get his schedule," said Benny, "without tipping off your dad?"

"You're gonna like this," I said, and I told Benny about the NFL players' strike and the *Wide World of Sports* and our game of Mastermind.

I had just arranged my first guess.

"Nope," said my father.

"You can't just say *nope*," I said. "You have to, like, illustrate where I went wrong."

"You were *totally* wrong," said my father.

"*None* of my pegs were right?" I said. "That's barely even possible."

My father shrugged, and I got an idea.

"Uncle Stan knows how to play."

"How nice for Uncle Stan."

"It *is* nice. He's really good, too."

"Maybe I should call him up and congratulate him on his skill with shitty children's games."

"Maybe you should, you know, unless he's at work?"

My father snorted.

"It's hardly a children's game. Look. It says *six and up* on the box."

"If a seven-year-old can play it, then the goddamn cat can probably play it." But then something twinkled behind my father's eyes. "He *does* have today off, though. I should call and see if he wants to pop on down to the Chalet." My father waggled his fingertips in anticipation of a frothy pint at his favorite nearby tavern.

My mother came out of the bedroom, holding a dress on either side of her.

"No one's going to the Chalet. We're having dinner with the Marklesons. Which one of these should I wear?"

It was as if someone had opened a valve and let all the air out of my father. He deflated back into the couch as, onscreen, a tetrahedron of swimmers kicked their legs in unison.

"The one on the left."

"Really?" my mother said. "I like the other one."

Making eye contact with me, he said, "So then why did you ask?"

"I just wanted my opinion confirmed. Which you've done. Thank you."

My father shook his head as if to say, *You see what I have to deal with?*

Dodging puddles down Beech Street, it occurred to me that our predicament with the reward money was not unlike that of the NFL players trying to get a proportionate slice of the financial pie they risked injury, week after week, to produce.

Benny said, "I give your performance a B." He paused and added, "Minus."

"What? We know he's home."

"We know he's *not working*. Why, in the name of Yoda, did you not simply call him?"

"You're like the mayor of duplicity! I'm following *your* lead."

Benny shook his head and we climbed the front steps of Uncle Stan's house and rang the doorbell. "If he's not home I don't know what we're gonna do."

But Uncle Stan opened the door.

"Well, if it isn't my favorite nephew and Little Lord Shortpants! Come on in."

Still a bachelor, Uncle Stan's place suffered, both decoratively and olfactorily, from a lack of female inhabitance. Wrinkled pants lay jettisoned across furniture. Mismatched shoes rested wherever they'd been kicked off. Across from the couch, a recliner was aimed directly at the television instead of at an angle that promoted conversation. The whole place smelled as if someone had just prepared French onion soup, in bare feet, while farting nonstop. Benny, who was accustomed to a meticulous organization of toys and regularly vacuumed rugs and a rigidly charted rotation of Minuteman Candle Company fragrances at his apartment, now walked into my uncle's house and sat down and said nothing. It took me a moment to realize he was holding his breath.

Uncle Stan fell into the recliner. "To what do I owe the pleasure?"

I said, "We've got some information. Kind of a lead."

"Go on," said Uncle Stan.

Not sure how to proceed, and getting no help from Benny, I said, "Well, there's this house across the street from our school."

My uncle said, "I'm with you so far."

I turned to Benny, who only nodded.

"The one with the pizza place and barbershop."

"I'm familiar with it," said Uncle Stan.

Beside me, Benny began to turn blue.

I said, "We think Mickey Thurston is hiding out there."

Benny's withheld breath exploded in a great salivary wheeze.

"No! Not like that!" he cried.

"Take it easy!" I said.

Benny let out an animal wail as if his brain had short-circuited. "Goddamn it! You *dangle* the information! You don't come right out with it!"

He gasped for air and said, "Mr. Zinn, are you running a dog kennel in here? Or maybe you've got a barrel of vinegar fermenting in the kitchen?"

"Well, well, well," said Uncle Stan. "If it isn't Woodward and Blowhard. What makes you think it's him? I mean, hiding out this close to Walpole seems reckless, even for ol' Mick."

"That's what *I* said!"

But then we told him about the bandages and the raccoon eyes and the lingering in a third-floor window all day and pacing the sidewalk as if his getaway were imminent. Uncle Stan scratched his chin and got up to fetch a beer from the kitchen and Benny lunged for the window and sucked the outdoor air. When he came back into the room Uncle Stan told us to run on home, that he had some things to look into.

We were in English class the next afternoon when we heard the sirens.

"And so our unnamed narrator attempts to tell us not that he is innocent of murdering the old man, but what?" Ms. Hannum surveyed the room.

Generally speaking, I took a casual approach to reading assignments. I'd skim the material or buy CliffsNotes and wing my essays with an above-average degree of success. But "The Tell-Tale Heart" was like four pages long, and I enjoyed it, so I raised my hand.

Before Ms. Hannum could call my name Benny said, "That he's not crazy."

"Very good, Benjamin," said Ms. Hannum.

I said, "If you cut me off one more time I will knock you the fuck out!"

Everyone froze. Ms. Hannum's jaw hung slack. Dead leaves rattled outside the window.

"*Mister* Zinn. I, for one, am shocked by your vulgar tongue." Beside me, Benny snickered at her choice of words. "Apologize to Mr. Silver this instant."

"Me? He's the one who didn't raise his hand. What about protocol?"

"Broken protocol is no cause for profanity. Apologize."

"It's okay, Ms. H. Ollie's a little on edge today," said Benny. "Speaking of protocol, I have a question of my own."

She gripped the bridge of her nose. "Proceed."

"The guy put the body parts 'under the floorboards.' Wouldn't the cops have smelled something?"

Ms. Hannum sighed. "The police arrived very shortly thereafter."

"Okay, fine. But let's say he managed to keep it together for the interview. He still would've had to live with the smell for a while. Why didn't he just bury him? And how, in eighteen-whatever-year-this-was, did he get all those body parts from the tub to the living room without leaving a trail of blood? It's not like he had trash bags or a plastic tarp."

"Mr. Silver, literature needn't always be taken literally."

Ms. Hannum turned to erase the chalkboard, which was when the police cruisers arrived out on Chickering Road with much fanfare, shattering any plans she might have had for the rest of the period. We craned our necks to see over the windowsill from our seats, until finally she said, "Go," and we dashed to the windows.

The cops surrounded the building, backs to the wall, guns drawn, beacons blazing atop the cruisers. One of them kicked in the door and they raced up the stairs. Now that he was on the verge of capture, I wanted Mickey Thurston to burst from the third-floor window and leap to a power line and swing safely into a convertible and outrun the cops all the way to the border. I didn't care about the money. I now realized that we were more like the greedy NFL owners than the underpaid gladiators on the field. Mickey was the real hero here, stealing from the fat-cat bankers, and Benny and I had to go and rat out Robin Hood just so we could buy more *Star Wars* figures than we'd ever need in three lifetimes. *We were wrong,* I mouthed to him, and he squinted at me, misunderstanding, but when we turned back to the window, the cops came out of the building empty-handed, scratching their heads.

The following Friday night, Benny and I were in my living room watching TV, my mother squeaking her highlighter over the pages of her anatomy textbook, when the sliding glass door flew open.

"Weekend's here! Who wants to go out for pizza?"

My father rarely entered rooms quietly. He preferred to burst into them as if streamers and balloons followed closely behind.

My father's car was a 1973 Saab Sonett, a weirdly esoteric limited-edition car. By the early '80s it had acquired a cult status among its owners—and its owners *alone,* one of those clubs that absolutely no one but its members even remotely give a shit about. His Sonett was a very singular shade of red-orange, three parts ketchup to one mustard, and that, coupled with its peculiar nose-heavy contour, didn't so much turn the heads as furrow the brows of pedestrians, as if the car's presence suddenly made people question what country they were in. The point is that my father's two-seater would never accommodate the four of us—though this isn't really the point, is it? I've gotten so far off point with board games and bank robbers and human anatomy and *Star Wars* and the body under Poe's floorboards, a shield I've erected to block the thing I've been trying so hard *not* to look at directly this entire time—so he climbed behind the wheel of my mother's car, a brand-new Oldsmobile Delta 88, and she and Benny and I piled in. Gone are the days, I'm afraid, when a plating line manager and his nursing student wife could get a loan for a brand-new sedan, gleaming white, with a plush velour interior. As far as I was concerned, it was the stretch limo of a country music star.

I should have seen what was coming when we pulled up in front of King's Pizza.

"King's?" I said. "We always go to Star Pizza."

My parents exchanged a look I could not decipher.

Inside, we gazed up at a menu that was nearly identical to Star's and yet all wrong and foreign-seeming, like my father's Saab. He mused, loudly, to the guy behind the counter, "Thought I saw a FOR RENT sign outside. You got a recent vacancy upstairs?"

The guy shrugged. "I just work here. I don't own the building."

At dinner my father managed to drop the words *bank, rob, escape,* and even *fugitive* into our conversation. As we awaited the falling ax, my father chomped joyously on pizza crust, loving every minute of it.

Afterward, back in the car, he said, "Anyone feel like swinging by . . . *Shoemaker's?*"

Before I could answer, Benny said "I do!"

Goddamn him. What did he care, anyway? A lecture from somebody else's parents was meaningless, irrelevant as a Belgian tax schedule. My father dragged us all down there to witness an obvious burlesque of his being very interested in a black-and-white photo of the actor Mark Hamill, encased in bandages. Naturally, they had never stocked nor heard of such an item.

"Oh, *really?*" He turned around to face Benny and me while my mother leafed through the latest issue of *Wonder Woman.* "What do you two have to say for yourselves?"

"Sorry," we said in unison, and he led us back out to the car. Statistically speaking, it was more likely that our mysterious bandaged man was a race-car driver, or a boxer, or a fighter pilot, or any number of other possibilities, rather than one specific bank robber on the lam. But we believed what we believed. We manufactured certainty out of thin air and headlines and wishful thinking. My father thought he could teach us a lesson, something about deception, about how you weren't supposed to lie to people in order to get something you wanted. Especially your family. But we didn't learn *not to lie;* we learned where our lies had met resistance. We got better at it. And that night we drove away from Shoemaker's, safely contained in the Oldsmobile's interior of cornflower blue.

Like a shuttled roll of microfilm, thirty years would scroll past with shocking speed and have their way with all of us, leaving rapidly growing masses in my father's lungs.

On the same coffee table beside the same couch, I set the same board game down between my father and me, the one with the colored pegs and the plastic shield and the guesswork. Twelve moves to get it right. It's not enough. You could have a thousand moves and still get it wrong.

An oxygen tank helps my father breathe. My mother naps in the bedroom, exhausted, her professional expertise now called upon at great length in the home. Clear plastic tubes loop over each ear. The periodic aerosol burst of the tank keeping the oxygen saturation in his lungs above a specific threshold. The rhythmically identical coughs lighting up his chest from the inside.

"This time I'm code-maker," I say.

"Fine." He coughs and says, "Let me ask you something. Remember that house?"

"What house?"

He shakes his head. "You know what house. Who was in it?"

"I don't know."

"You told your uncle it was Mickey Thurston."

"I told him I *thought* it was."

"What's the difference?"

"I don't know," I say. "Certainty?"

"You were certain enough to call the cops."

"There was a big reward. That kind of cash, what's the harm in a shot in the dark?"

"No harm for *you,* but for the potentially innocent guy upstairs . . ."

"Everyone's *potentially* innocent," I say.

He chuckles, which induces another coughing fit. "Don't make me laugh."

"Sorry. Besides, they never found ol' Mick."

"That's not the point. My point is, the reward made it okay for you to take a leap of faith, as long you didn't have to absorb the risk if it turned out you were wrong."

"Why are you asking me this?"

"I think you know."

We look at each other over the coffee table, the clean slate of Mastermind's pegboard between us. This time I can see the answer but my father cannot. Or maybe neither of us can. Maybe nobody can.

The word *regret* comes from the Old French, fourteenth century, "to lament someone's death; to ask the help of." An impossible contradiction, asking for help from the last person on earth who can provide it. Right now I want invisible strings to yank my father up off the couch just so he can burst through the sliding glass door again, accompanied by his high-decibel cacophony, freed from the workday's vaporous confines to prance around the apartment, loudly in charge again. I want to do the whole thing differently this time, without all the puzzles and deception. Nothing would slow the passage of time, but the time might be better spent.

Still awaiting his first move, I say, "I don't know the answer."

And my father laughs again. And coughs.

And says, "Anyone who says they do is full of shit."

ANNE THERESE MACDONALD

That Donnelly Crowd

FROM *False Faces*

I WANTED PEACE of mind. I took the rattle and bang of cocaine.
I wanted to be an English scholar. I traded stocks and bonds. I
wanted the gentle rain of my Washington coast. I took the deadly
smog of West LA. I wanted out. I stayed in. The year was 1983. President Reagan had our backs. We were young and rich. I needed to
pay attention, watch my backside and know where I was headed. I
needed God not to find me.

I tiptoed through the upmarket wedding gifts scattered about
the floor, past the white-satin wedding gown hanging on the door. I
stopped at the three-tiered wedding cake, destroyed its fluffy white
texture by burying the bride deep inside, and quietly, at two in the
morning, I sneaked to the parked Audi with my new tapestry suitcase, a suitcase more elegant than the wedding dress, more 1980s
than my future husband, more with-it than my wedding, more cool
and fashionable than my crowd. The wedding, meant to take place
the next day, Christmas Eve, was off. The drugs were done. I swore
to live only in hushed rains and sleep with gentle people. I wanted
a life shielded by the veil of a not-so-perfect existence. I needed
God not to find me.

I met Bridget Donnelly before I met Joe. She was a witch of a spinster who ran the only Dublin B&B open on Christmas Eve. She
was a tall, thin woman in a straight black skirt and white blouse, a
Dickensian crone in a long black dress and sweeping cape. I had
hopped on the first overseas flight available. Once in Dublin, I
hooked up with an American tour, a pretentious crowd of the re-

tired and leisurely bored. We sat around a heavy oval table in flickering candlelight. Bridget's hair was short and permed, her face small and round with a pointed nose and a receding chin, a chin in constant judgment of others. With bulging eyes of no apparent color—because no one ever cared to look at her eyes—Bridget Donnelly huddled in the corners of life. I hated Bridget Donnelly.

Her brother, Joe, walked in. The story of my life. My narrative. My history. Light as a breeze, he exuded a laughter that diminished every other man I had ever known, every golden penny I had ever earned, every rec-drug I could have afforded. A divorced man, an international computer specialist with an apartment in Germany, a house in London, an ex-wife in Sweden, a spinster sister in Dublin, an IRA brother buried in a rebel's grave. How dangerously romantic. His dark auburn hair reflected strands of red in the firelight —his lightly freckled face, darting blue eyes, his tall, rough build.

Our Christmas tour went to midnight mass. I dawdled behind until the chemistry shot across the room, landed on Joe, and two beings meant to be more than a blink of the eye sauntered into the church. We talked through the service, through the tour's after-mass breakfast, through the quiet slumber of the old people. At four in the morning, after extraneous, superfluous, and diversionary banter about Ireland, the Troubles, his life as an international computer specialist, how he was back in Ireland to purchase land for some factory, I steered the conversation on to me. I told him how I came to Dublin, my quick escape from my own wedding meant to take place in LA on Christmas Eve.

Joe put down his whiskey. "The thing I don't understand, Colleen, is why wouldn't you just marry him? Why would you run away?"

Until that moment, I had thought it quite amusing—leaving my man at the altar, sneaking out of LA, secret savings stashed. What would have been funny among my very trendy LA crowd didn't seem so clever that early Christmas morning, in a Victorian B&B, during a dark and rainy night, on an economically troubled and insignificant island. His seriousness sobered me.

"It stopped being fun, I suppose."

"You ought to think about what you're running from. Life is serious, you know. You've got to pay attention."

But I was too busy that Christmas morn to pay attention. I loved how he pronounced *Colleen* with the long *o*. My goal was to rein in this good-looking, sophisticated man. I needed to impress him

with my worldliness, my experience, money, trading in stocks and
bonds with commissions out my wazoo, with the fact that the major
partner in my firm would soon be mayor of Los Angeles, so my
crowd would not only be among the wealthiest young professionals
around, but we'd be the most politically connected. Joe remained
unimpressed.

Okay, I thought, a serious type. Begging to become his weak
point, I searched every inlet and bay of my life for the serious spots.
I pulled from my mind every grave section of my memory, things I
had discarded, covered up, repressed. I told him of my childhood
in Grays Harbor on the Washington coast, my duty-bound, dedicated people. I even wandered outside my safe zone and told him
of the coastal storm that killed my father and brother. Yes, I used
their tragedy, my tragedy, to impress him. I moved on. Intellectual
activity? I told him of my graduate studies in English literature, how
I ended my PhD pursuits only after I was fired as university journal editor for writing a scathing deconstruction of E. L. Doctorow's
major work.

"Why didn't you stay in that field?"

"I had this great fear of one day hating it, or my love for it would
end."

"Won't that happen with the stock-trading profession?"

"No. I hate stocks so God can't take that from me. You see, God
is out there lurking about, waiting for my mistakes. The minute I'm
happy, he'll find me, sweep down tragedy, take away my happiness,
replace it with panic and depression or something of that sort. My
goal in life is to keep God on edge."

Joe thoughtfully took another drink. Humor and seriousness,
opposite sides of the human psyche, worked best with Joe Donnelly. In a matter of minutes, he presented his gifts to me—the
stillness, the smiles, the winks of intelligence, the cosmopolitan atmosphere of his being, the dedication. That morning, full of hope
and desire, we lived out those feelings. The passion between us
overwhelmed me. We became one person, one whole being meant
from inception to eternity to be together. We made love past dawn.

The Christmas tour was to leave midmorning. I packed slowly,
still high from the lovemaking, unsure how to sneak around Bridget, fearful of facing Joe, who had fallen asleep with no promises.
Too, I was unsure of where or how to get around, through, and out
of Dublin.

Joe awoke. "No, no, no. You stay put, Colleen. We'll tour to-gether. I can show you the country."

I closed my tapestry suitcase. This was what I wanted, uncondi-tionally, truly, madly. I envisioned what I would tell my friends. The LA envy I would engender. The pictures I would take.

Bridget burst into the room in what surely was a black mourning dress. "Get on with the tour, girlie. I think we've all had enough."

Joe jumped out of bed, uninhibited in his nakedness. Bridget gasped and turned her head. "We're staying here, Bridget. It's Christmas Day."

"I don't care." She spoke to the wall. "You two are not staying here. That behavior will not take place in a reputable house. I want this girl out."

"Reputable? Here? That's a fine tune to play." Joe grabbed his clothes. "I'll take her into the city. I'm on holiday, anyway."

Bridget waved us both off. Her old-fashioned dress swished as she hurried out of the room.

"Are you packed, Colleen?"

I pointed to my tapestry suitcase. He dressed and lugged it out the door.

In Ireland's northwest coastal region, during the Troubles, there were still sights where only ghosts would walk. Ireland was a lonely island, dark and rainy, with a brooding cloudy atmosphere. I felt I had stepped out of the boundaries of sanity, history, reality. With no native language to describe it or label it, I became one with whatever the earth and wind and water was to its universe. Ireland made no sense to me. But I was with Joe Donnelly, and Joe Don-nelly was what I wanted.

Joe sat still and quiet in an abandoned core of an early-Chris-tian church. We'd spent five days searching ruins, visiting muse-ums, tracking down O'Casey, Joyce, Yeats. We were both exhausted, reserved. The walls of the ancient structure were barely two feet high. Joe sat silently and stared at an altar that no longer was, in one of those manic-depressive undertows that had periodically ap-peared in the midst of our passionate days in Dublin, Cork, Kildare, Connemara—a time full of sex and drink and James Joyce. There was peace on that coastline. It was still, empty. I teetered on an old stone wall, carefully balancing, challenging myself to keep from falling to my left, which would land me in the ocean several hundred feet below the cliff, or falling to my right, where I would land on soft, wet, chalk-like sand just feet from Joe. But I was confident in my happiness that week, and I knew I could balance and by balancing could enjoy both worlds on each side of me—the vast, rough, raging sea to one side and the quiet stillness of Joe on the other.

"Come here, Colleen, before you fall to your death."

Ah, he sounded like a man who would raise children, love a wife, work hard and long, build a home, a future, a life with a good-looking, accomplished, quite intellectual American woman at his side. If not for the pain and horror to come, those words, spoken in a deteriorated church on an empty coastline in a dilapidated country, would be the words that still echo from that short week. I jumped from the stone wall and stood at the entrance of what was left of the church.

"Colleen, did you ever think about the humiliation that poor bugger felt when you left the night before your wedding?"

"No, I didn't. LA people are incapable of feeling humiliation."

"Why did you do it?"

"I didn't trust it would last forever. I told you that." I sauntered over and sat next to him. "I knew that happiness would end with the vows. God would find me and make me miserable."

"Are you capable of love, then?"

"I don't know. It depends upon how much happiness is involved. I'd hate to see myself happy then lose it."

"Have you ever loved a man?"

"What odd questions. I don't really know."

"Will you marry me, then?"

"Marry you?" My heart leapt, my body shook. Such words from the man I dared not dream would spend his life with me.

"Yes, I want to marry you," he said. He looked young and innocent at that moment in his black trousers and new sweater, like an earnest schoolboy. "You'd get happiness that could last forever. I'd get, well, I suppose I'd get everything I wanted."

While traveling with Joe during the previous five days, I had occasionally found him resigned, perhaps fatalistic. Once, in a small pub near the university in Cork, an old school chum joined us. This happened everywhere we went, an old mate here, a school chum there, a childhood buddy down the row. In Cork, the man plopped down at our table and ordered us three pints. From his rumpled suit, white shirt, and food stains on his tie, I assumed he was university stuff. I kept guessing all the while he talked. A surveyor? An out-of-work grade school teacher? A government worker?

Oddly, Joe never introduced us. He let the man ramble on about his and Joe's childhood. Had he seen the new parish priest, Tommy Casey? Their old schoolmate? The one who had a thing for your sister, Bridget? Joe chuckled. The man took the chuckle as encouragement to go on about Bridget. Was she still running the family B&B? Should have kept it as your home, Joe, "'stead of running all over Europe trying to make something of yourself. You can run, but as they say, you cannot hide."

He turned to me. "Have you met Bridget?" He wiped foam from his mouth. "Bridget Donnelly is the type of woman who would make a man a wonderful grandmother." He laughed at his own joke. "A wonderful grandmother, except the explosive parts." He snorted until droplets came from his nose. "The Donnelly family. What a bunch—"

I started to ask what he meant when Joe stood, grabbed my hand, and we left. He remained silent the rest of the day. No amount of gentle humor could bring him out of it. I had quite enjoyed his chum. Traditional Irish pub, red-faced, curly-haired drinking mate, dark ales, laughter—quite a picture postcard. I said nothing to Joe. I don't think I wanted to know. I let Joe brood.

But in the unexpected proposal of marriage, he'd also sounded depressed. If I had not been so distracted by the idea of it, by his gorgeous being sitting alone in that ruin, by the romance of the brooding Irish, I would have cared enough to question him. But the perceptions of love levitate a woman. I melted every time I looked at Joe, awake or asleep. As I lay next to him, I dared not think of a life without him. My emotions were so deep, my reactions to his body, his mind, his sexuality so fulfilling. We had been like two beings sailing into oblivion, with no anchor, no stopping point, no handle. So powerful was our lovemaking, I felt like a feather or leaf floating from the heavens, touching earth only when the morning light hit the lace curtains. I felt that if I could take a deep breath, I would swallow the world, as he had swallowed me. For that second, I felt there was a rewarding God, there was a heaven and angels and life ever after. I stopped watching my backside.

"But," Joe said, "you have to marry me now."

"Now?"

"Back in Dublin. Tomorrow. I want to get married tomorrow."

"Why tomorrow?"

"Because, Colleen, you have a history of leaving the chap at the altar. The reason is no *fookin'* mystery." He waved me off as though I were a child. At the time, I liked the off-handed way he controlled my questioning, the drawn-out owl-type *oooo* that turned *fuckin'* into *fookin'*. The style gave him a bit of shabby sexiness. "We'll marry tomorrow. I have to get back to work on Monday."

"To London?"

"I can clear things up before we go to America. We'll start a new life in America."

A dart hit my inflated ego. Foreign man looking for a lonely American woman, his ticket to the New World. For a nanosecond, questions flew through my head, his background, his life abroad, his Swedish ex-wife, his apartment in Germany, the house in London, the IRA brother in a rebel's grave. Just as quickly, I dismissed such questions. In the silence of the landscape we returned to his little car, then to Dublin.

Bridget did not come to our small wedding. Through the whispered arguments in her makeshift lobby, I learned that I wasn't to get their mother's wedding ring or their parents' marriage bed that night, or any of the essentials a family would bestow on a new bride. I didn't contact what was left of my own family. My mother had a new husband, and she had long ago tired of my antics, my frivolous lifestyle. In truth, I never once thought I was being impulsive. How easily we discard all sense when love is involved. We're left with decision-making that is limp, unsupportable, without anchors. No wonder such massive, earthquake-size mistakes are made. No wonder people die.

I relied on Joe to diddle with Catholic rules and regulations and put together a wedding in one afternoon. Both of us were sure of our plan. I felt lightheaded as I vowed to a life with him. He looked smug and sure in his words. As the priest, Tommy Casey, Joe's old schoolmate, spoke the words, and as I repeated them, Joe put his arm around me and held me tightly. If he hadn't, I would have fallen.

The next night, a storm arose on the Irish Sea. We went to the dock to board the ferry for Holyhead, then on to London, only to find that gale warnings were in effect. They canceled the crossing.

A small crowd of passengers, Joe included, put up a fight. They argued with the dock man, the ticket man, and finally, the captain. The others chose Joe as spokesman. Eventually he convinced the captain and crew to make the crossing and get us all to England.

I saw the danger of the rising storm. I was too familiar with the pounding waves, the rain and cold, the growing winds, the shattered, empty boats returning to shore. I felt the fear my brother must have felt that night he drowned in such a storm. I pulled Joe aside and begged him to return to Dublin.

"You're a coastal girl, Colleen. This will be nothing."

"My father and brother were killed in a storm like this. I don't want to go."

He pushed my hand from his sleeve. "I can't think about that now. I have to get back."

Out on the sea, the waters became even rougher. The passengers retired to the belly of the ferry. I sat with them, my tapestry suitcase at my feet, waiting for Joe, who had not come down with the rest of us.

The ferry bounced and banged against the raging sea for another hour when I finally left my bench to find him. The black sky met me at the door, that ethereal darkness I so hated. The ratty boat, in a sickly pitch, flew into vertical upheaval, crashed down to the white foam of the beating waves and banged hard against the dark sea. It rose again, rested a second in midair, then plunged hard against the waves. I grabbed the handrails and pulled myself forward. I staggered out the door, stood for a moment while the boat rose to the sky, then crashed down. I took that opportunity to get on deck.

Joe was under the awning, his back to me, one arm around a pole. He was wearing a slicker, and for a second, I wondered where he had gotten it, but I discarded the question as immediately as it entered my mind. He smoked a cigarette and leaned to and fro with the rhythm of the boat. A man stood next to him, grasping the railing. He, too, swayed. I yelled to Joe, but the crashing and clambering of the raging sea swallowed my words. I shouted again, to curse that dark being that had taken my brother and father, to apologize for the thoughtless way I had used them to get Joe, to beg them to keep this flimsy junk of a ferry in one piece. Joe didn't hear me. He continued to shake his head and wave his cigarette at the

man. They seemed to be arguing. The man finally noticed me. He
alerted Joe, who turned, looked surprised, and motioned the man
off. The man lurched away into the rain and darkness.

"Get downstairs," Joe shouted as he staggered toward me.

"Who was that?"

"Nobody. Just a passenger."

"But I didn't see him when we all boarded."

"What does it matter?"

At that moment, it seemed odd to hear him ask such a question
in the middle of a deadly storm on the Irish Sea. The question
antagonized me.

"Where did you get the slicker?" I clutched the railing behind
me with both hands. Joe removed my hands, turned me around,
and steered me down the stairs.

"Go. Passengers are supposed to be below."

"But you're a passenger."

"Colleen, get down there." At the third step, I lost my footing
and caused him to fall. "*Shite,* Colleen. Don't bring us both down."
He got up, shook his head, grabbed the hand railing, stepped past
me, and found his own way to an empty bench. I struggled, found
the railing, and, by small steps and sways, staggered to his side. He
scooted over an inch or two as though disgusted by my inability to
handle the boat's pitching and twisting. Unlike the rest of the passengers, either ghostly white or sickly green, moaning and vomiting without embarrassment, Joe sat still, his arms spread across the
back of the wooden bench as though he were sitting in a city park.

"I thought you were born on the American coastline."

"It's been awhile."

My upper lip perspired and my mouth felt dry. My attempt at humor, just like my shouting on deck, simply flew through the dank
air and found its way out the door and into the storm. Joe stared
ahead. I looked in the same direction but only saw a dirty fire hose
wound several times on a rusty hook. The sick odor of vomit per-
meated the stuffy passenger area. I spied the women's room and
stumbled to it. Inside, the toilet water spilled and splattered with
every movement of the ferry. I held myself over a sink and vomited.

"Feel better?" he asked when I returned.

"No."

He looked away.

After two more hours of beating against the sea, of vomiting and nausea all around me, of silent abuse from Joe, he looked at his watch, stood, and rubbed his face. "Come on. We're docking in a minute. I'm not feeling so well."

"No one feels well, Joe. In hell, no one feels well."

"You have no idea of hell."

He led me upstairs as the boat limped into dock. Dragging my tapestry suitcase, battering it left and right up the stairs, I stopped at the top to catch my breath. Joe stood impatiently, his leather bag slung over his shoulder. He turned and started down the gangway. The sky was jet-black, the rain fell heavily, and my wool coat smelled like dirty, wet sheep. I used both hands to lug my suitcase down the gangway and onto the dock.

On stable ground, it took me a moment or two to find my equilibrium. I dizzily kept pace with Joe. He had not spoken to me since we docked, and now moved impatiently through the small crowd of dock and ferry workers and the few passengers still walking. I followed him out of the waiting shelter. My hair was dripping wet, and I desperately needed a bathroom. When I said so, Joe stopped, motioned to the ladies' room, and remained in place.

Inside, I went to the mirror. "New husband," I said aloud. What a laugh. Words can be miles from reality, from correct labels and titles. Joe was a stranger to me. His carefree demeanor, his smiles, his joking manner had all disappeared in the black slicker and rough ferry ride. I looked like hell.

He pounded on the ladies' room door. "Come on, Colleen. I need to get going."

By the time we were in the parking lot, I had enough. "Wait, Joe."

He turned.

"Why are you doing this?" I shouted over the rain and wind. I dropped the suitcase and kicked it toward him, each kick moved it an inch or two across the muddy parking lot. "Why are you being so awful to me?" The words sounded ridiculous, like a pathetic housewife begging for attention or a useless girlfriend who knows the relationship is over—silly, pleading, and naïve.

Joe picked up my suitcase.

"I'm not moving until you tell me why you're doing this!"

He threw the suitcase to the ground and kicked it several times. "Doing *fookin'* what?"

"This—ignoring me, being rude to me, not talking." Thin, elementary words that represented nothing of substance or need or importance. "Are you mad you married me? Are you embarrassed for bringing me to London? Embarrassed for me to meet your friends?"

"I don't have time for this, Colleen." He stopped at a small white car and pulled out his keys.

"Where did you get this car? You didn't tell me you had a car here. Why do you keep a car in Dublin and one here? Where do I fit into all this? I should know these things."

"Are you coming, woman?"

"Woman!" I marched up to him. "Don't you ever call me that. I'm your wife, whether you like it or not." More asinine, foolish words that simply voiced naïve, needy emotions that would have been better left unsaid.

He picked up my suitcase, dragged it across the mud, and shoved it into the backseat. I continued to shout at him like an old fishwife — *this was wrong, this was a mistake, I don't know what I was thinking, how do we get a divorce, was it a legal marriage* . . . on and on I went.

He slammed the car door. "I've got the *fookin'* flu, Colleen. I want to get home."

"You've got the *fookin'* seasickness, Joe."

He put his head to the top of the car. "You haven't a clue. Get in."

I opened and slammed the door, but I did not get in — a stupid gesture, overdramatic, adolescent behavior.

He leaned across the top. "Damn it, Colleen. I'm sicker than a *fookin'* dog."

I got in, plopped onto the seat, and folded my arms. What a pathetic sight. He needed someone strong at that moment, and I proved weak. He needed some support, and I proved selfish. He needed a woman on whom he could rely. I proved useless and needy.

We drove in silence through the wet English countryside. After an hour or so in the dark and rain, I settled down. The sights and smells around me — pine woods, moist soft grasses, the earthy fragrance of wet dirt — were comforting, like home. A warm excitement about seeing his home, my new home, my chance for a new, clean, clear life changed my bad humor. I pictured myself introducing Joe to my friends: *This is Joe Donnelly, an international computer specialist. A man with a home in London, an apartment in Germany, an ex-wife in Sweden, a sister in Dublin, an IRA brother in a rebel's grave.* My self-image puffed up with every thought of him.

Eventually, Joe left the highway and drove toward the lights of a big city. He drove slowly, squinting through the windshield. A mile or so on side streets and we came to a downtown. We stopped in front of a drugstore.

"There's a hotel around that corner. We'll stay there for the night. I can't drive on."

"Aren't we in London?"

"No, we're a couple of hours from London." He rubbed perspiration from his upper lip, pushed his hair from his forehead, and opened the door. "I've got to get to bed."

Disappointed, estranged but too tired to fight, I opened my door, pulled up my seat and struggled to remove my suitcase. The suitcase was caught on a small metal case sitting upright on the floor. When I finally dragged the suitcase to the curb, Joe got his bag from the trunk, locked the door, and led me around the corner to the front of the hotel.

"Wait right here. I forgot something."

Both our bags at my feet, I watched as he jogged down the street and around the corner. He disappeared for several seconds, returned quickly.

"What's the matter?"

"Never mind." He took my arm and steered me into the hotel.

The shabby hotel reminded me of the other side of Grays Harbor — the dankness and musty smell of seaside buildings. Joe registered us as Mr. and Mrs. Joseph Donnelly, which affirmed our marriage. He led me up a dark, narrow stairway and down a stale-smelling hall, rattling his keys all the way. Our corner room, covered with flowered wallpaper, had worn shades and torn curtains.

"Not much of a honeymoon suite," I said.

Joe fell onto the bed and buried his face in the pillow, covered it with his arms. Used to the silence between us, I simply pulled the shades and curtains and peeked into the WC. Both the toilet and sink were clean but old-fashioned. I hated chain-pull toilets and detached bathtubs, coin water-heaters and old sinks — more small-minded chatter in a brain that should have been active, inquisitive, and alert.

Joe raised his head. "Get me that waste bin. I'm going to retch."

I quickly did as I was told. He leaned over the bed, choked and splattered into the basket. Attempting the role of the dutiful new wife, I sat next to him, stroked his head, helped him remove his shoes. He shook me off and tried to stand up, but fell back onto the bed. I emptied the wastebasket into the toilet and washed it out. When I returned, Joe was back in bed, his head buried. I opened my suitcase.

When Joe spoke again, he said something that sounded like "Stay away from the window."

"What did you say?" As I stood, I was flung hard onto the bed by an unnatural force, as though shoved from behind by a giant fist. The window shattered, an explosion lit the room, a blaze of fire rose up then receded. Instinctively, I threw myself onto the floor and buried my head in my arms. My heart pounded, a loud, thumping rhythm. I blocked out the sirens and human screams. A familiar panic overtook me—fear of the dark, horror of strangers in a window, of dark corners, manic behavior, endless black oceans, loose limbs and bodies. Neither of us moved. I dared not speak. I heard Joe say over and over again into the pillow, "*Fook, fook, fook.*"

He grabbed the wastebasket and vomited. This time I didn't move to help him. When finished, he scooted onto his back. I watched through the corner of my eye. He stared at the ceiling, like he was counting the tiles or waiting for something, killing time. In the moments that followed, sirens blazed toward our hotel, but even then I couldn't hear them—the room was so silent. I sensed the heart-beating shock of death, of being in the wrong place at the wrong time, of two worlds, edges of two planes, teetering between two modes of living, a darkly lit future, fear of ghosts and of the dark. God had found me. I was scared to death of Joe Donnelly.

It took all of twenty minutes for them to start banging on the door, the landlord shouting, "There they are, the two Irish ones." Three policemen stood above us.

"Joseph Donnelly?"

Joe nodded but didn't move. One of the policemen pulled him up. "Get to your feet!"

"I've got the *fookin'* flu. I just want to sleep." He plopped back onto the bed.

The policeman looked at me. I quickly stood. "Who are you?"

"She's my wife," Joe answered.

Joe must have guessed back in the ferry boat that I would be speechless at this point. I'd be useless. I'd be stunned. His plan would backfire. His smart and urbane woman would fail him. A strong worldly, defiant type was what he needed, not some weak, confused thing.

"Leave her alone." Joe pulled himself from the bed. "She's American. Doesn't know shit about what's going on here."

"I'm bringing you both in."

My hands shook and my chin quivered. The officers' arrival had me torn between relief and fear. Their accents sounded imperial and brutish after a week of the melodious Irish. Joe pulled a second sweater from his bag and put it on. I picked up my wool coat, but it was soaking wet and covered in fine pieces of glass. I threw it on the floor and grabbed a sweater from my opened suitcase. The three policemen and the landlord led us down the hall, down the damp stairs, and out onto the crowded street.

All eyes and fingers pointed to us, people pushed and shoved us, shouted obscenities as we drove away. My brain, cleared of the naiveté of the simpering new wife, replayed, almost at a mental distance, what had gone on that night—the insistence and negotiation for the ferry ride during a gale, the meeting on the deck, the suddenly appearing slicker, the hurry to the waiting car, intense drive, hotel instead of the house, his return from the corner, covering his head, the sickness, fear . . . *that metal case.* That was where my mind stopped. No matter how I urged it on, how I tried to think beyond, how much I tried to see a clear path to a solution, every thought became muddled within what had just happened, where I was, how I got there. We sat in silence as we sped through the countryside, a Nazi-esque siren screaming loudly. I felt like a war criminal in some old movie.

Joe took my hand. "I didn't do it."

I pulled away. Joe looked larger to me, more straggly, his sweater hand-knitted and worn. I couldn't remember when he had changed from shoes to black boots, from trousers to jeans. How could he look like a computer specialist one hour and a terrorist the next?

We entered the station together. It smelled like the Grays Harbor Police Station. They registered us, took our fingerprints. As they did, Joe hollered, "Better watch your steps, mates. She's an American, and she's my wife."

An older cop in plain clothes came into the station. "Ah, one of the Donnelly's. Joe, right?" He became serious. "How long you two been married?"

With a chuckle, Joe answered, "About a day."

"You Donnelly's get the best alibis. Your brother is still about, I see, even though we got him locked up. How's our lovely Bridget? Still in the explosives business?"

"I had nothing to do with this. I don't know about my *fookin'* brother."

Muddled . . . I had to think back to our first night. Surely he had told me his brother was dead. The rebel's grave and all.

"That's what they always say, Joseph Patrick Donnelly, and always, always, a Donnelly is where it happens."

"Lookit, man, I'm really sick. I need to lie down. I don't do explosives. I'm here for that factory in Kildare and you know it."

This was the nightmare that had been waiting for me since childhood—defenseless, surrounded by lies, explosions, strangers, imprisoned in damp, dark rooms.

"Just think, Colleen," Joe shouted as they dragged him toward a cell. "God came looking for you and he found me. Funny how that happens with people who . . ."

I never heard the rest.

MARK MAYER

The Clown

FROM *American Short Fiction*

THE CLOWN COUNTED his murders as he drove the new couple to
the house on Rocking Horse Lane. Not few. The Lexus needed air
again, according to the little orange light, the man in his passenger
seat was offering original commentary on the Clintons, and behind
the clown's left eye a toothache and an earache were collaborating.
Not few at all, and some of the murders had been admirably painful, admirably patient. Outside the Lexus it was seventy-two degrees
in October, and inside the Lexus, according to a different screen, it
was also seventy-two degrees, the car's climate system blowing hard
even so. The clown hated the Lexus and was wearing a blazer he'd
bought to match it. In the backseat, the woman, very pregnant, was
picking her teeth with the aid of her phone. The clown's mouth
—thirsty—tasted like waffle fries and crispy chicken sandwich, and
so did all the rest of him. Salt, grease, a synthetic drive-thru savor
—he was likely composed of it by now. No matter how many times
he sucked the straw the soda was still out.

"We hate to leave the downtown," the man, Seamus, was saying
again. "Our apartment is five minutes from Pinche Taco, five minutes from Cerebral Brewing, like two minutes from Über Dog, but
how fast I got her pregnant, we're going to need rooms."

"Congratulations," said the clown, shaking his ice. Any kind of
knife murder, some hooks, some rod-and-fire stuff. One dehydration. He tried to recognize himself, his life and effort, in the ré-
sumé, but it was like he'd consigned his life effort to a secret man.
What was left ate waffle fries, sold houses, awaited the secret man's
return.

But he had a good feeling about this couple. Early thirties, Apple Watches, fecund. He *wanted* to kill them. That was something. The woman, Eliza, was very quiet. All she had said since the place on Ridgeway Row was "Hi, Daddy" when they passed a trim tort lawyer's billboard. Seamus was lavishly freckled, in an overlaundered polo probably assigned to lazy weekend wear, curling collar leaning toward the postnuptial paunch.

The houses on Vinci Park and Ridgeway Row, where the air still smelled of other people's lentil soup, had been staged disappointments, unmowed drabnesses after which 404 Rocking Horse would gleam like a mirror. It was the perfect place for Eliza and Seamus; Eliza and Seamus were the perfect pair for it. The clown had been preparing this for a while.

"We're thinking high fours, maybe low fives," Seamus was lowballing already. "They're reviewing me for associate sooner than anyone in my cohort, so it's not that. I'm just not ready for *the* house yet, you know?"

The clown did know. The man wanted granite counters, sectional couches, a pop-up soccer goal. There was time yet for Japanese fountains. He wanted the yard the kid could mow for iTunes money, not the one that needed a koi specialist. Happiness was not so hard to engineer for the typical, but it did no good to say it. The house on Rocking Horse would speak for him, a three-bedroom with a power study and a crafts room with a guest loft. You had to let the clients spin twice in a living room and recognize themselves. Not just themselves—the selves they knew and also latent selves they just suspected. Only then, when they saw their books in the cases and their mugs in the cabinet, could the murderer emerge from the basement, where he'd been waiting all along.

"Downtown, it's fun and all, but it's not safe for Eliza or the kid. All the money the city has now, you think they'd clean that shit out. Our alleyway, every morning someone's given them all hot coffee and doughnuts. These bums are glamping."

The clown, forty-eight, amicably divorced, amicably depressed, real-estate licensed, was aware that he was a type too. Apart from murder, his interests were no less predictable than Seamus's. He'd offered lunch after the Ridgeway place—he often took clients out —but now he was thinking about Tums—he loved Tums—about gin, about juice cleanses, about smothering Seamus's face with the wet side of Seamus's scalp. He rarely spoke his mind. He let his thoughts imbue his smile.

He'd set about it in earnest ten years ago, full sails with research and planning, whiteface and greasepaint, professional grade, learned to accentuate a menace, if there was one, already present in his face. The wig had cost a fortune, real hair, bruised strawberry, but it had lasted. The teeth too, cutlery porcelain, filed, stained. Ought to be tax deductible. The nails he made himself with molded tin. It took most of an hour to put it all on, but people did react—more so than they would to rubber stuff, he hoped. "That tall building over there would be your closest hospital, if anything happens," he said. "Terrific obstetrics center, though I'm sure you've already made plans. There's the Whole Foods coming up and here's a mosque, should you be needing one of those. I believe it would be your polling place were you to move before the election."

Seamus grumbled something about voting early. For the rest of Seamus's life, a diminishing proposition, indignation would race cholesterol. He would make a colorful choking victim, but the clown had promised himself patience, intentionality. Cruelty and pain were easy quantities, but murder used to *express* something in him. Take the kings of Greece and Persia who entertained guests with hollow bronze bulls that seemed to bay when wheeled over a fire, when in fact it was condemned queens screaming from inside. It was cruel, it was painful—but it was so kingly too. The court clapping and marveling, pretending they didn't know, while the king spat seeds from his grapes. The Aztecs murdered like Aztecs, the Nazis murdered like Nazis. The clown, meanwhile, had groomed himself to match the Lexus that was supposed to give him credibility regarding other people's homes.

"Been saving this place for a special family," he said, pulling into the driveway. It was true.

During the walk-through, Seamus stuck close by, explaining everything to the clown: "I never liked these kind of light switches . . . Chessboard, huh? I want to learn some chess strategy, some real chess systems . . . No disrespect to your grill here, but it's all about the smoker."

Noted. The clown had to remind himself it wasn't about killing Seamus, no matter how urgently he deserved to be murdered. Murder had to come from the inside. The urgency must be in him.

"We're only two crosswalks to Langston Elementary, where Mark Zuckerberg's nephew went to school," he said. "Langston's a recipient of a 2016 tech-arts grant from the George Lucas Foundation, the one on NPR." That was enough to provoke several more minutes of opinionation from Seamus. It was an old trick: the more a client heard his own voice in a house, the more he felt the house was his. Eliza, meanwhile, was going around seeing how the toilets flushed.

The clown liked knives, big knives, little knives—but what even was a knife? Something very narrow but no less hard. The set stashed in the crawl space of 404 Rocking Horse had chef's knives, cleavers, a straightedge razor, a few more theatrical things, toothy, curving. Almost every night since the house had been vacant, he'd let himself in, retrieved his things from the crawl space, and, fully kitted out, sharpened his knives, grind by meditative grind. Just last night, he'd sat thickly painted under this floor. Breathe. Intuit the killer already implied by the house. On the iPhone on his knee, his Facebook feed worked the cud of another late-breaking candidate scandal.

Touring the basement ("Here's your water heater . . . These guys here are for bolting a safe . . ."), he found one of his fingernails. "Huh? What do you think this is?" He showed the man, but the shrug was a shrug, not a shiver.

Whatever. He'd imagined stashing acids and paralyzing agents down there too—imagined how shocked and impressed Eliza and Seamus would be if they woke to find themselves prepped for a chemical flaying or immobilized beneath a swinging blade. He wished he could do something like that, but it was too much contraption. The engineering and constructing, the procurement of regulated chemicals—it was beyond him. He was a knife clown. He could never pretend to be what he was not.

Eliza said the house was perfect. Seamus, saving face, said they'd "have to do a little thinking through." The deciders, the clown imagined, were Eliza and her billboard dad. "Well, I think you're perfect for it," the clown said. They were. Their smug veneer would rip right through. The clown expected to hear from them Monday or Tuesday at the worst. He would throw in a moving service if the sale called for it, and they'd be dead before Thanksgiving. He promised it to himself the way he'd promised Owen ski camp, which now he would actually be able to pay for. A thing to look forward to, as the boy's therapist had suggested. Something the best version of you, if not you yourself, would want to do.

After he returned Seamus and Eliza to the RE/MAX lot, the clown accepted a Friday nachos invitation. Usually, a birthday or two had accumulated during the week. This time Lauren had made her first sale since licensure. "*I'm* going to buy *you* a drink," she said to the clown, poking and sweeping a fingertip accidentally enough across his nipple. She leaned in and whispered behind her nails, "It's a lie . . . you're going to buy *me* a drink." He doubted she actually wanted to fuck him, but he was pretty sure she wanted him imagining it, so he did imagine it, let it imbue his smile, and told her he'd be there.

He pulled over on his way to Baja's and made notes on the couple in his phone. Arrogance, wealth, an anxious hatefulness, the unconscious rivalry between them. There was some authentic American fearfulness in them perfectly suited to the Rocking Horse property, away in its little suburban circlet of fast-growth trees and prize schools and four-cheese macaroni chains. He worried for a second that someone else might murder them first.

At Baja's, Haru and Leroy hailed him from the corner booth. Lauren didn't even look up from her eye tunnel with Monique, who was telling the story of the movie she'd watched last night. Haru and Leroy were comparing notes on the BioShock installment they both were playing. Haru liked spicy food, shoes, and video games. Leroy liked Bernie Sanders, video games, and the Cleveland Cavaliers. Monique liked movies, her husband, and coconut oil. Everybody was a person. And the clown? For his birthday, the office had given him a Starbucks card.

After ten minutes, he proposed a toast: "To virtue!" he said and sat quickly down. Lauren made a wounded scoffing sound, and everyone laughed, and the clown stood up quickly and amended: "To the conquests of Lauren—may they be many."

They shared a smile then, escaping for some seconds the commotion of the nachos. He hadn't been fair. These were real people, not portfolios of interest. He searched her. Lauren had bobbed black hair, wore silver; the purple in her veins made her neck seem almost tattooed. She did have at least one tattoo, some text on her side you could see through the white of her work shirts. She liked Heart, she hated baby carrots . . . He searched harder. Maybe his own self had become small through a habitual disregard for the uniquenesses of other selves. So he studied her for particularities. At RE/MAX Reservoir Day, Lauren had spat arcs of water through her teeth. She called her car Thumper. She could do fingertip push-ups. For Halloween she was going to be the *Terminator* mom. He waited for a reciprocal sense of selfhood to reveal itself in him, but all he saw was Seamus trailing entrails through his perfect home.

"I don't think I should drive," she said. It was the third or fourth time she had said it, but they'd stayed there drinking beers. The others—Monique with her eyebrows—had long ago waved bye.

"How bad is the Uber from here?" He waved for the bill.

"I don't trust Ubers. Could be anyone," she said. "Could be—"

He waited. "Could be who?"

"A serial fucker." She was drunk. She laughed.

"Really. What's the worst that could happen?"

"Are you kidding?" She chipped off a dot of toasted cheese.

She was right. He apologized. He was just fishing for ideas. He said, "You never told me though. What'd you sell?"

"Four-oh-four Rocking Horse," she said, reviving. She popped up and did her little dance again, tossing invisible cash onto the table.

He supposed now he'd just have to murder her instead. Baja's didn't take American Express, so he put down the Banana Republic Visa and the cash he had, distractedly trying to make a plan.

She was drunk enough. In the Lexus, he leaned over and kissed her, and she reached almost immediately for his belt. She could barely kiss, all the hurry-up in her hand. "Not here," he said, but she unbuckled him and lifted it out.

Cheese and chips and too many Sam Adams and still that crispy chicken flavor. The Lexus needed air, according to the little orange light, and the woman in the passenger seat was now fellating him like she wanted to get things over with. "Not here," he said again.

"I don't want to go home," she said. "I hate my place."

"But this is a Baja's parking lot."

She laughed, only in order to say, "You make me laugh." Perhaps everyone had done this before, accidentally fucked a coworker on nacho Friday, but did it have to be done as a grim reenactment of the last time? Back in the corner booth, she'd had him defending *James and the Giant Peach,* denouncing nutmeg (not a happy flavor), describing the brazen bulls Greek kings used to kill their queens, now he felt anonymous again. "I better go pee," she said, but she didn't sprint for Thumper. She squatted between two pickup trucks and climbed back in.

He took her to the house on Rocking Horse Lane and let her fall asleep on the couch. In the basement, he retrieved his kit and knives and changed. He listened to the subterranean sounds of the neighborhood as he greased beneath the naked bulb—the switches of preprogrammed sprinklers, the swamp coolers falling back to work, even in October. He glued on the charred eyebrows, sealed the sharp teeth in. He washed the yellow, snake-slit contact lens in saline and eased it on. He combed the wig up, full fry, cinched the big belt tight atop his happy sooted tatters. He slid a few unscabbarded knives through the belt. The nails came last or he'd shred everything in the process.

He approached the couch in squeaking shoes, leaned over the back, and watched her sleeping. Now was when the menace should awaken something in him. The secret man was here.

He leaned further, grazed his nails across her face, punctured the couch leather claw by claw next to her ear. He bit down on his gums with his cutlery teeth until a drop of blood rolled over his lips, oiled itself redder on his smile, and fell onto her neck. She didn't wake.

Fine. He had too much beer in him for a chase scene, anyway. He aimed a fingernail for either side of her trachea. He would just rip it forward and hold her down while she drained. Then he'd get a U-Haul, find someplace to torch the couch (a show-house couch might not be missed), torch her, grind her teeth and any stubborn bones, Clorox the living room and the Lexus, and return the van. He'd have to chainsaw the couch to move it by himself. That would be dusty. Sometime in the a.m. you could expect Eliza and her dad to come peeking through the windows. He was supposed to FaceTime with Owen's therapist at noon.

He didn't mind hard work. He hadn't become a murder clown following paths of least resistance.

There were Tums in the glove box. He loved Tums, but he was afraid to go even that far in his suit.

He woke her up at 5 a.m. "I fell asleep," she said. A couch crease had left a rather gorgeous scar along her face.

"Let's get doughnuts. I'll drive you home."

She blinked at him. "We didn't even—"

"You mean you don't remember? You cooed, you cried . . ."

She yawned, squeezing her eyes to size her headache. "That's fucked up, Dennis."

He apologized. "I took a long shower and slept upstairs. We'll never speak of it again."

It didn't mean he was *never* going to murder her—just because he hadn't murdered her last night. When the morning papers were dropped off at Donut Time, he spread the crossword and watched her make quick work of it and the Jumble.

The sunrise woke up a little rain. Saturday was supposedly a workday, but hooky made things sweet. "I like your face," she said. "It's a real face. Some faces look like you could reach right through them."

He leaned forward and she tested the reality of his scruff. "You shave like a dad," she said.

He thought he understood what she meant by that—she meant she'd finally realized she didn't want and hadn't wanted him. That was okay. A lover you always half-suspected was trying to kill you. He'd never killed a friend before.

"I am a dad."

"I know. Riley? Jonas?"

"Owen."

"*Owen.* And you never miss a soccer game?"

The black jelly in a halved doughnut trembled as a cement mixer drove by. "The soccer games are in San Jose, actually."

"Christmases and campouts?" He looked at her, but she was already looking at him. "Your ex won't even let you have a campout? Really? You shave like such a great dad."

"It's not her. Owen never liked me very much," he said. "I thought I'd be a fun dad. Nieces and nephews always liked me. I've got all the Roald Dahls."

She waited.

"He'd get hysterical if his mom tried to leave us alone."

"He didn't grow out of it?"

"He was four when we divorced, and she waited three years before they moved away. My days were impossible. He refused to get out of the car when she brought him over. They've been in California now for seven and a half years."

Lauren's forehead wrinkles were legibly sympathetic. Her eyes, though, were wondering what had scared the kid. "He's old enough to explain himself, isn't he?" she said.

He told her about the therapist he paid for. "Part of me is a little proud of him, for figuring me out so fast. How long did it take you to learn to hate your dad?"

"He said he was voting for Trump and I pretty much declared it." She'd noticed the drop of blood on her collar, was scraping at it casually, unsurprised to find it there. "I couldn't believe him. But I figure I only need to hate him till Hillary wins."

Lauren admitted her plan for the day was to carve pumpkins and decorate her place for Halloween. He should help. When it was time to FaceTime the therapist, she'd leave him alone. "Do you like pumpkins?"

"I like knives," he said.

At the Safeway next to Donut Time, Lauren turned the pumpkins carefully, examining their personalities, she said. She asked him what candy they should get, and he realized his tooth- and earaches were gone. She directed him to a costume store, just opening, where she bought cobwebs and some cartoonish plastic bones, and then to an art supply where she got a large roll of black construction paper. He drove slowly in and out of parking lots so the knife kit in his trunk wouldn't clank.

He followed Thumper from the Baja's lot back to her duplex. The street looked vaguely familiar—maybe he'd bought a kayak off Craigslist somewhere over here?

She brewed them coffees that bore no relation to the Styrofoam stuff from Donut Time. He could feel its strength right through the mug. He leaned back against the counter, savoring, while she, with impressive fluidity, ran a razor over the blackout paper, tracing the profiles of cats and crones. She didn't even draw the line in pencil first. He held the paper to the windows and she taped it on.

She brushed the shreds off the kitchen table and got out a mixing bowl and knives. She looked at him. "I'm going to say it even though I don't think it needs to be said."

"Friends."

"And not the kind who fuck each other."

"Agreed."

"Good." She set down her pumpkin heavily, its thud and her *good* coinciding. "Now, what else is there that friends do?"

Her kitchen had banged-up wood cabinets and wallpaper that reminded him of bed-and-breakfast sheets. The place wasn't her, but you could see how she'd exerted herself against it in little ways, her pretty mixing bowls and denim apron on a peg. Big Boggle was with the cookbooks on the fridge top, a duck skull she must have found on a hike was on the window ledge over the sink. She'd hung a pull-up bar in the doorway and a string of prosperity hens from the bar. She played Bessie Smith and warmed up empanadas she'd made with minced lamb. She had a homemade chimichurri.

He carved his own face onto the pumpkin. She seemed amused. "It's Dennis," he explained.

She looked back and forth. "I suppose it is."

At noon, he sat with his iPad in the Lexus and talked to Dr. Jordie. She was at home, in a living room—he saw an adult son walk behind her with a cereal bowl. She asked how he was in a tone that indicated small talk, not therapeutic concern, and pretended not to observe that he'd hidden himself in a car.

"I might not be able to pay for ski camp after all," he said. "I'm sorry. I haven't told Tina."

"Ski camp might have been ambitious," she said in her Terry Gross voice. "Tina had to promise Owen he wouldn't have to go."

He opened his mouth to say he didn't know what to say and couldn't say even this.

"It's been a rough week," Dr. Jordie said. There was a wobbling view of her chin and blurred arm skin as she scratched something off the laptop screen. "Owen refused to go to school. He refused to eat or shower. Tina was making any deal he'd take."

The clown thought his face looked relaxed in the little frame superimposed on Dr. Jordie, but he felt a sour pain in his saliva glands, as if they were being squeezed. He'd been made to believe Owen wanted to go to ski camp. Now he scrubbed away his image of the boy watching ski videos on his phone and intuiting potential future freedoms. A yipping alpine skier dropping through blue sky —he'd thought maybe Owen had glimpsed his own secret man, and not a bad one. Behind his face, where the therapist couldn't see, the clown scrubbed at the free skier, until the white snow and red Gore-Tex rinsed away except for a few persistent smears.

Meanwhile, he'd missed a few sentences. ". . . got or gave himself a bloody nose and refused to hold it closed," the therapist was saying. "He sat there in English class with blood dripping onto his shirt." She paused for him to react.

"Was it a lot of blood?" the clown said.

"We talked at some length about it. He said he wanted to show them what a freak he is."

"He's not a freak."

She smiled to indicate that the reply to follow was worth her fee. "That's actually not for us to say, Dennis. He feels like one—but the crucial thing isn't that. It's that he wants to *show* everyone. He wanted his whole class to know who he is."

The clown felt like a dummy for not using Lauren's bedroom as she'd offered. It was finally a little cool out and the windows were fogging up. He'd imagined she didn't really want him to see her room—her unmade sheets, the twisted-up workout clothes flung to the floor. Like the blazer he still had on, his bedroom furnishings were selected to match the Lexus: king mattress made of some proprietary foam, tall vase of reeds in the corner, woodblock prints of some samurai character talking to the breeze. Guests to his bedroom were rare and left knowing no more than he let them.

Dr. Jordie's son walked by again, this time wearing a towel over his neck. So they had a pool. He imagined the son facedown, afloat on his own bleach-clean blood. "Very intimate in its way," Dr. Jordie was saying. He thanked her and PayPalled the fee.

When he came back into the kitchen, Lauren was the *Terminator* mom. Witches and arched cats made of sunlight shined through the blackout paper into the room. "How did I do?" she said. She had on Linda Hamilton's black tank top, utility belt, and sunglasses, and a water gun. "Sarah Connor, 1995." She did a one-arm pull-up on the bar in the kitchen door and landed looking at him. Maybe she thought he'd gone outside so he could cry, but there was no scrutiny in her eyes, only attention. "I'm going to smear on some greasy war-zone-looking shit later. Do you do Halloween?"

"I was thinking," he said before he could stop himself, "of being a scary clown."

"Classic. For a party or for the kids?"

It felt like the fog from the Lexus was coating his skin. He shouldn't have said anything. Halloween was Monday, any parties would be tonight. She attempted a second one-arm pull-up with no luck. "Do you have your costume yet? You should have got it when we were at the party store."

"I have it," he said. His voice was weird. "From last year."

"Wait a second." She squeezed out another pull-up with two arms and thudded to the floor. "You're not one of those clown prankers, are you? Is this a thing you do every year?"

He instructed his face not to do anything, but she was already grinning and shaking her head. "Holy shit."

"I'll be right back," he said.

Up and down her street were Hillary-Kaine signs, yes on Prop 200, yes on Amendment C, plastic gravestones, broom-crashed witches, jack-o'-lantern leaf bags, Love Trumps Hate. He got the kit from the back of the Lexus and carried it in. He laid it in a kitchen chair and undid the clasps. He set the wig between the pumpkins and showed her his greasepaint and his sponges, his red curtain-cloth pants with their ragged patches, his floorboard-slapping shoes, his shirts with their bloodstains and chipped buttons, his long stained teeth, his yellow metal nails. He didn't look up at her the whole time. He couldn't. He searched for more things to show her, so he could delay meeting her eyes. He unscrewed the contact case, so she could see the jaundiced snake-eye floating in its sterile cup. It scared him how violently it shook.

Finally he had to look up, so anxious now he couldn't pretend otherwise. "I'm glad to know you, Dennis," she said. She laughed. "I've known some geeks, I mean I thought I was a connoisseur . . ." She picked up the wig ("May I?") and pressed it on over her Sarah Connor do. She giggled as she fluffed it up, brushing loose plaster dust from the Rocking Horse basement or else trapped flecks of bone. She Jokered up her smile but couldn't hold it. Her giggling quivered the whole wig. She held one of the jack-o'-lantern knives, classic Bates Motel grip. "So you stalk around like this? People must flip out. I'd straight-up mace you before you could say 'punked.' I hope you're safe out there."

He laughed, but it was not his Lexus laugh. It started sociably enough, a laugh at himself, at how he must look, but it cracked down the middle when it reached his belly and something wet and maniacal blurted out of him. Lauren blinked and put a hand on his shoulder. She looked him in the eye, trying to see if he was crying or what. Whatever it is, let's hear it, she seemed to say. He didn't know what to do.

He started to say something but was laughing again—bilious, hot, disgusting, straight from his gut. It was mirthless and too loud and chicken flavored. She was backing away from him now ("You okay, Dennis?"), the wig sliding off her head.

"Give me the knife," he said.

To his surprise, she did, the safe way, gripping the blade and offering him the handle.

"You said you wanted me to show you," he said. It was the clown's voice, not Dennis's. "I'll show you, then." It terrified him what he was saying. He had to stop for breath between each word. *I'll show you. I'll—show—you.*

All the fun was happening downtown, five minutes from Pinche Taco, five minutes from Cerebral Brewing, about two minutes from Über Dog. There were scarecrows and Wonder Women and Cookie Monsters marauding through the early dark. Med students and waitresses, guised as Amelia Earhart, as swan-Björk, swung arms overhead to taxis, to the songs of passing cars, to friends stepping out of corner liquor stores across the street. A quartet of speeding Harleys ripped a seam in the night. A foam Hulk fist fell from a balcony and bounced into the road. Everyone was hidden in the clamor, welcomed and exalted by it. The clown felt simultaneous with himself. It couldn't be explained.

The clown and Lauren waited at the crosswalk with two scanty pirates. They eyed him. He was suspiciously uncostumed. The clown wore just his blazer and slacks, his graying temples, but beside him Lauren was to the nines. The happy tatters ill-fit her even better than they ill-fit him. He'd whited her face and drawn a great big ripping smile, almost to her eyes. Her forehead was smaller than his and the charred eyebrows reached up and tangled in the frizz of the wig. The teeth bulged her lips into a psychopathic grin. The tinsel nails made a little music as they walked.

Seamus and Eliza's apartment complex was exactly what he'd imagined, a high cube of condos with mountain bikes on the balconies, fake brick on Tyvek, banners over the office. He could picture the police tape, the office phone ringing, the men encamped in the alley shooing off the sirens and lights.

What he'd tell Owen, if Owen wanted to hear him, was that it was the scariest thing in the world to let yourself be known. You might not be liked. In fact, you wouldn't be. There's plenty in each of us that's unforgivable, he'd say. In a political world, it would always make a kind of sense to hide yourself away. But, he'd say,

I want you to know me, even if sometimes you hate what you see. And I hope you'll find a way to let me know you too.

He led Lauren up the courtyard stairs and along the balcony past potted cactuses and airing yoga mats. He gestured for her to listen. Behind the door, Seamus was making original commentary on the Clintons. Lauren seemed nervous. She kept whispering, was she supposed to say something or do something scary? "Do I say trick or treat?" The clown took a deep breath and let it all imbue his smile. He told her to relax. It was going to be great. The knife was in his blazer, his heart was in his smile. He knocked and said, "Don't worry. Just keep your eyes on me."

REBECCA McKANNA

Interpreting *American Gothic*

FROM *Colorado Review*

CHLOE RECEIVED THE first letter in December. She worked at the American Gothic House in Eldon, Iowa, and spent that afternoon helping a middle-aged couple put their golden retrievers into two of the museum's many replicas of the clothes the couple in Grant Wood's painting wore—a black dress and colonial-print apron for the woman; denim overalls and a black jacket for the man. Both dogs endured this stoically, much more stoically than Chloe thought she would have been able to do.

The house looked salmon colored in the fading winter light. It was only four thirty, but with the time change the sun would set soon. She walked toward the visitors center next to the house. Her hands ached from the cold. As she walked, carrying the pitchfork and costumes, she thought about Grant Wood. Was there any way he could have predicted the bastardization of his creation? Bougie people driving from suburbs of Chicago to pose their dogs for an insipid picture they would probably frame and hang above a piano no one played.

Inside the visitors center, Mark was behind the front desk, listening to someone on the phone. He was in his mid-twenties, a few years older than Chloe, and had worked at the museum longer than she had. He was tall and skinny with pale skin, wire-rimmed glasses, and hair the same color as Van Gogh in *Self-Portrait with Palette*—hair that was a golden red and seemed to be lit from within. Mark usually answered phone calls from people with questions about the house and its history or teachers who wanted to schedule field trips; he sometimes, however, talked to elderly people who called under the pretense of sharing their story about Grant Wood or the painting but who just wanted someone to talk to. He was always kinder and more patient with those people than Chloe thought she would be, making active-listening statements like *I'm sorry. That must have been difficult. I see. Good for you.*

The museum was closing soon, and one visitor remained—a man in his late fifties with graying hair and a long black coat. Chloe left him in front of an exhibit about Grant Wood's childhood and went into the break room, where she propped the pitchfork against the wall, took off her coat, and grabbed a pile of mail from the counter to sort.

She heard the documentary about *American Gothic* playing on repeat in the media room. She always found the name "media room" a little too ambitious for the tiny space with a few wooden chairs and a TV and DVD player. She almost had the documentary memorized: "It is one of the most familiar images in American art, and its story starts here, in Eldon, Iowa, in the year 1930, when a young artist named Grant Wood saw a small white house built in the Carpenter Gothic style." She found the narrator's deep voice comforting.

She threw away a lot of junk mail—magazine-subscription ads and coupons mostly—and then sorted through the remaining letters. One was a thank-you card from a fifth-grade class that had visited the house a month before. Another was a clipping about the house that was in some art magazine recently.

Finally she got to the last letter. Its Daffy Duck postage was out of step with what was stamped across the back of the envelope in red: NOTICE! *This correspondence was mailed by an inmate confined in a facility operated by the Kentucky Department of Corrections. Its contents are uncensored.*

When she ripped it open she found creamy paper, the surface covered with neat, old-fashioned cursive from a pencil. The letter was formal, polite. A man asking what the painting was truly about. Was it a parody of Iowans? Or a tribute? Or something more serious—possibly a mourning portrait? He said he'd read a variety of different interpretations, and he was curious what the "official" interpretation was.

This may seem silly, he wrote. *But as you can understand, I have nothing but time on my hands to ponder these things. I want to understand what Grant Wood's intentions were.* He signed the letter: *Peace, Jon Allan Blue.*

The name nagged at her. It seemed familiar, but wouldn't she remember someone with the last name Blue? She looked up "Jon Allan Blue" on her phone. The number of results surprised her. The media had dubbed him "The Midwest Mangler." His victims were young women in Iowa, Kentucky, and Nebraska, bodies mutilated beyond recognition, skulls bashed in, bodies stabbed repeatedly. He had been on death row at the Kentucky State Penitentiary for over a decade, since Chloe was ten years old.

There were photos of him online. He was handsome—even the media commented on his "all-American good looks." His eyes were gray, his lips full. His forehead was heavily lined, and there were tributaries of wrinkles fanning out from his eyes. There was something appealing and youthful about his smile. He looked more like a CEO than a serial killer, although Chloe had read once that people in both occupations often had psychopathic traits.

Chloe held a letter written by someone who had stabbed several women to death, and this was terrifying—and the most exciting thing to happen to her. She was desperate to understand how someone who did so many horrific things could write such a polite, reasonable-sounding letter in perfect Palmer script.

While she read an interview with one of Jon Allan Blue's lawyers, Mark entered the break room. He sat next to her, his shoulder touching hers, his head craned to look at her phone.

"What are you reading?"

Although there was no reason not to tell him, although the letter would have made for an interesting conversation, she darkened her phone's screen, shrugged, and said it was nothing.

She did not write back, but she did not throw Jon Allan Blue's letter away. She took it home and kept it in a drawer in her nightstand. She read through websites about his crimes each night when she got home from work.

Some of the websites said the women Jon Allan Blue murdered resembled an old girlfriend who scorned him. People pointed to this woman as the reason he began to hate and want to hurt women. This seemed much too simplistic to Chloe. Besides, when she pictured him murdering young women, they were never brunettes like his old girlfriend. They were always blondes like Chloe.

Then, in January, Jon Allan Blue sent a second letter. It was almost identical to his first letter, asking the same question about the painting's meaning with the same polite tone. At the end he wrote, *I am sure it would be more convenient for you to answer my question through email. Unfortunately, Kentucky inmates are not allowed Internet access, so I would greatly appreciate your written response.*

After work Chloe went to Eldon's post office, a red brick building on Eldon's main street, across from the diner and a heating-and-cooling business. She paid thirty-five dollars, not an insignificant sum on her paycheck, to rent a PO box for a year and mailed her first letter to Jon Allan Blue. She kept her response short. She told him she worked for the museum and his question was a valid one. There was no consensus about what the painting meant. All the suggestions he floated were possibilities. Wood himself, however, had always maintained it was a tribute to Iowan life. Before she closed the letter, she encouraged him to respond with other questions he might have. As she drove home, she felt the thrill of expectation, a blooming in her chest. She felt the same way when she was a little girl and stole a candy bar from a gas station — guilty yet buzzed on adrenaline and the satisfaction of doing something inadvisable.

The next day after work, she and Mark went to Eldon's only remaining bar. The town's population was nine hundred, but with each census it continued to dwindle. There were a lot of shuttered businesses, mobile homes with busted windows, and plastic toys left in front yards to bleach in the sun. On the sign in front of Eldon's high school, the motto "Do No Harm" had been posted, which summed up the school's aspirations for its students pretty well. The people who did leave for college rarely returned.

Chloe had never gone to college, never left Eldon at all. At eighteen, she hadn't known how to afford it and wasn't sure she was college material. She'd never performed particularly well in her classes, other than art, and was often lost in daydreams when she should have been listening to her teachers. She told herself someday, when she saved some money, maybe she'd study art. But years passed and the day never came.

The bar smelled like stale beer and cigarette smoke. Other than the Johnny Cash song playing, the only sounds were pool balls hitting one another and the occasional smoker's cough. She and

Mark ordered beers and talked about the girl who'd tried to shop-lift from the museum gift store earlier that day.

"What kind of teenager tries to steal a tote bag printed with a Grant Wood painting?" Mark asked, although to Chloe the answer was obvious—a desperate one. She opened her mouth to say that, but a hand on her shoulder interrupted her.

"Your mama let you out to play?"

It was her mother's ex-boyfriend, Frank. He flashed yellow teeth at her in a smile. He was tall and skinny, and his jeans, work boots, and the hairy backs of his hands were flecked with white paint. She had never liked him—a mean drunk who always looked at her like she was a flank steak rather than a human being. He leaned forward and slurred something else. By his inflection, she could tell it was a question. She did what she often did in such situations —appeased him and nodded and laughed, hoping she could make the interaction end, hoping his beer breath would move out of her face.

She realized she could have been agreeing and laughing about anything. He could have been asking if she were a dumb cunt, and she would have just laughed and nodded. The realization made her angry.

Frank leaned back and laughed, too. Then he continued on to the bathroom.

"Dick," Mark said, but long after the man was out of earshot.

Jon Allan Blue responded to her letter a week later, thanking her for her response and asking what it was like to work at the museum. This started a series of short letter exchanges. They wrote about innocuous things—her job, his interest in art and Grant Wood in particular, their shared love of the Midwest landscape. Eventually, he began to write about his daily life in prison.

His cell on death row was 6 x 9 x 9.5 feet high. He woke at five a.m. to the rattle of the breakfast cart—powdered eggs and toast served on a Styrofoam tray with a plastic spork. At least once an hour a guard checked on him. Other than phone calls, legal visits, or exercise, he stayed in his cell. Death row had a particular smell —body odor and fecal matter. *It was better back before 2011 when people were still allowed to smoke,* he wrote. *The smoke masked the stink. Although, you get used to it after a while.*

He owned a 13-inch TV and said his favorite shows were *American Idol* and a drama about young lawyers. *In another life, I would have liked to be a lawyer,* he wrote.

Multiple prisoners in the wing watched *Jeopardy* together, each trying to yell out the right answer first. Men in the wing talked to one another, moving to the front of their cells and speaking loudly enough for their voices to echo down the hall. However, the talk was frequently the rambling of isolated, crazed men, so he put on his headphones and listened to the radio. He read a lot: news magazines and, lately, books about regionalist art and Grant Wood.

I'm not sure why American Gothic interests me so much, he wrote. *I guess there's something funny and sad and disturbing about it—all at the same time. I guess life is kind of like that, too.*

One evening in March, she sat in her apartment reading his most recent letter.

She lived on the first floor of an old, creaky house sectioned off into apartments. As was often the case, she heard the girl who lived upstairs talking to her mother on the phone, telling her, yes, she was making good decisions, yes, this guy was a good guy, different from the last one.

Things are much the same here, Jon wrote in his latest letter. *The appeals process drags on, but you know I doubt my attorneys' skills and competence. It's hard to describe how lonely this place is, especially in the evening. Your letters help make it bearable. It's strange—I feel like I know you, yet we've never met. I would love to talk to you on the phone, if you'd be willing. I'm allowed limited phone privileges each week, and I can't think of a better way to use them than hearing your voice. Please consider it. If you're willing, let me know, and I'll tell you how you can go about getting on my approved callers list.*

As always, I wish you all the best, Chloe, and I think of you often.

She leaned her head against her futon. She'd bought it at the Salvation Army, and despite her best efforts, it still smelled of onions.

He was taking up more and more of her thoughts. She was painting again, something she hadn't done since high school. She was good enough to be decent, but not good enough to be great or ever have a show in a gallery. She found herself sketching Grant Wood photos she looked up online, copies of copies. She mailed them to Jon, who told her he taped them up on his cell walls and complimented her on her proficiency. She started a sketch of him, but every time she worked on it, after about a half hour she realized she was sitting alone in her apartment drawing a flattering portrait of a serial killer. She would close her sketchbook and watch TV instead.

Chloe drank a beer to calm her nerves. When the phone finally rang, she heard an operator asking if she would accept a collect call from an inmate at the Kentucky State Penitentiary. She said yes but had a hard time catching her breath. She was perched on the edge of her futon and found herself staring at her bare feet on the hardwood floor, her calluses and chipped pink polish looking in step with the warped wood, two of the oak boards water stained and bowing like they were inflated.

She'd already heard his voice from interviews posted online, videos of him in the scarlet-red jumpsuit designating the prison's death row inmates. In them, he talked like a teacher—someone comfortable with the sound of their own voice, comfortable explaining things to people, and confident they had the knowledge to make people understand. In more recent interviews, he said killing people was like being possessed by a demon. The next day, he felt great remorse for what he had done, and it weighed on him that, "in the eyes of God and in the eyes of the law," he was responsible for what a "great force" had made him do. He squeezed his eyes shut when he talked like this.

The lines on his face were deeper than they had been during pictures taken at his trial, and his eyes appeared sunken, with dark circles surrounding them. Although he would spend long portions of the interview looking at his hands, choosing his words with care, when he did look at the interviewers, his stare was intense and penetrating. Chloe wondered what it would be like to be on the receiving end of such a gaze.

There was a thrill when she heard him say her name. He asked her where she was. After she answered, he said, "You have a lovely voice with just the tiniest bit of a lisp."

She blushed. She'd endured years of special speech classes in school because of her lisp. It used to be much worse. She and a girl who couldn't say her *R*s read aloud from books about jungle cats. Both she and the other girl had only slight traces of their speech impediments by the time they graduated from high school.

"Oh, God," she said. "That's embarrassing."

"No, no," he said. "It's endearing. It's sweet."

She felt profoundly grateful to him in that moment. He had only twelve minutes of phone privileges. They talked about his daily routine—apparently the prison gym's treadmill was broken —and she talked about her job.

"I saw the painting in person once," he told her. "In Chicago. It was," he laughed drily, "before all this happened. It's an amazing piece."

Chloe told two lies to get her job at the center. The first was that she liked *American Gothic*, when in fact she found it hideous. The second was that she had seen it in person. The truth was, although she had lived in the Midwest her entire life, she never had the opportunity or funds to travel to Chicago.

Still, she found herself nodding, even though he couldn't see her. "Amazing," she agreed. "I felt the same way."

Finally, when they had to hang up, he said, "Thank you for this. You don't know how much I looked forward to talking to you."

"You're welcome," she said. Once they were off the phone, she sat on her futon and continued to stare at her feet. She wondered what she was supposed to feel. Possibly guilt? Possibly conflicted? Instead, she tried not to smile.

Several phone calls later, he asked her to tell him something she hadn't told anyone.

"I'm not that interesting," she said.

"That's obviously not true," he said. "You were willing to become my friend. Not everyone would do that."

She felt pleased he considered her a friend, and slightly unsatisfied—like when someone gave a hungry person only a bite of chocolate when they craved the whole bar.

"I guess there's one story," she said. "But it's kind of weird." Even thinking of it made her feel queasy.

"I like weird," he said. So she told him.

She told him how her real father left when she was a baby. How he returned only once—when she was fourteen he came through town and asked to take her to dinner at a steak house in Fairfield, so they could catch up. Her mother hadn't wanted to let her go, but Chloe wheedled until she got her way. The meal was good, a nice change from peanut butter sandwiches and ramen noodles.

She learned he had done okay for himself, starting his own construction business in Illinois. He was ready to pay the back child support, to try to support her as best he could.

"You deserve that," he said while they chewed their steaks. While he was paying the bill, she thought how lucky she was to have this man as her father and not her idiot stepfather, the father of her half siblings.

They had so much to talk about he drove down by the Des Moines River once they got back to Eldon, and they parked and sat and talked. It happened naturally. First he hugged her. Then he kissed her forehead. Then he kissed her neck. And then he reached up her skirt. The water lapped at the riverbanks. She put her hands where he told her, but she didn't allow herself to think about anything. She kept her eyes closed, kept listening to that rushing water, kept letting it drown everything else.

When he dropped her off at her house, he kissed her on the forehead. He never visited again, but the child support payments continued coming until she turned eighteen.

When she finished her story, Jon cleared his throat. "It makes me regret I'm in here and not able to find your father and give him some nice whacks with a crowbar. That often does wonders for a person."

That was the first night Chloe started fantasizing about Jon murdering people she knew.

She couldn't deny his phone calls were becoming less a curiosity and more a thing stilling the loneliness beating inside her. The darkest thing he had ever done was out in the world for everyone to see. There was something comforting about that.

She didn't fantasize about having sex with him. She didn't know why, but she didn't. Maybe because she had never enjoyed sex? Maybe because it always hurt in all the wrong ways? Instead, she pictured him putting a choke collar around her neck and leading her into the woods. She pictured him cutting off her clothes and making her kneel, naked, in the leaves. He would pull on the choke chain and grab a handful of her hair, yanking hard. For a while, that was the extent of the fantasy, and it was enough to get her off late at night, her fingers moving between her legs. But eventually, it changed. After he yanked at her hair, she would grab a sharp stick from the forest floor. She'd wait for him to let go of her hair, for him to give her chain some slack. Then she'd stab him in the neck with the stick, his warm blood flowing out across her hands and her naked chest until she was sticky with it.

"I think about stabbing you," she told him once on the phone, surprising herself by saying it aloud.

"Do you?" he said, as though this amused him. "What else do you think about?"

She told him in precise detail, and when he finally spoke, his voice sounded deeper than before. "The first part of that sounds just fine," he said. "But if you tried the second part, you would regret it." He said this almost cheerfully.

"Would I?" she asked.

"Yes," he said, this time more firmly. A few moments later, the operator cut in, signaling their time was up.

"How would you kill someone and get away with it?" she asked Mark.

"What?" They were in the break room, eating sandwiches during lunch. He was sitting so close she felt the heat of his arm.

She repeated the question. He stared at her. "You've never thought about it?" she asked.

"No," he said. "I can honestly say I never have." They lapsed into silence. The subject was all Chloe thought about. Killing and those who were capable of it. She wasn't the only one fascinated. She couldn't be. There were too many TV shows and movies and books all based around it. Too many fictional serial killers who were memorable in pop culture. But they couldn't give her what Jon Allan Blue could. They were glamorized, flashy, unreal—pretty actors covered in corn syrup and red dye. They knew nothing about what it really felt like to take a life, what allowed you mentally to ascend to that ultimate assertion of power, erasing another person's existence.

Mark bumped her shoulder with his and smiled. "What are you thinking about? The perfect crime?"

She smiled and shook her head.

"I think I've figured it out," Jon said. It was early June, and Chloe was drinking a beer and sitting in front of her window air-conditioning unit, trying to dry the sweat that collected between and under her breasts.

"Figured what out?" she asked.

"The painting," he said. "I think I understand what it means." Jon told her Grant Wood lived in the attic of a funeral home's carriage house and had replaced his front door with a coffin lid. He talked about the reaction to *American Gothic*—how one Iowan woman was so incensed by the painting, she threatened to bite Wood's ear off. He started talking faster and faster, and Chloe struggled to follow what he was saying. He talked about all the black in the painting —the man's black jacket, the woman's black dress. He talked about the symbolism of the farmer's pitchfork and of the plants on the doorstep—the geranium for melancholy.

"Look at the people in the painting," he said. She had never heard him so agitated before. "Really look at them. These are people seething with repressed violence. These are people fixated on death."

She pulled the painting up on her computer and stared at the expression on the man's face. She studied how his bushy eyebrows came to points, how his long face and pinched mouth added to how sinister he looked. The woman, on the other hand, just looked lost. Chloe had read that originally Wood said the woman was the farmer's wife, but after the age difference scandalized people, he began telling people she was the farmer's daughter.

Despite what Jon said about it, Chloe saw something sad about the painting. Despite their severe expressions, the two figures looked powerless and defeated, like people who had felt small their whole lives, standing in front of a cheap farmhouse with fancy windows.

After five minutes, Chloe ended the conversation, much to her reluctance. The collect calls from the prison cost five dollars a minute. "It's a racket," Jon told her once. "And the prison gets a cut of the money." After saying goodbye to Jon, she walked to the bar to meet Mark.

It was hot, and they were thirsty. Instead of pacing themselves with waters in between rounds, they both downed beers quickly, getting much drunker than usual.

After their fifth round, Mark leaned toward her. "I think you're beautiful," he said, and kissed her. She let him. She felt dizzy and light and took his bottom lip between her teeth and bit. At first he moaned as if he were aroused, but a second later, the moan changed to one of pain, and he pulled away from her. She tasted blood.

"What the fuck?" he demanded, dabbing his bloody lip with a cocktail napkin.

She stared at him. She liked the way he was looking at her—as if she were some fearsome creature he had never seen clearly until now.

He rose from his stool and threw some cash on the bar. "Look, we're both drunk. I'm going to go." She didn't stop him.

She saw Frank, her mother's ex-boyfriend, facing away from her, resting his arm on the edge of the pool table. The adrenaline flowing through her, coupled with the alcohol, made her feel like she took up all the space in the bar. She finished her beer and stood to grab a pool cue.

JENNIFER McMAHON

Hannah-Beast

FROM *Dark Corners/Amazon Original Stories*

Halloween 1982

Please, Hannah, please, come out with us tonight.

It won't be like before, we promise.

Please, please, please, please, say you'll be our friend again and come with us.

We'll get candy. So much candy. Whole pillowcases stuffed full of Kit-Kats, peanut butter cups, Mars bars.

So much sugar, we won't sleep for a week.

Trust us, Hannah.

Come with us, Hannah.

It'll be a night you won't ever forget.

Halloween 2016

"There's no way you're leaving the house like that." Amanda spoke in her flat, level I'm-the-mom-here tone, doing her best to hide the shaking in her voice. Really, she wanted to scream. Scream not in fury, but horror. She wanted to run from the kitchen and hide in her bedroom, slamming the door maybe, like *she* was the teenager. Her skin prickled with cold sweat. Her stomach churned. She worked to steady her breathing as she made herself look at her daughter, take in the whole grotesque costume.

It was like some hole had been ripped in time, and Amanda was twelve years old again, dressed in her lame cat burglar costume with a striped shirt and pillowcase money bag, handing her mask over so that Hannah-beast's costume would be complete. *Thanks, Manda Panda!*

Erin's face was painted blue with thick greasepaint. There was a black plastic eye mask held in place by elastic. A pink feather boa. A silver cape. Topping it all off was a rainbow clown wig.

Jesus, how many rainbow clown wigs did the drugstore in town sell each Halloween?

The costume was spot-on; a near-exact replica with the exception of the face paint—it was the wrong shade of blue and too thick. The real Hannah-beast had worn makeup that was thin, patchy, a dull pale blue that had made her look cyanotic.

"That is totally unfair," Erin said.

"I thought you were going as a cat."

"I'm a cat every fucking year, Mom."

This was a new thing for Erin, the swearing all the time. She'd never done it back when Jim was here. He wouldn't have stood for it. But Amanda had decided to ignore it. To ride it out and let Erin blow off steam by dropping a few f-bombs here and there.

Pick your battles, Amanda told herself. And besides, didn't letting the swearing slide make her the cool mom as opposed to the up-tight dad? The dad who had walked out on them four months ago, claiming Amanda was too distant, too walled off, and he couldn't live his life with a woman he didn't know how to reach.

"You know the rules," Amanda said to her daughter. "You are not going out like that."

"Your rules suck and make no sense," Erin said with disgust. "They're totally *arbitrary.*"

Erin always thought she could win an argument if she used big words. Jim had often let himself be distracted or amused. Not Amanda. Amanda said nothing.

"It's my last year of trick-or-treating," Erin whined. Next year she'd be a freshman in high school. "Why do you have to *ruin* it?" Her voice broke a little bit, and Amanda thought Erin might start crying.

She cried a lot lately, mostly while fighting with Amanda over perceived unfairnesses. It had been so much easier when she was younger, crying over a scraped knee or some hardship she'd endured at school—not getting enough turns on the big slide or her teacher saying she hadn't shown her work properly on a math worksheet. Then, all problems could be solved with a hug—*Give me one of your boa constrictor hugs, Mommy, real tight like you'll never let me go!*—and a trip to the ice-cream shop, where they'd split a cookie-dough sundae with extra whipped cream.

Now Amanda took in a breath, forced a smile. "That's my job. Fun ruiner."

Erin stared at her through her mask, her eyes angry and a little desperate. They could have been the real Hannah-beast's eyes.

Manda, the eyes pleaded. *Manda Panda, please. Don't let them do this to me.*

Amanda had to look away, glancing over at the kitchen island, where the pumpkin they'd bought last week at the farmers market still sat, uncarved. Pumpkin carving had always been Jim's job, a task he'd taken seriously, downloading templates from the Internet, spending hours cutting out perfect cat faces, witches flying on brooms, and one year, a raven with intricate feathers and glowing eyes.

"Go change," Amanda told her daughter. "Now."

Erin sighed dramatically. "Can you just explain why? Can you be *that* fair?"

Every year since she was in third grade, Erin had asked to go as Hannah-beast. She'd seen the older kids doing it, a handful each year, and she'd heard the stories. How the real Hannah-beast came back each year at Halloween, came back with a box of matches in her pocket, so you better look out, better be careful, better hope you didn't run into her. She was a crazy ghost girl, Hannah-beast was. She'd killed in life and she'd kill again in death, given half a chance.

But the stories were just that: stories. Myths with pieces of truth hidden inside.

Over the years, Erin had seemed eager for these nuggets of truth.

"But Hannah-beast was a real girl, right?" Erin would ask.

"Yes," Amanda would tell her.

"A girl who died a long time ago?"

"Yes."

"And she set a fire?"

Amanda would nod, always having to look away. "Yes," she'd

say, the same reply she'd given hundreds of times, beginning back when she was Erin's age and the police first questioned her about it.

"And people died?"

"Yes."

"Did you know her, Mom?" Erin would ask, eyes wide and hopeful. "Did you know the real Hannah-beast?"

"No," Amanda would say, the lie so practiced it rolled off her tongue in a loose and natural way. "I didn't know her at all."

She looked at her daughter now in her blue face paint—thirteen years old, gangly as a scarecrow.

"Please, Mom," Erin said, voice quiet and pleading now. "Seriously, it's not fair. At least tell me why."

"Because," Amanda said, pausing for a moment to breathe and keep her tone calm. "Because I said so."

Erin shook her head to express her utter contempt, the bright rainbow wig slipping slightly. She stomped off, out of the kitchen and up the stairs to her room, slamming the door with impressive force. Amanda went into the living room and sank down into the couch, eyes focused on the overflowing bowl of brightly wrapped candy in a plastic pumpkin bowl.

Erin came downstairs half an hour later, face cleaned of blue makeup, replaced by cat whiskers drawn with eyeliner, cherry-red lipstick. She wore black leggings, a black hoodie, and a headband with furry black ears gone mangy from one too many Halloweens. She had on her school backpack, which would soon be stuffed with candy, popcorn balls, and glow sticks given out by the police officers who were out in full force each Halloween, as if by sheer numbers they could ward off what was coming: the small army of Hannah-beasts, the little fires all over town—dumpsters, trash cans, vacant buildings, the old salt shed. And somehow, they never managed to stop a stuffed effigy of Hannah-beast from being hung by a noose from the town gazebo each year, cloth body stuffed full of newspaper and rags, pillowcase face painted blue, rainbow wig stapled on, pink boa ruffling in the breeze as the creepy doll swung in circles from the thick rope.

Erin went straight to the front door, passing Amanda in the living room without a word. There was a rapid-fire knocking, and she flung the door open. Her friends were gathered on the front porch—they must have texted Erin that they were there. Two Hannah-beasts, Wonder Woman, and a red devil in a too-tight, too-short dress.

Erin walked out and slammed the door behind her, but not quickly enough to drown out the first words she spoke: "I fucking hate my mother."

1982

"Please, Hannah, please, come out with us tonight," the three girls cooed like sweet little doves, funny partridges, as they stood gathered outside her first-floor bedroom window. They knew better than to come to the front door, deal with Daddy and his fire-breathing bourbon breath telling them they weren't good girls, they were trash, little dipshit whores.

Girls like that, they're going straight to hell. That's what Daddy said. *You stay away from them unless you want to get burned.*

Their porch light was dark, no smiling jack-o'-lantern to greet trick-or-treaters, no bowl of candy waiting by the front door.

Hannah bit her lip, looked through the screen at the girls gathered outside smiling in at her from the shadows, begging: "Please, please, pleeeeeaze."

"It won't be like before, we promise."

"Please say you'll be our friend and come with us," they begged.

Hannah shook her head. "I'm not supposed to."

It was more than the fact that her daddy would skin her alive if he caught her going out with these girls. It was that she didn't trust them. Not one bit.

They'd given her dog biscuits, telling her they were oatmeal cookies, then barked out their own laughs, saying, "Hannah's a dog! Bowwow, Dog-face! Bow-fucking-wow!"

Then she'd cried, actually cried, and they'd said they were sorry, sorry, so, so sorry. It was a joke. Just having a little fun is all.

Some days they took her lunch money, saying it was a tax she had to pay, and if she didn't pay it, they wouldn't be her friends anymore, wouldn't let her sit with them, not ever. Not like they did all that much anyway. Mostly she was greeted with disgusted snarls of "Go away, Hannah."

The worst was the time they'd tried to turn her into a real girl. "Trust us," Mel said. "We'll make you pretty. You want to be pretty, don't you, Hannah?"

And they took her to Katie's house, where they made her soak in a tub full of "pretty-girl bath salts" that made her break out in a hot rash all over her body. Then they coated her legs with shaving cream, and Mel shaved her with a pink razor, saying, "You've got quite the pelt going on here, Hannah. What are you, a wolf-girl?"

And Hannah had bared her teeth, laughed, and said, "Maybe I am. Maybe I'm going to eat you up." She gave them a growl, deep in her throat, and snapped her jaws at Mel, made like she was going to bite her.

This had startled Mel. Or maybe she just pretended to be startled. Maybe she slipped on purpose.

The next thing Hannah knew, she was dripping blood down her leg, not like little weeping dots, but like a spring stream that runneth over.

"Fuck," Mel said. "Sorry." But then she smiled ever so slightly and shot a quick glance at Manda and Katie, and Hannah knew she wasn't sorry. Not one bit.

Hannah still had the scar.

"It's Halloween, Hannah," Manda said now, pleading. She was dressed up like a cat burglar with a striped shirt and watch cap, a black mask, and a pillowcase with a huge dollar sign drawn on the outside. Katie was a girlie clown, a feather boa draped around her shoulders. And Mel, she was some kind of superhero space princess with a silver dress, tall black boots, a silver cape, a tiara, and a big plastic laser gun strapped to her back.

"Don't you want candy?" Katie asked as she stood shoulder to shoulder with Mel. "We'll get candy. So much candy! Whole pillowcases stuffed full of KitKats, peanut butter cups, Mars bars."

"So much sugar we won't sleep for a week," Mel promised.

"Then we can swap," Manda said. "I know you love peanut butter cups—I'll give you all of mine."

Hannah let herself imagine it: roaming the streets, going door-to-door with these girls, opening her sack up, and watching the candy fill it until it was heavy, so heavy that it was hard to carry, bulging with chocolate, lollipops, wax lips, candy she'd never even heard of, never even tried.

"Come with us," Mel said.

"Come with us," Katie begged, an echo of Mel. Which was how Hannah thought of her. Not a person all her own, just an echo. Whatever Mel said, Katie did. Whatever Mel wore, Katie wore. She even brought the same kind of sandwich as Mel to school each day —peanut butter and fluff, with the crust cut off.

Hannah looked at Manda. The only one she half-trusted. She'd been to Manda's house before, spent the night once even. It had been during February break, and the other girls were away; Hannah knew this would never have happened if they'd been around, if there'd been even the slightest possibility that they'd find out.

Manda's house was big and beautiful. Her parents were real nice too. They took Hannah and Amanda to the video store, let them pick out whatever they wanted; then they stopped at the grocery store and bought a pan of popcorn that they cooked on the stovetop—pop, pop, pop—and the foil over it puffed up as it filled, turning it into a crinkly, metallic mushroom. She and Manda made pink cupcakes with purple sprinkles, and Manda's mom wrapped the leftovers up for Hannah to take home. Hannah stayed in her clothes at bedtime, and Manda's mom was all like, "Where's your nightgown, sweetheart?" and Hannah said, "I forgot it," when the truth was she didn't own one at all.

"Well, I'm sure Amanda has something you can borrow! Let's go see." Then Amanda's mom was opening all the drawers in her dresser and going through the closet and making a whole pile of stuff that she said was either too small for Amanda or that Amanda never wore anymore. Not just nightgowns, but jeans and a dress and shirts and this pair of pink cowboy boots that Hannah tried on, and they fit perfect, like her feet and Manda's were the same shape and everything. "Take them," Manda's mother said. "Take all these things. Amanda doesn't wear any of it anymore." Amanda looked kind of surprised, a little angry maybe even, so Hannah said, "No, thanks. I'll just borrow the nightgown for tonight." Manda's mom gave Manda a look, and Manda smiled at Hannah and said, "No, you should take all this stuff. I was just gonna give it to the Salvation Army anyway."

Hannah went to sleep that night curled up against Manda, wearing her white nightgown, Manda's heavy comforter on top of them, and it was the happiest she'd ever been. "I love you, Manda," she said. "Manda Panda," she added, giggling the new name into Manda's shoulder.

"Go to sleep," Manda said.

She wore Manda's pleated acid-washed jeans and lavender polo shirt (with the collar turned up, the way Manda always wore it) to school when they all came back from break the next Monday, and Mel had laughed, then got all angry, and asked, "Amanda, isn't that your shirt? And your jeans?" and Manda turned bright red, and Hannah said, "Yeah, they are. I stole them. When I was at her house."

Mel glared at Manda. "When was Dog-face at your house?" And Manda—she looked all frantic, little drops of sweat dotting her forehead.

"I broke in," Hannah said quickly. "Broke in when no one was home."

"Thieving little bitch," Mel said. "Give them back. Right now."

"Yeah, go take them off, or we'll do it for you," Katie said. She took a step closer to Hannah like she was going to start ripping them off right in the hall.

"It's okay, really," Manda had said. "They're like a hundred years old, they don't even fit, just let her—"

"It is *not* fucking okay," Mel snarled. Manda hadn't said any more.

And Hannah had gone into the bathroom and taken off the clothes and put on her gym clothes and worn those all day instead —her stinky T-shirt and too-tight shorts. She'd folded Manda's clothes up neatly and returned them to her during study hall. Manda slipped them into her book bag without saying anything, but she smiled apologetically at Hannah. When Hannah got home from school that day, she put the rest of the hand-me-downs in a kitchen garbage bag, sealed it tight, and hid them in the bottom of the trash bin in the garage. One of her chores was rolling the bin to the curb every Friday night, so she knew it'd be gone soon, and her daddy would never know.

But the boots, those lovely pink boots, she kept those. She knew better than to wear them to school. She put them on every day when she got home and danced around in her bedroom, imagining she was Manda, and she lived in a big house with a big closet full of clothes she never wore and sweet pink cupcakes baking in the kitchen.

The real Manda, just outside her bedroom window, smiled at

her now, held out her hand. "Come on," she said. "Come trick-or-treating with us. It'll be so much fun. Promise."

"I . . . I don't even have a costume."

"It's cool. We'll make you one," Mel said. "We'll give you parts of ours."

Then Mel reached up, untied her beautiful silver cape, and held it out.

It sparkled in the streetlights.

"Katie will give you her wig," Mel said.

"But the wig is—" Katie started to protest, then Mel shot her a glance.

"The boa too," Mel ordered.

Katie took off the wig and boa without question and held them out to Hannah.

Hannah lifted up the screen, wiggled her way out the window.

It was only when she dropped to the ground that she realized she was wearing the pink boots, Manda's boots, but no one said anything; no one seemed to notice, not even Manda.

"Oh, Hannah," they all said, putting their hands on her, patting her back, stroking her hair like she was something truly great, like their own pet unicorn. "We're going to have so much fun. It'll be a night you won't ever forget."

2016

Amanda stood looking out the living room window, watching Erin and her friends saunter off down the street. They moved so easily together, bumping against each other, moving the same way, the same direction, like a school of fish. She'd walked that way once with Mel and Katie, like they were one being, a three-headed beast, finishing each other's sentences, breaking into Journey songs: "Don't Stop Believin'" and "Who's Crying Now."

It was just past six now, already full dark. Amanda went out onto the porch, plugged in the plastic glowing witch, the strings of tiny orange lights wrapped around the porch railings. Putting up the lights had been Jim's job too, but Amanda had gone out and bravely gotten up on a stepladder, wrapping them around the posts, but no matter how she'd tried, she couldn't get them to come out even.

"Being honest? Looks like shit, Mom," Erin had said with a shrug. And she'd been right.

Amanda didn't even attempt to do the fake cobwebs and dangling plastic spiders Jim usually decorated the porch with. He loved Halloween.

Amanda hated it.

She shivered now, looked down the street at a group of small ghosts and witches heading her way with their parents. Amanda went in, readied herself with the giant plastic bowl of chocolate bars and lollipops.

Jim had dressed up every year, answering the door dressed as a zombie, a vampire, a mummy. Always a monster. Always something slightly frightening.

The trick-or-treaters had loved it. Erin had always made a show of running from him as he chased her around the house, arms outstretched, reaching for her as she screamed in mock horror.

Amanda had hidden in the back of the house, claiming she had so much work to catch up on, or a migraine coming on.

"Trick or treat!" the little crew gathered on her porch now called. She forced a smile, opened the door.

"Oh my goodness, what do we have here?" she said, holding out the bowl. "A ghost, two witches, and—what are you, sweetie?"

The girl in the back stepped forward, into the light. She looked about five or six years old.

"I'm a chicken," she said, showing off her cardboard wings with yellow feathers glued on. She wore a yellow shirt all splattered in red.

"And what a fine chicken you are," Amanda said.

"I'm a *dead* chicken," the little girl said delightedly. "See my blood?"

"Oh my," Amanda said. The woman with them (too young to be a mother, surely—must be an older sister, or a babysitter maybe) gave her an apologetic you-know-how-kids-are smile.

Amanda spotted another group coming down the street. Older children. One of them wearing a rainbow wig.

"Happy Halloween," she said, closing the door on the small children, wanting to lock it.

She went back into the kitchen, opened a bottle of merlot, and poured herself a full glass. The uncarved pumpkin sat on the island, taunting. She took a good swig of wine, caught a glimpse of her reflection in the dark window over the sink: a frazzled-looking woman in jeans and a black turtleneck, dark circles under her eyes. She took another long sip of wine, feeling it warming her from the inside out, and turned toward the pumpkin.

She could do this. And wouldn't Erin be surprised when she got home and saw the soft glow of a grinning jack-o'-lantern decorating their porch?

See, your old mom's not such a Halloween party pooper after all.

Amanda opened drawers and cabinets, pulled out a large carving knife and small paring knife, a big metal spoon, a plastic bowl for the guts, and a baking tray for the seeds because that's another thing Jim had always done—roasted the seeds after sprinkling them with cinnamon and sugar. Erin loved them that way. "These," she'd say, holding a handful of seeds, "are the *epitome* of fall." Then she'd give a coy grin, clearly pleased with herself for showing off her vocabulary.

There was a knock on the door. Amanda set her glass of wine down, picked up the bowl of candy, and opened the door.

Not one but two Hannah-beasts greeted her, blue faces leering, smiling, rainbow wigs glowing.

"Trick or treat," they said.

Amanda took a step back.

There was a third girl, wearing a white lab coat and big black-framed eyeglasses, just behind them. She said, "Dumbasses, you're supposed to say *boo!* That's what the real Hannah-beast said."

Amanda's breath caught in her throat.

Say boo.

Say boo, Hannah.

1982

"Say *boo,* Hannah," Mel instructed as they stood on their first porch, holding open their bags.

Hannah's face itched and felt tight from the blue makeup they'd put on, left over from Katie's clown kit—she'd used up all the white and red on her own face, and blue was the only color she had left, so they'd coated Hannah's face in it. At first it had been greasy, sticky as they rubbed it on. Now, as it dried, it itched.

The old man passing out candy stared at her, taking in her rainbow clown wig, feather boa, and silver cape. He asked, "And what are you supposed to be?"

"She's a Hannah-beast!" Mel crowed. "Say *boo*, Hannah. Say *boo* and show the man how scary you can be."

"Boo," Hannah said quietly.

The man shook his head, laughed. The girls laughed too.

Hannah stood up taller, rocked back on her heels, and lunged forward like a snake about to strike. "BOO!" she screamed.

The old man jumped, startled. Then he frowned, muttered, "Crazy kid," and closed the door in their faces.

The girls squealed, squealed with joy, patted her on the back.

"Nice job, Hannah-beast."

"Holy shit, did you see his face?"

"Hannah-beast is scary!"

"Hannah-beast is crazy!"

"Hannah-beast is spectacular!"

They ran down the sidewalk, laughing. All the other groups of trick-or-treaters, all the adults on porches, turned to look their way.

The soles of Hannah's pink boots clapped as loud as a horse's hooves along the sidewalk. "The boots look good on you," Manda whispered in her ear, her breath sweet with sugar.

They ran through the center of town, past the park where the Halloween party for the little kids had been earlier—the park where tiny ghosts and goblins and princesses had bobbed for apples, played pin the arm on the skeleton, and attacked a ghost piñata strung up with heavy rope from a beam in the center of the white gazebo.

They ran and ran until Mel stopped them at a house with a porch decorated with Halloween lights, several happy jack-o'-lanterns, and a patchwork scarecrow slumped in a chair.

They all crowded together on the tiny front porch with sloping floorboards, shoulder to shoulder, and it felt good, so good to be bumping against these girls, laughing with them under the Halloween wind chimes hung above the front door—little ghosts dancing, banging into each other, making music. They were like those ghosts, Hannah thought, smiling up at them.

They knocked too loud on the door, sang out, "Trick or treat, trick or treat!" and a woman answered, held out a bowl of candy, said, "Happy Halloween!" A poodle danced around the lady's feet, barking in that little yappy-dog kind of way, a pink collar with fake diamonds glittering around its neck.

And the girls didn't have to tell Hannah this time; she did it without being asked. She pressed forward, stood on her tiptoes to make herself taller. She held up her arms, cape flapping behind her, got right in this lady's face, and screamed, "BOO!" which made the poor lady recoil and scream a little, and once she caught her breath, she asked, "What is *wrong* with you?"

"She's Hannah-beast," Mel said, giggling. "That's what's wrong."

"She can't help it," Katie said. "She's crazy. I'd bring your puppy inside if I was you. She might just eat it up!"

And Hannah bared her teeth and growled. The lady pulled her dog inside, slammed the door in their faces.

The girls all laughed loud and shrieking laughs.

"You're the real thing, Hannah-beast," Katie said, twirling around her like Hannah was the sun and she was just a little planet trying to get warm.

"I am spectacular!" Hannah crowed to the night as she flew down the steps, the others following her now, chasing her, calling after her: *come back, slow down, don't leave us, we love you, Hannah-beast.*

2016

Amanda cut the top off the pumpkin in six quick slashes, lifted it off, a neat little cap with a curved stem. She went to work hollowing the thing out. She hated the cold, squishy feel of the pumpkin's insides — "the guts," as Erin called them.

She thought of that long-ago Halloween, the week before, actually, when Mel had presented her carefully laid-out plan.

"I think it's totally brilliant, but are you sure it'll work?" Katie asked.

"Of course I'm sure. She'll come with us. She'll do what we say."

"But don't you think it's kind of . . ." Amanda hesitated.

"Kind of what?" Mel snapped, eyes daring Amanda to continue.

"I don't know." Amanda bit her lip. "Think of all the trouble she's going to get in."

Mel looked at her, head cocked. "So? Come on, Amanda. It's not like she doesn't deserve it. Think about it. Always pestering us all the time. Being so fucking weird."

"And don't forget, the bitch broke into your house and stole your old clothes!" Katie added. "She's probably, like, all obsessed with you or something. Gross. Plus, it will be hilarious and you know it."

Amanda frowned.

"What if she tells?" Amanda asked.

Mel laughed. "As if anyone would believe her."

"As if," Katie repeated, trying to copy Mel's laugh.

Mel smiled. "It's the perfect plan."

Now, Amanda topped off her wine, told herself to stop it. Stop thinking about that night, stop reliving every moment, every terrible decision she'd made, stop playing the "if only" game. She'd trained herself well over the years. If you spend enough time blocking something out, built sturdy enough walls around it, then it's almost like it didn't happen.

Except on Halloween. One night each year it all came back when the parade of Hannahs showed up at her door, when the life-size rag doll dressed as Hannah-beast was cut down from the gazebo in the center of town, a noose around its neck.

Say boo, Hannah.

Now she picked up the knife and started on the eyes of the jack-o'-lantern. Round eyes, she decided. Jim had always done scary slit eyes with dramatic, angry arched eyebrows. A frowning mouth full of jagged, dangerous teeth.

Her pumpkin was going to be happy. Cheerful.

She was finishing up the second eye when there was a knock at the door, another round of trick-or-treaters. Supergirl, a soldier, two zombies, and one Hannah-beast who made sure to say, "Boo!"

Amanda gritted her teeth and held out the bowl.

She'd just started on the nose when there was another knock. A Hannah-beast and a vampire.

Trick or treat.

Boo!

This Hannah-beast was collecting candy in a red plastic gas can with a hole cut in the top. Too goddamned much. Amanda stared at the gas can full of bright candy wrappers, thought of saying something, something adult, like "You've taken this too far" or "Don't you think that's in poor taste?" But before she got the chance, the girl was gone.

Before she even got to close the door, another group was coming up the walkway toward the porch.

Jesus. Why so many Hannah-beasts this year? It had to be a record.

This time it was a boy dressed as Hannah-beast. He was accompanied by a girl who looked to be dressed as a prostitute, and another boy in a long black trench coat and a ski mask.

This Hannah-beast had visible stubble on his chin under the thin blue makeup. "Boo," he said, voice bullfrog deep.

Fuck you, Amanda said back to him in her head. She kept her lips tightly pursed so the words wouldn't find their way out and thrust the bowl of candy in the boy's direction. He took a whole handful, then was gone, the others trailing behind him.

Come back, slow down, don't leave us, we love you, Hannah-beast.

"You're only supposed to take one!" Amanda shouted at him. He gave her the finger behind his back, not even bothering to look at her.

Amanda closed the door, refilled her wine (the bottle was almost empty now), and went back to the pumpkin. She was further along with it than she'd realized. The nose was done and had a delicate triangle shape. Now for the mouth. A happy pumpkin needed a big grin. Some chunky teeth maybe. Cheerful, but not too goofy. She picked up the paring knife and started at the left corner of the mouth, working her way down, doing a light line at first, just breaking the skin to get the design roughed out, then going in deeper.

The pumpkin was soon smiling back at her.

"Hello, you," she said to it, thinking, *Won't Erin be pleased?*

Job well done, Mom.

A shadow passed in front of the kitchen window. Amanda glanced up just in time to see a figure moving by the living room window—someone in a cape with a black eye mask and a rainbow wig.

"Fuck!" Amanda jumped back off the kitchen stool, the knife slipping. She'd cut herself at the base of the thumb. There was blood on the mouth of the pumpkin, covering its lower teeth. "Fuck, fuck, fuck!"

There was a knock at the door.

"Trick or treat!" voices called. Amanda wrapped a kitchen towel around her hand, went to the door. A Hannah-beast and a slutty devil.

"You're not supposed to cross the yard!" she scolded. "You're supposed to stay on the walkway."

"Um. We did," said the girl devil.

"You crossed the yard. I saw you from the kitchen."

"It wasn't us," the devil said with a shrug.

"Boo?" the Hannah-beast behind her said, cautiously.

"Fuck off," said Amanda, slamming the door in their faces, looking down to see the blood had soaked through the towel.

1982

They went from house to house until her pillowcase was heavy, heavy like she really did have a dead dog inside it, which was what the girls were telling everyone they met.

Hannah-beast's a real monster, that's for sure! Be careful, or she'll eat you up! She's got a dead poodle inside her bag. She's gonna snack on it later. Yum, yum, yum.

You're doing so good, Hannah. We love you, Hannah. You're scaring the shit out of the whole town, Hannah. This is your night. The night of Hannah-beast. Say boo. Boo! Boo! Boo!

They flew through town; Manda was holding her hand as they ran, and Hannah's heartbeat pounded in her ears. Her face felt tight, her head itched under the rainbow wig, but she was happy, so happy, the feathers of the boa tickling her as she ran, the cape flying out behind her. Everyone in town, all the kids from school, they all saw her. They saw her with the other girls, and they knew . . . they knew she was something special.

But now it was late. Nearly ten. The streets were clear of trick-or-treaters. Porch lights had been turned off. They sat on the wooden floor of the gazebo in the park, eating candy, trading favorites. Manda didn't like anything with nuts. Mel hated Mounds bars (which meant Katie did too). They gave Hannah all their peanut butter cups, didn't even make her trade for them.

"I should go home," Hannah said. Even though she knew Daddy would be sleeping his bourbon sleep until the alarm went off at seven tomorrow.

"No way! Not yet!" Katie said, grabbing her arm.

"We've got one more special surprise, Hannah," Mel said.

"What's that?"

"It's a scavenger hunt," Katie explained.

"Do you know what that is?" Manda asked.

"Sure, I guess," said Hannah, thinking it sounded like a thing from birthday parties, even though she hadn't been invited to a birthday party since second grade.

"It's where you follow clues, gather objects, and find a prize."

"Like a treasure hunt?" she asked.

"Yeah, like a treasure hunt," Katie said, smiling, bobbing her head.

"Well, what's the prize?"

Mel laughed. "Think about the word *prize*, Hannah. It's short for *surprise*, right? And it wouldn't be a surprise if we told you."

"It's gonna be good, Hannah," Katie promised. "Something you'll never forget."

"Are you ready?" Mel asked. "Ready for the first clue?"

"I don't know," Hannah said. "It's late, and my dad—"

"If you don't want to do it, you don't *have* to," Manda said.

"Of course she wants to do it," Mel said, giving Manda a disgusted look.

"Yeah," Katie said. "You want the surprise, don't you, Hannah?"

Hannah hefted her sack, heavy with candy, over her shoulder. "BOO!" she howled at the top of her lungs, and the girls all laughed and patted her on the back, and she was the star of the show. It was the night of Hannah-beast. *Hannah-beast unleashed,* that's what Mel said.

"You can leave your candy with me," Manda said. "It'll be easier without it. And I'll keep it safe, I promise."

Mel handed her a piece of paper, and Hannah squinted down at it through the eyeholes of her mask. "'You'll find me in Old Man Jarvis's garage. I'm made of metal. I ring but I'm not a phone.'"

Hannah looked up from the paper to the others.

"What are you waiting for?" Mel asked. "Go!"

Hannah started off running toward Old Man Jarvis's place. She looked back and saw the girls standing in the gazebo, watching her. "Aren't you coming?" she called.

"We'll meet you at the end."

"But how will I know what to do?"

"Just follow the clues," Katie said. "You can do it!"

"Yeah, you can do anything!" shouted Mel. "You're Hannah-beast!"

2016

Amanda wrapped up her hand in gauze and surgical tape. The bleeding had finally stopped.

"Fucking idiot," she mumbled to herself.

She went back out to the kitchen, poured the last swallows of wine into her glass. She lit the votive and dropped it inside the pumpkin, stepped back to admire her handiwork.

The smiling face leered back at her—round eyes hopeful, expectant, a slack-jawed grin giving the thing a bewildered look.

Her stomach twisted, the wine turning to acid.

Hannah. It was Hannah's face.

Hello, Manda Panda.

Long time no see.

The air seemed to go out of her. The cut on the base of her thumb throbbed in time with her heartbeat.

At that moment, the power went out, plunging the house into darkness and silence.

The wineglass slipped out of her hand, crashing onto the tile floor.

1982

I ring but I'm not a phone.

Hannah worked the clue around in her brain as she entered Mr. Jarvis's garage through the open door. She squinted in the darkness as she walked around the old Plymouth parked there. There were tools hanging on the wall: rakes and hoes and shovels. And a workbench at the end. She walked over to it.

I ring.

Ring around the Rosie.

She looked at the tools on the bench and the wall: hammer, saws, screwdrivers, wrenches.

"None of you ring," she said.

She bit her lip. She could do this. She had to do this. Show them that she wasn't a dummy. Not like everyone thought she was.

"I'm Hannah-beast," she whispered. "I can do anything."

Then, like a miracle (the power of Hannah-beast brought miracles!), she saw it! There on the shelf above was what she'd come for: an old brass cowbell. It was sitting on top of a crowbar. She picked up the bell, saw it had a note tied to it. She moved closer to the window and read the note by the light coming in from Mr. Jarvis's front porch.

> Ring me for one FULL minute. NO CHEATING. Then take the crowbar underneath and go to the Blakelys'. Use the crowbar to pry open the door to the shed. Inside, look for something red. Bring this note with you.

Hannah stuck the note in her pocket, held on to the bell, and started ringing it and counting, "One, two, three . . ."

She was at fifty-five when the front door to the Jarvis house banged open, and Mr. Jarvis came walking stiffly toward the garage, calling, "Who's there? What the hell is going on?"

She started counting faster: "Fifty-five-fifty-six-fifty-seven-fifty-eight-fifty-nine-sixty!" She dropped the bell, grabbed the crowbar, and tore out of the garage, nearly running into Mr. Jarvis in the driveway.

"Hey, come back here!" he yelled. But she did not slow. Did not turn. She zigzagged her way through backyards, across the Caldwells' field, and over to the Blakelys'. The old wooden shed was in their backyard along a split-rail fence. She tugged on the door handle, but it was locked, as the note had said, so she slid the chiseled end of the crowbar between the door and frame, pushing it in as far as it would go; then she pulled her full weight behind it. The old wood on the doorframe cracked and splintered and the door flew open.

She laughed. She was Hannah-beast. No locks could stop her.

The red thing was waiting for her right in the middle of the shed: an old gas can with a note tied around the handle.

> Use the crowbar to smash out the window of the shed, then leave it behind. Take the gas can to the Caldwells' old barn. Look for something small and brass. Keep all the notes with you.

Without pausing to think, she smashed out the old single-pane windows with the crowbar, then threw it to the ground. As she sprinted across the yard, lights came on in the house. A man shouted, "Stop right there!" but she didn't even turn around, just ran faster, harder, the wig bobbing around on the top of her head, the cape flying out behind her.

"BOO!" she screamed as loud as she could.

2016

"What the fuck?" Amanda said, blinking in the darkness. All the background noises of life were gone: the humming refrigerator, the ice maker, the furnace clicking on, and fans starting.

She tried to remember where the breaker box was in the basement. What you were even supposed to do to try to get the power back on — flip a switch, change a fuse? This had always been Jim's department.

She stumbled forward, stepping over the broken glass and spilled wine, toward the window, saw it wasn't just her house that was out. It was the whole street. The whole town, maybe. She didn't see a hint of light anywhere.

Amanda held still, watching, listening.

A siren whined far off. A girl screamed. Someone laughed.

Amanda thought she smelled smoke.

Her throat grew tight.

The grinning jack-o'-lantern, with the candle sputtering inside, was now the only light in the room, filling the kitchen with a fiery-orange glow. The flickering eyes were watching, following her, saying, *I know who you are. I know what you've done.*

"I'm sorry," she said out loud, the words tumbling out before she could stop them. "I didn't know what would happen. I should have stopped it, but I had no idea. None of us did. I was young and scared and stupid."

Tears filled her eyes; her throat grew tight as she tried to keep down the sob she felt coming.

"I'm sorry," she said again. "Sorry for being such a fucking coward."

The pumpkin only stared, the hideous grin seeming to grow wider, more taunting.

She was not going to be forgiven.

Not this easily.

1982

Running, running, wind in her blue face, blowing the cape back, and the hair, oh the hair, the great rainbow happy clown wig. She's a wild thing. Hannah-beast unleashed. The gas can bumped against her thigh, the gas in it sloshing around like water in an empty belly. Her brain buzzed from sugar, from the high being around those girls had given her, and now, now she was on a hunt, a scavenger hunt, and she was going to get a prize, a SURPRISE, something good, something wonderful, something that would make the girls love her even more.

Love her more, more, more. Her heart pounded as she ran, felt like it was going to explode right out of her chest. The barn was in sight, a big old leaning thing—miracle it was still standing. The Caldwells were sleeping, tucked safe in their beds, the lights in the white farmhouse all turned off, too late for trick-or-treaters. Mr. and Mrs. Caldwell had two kids, little kids, still in elementary school, fourth and fifth grade, lucky little buggers. Elementary school wasn't like middle school, where the halls were long and dark, and people jumped out at you, shoved you, kicked you; people left horrible stuff in your locker—dog shit in paper bags, notes that said "Why don't you just curl up and die, Hannah?"

She entered the barn, ducked into the shadows, pausing to catch her breath, trying to slow her racing heart. The barn was open at one end and had a hayloft with a wooden ladder leading up to it, and it was still full of old hay bales from back when there used to be cows and horses. There was a long row of windows, most with the glass busted out. The floor was dirt. There was a broken tractor. An old motorcycle. Engine parts. Kids' bicycles. The barn smelled like old wood, grease, and gasoline.

Something brass.

How was she going to find something brass in here? Needle in a haystack.

But they'd made it easy for her.

So easy.

Too easy?

Did they think she was that dumb? Or were they just being nice?

Nice, nice. Nice as spice. Manda Panda maybe, but not the others. Maybe Manda had left this for her, right where she could find it. Manda was on her side. Manda wanted her to win, to get the big surprise of a prize.

At the other end of the barn, there was a dim glow. A flashlight turned on, left on the floor. And there, in the beam of the flashlight, was an old brass lighter with a note tucked underneath.

She picked up the lighter, opened it up, and flicked it to see if it worked. The wheel struck the flint, and a flame came to life. Hannah knew how to work lighters. She sometimes lit Daddy's cigarettes for him while he was driving. "Light me up, Hannah Banana," he'd say. She'd pull a Camel out of his pack and get it going for him, take a few puffs herself first just 'cause it made Daddy smile.

She picked up the note:

> You're almost done! Take the three notes and burn them with the lighter. Leave the ashes in the barn. Take the lighter and gas can and bring them to the tallest oak tree at the edge of the yard. We'll meet you there and give you your prize.

Hannah scrabbled the notes out of her pocket, held them with this final one, and flicked the lighter, watched the flame swallow them up. She held them until her fingers were hot and she couldn't stand it any longer; then she dropped them, watched what was left of the pages sink and flutter to the dirt floor like burning moths. Once they were down there and had burned out, she stomped on them to make sure — didn't want to leave anything smoldering, not in this old barn.

The wind blew hard outside, rattling the glass left in the windows. She thought she heard something up above her, coming from the hayloft. A board creaking like a sigh.

She pocketed the lighter, picked up the gas can, and headed out, scanning the tree line, looking for the tallest oak. She didn't know her trees, didn't know an oak from a maple from an ash, especially now that most of them had their leaves off. She headed for the tallest tree she could see, walking across the big yard, through grass that needed to be cut, so long it was like a hayfield.

She got to the tree and looked around for the girls. Nothing.

"Manda?" she called, keeping her voice low, not wanting to wake up the Caldwells. "Mel? Katie?"

She was there before them. She'd been faster than they'd

thought she'd be. Wouldn't they be impressed? Hannah-beast was fast. Hannah-beast was clever.

She stood next to the tree, fidgeting with the lighter. It made her fingers smell tangy and metallic, like raw metal. She flicked it, watched the flame. They'd see her now as they came. See her and know she had the lighter.

She was like the Statue of Liberty with her torch. She held it up high, her eye on the flame.

I got it.

I found it.

I win.

The acrid lighter-fluid smell filled her nostrils.

But there was something else. Another smell behind it. A campfire smell.

Smoke.

She smelled smoke.

She looked over at the barn and saw flames curling out through the windows, reaching up like long fingers, all the way to the roof.

Her heart jackhammered in her chest.

Had she done this? Had the paper not been out?

No. It had been. She'd made sure.

She stood, frozen. She thought of running, but then the girls would never find her. So she stood and watched from her safe place tucked behind the thick old tree. The lights from the house came on, and Mrs. Caldwell came out, screaming. She tried to run into the burning barn, but Mr. Caldwell was running now too, grabbed her from behind, stopped her.

There was another sound too. Screaming. High pitched and hysterical, from inside the barn.

Animals, Hannah thought at first. *There must have been animals in there after all—a horse or cow, a couple of pigs maybe tucked away in a dark corner.*

"Ben! Brian!" Mrs. Caldwell called. She fought against Mr. Caldwell, kicking, digging her nails into his arms. "Let me go!"

"For God's sake, Margaret," he said. "You can't go in there."

"Brian! Ben!" she howled.

The Langs came over from across the street. The barn was completely engulfed in flames now—it seemed to have taken only a minute. Mrs. Caldwell was screaming, sobbing, hysterical, and Mr. Caldwell kept his arms wrapped tight around her. More people came, people from down the street. Sirens started in the distance. Too late now. The VFD boys with their pumper trucks and miles of hose could never save that old barn.

Hannah watched from behind the tree, feeling like she was watching some show on TV, not something from her very own life. The barn roof caved in with a terrible cracking, roaring sound, and Mrs. Caldwell sank to her knees, howling like she was the one on fire.

Then Hannah saw the girls, her girls, coming down the street, twittering and bobbing like a flock of birds. They slowed, all three staring at the burning barn. Manda grabbed Mel's shoulder, leaned in, said something Hannah couldn't hear. Then they all ran to the sidewalk in front of the barn, to the group of neighbors gathered there.

Hannah stepped out from behind the tree, waving, trying to get the girls' attention, not sure if she should run to them or wait right where she was. That was what the note said, to wait. So that's probably what she was supposed to do?

Mr. Jarvis was there in the circle of men the girls were talking to. The fire was so loud she could make out only snippets.

"I saw her," she heard Mr. Jarvis say.

Mr. Blakely was there. She heard "Gasoline."

A lady in a fluffy turquoise bathrobe—it might have been Mrs. Novak?—spoke to the girls grimly. Hannah heard every word this time.

"Benjamin and Brian were sleeping in the hayloft. They do it every Halloween."

Hannah looked back at the fire, showers of sparks going up and up and away.

It was like hell. Like what she'd imagined hell might be like. That hot. That smoky. That loud.

Then Mel turned toward Hannah's hiding place by the tree, pointed. Her eyes blazed with the reflection of the fire—devil eyes. "There she is!" she shouted. "She did this!"

Everyone looked her way. Saw the gas can by her feet. The lighter in her hand.

Katie stared, stunned, slack-jawed, but slowly, she reached up her hand and pointed too.

Some of the men, they took a step in Hannah's direction.

Hannah looked right at Manda, her eyes pleading: *Please. Say something. Don't let them do this to me.*

Manda was crying now, crying hard. "But she—" she began, and Mel clamped a hand down on Manda's shoulder, held tight with a clawlike grip that would surely leave a bruise. Manda looked down at the ground, then back to Hannah. "Yes, that's her," she said through her tears. "That's Hannah-beast."

And Hannah, she turned and ran.

2016

It had been Mel who'd set the fire. Amanda should have stopped her. She should have done something—actually fucking stood up to her for once. Now, as an adult, she couldn't believe how much power Mel had had over her. What had she been so afraid of? Being shunned from the lunch table? Having nasty notes left in her locker? It all seemed so trivial compared to what had happened to those Caldwell boys, what had happened to Hannah.

Over the years, Amanda had told herself that she didn't think Mel would really do it, that she'd been sure it was just another of Mel's grand schemes that would come to nothing. Like the way she said one day they'd go to the mall and hide in the bathroom with their feet up during closing time; then they'd sneak back out and have the whole mall to themselves, and they'd get skateboards from the sporting goods store and go up and down the mall, eating all the candy they wanted from the Sweet Spot, then play Ms. Pac-Man all night at the arcade. Mel would go on and on about everything they'd do that night at the mall, but Amanda knew it would never happen. Amanda had told herself the barn fire would be like that.

So when Mel came sprinting out of the barn, grinning wildly, saying she'd done it, Amanda was sure she was just fooling around. Until she saw the smoke.

She could have run in then, tried to put it out. Or gone and pounded on the Caldwells' door and told them to call the fire department quick. She could have done something.

Instead, she saw the smoke, the orange glow of fire from deep inside the barn, and she ran like the coward she was, the coward she would always be.

She took off right behind Mel and Katie. They were laughing, giddy, and hadn't Amanda laughed too? Sure she had. It was terrible, but it was also exciting and crazy, like nothing she'd ever done. Thrilling. They'd had no idea the Caldwell boys were sleeping up in the hayloft. The plan was to make people think Hannah had burned down the barn. Get her in a little trouble. Not have the whole town think she was a murderer. Not to be murderers themselves.

The pumpkin watched, smiling stupidly at her, looking more like Hannah than ever.

I love you, Manda Panda.

Amanda remembered feeling Hannah's warm breath on her neck the night she'd slept over, snuggled up against Amanda in her twin bed.

Go to sleep, Amanda had said that night, irritated that Hannah was there, that she was so pathetic and desperate, but also a little thrilled by the power she had over this girl, this girl who loved her so completely. Who called her Manda Panda, which was incredibly stupid but kind of sweet.

Amanda had hated it and loved it all at the same time. Which was the way she'd felt about Hannah, wasn't it?

Amanda wondered for a moment if Katie or Mel ever thought about that night, about Hannah, about those boys in the barn — she hadn't spoken to either in years, couldn't even bear to keep up with them on social media. *No,* she thought. Neither of them ever understood the enormity of what they had done. Neither of them could.

The candle flickered, making the pumpkin seem to open its eyes wider, looking frightened, desperate.

Please, Manda. Don't let them do this to me.

"Enough already," Amanda said, picking up the carving knife, digging it into the pumpkin's left eye, determined to change its shape, to make it look less Hannah-like.

In the darkness and silence, she worked to make the eyes more triangular, angrier, more like one of Jim's devil-faced pumpkins.

When she finished with the eyes, she stepped back. It was no good. It just looked like a furious version of Hannah leering back at her.

You can't make me go away this time.

She picked up the knife again, thinking she'd fix it—change the nose and mouth, banish Hannah-beast once and for all.

She froze, sure she'd heard a giggle from somewhere behind her, deep in the dark center of the house.

She listened hard, and it was not laughter she heard this time but the *clip-clap* sound of boot heels moving across the floor. The sound of her old pink cowboy boots—the boots her mother had shamed her into giving to Hannah.

The boots Hannah had been wearing that night.

The boots look good on you, Hannah.

"Hello?" she called. She waited, knife clutched in her hand, heart pounding in her ears.

"Hannah?" she asked, choking out the name.

The jack-o'-lantern grinned, seemed to give her an evil wink. *I'm right here. I have been all along.*

1982

Sometimes the best place to hide was right in plain sight.

She sat, cross-legged, in the dark gazebo right in the middle of town, the same spot where she'd been just hours before, trading candy with the girls, taking all their peanut butter cups. The floor of the gazebo was littered with the wrappers they'd left behind.

She sat for so long her legs turned to pins and needles.

The sirens went on and on. It seemed everyone in town was up and awake, walking the streets, talking. They talked over each other, shouted across the street to friends and neighbors.

Did you hear, did you hear? Bad fire at the Caldwells' place. Both their boys dead. They were sleeping in the barn. It was that Hannah Talbott girl.

She came to my house tonight, dressed all crazy, acting like some kind of animal. Threatened my dog. Screamed right in my face.

Mental, that one is.

What was that crazy costume she was wearing, anyway?

Said she was some kind of beast.

She was all over town, wicked girl running wild. Broke into the Jarvises' garage, stole a crowbar. Used it to get a gas can from the Blakelys' shed. Busted up the shed while she was at it. Then she walked right on over to the

Caldwells' place, soaked that old barn in gasoline, torched it. Those poor boys never had a chance.

She could tell, of course. She could tell, but who was going to believe her? Who ever believed a girl like Hannah? A girl who'd been caught with a gas can and a lighter.

That's her, Manda had said. *That's Hannah-beast.*

She was still in her costume, now dirty, stinking of smoke and gasoline.

Girls like that, they're going straight to hell. You stay away from them unless you want to get burned.

Her face itched, didn't feel like her face at all. The wig was on crooked. The cape was torn.

She looked up, saw a rope dangling down—an old piece of clothesline maybe—looped around the overhead beam. The rope that had held the ghost piñata earlier. The little kids had swung at it with a stick, the ghost bobbing, dancing in circles until it was hit dead-on, torn open, candy flying out, the little kids all pushing each other, scrambling to collect the most pieces.

Hannah stood, reaching for the rope, hands shaking a little. She gave it a tug like she was ringing an invisible bell.

I ring but I'm not a phone.

The rope was looped over one of the rafters, tied tight with a string of knots. She gripped it with both hands and swung, feet drifting over the refuse of the evening—the clear cellophane of Manda's Smarties, the bright scraps from Mel's Tootsie Pops, the wrappers from all those Hershey's bars Katie had eaten.

She was her own piñata, swinging. The rope held her weight.

She climbed up on the low wall of the gazebo, cape flapping in the breeze like she really was some kind of superhero about to take flight. The cowboy boots were slippery and she had to lean quite a bit to reach the center, but she kept her balance. She made a careful slipknot in the rope. Her hands didn't feel like her hands at all.

It was like it was some other girl. Like she was watching some other version of herself in some far-off place tie the knot.

A ghost of a girl.

A beast of a girl.

Hannah-beast unleashed.

The real Hannah was home, tucked up all safe and warm in her bed like a good girl, right where she belonged, a girl who wasn't going to hell. A girl who had a best friend named Manda who'd given her a pair of special pink boots, boots that fit so perfectly it was like she and Manda were one.

The candy wrappers got caught in the breeze, skittered across the floor below her, empty and forgotten.

Hannah looped the rope around her neck over the rainbow wig, over the pink boa. She heard the girls' voices in her head as she jumped off the wall — *Hannah-beast takes flight!* — swinging, flying, legs dangling over the floor.

Say boo!

2016

Amanda held her breath, listening to the footsteps come up behind her. They were real; she was sure of it. Not born of paranoia and too much wine, right? She glanced down at the pumpkin, her knife now turning the blocky teeth into pointed ones, giving it a vampire grin.

Hannah-beast's a real monster, that's for sure. Be careful, or she'll eat you up!

Amanda looked up, out across the kitchen at the window over the sink, and saw the reflection in it: the dim kitchen lit only by the candle in the jack-o'-lantern; herself, hunched over before it, whittling away; and a figure behind her — a girl with a blue face, a bright clown wig, a pink feather boa, a silver cape.

She blinked, but it did not go away, just came closer, closer still.

I love you, Manda Panda.

She could hear the creature breathing as it drew near, could smell smoke and gasoline.

Amanda could not move, could not speak or scream.

She was twelve years old again, looking at Hannah as she stood with the gas can by her feet, the lighter in her hand, staring desperately at Amanda: *Please. Don't let them do this to me.*

But Amanda had only pointed. *That's her. That's Hannah-beast.*

"Boo!" Hannah roared in her ear, right behind her now.

"Go away!" Amanda screamed as she spun. They were the words she and the other girls had said so many times to Hannah when she followed them around like some pathetic dog at school, when she sat down at their lunch table, when she showed up at Amanda's house, wanting to ride bikes, wanting to sleep over again. *Why can't you just go away?*

Amanda plunged her carving knife deep into Hannah-beast's belly, shouting, "Go the fuck away!"

But the creature did not disappear like smoke, like the ghost she should have been.

Amanda's hands were warm and sticky with blood.

Hannah-beast looked down at the knife in her belly, slack-jawed, stupid.

When she looked up, Amanda saw her, really saw her.

And in that moment, she realized Hannah had won.

"No!" Amanda cried, the word a wailing sob. "No, no, nooo!"

Erin looked so surprised, so puzzled, as she reached down and touched the knife, like she couldn't believe it was real. Amanda could see traces of cat whiskers beneath the blue face paint.

"Mom?"

JOYCE CAROL OATES

The Archivist

FROM *Boulevard*

I.

HE WOULD PROTECT me. He promised.

Kissing the scar at my hairline. Smoothing the hair back, that he might press his lips lightly against the scar. Making me shiver.

He would *take measurement* of me. *Establish a record.* The size of my skull, the length of my spine, the size of my hands and feet (bare). Height, weight. Color of skin.

Then taking my hand. Pressing it between his legs where he was fattish, swollen like ripe, rotting fruit. Pressed, rubbed. When I tried to pull away he gripped my hand tighter.

Don't pretend to be innocent, "Vio-let!" You dirty girl.

Sometimes he called me Sleeping Beauty. (Which had to be one of his jokes, I was no *beauty*.)

Sometimes he called me Snow White.

"I am 'Sandman.' Do I have a *sandpaper* tongue?"

Seven months. When I was fourteen.

If it was *abuse*, as they charged, it did not seem so, usually. It was something that I could recognize as *punishment*.

Each time was the first time. Each time, I would not remember what happened to me, what was done to me. And so there was only a single time, and that time the *first time* as well as the *last*.

Each time was a rescue. Waking to see the face of the one who had rescued me, and his eyes that shone in triumph beneath grizzled eyebrows. Sharp-bracketed mouth and stained teeth in a smile of happiness.

Vio-let Rue! Time to wake up, dear.

Mr. Sandman was the teacher who'd sighted me lost in the ninth-grade corridor, when I was in seventh grade. When I'd first come to Port Oriskany as a transfer student. The teacher with the grizzled eyebrows and strange staring eyes who'd seemed to recognize me. As if (already) there was a secret understanding between us.

And now you are in my homeroom. "Vio-let Rue."

No alternative. Mr. Sandman was the ninth-grade math teacher.

At last, I was *his*. On his homeroom class list and in his fifth-period math class.

For both homeroom and math class Mr. Sandman seated me at his right hand where he could *keep a much-needed eye on you.*

He'd helped me to my feet. Before he'd been my teacher. Discovered me sleeping in a corner of the school library where I'd curled up beneath a vinyl chair as a dog might curl up to sleep, nose to tail, a shabby little terrier, hoping to be invisible and not to be kicked.

No one else seemed to see me. Might've been somebody's sheepskin jacket tossed beneath a chair at the back of the room.

Standing over me breathing hoarsely for so long, I wouldn't know.

Time to wake up, dear! Take my hand.

But it was his hand that took my hand. Gripped hard, and hauled me to my feet.

Why did you let him touch you, Violet! That terrible man.

Why, when you would not let others touch you, who'd hoped to love you as a daughter?

2.

"I am the captain. You are the crew. If you don't shape up, you go overboard."

Mr. Sandman, ninth-grade math. His skin was flushed with perpetual indignation at our stupidity. His eyes leapt at us like small shiny toads. When he stretched his lips it was like meat grinning,

we cringed and shuddered and yet we laughed, for Mr. Sandman
was *funny*.

He was one of only three male teachers at Port Oriskany Middle
School. He was advisor to the Chess Club and the Math Club. He
led his homeroom class each morning in the Pledge of Allegiance.

(In a severe voice Mr. Sandman recited the pledge facing us as
we stood obediently with our hands over our hearts, heads bowed.
There was no joking now. You would have thought that the Pledge
of Allegiance was a prayer. A shiny American flag, said to be a personal flag, a flag that Mr. Sandman had purchased himself, hung
unfurled from the top, left-hand corner of the blackboard, and
when Mr. Sandman finished the pledge in his loud righteous voice
he lifted his right hand with a flourish, in a kind of salute, fingers
pointing straight upward and at the flag.)

(Was this the *Nazi salute?*) (We were uncertain.)

Mr. Sandman ruled math classes like a sea captain. He liked to
shake what he called his *iron fist*. If one of us, usually a boy, was
hopelessly stupid that day he'd have to *walk the plank*—rise from
his desk and walk to the rear of the room, stand there with his back
to the class and wait for the bell.

On a day of *rough waters* there'd be three, could be four, boys
at the rear of the room, resigned to standing until the bell rang,
forbidden to turn around, no smirking, no wisecracks, *if you have to
pee just pee your pants*—a Sandman pronouncement shocking each
time we heard, provoking gales of nervous laughter through the
room.

Of course, this was ninth-grade algebra. We were fourteen, fifteen years old. Nobody in this class was likely to *pee his pants*.

(Yet we were not so old that the possibility didn't evoke terror in
us. Our faces flushed, we squirmed in our seats hoping not to be
singled out for torment by Mr. Sandman.)

It was rare that Mr. Sandman commanded a girl to march to *walk
the plank*. Though Mr. Sandman teased girls, and provoked some
(of us) to tears, yet he was not cruel to girls, not usually.

Boys were another story. Boys were *Schmutz*.

Bobbie Sandusky was *Boobie Schmutz*. Mike Farrolino was *Muck
Schmutz*. Rick Latour was *Ruck Schmutz*. Don Farquhar was *Dumbo
Schmutz*.

Was any of this funny? But why did we laugh?

Hiding our faces in our hands. Nothing so hilarious as the misery of someone not-you.

You'd have thought that Mr. Sandman would be detested but in fact Mr. Sandman had many admirers. Graduates of the middle school spoke fondly of him as a *character, mean old sonuvabitch who really made us learn algebra.* Even boys he ridiculed laughed at his jokes. Like a standup TV comic scowling and growling and the most shocking things erupting from his mouth, impossible not to laugh. Hilarity was a gas seeping into the room that made you laugh even as it choked you.

Mr. Sandman was a firm believer in *running a tight ship.* "In an asylum you can't let the inmates get control."

A scattering of boys in Mr. Sandman's class seemed to escape his ridicule. Not the smartest boys but likely to be the tallest, best-looking, often athletes, sons of well-to-do families in Port Oriskany. These boys who laughed loudest at jokes of Mr. Sandman's directed at other, less fortunate boys. *My goon squad.*

He'd get them uniforms, he said. Helmets, boots. Revolvers to fit into holsters. Rifles.

They could learn to *goose-step.* March in a parade along Main Street past the school. *Atten-tion! Ready, aim.* He'd lead them.

(Would Mr. Sandman be in uniform, himself? What sort of captain's uniform? A pistol in a holster, not a rifle. Polished boots to the thigh.)

Boys were goons at best but girls didn't matter at all. When Mr. Sandman spoke with a rough sort of tenderness of his *goon squad* it seemed that we (girls) were invisible in his eyes.

"Girls have no 'natural aptitude' for math. There is no reason for girls to know math at all. Especially algebra—of no earthly use for a female. I have made my opinion known to the illustrious school board of our fair city but my (informed, objective) opinions often fall upon deaf ears and into empty heads. Therefore, I do not expect anything from females—but I am hoping for at least mediocre, passable work from *you.* And *you,* and *you.*" Winking at the girls nearest him.

Was this funny? Why did girls laugh?

It did not seem like a radical idea to us, any of us, that girls had no *natural aptitude* for math. It seemed like a very reasonable idea. And a relief, to some (of us), that our math teacher did not hold us to standards higher than *mediocrity*—(a word we'd never heard before, but instinctively understood).

In fact Mr. Sandman didn't wink at me at such times. When he made his pronouncements which were meant to make us laugh, and yet instruct us in the ways of the world, he didn't look at me at all. He'd arranged the classroom seating so that "Violet Kerrigan" was seated at a desk in the first row of desks, farthest to the right and near the outer wall of windows, a few inches from the teacher's desk. In this way as Mr. Sandman preened at the front of the classroom addressing the class I was at his right hand, sidelined as if backstage in a theater.

Keeping my eye on you. "Vio-let Rue."

Each math class was a drill. Up and down the rows, Mr. Sandman as captain and drillmaster calling upon hapless students. Even if you'd done the homework and knew the answer you were likely to be intimidated, to stammer and misspeak. Even Mr. Sandman's praise might sting—"Well! A correct answer." And he'd clap, with deadpan ironic intent.

As Mr. Sandman paced about the front of the room preaching, scolding, teasing, and tormenting us an oily sheen would appear on his forehead. His stiff, thinning, dust-colored hair became dislodged showing slivers of scalp shiny as cellophane.

It made me shiver, to anticipate Mr. Sandman glancing sidelong at me.

Keeping an eye on you. "Vio-let Rue."

Ever since you came to us. You.

These were quick, intimate glances. No one saw.

Staying after school, in Mr. Sandman's homeroom.

This was a special privilege: "tutorial." (Only girls were invited.)

Told to bring our homework that had been graded. If we needed "extra" instruction.

Mr. Sandman stooped over our desks, breathing against our necks. He was not sarcastic at such times. His hand on my shoulder —"Here's your error, Violet." With his red ballpoint pen he would tap at the error and sometimes he would take my hand, his hand closed over mine, and redo the problem.

I sat very still. A kind of peace moved through me. If you do not antagonize them, if you behave exactly as they wish you to behave, they will not be cruel to you.

If you are very good, they will speak approvingly of you.

" 'Vio-let Rue' — you are a quick study, aren't you?"

With the other girls Mr. Sandman behaved in a similar way but you could tell (I could tell: I was acutely aware) that he did not like them the way he liked me.

Though he called them *dear* he did not enunciate their names in the melodic way in which he enunciated *Vio-let Rue*. This was a crucial sign.

Edgy and excited we bent over our desks. We did not glance up as Mr. Sandman approached, for Mr. Sandman did not seem to like any sort of flirtatious or over-eager behavior.

Leaning over, his hand resting on a shoulder. His breath at the nape of a neck. A warm hand. A comforting hand. Lightly on a shoulder, or at the small of a back.

"Very good, dear! Now turn the paper over, and see if you can replicate the problem from memory."

Sometimes, Mr. Sandman swore us to secrecy: we were given "rehearsal tutorials" during which we worked out problems that would appear on the next day's quiz or test in Mr. Sandman's class.

Of course, we were eager to swear *not to tell.*

We were privileged, and we were grateful. Maybe, we were afraid of our math teacher.

Eventually, the other girls disappeared from the tutorials. Only Violet Rue remained.

3.

Instinctively Mr. Sandman knew: I did not live with my family but with relatives.

Though each day came the hope—*Daddy will come get me today.*

Or, more possibly—*Daddy will call. Today.*

Running home expecting to see my aunt awaiting me just inside the door, a wounded expression on her face—"There's been a call for you, Violet. From home."

At once, I would know what this meant.

Even Irma understood that *home,* for me, did not mean the tidy beige-brick house on Erie Street.

And so, each day hurrying home. But even as I approached Erie

Street a wave of apprehension swept over me, my mouth went dry with anxiety . . .

For there would be no Daddy waiting for me. There'd been no telephone call.

In the meantime reciting multiplication tables to myself. Multiplying three-digit numbers. Long division in my head. Puzzling over algebra problems that uncurled themselves in my brain like miniature dreams.

Such happiness in the Pythagorean Theorem! Always and forever it is a fact, clutched-at like a life-jacket in churning water— *the sum of the areas of two small squares equals the area of the large one.*

No need to ask *why*. When something just is.

Math had become strange to me. "Pre-algebra"—this was our ninth-grade curriculum. Like a foreign language, fearful and yet fascinating.

"Equations"—numerals, letters—*a, b, c*. Sometimes my hand trembled, gripping a pencil. Hours I would work on algebra problems, in my room with the door shut. It seemed to me that each problem solved brought me a step closer to being summoned back home to South Niagara and so I worked tirelessly until my eyes misted over and my head swam.

Downstairs Aunt Irma watched TV. Festive voices and laughter lifted through the floorboards. My aunt often invited me to watch with her, when I was finished with my homework for the night. But I was never finished with my homework.

On her way to bed Aunt Irma would pause at my door to call out in her sweet, sad voice, "Goodnight, Violet!" Then, "Turn off your light now, dear, and go to sleep."

Obediently I turned off my desk light. Beneath my door, the rim of light would vanish. And then a few minutes later when I calculated that my aunt and uncle were safely in bed I turned it on again.

During the day (most days) I was afflicted with sleepiness in waves like ether but at night when I was alone my eyes were wonderfully wide-open and my brain ran on and on like a rattling machine that would have to be smashed to be stopped.

On my homework papers Mr. Sandman wrote, in bright red ink — *Good work!*

My grades on classroom quizzes and tests were high—93%, 97%, 99%. Because I prepared for these so methodically, hours at a stretch. And because of the secret tutorials.

It was true, I had no *natural aptitude* for math. Nothing came easily to me. But much that passed into my memory, being hard-won, did not fade as it seemed to fade from the memories of my classmates like water sifting through outspread fingers.

My secret was, I had no *natural aptitude* for any subject — for life itself.

Keeping myself alive. Keeping myself from drowning. That was the challenge.

They would ask *Why*. But lifting my eyes I can see the synthetic-shiny American flag hanging from the corner of Mr. Sandman's blackboard, red and white stripes like snakes quivering with life.

Listening very carefully I can hear the chanting. Each morning pledging allegiance. (But what was "allegiance"? We had no idea.) The entire class standing, palms of hands pressed against our young hearts. Reciting, syllables of sound without meaning, emptied of all meaning, eyes half-shut in reverence, a pretense of reverence, heads bowed. Five days a week.

Our teacher Mr. Sandman was not ironic now but sincere, vehement.

Pledge allegiance. To my flag. And to the Republic for which it stands. One Nation, indivisible. With Liberty and Justice for all.

Under his breath Mr. Sandman might mutter as we settled back into our seats — *Amen.*

4.

Each time was a rescue. No one would understand.

Boys had been trailing me, calling after me in low, lewd voices — *Hey baby! Baby-girl! Hey cunt!*

Not touching me. Not usually.

Well, sometimes — colliding with me in a corridor when classes changed. Brushing an arm, the back of a hand across my chest — "Hey! Sor-ry." At my locker, jostling and grinning.

Because I was a transfer student. Because I was alone. Because, like Mr. Sandman, they could see something forlorn and lost in my face, that excited them.

In a restroom where I'd been hiding waiting for them to go away after the final bell had rung I'd asked a girl, are they gone yet, she'd laughed at my pleading eyes and told me yeah sure, those assholes had gone away a long time ago. But when I went out they were waiting just outside the door to the faculty parking lot.

Shouts, laughter. Grabbing at the sleeves of my jacket, at my hair —*run cunt run!*

Crouching behind a car, panting. Hands and knees on the icy pavement. Desperate for a place to hide trying car doors one after another until I found one that was unlocked. Climbed inside, into the backseat, on the floor making myself small as a wounded animal might. On the rear seat was a man's jacket, I pulled over myself. Meant to hide for only a few minutes until the braying boys were gone but so tired!—fell asleep instead. Wakened by someone tugging at my ankle.

Mr. Sandman's dark face. Steel-wool eyebrows above his creased eyes. "Vi-o-lct Ruc! Is that you?"

His voice was almost a song. Surprise, delight.

"What are you doing here, Vio-let? Has someone been hounding you?"

Of course, Mr. Sandman knew. All of the teachers knew. Though I had not ever told.

How much worse it would be for me, if I *told*.

I was not sure of the names of my tormenters. It was a matter of shame to me, there were so many.

"Well! You don't have to tell me who the vermin are just yet, dear. You have already been upset enough." A pause. A stained-teeth smile. "I will drive you home."

Invited me to sit in the passenger's seat beside him. Astonishing to me, the math teacher famous for his sarcasm was behaving in a kindly manner. Smiling!

Though glancing about, to see if anyone was watching.

It was late afternoon, early winter. Already the sky was dim, fading.

In my confusion, waking from sleep, I seemed not to know exactly where I was, or why.

Mr. Sandman advised me, I might just "hunch down" in the seat. In case some "nosy individual" happened to be watching.

"One of my teacher-colleagues. Eager for gossip, you bet."

Quickly I hunched down in the seat. Shut my eyes and hugged my knees. I did not want to be seen by anyone in Mr. Sandman's car.

Mr. Sandman's car was a large heavy pewter-colored four-door sedan. Not a compact vehicle like most vehicles in the faculty parking lot. Its interior was very cold and smelled of something slightly rancid like spilled milk.

"You live on the east side, I believe? Is it—Ontario Street?"

This was astonishing to me: how did Mr. Sandman have any idea where I lived?

"Not Ontario? But nearby?"

"Erie . . ."

"You are wondering how I know where you live, Violet? And how I know with whom you live? Well!"

Mr. Sandman chuckled. It was part of his comic style to pose a question but not answer it.

When I was allowed to sit up a few minutes later and peer out the car window it did not appear that Mr. Sandman was driving in the direction of Erie Street. The thought came to me—*He is taking another route. He knows another, better route.*

And when it became evident that Mr. Sandman was not driving me home at all I sat silently, staring out the window. I did not know what to say for I feared offending Mr. Sandman.

In homeroom and in math class Mr. Sandman was easily "offended"—"deeply offended"—by a foolish answer to a question, or a foolish question. Often he simply glared, wriggling his dense eyebrows in a way comical to behold, unless you were the object of his ire.

However, Mr. Sandman was in a very good mood now. Almost, Mr. Sandman was humming under his breath.

"You know, Violet, it has been a pleasant and unexpected surprise—to discover that you are an impressively good student. Quite a surprise!"

Mr. Sandman mused aloud as he drove. There was no expectation that I should answer him.

"And also, a pleasant and unexpected surprise, to discover such an impressively good student in my automobile, hiding under a garment like Sleeping Beauty."

We were ascending hilly Craigmont Avenue. Still we were moving in a direction opposite to my aunt's and uncle's house on Erie Street and still I could not bring myself to protest.

". . . indeed there are some surprises more 'unexpected' than others. And discovering that Violet Rue Kerrigan is one of my better students has been one of these."

Violet Rue Kerrigan. The name suggested wonder, in Mr. Sandman's voice. As if referring to someone, or something, apart from me of a significance unknown to me.

Upper Craigmont Avenue was a residential neighborhood of older, large houses. Tall plane trees with bark peeling from them, like flayed skin. Storm debris lay scattered on expanses of cracked sidewalk and broad front lawns. If there had not been (dim) lights in the windows of houses we passed I might have thought that Mr. Sandman was driving me into an abandoned part of the city.

At last Mr. Sandman turned into the driveway of a stone house, bulbous gray stone, cobblestone? — with dark shutters, and a ponderous slate roof overhead.

Crabgrass stubbled the front lawn. A plane tree lay in ruins as if it had been struck by lightning. The long asphalt drive was riddled with cracks. My father would have sneered at such a derelict driveway though he would have been impressed by the size of Mr. Sandman's house. And Craigmont Avenue looked to be a neighborhood of expensive properties, or properties that had once been expensive. "I am the 'last scion' in the Sandman family," Mr. Sandman said, chuckling. "Since my elderly infirm parents passed away years ago my life is idyllic."

Idyllic was not a word with which I was familiar. I might have thought that it had something to do with *idle.*

As Mr. Sandman parked the large heavy car at the top of the driveway, some distance from the street, I managed to stammer, "I — I want to go home, Mr. Sandman. Please." But my voice was disappointingly weak, Mr. Sandman seemed scarcely to hear.

(By this time I needed to use a bathroom, badly. But this I could not tell Mr. Sandman out of embarrassment.)

"Well, dear! Why are you cowering there like a kicked puppy? Get out, please. We'll have just a little visit — this time. Just a few minutes, I promise. And then I will drive you home to — did you say Ontario Street?"

"Erie . . ."

"Erie! Of course."

A subtle tone of condescension in Mr. Sandman's voice. For the *east side* of Port Oriskany was not nearly so affluent as the *west side* nearer Lake Ontario.

My legs moved numbly. Slowly I got out of Mr. Sandman's car. It did not occur to me that I could run away—very easily, I could run out to the street.

At the same time thinking—*Mr. Sandman is my teacher. He would not hurt me.*

"We'll have just a little 'tutorial.' In private."

Badly wanting to explain to Mr. Sandman—(now nudging me forward, hand on my back, to a side entrance of the darkened house)—that I was concerned that Aunt Irma would wonder where I was for she often worried about me when I was late returning home from school . . . And this afternoon I'd lost time, might've been a half hour, forty minutes or more, in my stuporous sleep in a car I had not realized was Mr. Sandman's. . . . But I could not speak.

Inside, Mr. Sandman switched on a light. We were in a long hallway, my heart was pounding so rapidly I could not see clearly.

And now, in a kitchen—an old-fashioned kitchen with a high ceiling, the largest kitchen I'd ever seen, long counters, rows of cupboards, a large refrigerator, an enormous gas stove, a triple row of burners and none very clean . . .

"I was thinking—hot chocolate, dear? At this time of day when the spirit flags, as the blood-sugar level plummets, I've found that hot chocolate restores the soul."

In the center of the room was an old, enamel-topped table with solid legs. On it were scattered magazines, books. A single page from the *Port Oriskany Herald* containing the daily crossword puzzle, which someone had completed in pencil.

Shyly I agreed to Mr. Sandman's offer of hot chocolate. I could not imagine declining.

Daring to add that I needed to use a bathroom, please . . .

Mr. Sandman chuckled as if the request was endearing to him. "Why, of course, Sleeping Beauty. It has been a while since you have *peed*—eh?"

So embarrassed, I could not even nod yes.

"Even Sleeping Beauty is required, sometime, against all expectations, to *pee*. Yes."

Humming under his breath Mr. Sandman escorted me to a bathroom at the end of a dim-lit corridor, fingers on my back. He reached inside the door to switch on the light, and allowed me to close it—just barely.

My heart was pounding rapidly. There was no lock on the door.

It seemed to me, possibly Mr. Sandman was close outside the door. Leaning against it. The side of his head against it, listening?

Trying to use the toilet as silently as possible. An old, rusted toilet, with a seat made of dark wood. Stained yellowed porcelain at which I did not want to look closely.

Was Mr. Sandman outside the bathroom? Listening? I was stricken with embarrassment.

And then, flushing the toilet. A loud gushing sound that could have been heard through the house.

Washing my hands was a relief. Though the water was only luke-warm I enjoyed scrubbing my hands. Several times a day I washed my hands, took care that my fingernails were reasonably clean.

Noticing now that there were books in the bathroom, on the window sill. *Crossword Puzzles for Whizzes. Favorite Math Puzzles. Favorite Math Puzzles II. Lewis Carroll's Math Games, Puzzles, Problems.* The books were small paperbacks with cartoon covers, that looked as if they'd been much used.

When I left the bathroom it was a relief to see that Mr. Sandman was not hovering outside the door after all.

In the kitchen he awaited me with his wide, wet smile that made you think of meat. He'd placed two large coffee mugs on a counter and was preparing hot chocolate on the stove, shaking powdered, dark chocolate out of a container and into simmering water.

In my hands the mug of steaming hot chocolate was consoling. Shyly I lifted it to my lips since Mr. Sandman expected me to drink it; he would observe closely, to see that I did.

The liquid chocolate was thick, slightly bitter. Almost, I'd have thought there was coffee mixed with it. But I was weak with hunger, and with relief that Mr. Sandman had not followed me into the bathroom. And now that I had used the bathroom and washed my hands I could see that Mr. Sandman meant to be kind.

"Would you like to borrow these, Violet? Of course."

Mr. Sandman was leafing through *Lewis Carroll's Math Games, Puzzles, Problems.* Many of the problems had been solved, in pencil. On some pages there were enthusiastic red asterisks and stars.

"See here, Violet. This section isn't too difficult for you. Shall we do these together?"

Mr. Sandman sat me at the kitchen table. Gave me a pencil. I puzzled over the (comical, far-fetched) cartoon problems as he leaned over my shoulder breathing onto my neck. My head began to swim. "Careful, Violet! Let me take that cup from you."

Could not keep my eyes open. Would've fallen from the chair except Mr. Sandman caught me.

Light was fading. Small spent waves lapped at my feet. Whispers, laughter at a distance. My eyelids were so heavy, I could not force them open . . .

Waking then, some time later. Groggy. Confused. Not in the kitchen but in another room, and on a sofa. Lying beneath a knitted quilt that smelled of moth balls, my sneakers removed. (By Mr. Sandman?) Across the room, in a leather easy chair, Mr. Sandman sat briskly grading papers by lamplight.

"Ah! At last Sleeping Beauty is waking up. You've had a delicious little nap, eh?" Mr. Sandman laughed heartily, indulgently.

My neck was aching. One of my legs was partially numb, I'd been lying on my side. Still very sleepy. A dull headache behind my eyes.

"Dear, it's late—after six p.m. Your aunt will be worried about you, I will drive you home immediately."

How long had I been asleep? My brain could not calculate—an hour? Two hours?

Mr. Sandman set aside his papers. He seemed anxious now. His breath smelled pleasantly of something sweet and dark, like wine.

When I stumbled getting up Mr. Sandman gripped me beneath the arms, hard. "Oops! Enough of 'Sleeping Beauty.' You need to *wake up*, immediately."

Walked me into the kitchen, turned on a faucet and splashed cold water onto my face, slapped my cheeks—lightly!—but enough to make them smart. Bundled me into my jacket and walked me outside into the fresh cold air. My knee had begun to ache, I was limping slightly. Quietly Mr. Sandman told me in the car, "This is our secret, dear. That your math teacher has given you—*lent you*—the Lewis Carroll puzzle book. For others would be jealous, you know."

And, "Including adults. Especially adults. *They* would assuredly not understand and so you may tell them 'Math Club.' It's quite an honor to be selected."

Cautiously Mr. Sandman drove along Erie Street. When I pointed out my aunt's and uncle's house he drove past it and parked at the curb several houses away.

"Goodnight, my dear! Remember our secret."

Lights were on at the house. An outside porch light. I feared that Aunt Irma would be looking out the window. That she'd seen the headlights of Mr. Sandman's car pass slowly by.

But when I went inside Aunt Irma was in the kitchen preparing dinner. She asked where on earth I'd been and I told her without a stammer—"Math Club."

"Math Club! Is there such a thing?"

"I'm the only girl who has been elected to it."

If Aunt Irma had been about to scold me this declaration intimidated her. "They'd never have let me in any math club, when I was in school."

And, "Oh, Violet! Did you go out this morning with your shirt buttoned crooked? Look at you . . ."

I did. Cast my gaze down on myself, seeing that indeed my shirt was buttoned crookedly. Shame.

But why would you go back with him again, Violet? Why—willingly?

5.

Soon then, announcing to Aunt Irma that I'd not only been selected for Math Club but elected secretary.

Which was why I was often late returning home after school. In winter months, after dark.

(And it was true. True in some way. From his several classes Mr. Sandman had "elected" eight students to comprise Math Club. Six boys, two girls. Boys were president and vice president and I was secretary.)

Uncle Oscar seemed impressed, too. When I showed him *Lewis Carroll's Math Games, Puzzles, Problems* he leafed through the little paperback with a wistful expression.

". . . once, I could probably figure these out. Now, I don't know . . ."

Later I would find the little book on the kitchen counter where he'd left it.

Living with adults you live with the husks of their old, lost lives. Like snakes' husks, or the husks of locusts underfoot. The fiction between you that you must not allow them to know that you know.

How many times Mr. Sandman drove me after school to the stone house on Craigmont Avenue. When I was asked I would say truly I did not know, could not remember for always it was the first time and not ever did I seem to know beforehand what would happen nor even, in retrospect, what had happened.

How many times do you dream, in a single night? In a week? A year?

Snowy nights. The heater in Mr. Sandman's car. Windshield wipers slapping. Sheepskin jacket, boots. Mr. Sandman taking my hands in his and blowing on them with his hot, humid breath— "Brrrr! You need to be warmed up, Snow White."

Hot chocolate, with whipped cream. Spicy pumpkin pie, with whipped cream. Jelly doughnuts, cinnamon doughnuts, whipped cream doughnuts. Sweet apple cider, *piping-hot*. (Mr. Sandman's word which he uttered with a sensual twist of his lips: *piping-hot*.)

One evening he had a favor to ask of me, Mr. Sandman said.

For his archive he was taking the measurements of outstanding students. All he required from me was a moment's cooperation— allowing him to measure the circumference of my head, the length of my spine, etc.

"An archive, dear, is a collection of facts, documents, records. In this case, a very private collection. No one will ever know."

I could not say *no*. Already Mr. Sandman was wrapping a yellow tape measure about my head— "Nineteen point six inches, dear. Petite."

The length of my spine— "Twenty-nine point four inches, dear. Well within the range of normal for your age."

Height— "Five feet three point five inches. A good height."

Weight— "Ninety-four pounds, eleven ounces. A good weight."

Waist— "Twenty-one inches. Good!"

Hips— "Twenty-eight inches. Very good!"

As Mr. Sandman looped the tape measure about my chest, brushing against my breasts, I flinched from him, involuntarily.

He laughed, annoyed. But did not persist.

"Another time, perhaps, dear Violet, you will not be so skittish."

So many books! I stared in wonderment. I had never seen so many books outside a library.

Proudly Mr. Sandman switched on lights. Bookcases of elegant dark wood lifting from the floor to the ceiling.

Many of the books were old, matched sets. On the lowermost shelf were *Encyclopedia Britannica, Collected Works of Shakespeare, Collected Works of Dickens, Great British Romantic Poets*. There was an entire bookcase filled with books on military history with such titles as *A History of Humankind at War, Great Military Campaigns of Europe, The Great Armies of History, Soldat: Reflections of a German Soldier 1936–1945, Is War Obsolete?* In an adjacent bookcase, *The Coming Struggle, Free Will and Destiny, The Passing of the Great Race, Racial Hygiene, A History of Biometry, The Aryan Bible, Adolf Hitler's* Mein Kampf: *A New Reading, The Dark Charisma of Adolf Hitler, Origins of the Caucasian Race, Is the White Race Doomed?, Eugenics: A Primer.*

On a special shelf were oversized books of photographs. More military history: US, Germany. Tanks, bomber planes. Fiery cities. Marching men in Nazi uniforms, swastika armbands. Saluting stiff-armed as Mr. Sandman saluted the flag in our classroom.

On the shelves of other bookcases were boxes of old, photocopied records, documents. Mr. Sandman gestured toward these with an air of casual pride—"Transcripts of meetings of the *Race Betterment Society, 1929–1943*. A photocopy of the original manuscript of *The Bible of Practical Ethics and the 'Final Solution.'* And other rare materials I've acquired through antiquarian dealers."

On a table were unframed photographs of local landscapes, skies of sculpted clouds, the mist-shrouded Niagara Falls, which Mr. Sandman had taken himself. And one, apart from the others, that had begun to slightly curl, depicting a girl of about my age lying on a four-poster bed, partly clothed, hands clasped over her thin chest. Long straight pale hair had been spread about her head like a fan. Her eyes were open and yet unseeing.

A girl I'd never seen before, I was sure. I felt a pang of alarm. Jealousy.

Mr. Sandman saw me staring at the photograph and quickly pushed it aside.

"No one you know, dear. An inferior Snow White."

I would not recall the part-unclothed girl afterward. I don't think so. Though I am recalling her now, this *now* is an indeterminate time.

Against the windows of Mr. Sandman's cobblestone house, a faint *ping* of icy rain, hail. An endless winter.

"It is a fact kept generally secret in the United States that Adolf Hitler acquired his 'controversial' ideas on race and on the

problems posed by race from us—the United States. Our history
of slavery, and post-slavery, as well as our 'population management' of Indians—on reservations in remote parts of the country. How to establish a proper scientific census. How to determine
who is 'white' and who is 'colored'—and how to proceed from
there."

Mr. Sandman spoke casually yet you could hear an undercurrent
of excitement in his voice.

Adolf Hitler was a name out of a comic book. A name to provoke
smirks. And yet, in Mr. Sandman's reverent voice *Adolf Hitler* had
another sound altogether.

I'd left my mug of apple cider in the kitchen, half-empty. I had
not wanted to drink more of the hot sweet liquid that was making
me feel queasy. But Mr. Sandman brought both our mugs into the
library, and was handing mine to me.

"Finish your apple cider, Violet! It has become lukewarm."

Helplessly I took the mug from him. Shut my eyes, lifted the
mug to my lips, to drink.

Sweet, sugary apple juice. A taste of something fermented, rot-
ted.

They would ask— *But why would you drink anything that man gave
you? Why, after what happened the first time?*

There'd been no first time. All times were identical. There was
not a *most recent time,* and there was not a *present time.*

"Some of us understand that we must archive crucial documents
and publications before it's too late. One day, the welfare state may
appropriate all of our records. The *liberal welfare state.*" Mr. Sandman spoke with withering contempt.

Entire populations were falling behind others, Mr. Sandman
said. The birthrates of those who should reproduce are declining
while the birthrates of those who should not be allowed to reproduce are increasing— "Mongrel races breed like animals."

When I stared blankly at him Mr. Sandman said, "Violet, you're
a smart girl. By Port Oriskany standards, a very smart girl. You understand that the Caucasian race must preserve itself against mongrelization before it's too late?"

I had heard that a *mongrel dog* is healthier and likely to live longer than a *pedigree dog.* But I did not often reply to Mr. Sandman's
questions for I understood that he preferred silence.

"'Mongrelization' is the natural consequence of the slack, liberal illogic—'all men are created equal.' For the obvious fact is, in human nature as in nature itself, all men *are created unequal*."

This seemed reasonable to me. I did not feel *equal* to anyone and certainly not to any adult.

My legs were growing weak. Mr. Sandman took the mug from me, and seated me on a sofa. In his kindly lecturing voice, which was very different from his classroom lecturing voice, he told me that there are hierarchies of *Homo sapiens*, the product of many thousands of years of evolution.

At the top were Aryans, the purest Caucasians—the "white race." Northern Europe, UK, Germany, Austria. The *crème of the crème*. Beneath these were Middle Europeans, and Eastern Europeans, and beneath these Southern Europeans. By the time you got to Sicily you were in another, lower level of evolution—"Though some of the people are very physically attractive, paradoxically."

There were the Eastern civilizations—Asian, Indian. Here too the lighter-skinned had reigned supreme for many thousands of years though in continuous danger of being infected, polluted by the darker-skinned who resided in the south.

In Africa, Egypt was the exception. A great ancient civilization, and (relatively) white-skinned. The remainder of the continent was dark-skinned—"Indeed, a 'heart of darkness.'"

Earnestly and gravely Mr. Sandman spoke, facing me. His words were incantatory, numbing.

"Black Africans were brought to America as slaves, which would prove a disaster to our civilization. For the enslaved Africans would not remain enslaved through the meddlesome efforts of Abolitionists and radicals like Abraham Lincoln, and so it was to be inevitable that black Africans were granted freedom, and seized freedom, and wreaked havoc upon the white civilization that had hitherto given them shelter and employment and nurtured them . . . First, the military was 'integrated.' Then, public schools. Then, the Boy Scouts of America!" Mr. Sandman shook his head, disgusted.

"With *integration* comes *disintegration*. Some Negroes wish to dilute the white race by interbreeding while others wish to eradicate the white race of 'demons' entirely. Revenge is only natural in humankind. As species have to compete for food to survive, so races must compete for the dominion of the earth. The Führer understood this and launched a brilliant preemptive strike but his fellow Caucasians idiotically opposed him—who can forgive them! One day there will be a race war. To the death." Mr. Sandman's voice rose, vehemently as it sometimes did in class.

Führer. This too was a word out of a comic book. Yet, there was nothing funny about *Führer* now.

"Violet, have you heard of the fearful science of eugenics?"

To this, I could shake my head *no*.

"Why is it 'fearful,' you're wondering? Because it tells truths many do not wish to hear."

According to eugenics, Mr. Sandman explained, interbreeding—"miscegenation"—was a tragic error that would result in the destruction of Master Races, and free-breeding—"promiscuity"—would result in inferior races having as many babies as they could and overwhelming Master Races with their sheer numbers.

"We have seen how the black race is being contaminated by its own thugs—cities like Chicago have become overrun with gangs and drug addicts. They breed like rabbits—like rats! Slavery is the excuse their apologists give—its shadow has fallen upon all blacks, and renders them helpless as invalids. They have no morals. They are greedy and lustful. Their average IQs have been measured many degrees lower than those of whites and Asians. How many great mathematicians have been Negro? That's right—none."

Relenting then, "Well. Almost none. And they were light-skinned blacks, Arabs. In medieval times."

And, "In all fairness, some dark-skinned persons have realized the danger of promiscuity. Certain black intellectuals and leaders like W. E. B. Du Bois believed that only 'fit blacks' should reproduce—not thugs! The 'Talented Tenth' of all races should mix." But Mr. Sandman shuddered at the prospect.

In my fifth-period algebra class there were just three black students—two girls and a boy. Not often but occasionally Mr. Sandman would call upon Tyrell Jones, a stolid, solemn dark-skinned boy with thick glasses: "Ty-rell, come to the blackboard, please. Solve this problem for us." Because Tyrell was one of the better students in the class, and black, Mr. Sandman seemed bemused by him. Tyrell was not a *thug* certainly. Yet Tyrell was not what Mr. Sandman called *light-skinned*.

"Here, Ty-rell. We are waiting to be impressed."

Mr. Sandman handed Tyrell the chalk, which Tyrell near-fumbled in his nervousness.

Tyrell Jones was in two other classes with me. Teachers were protective of Tyrell for he was cripplingly shy, with few friends even among the black students. He wore heavy tweed jackets that might've belonged to his grandfather. He had allergies and was often blowing his nose, sucking air from a plastic device he kept in a pocket. He did not seem young. Standing at the board in Mr. Sandman's class, chalk in his fingers, he appeared to be paralyzed with fear, staring at the problem Mr. Sandman had scrawled on the blackboard as if he had never seen it before though (probably) he'd successfully solved it in our homework assignment. His eyes magnified by the thick lenses skittered over the class of (mostly) white faces as if, desperate, he was looking for a friend.

I would have smiled at Tyrell Jones if he'd looked at me. Just a quick, small smile. For if I smiled at anyone, I did not (really) want them to see; I did not want to be responsible for a smile.

But I was seated too far to the right, out of Tyrell's range of vision.

Mr. Sandman had been peering at me, frowning. Could he read my thoughts? In my fear of the man was a numbness of intellect: I had ceased thinking rationally.

". . . race war, inevitable. If they can't mongrelize our civilization they will attack us directly. Even Tyrell Jones of whom you seem fond . . . he is no friend of ours."

I could not bear it, the way Mr. Sandman read my thoughts. Often I felt as if my head must be transparent, Mr. Sandman could peer inside.

"Most politicians shrink from associating themselves with the 'race issue' at the present time—they're cowards. As a public school teacher, I am in an awkward position. At least, in this northern state. All around me, I believe are sympathizers—embattled 'whites.' And yet, we must not acknowledge one another. I've had to be the very soul of discretion. I never 'discriminate' against Negro students, when they are in my classes. Nothing could be proved against me if the NAACP tried to sue. I never go out of my way to help, or to hinder. But I rarely acknowledge them, either. For the most part they are invisible to me."

This seemed sad, and wrong. I dared to ask Mr. Sandman why he didn't like Ethel, Lorraine, and Tyrell, in our class? They were all nice, and Tyrell was smart.

"It isn't a matter of 'liking' them as individuals. As individuals they might be inoffensive. They do behave themselves in our class.

It's the race that is a threat. Suppose the Negroes were carrying plague virus? You'd avoid them then, even if they are 'nice.'"

"But—they don't have the plague . . ."

"Silly girl! They have something worse than the plague. They have the virus that will destroy the white race, from within. Look, I am one of the most fair-minded teachers in the Port Oriskany school district. I give everyone the benefit of the doubt. But the Negroes, I do not. I draw the line. I don't 'see' them and I don't want to teach them. I am obliged to teach them, but I am not obliged to 'see' them."

"Did a black person hurt you, Mr. Sandman?"

"Don't be ridiculous! No one has hurt *me*. I've tried to explain to you! This isn't personal, it's principle. Even if I 'liked' one of them, I would not want our race to be contaminated by their genes . . . Some of them are attractive, yes, and even intelligent, to a degree. I grant you, there are astonishing black musicians, singers, dancers. Athletes—of course. But their cousins, brothers, fathers—those are the problems. The race issue in the US isn't black people we know, our students, our servants, and the people who work for us, for instance in the school cafeteria, or collecting trash, it's the ones making trouble politically, and the ones who are their relatives. *Thugs* just getting out of prison, or on their way in." Mr. Sandman spoke meanly. Words bubbled up like bile.

My eyelids were becoming heavy. Mr. Sandman's vehement words were like blows of a mallet that has been wrapped in a material like burlap. Hard, harsh yet numbing.

It was not an unpleasant sensation, sinking into sleep. For now my heart was beating less rapidly and nervously and my thoughts were not flashing and darting like heat lightning.

Gently the voice nudged: "Vio-let? Time to wake, dear."

Gently the hand nudged my shoulder. With an effort I opened my eyes. Seeing a man stooping over me, feeling his humid meat-breath.

Seeing with alarm that the sun had disappeared entirely from the sky and night pressed against the windows.

In a silk robe I was lying on a bed. A four-poster bed that creaked as the man's weight settled heavily upon it.

The silk robe was royal blue on the outside, ivory on the inside. It required some time for me to realize that something was wrong.

Was I naked, inside the robe? My skin tingled, as if I'd been bathed. Lotion rubbed into my skin. Talcum powder on my breasts, belly.

A shock to comprehend. I could not allow myself to comprehend.

The ends of my hair were damp. At the back of my mouth was something dry and gritty like sand.

"Sleeping Beauty! Time to open those beautiful myopic eyes."

My eyes were open. But I was not seeing clearly.

Did he—bathe me? Remove my clothes, carry me into the bathroom?

In the bathroom was a marble tub with claw feet. An antique tub, deep as an Egyptian coffin. Vividly I remembered.

A worn tile floor, slick with wet. A camera flash, blinding.

"Ah, good! You're waking up, are you? Yes."

Mr. Sandman spoke distractedly. Perhaps I had slept too long.

He had freshly shaved, his skin exuded an air of heat. His thinning gray hair too was damp, brushed back from his creased forehead. Had Mr. Sandman changed into a fresh-laundered white shirt?

A panicked thought came to me—*He is naked, below.*

But no: Mr. Sandman was fully clothed. White shirt, dark trousers. At school he wore a white shirt, dark trousers, tweed coat. No necktie.

I was very confused. Sitting up, foolishly clutching the silk robe around me. It was shocking to me, to see my bare feet.

You can't run away. Can't run far. He would catch you.

He could kill you if he wished. Strangle you.

The man was waiting for me to realize. To scream. To become hysterical.

His fingers were poised. It was up to me.

Lying very still trying to summon my strength. Like water, that falls through outstretched fingers. Despair filled me, yet the calm of reason—silly bare feet, I could not run far.

"Your clothes are here, Violet. I had to launder them—they were soiled . . ."

Mr. Sandman spoke briskly, disapprovingly. Indicating, at the foot of the bed, clothes neatly folded. Strange to see, how neatly folded.

So grateful to see my clothes! I'd been clutching the silk robe around me, in terror that Mr. Sandman would snatch it away.

But he was a gentleman, you could see. The cobblestone house on Craigmont Avenue. So many books.

Could have wept, suffused with gratitude. For he would allow me to live, and he would forgive me the fear and repugnance in my face.

"Our secret, Violet. Do you understand, my dear?"

Yes. I understood. Understood something.

Understood that I'd been allowed to live. To continue.

Discreetly now Mr. Sandman retreated. Allowed me some privacy.

(A bedroom, dimly lighted. At the windows, darkness. The floor was covered in a thin carpet, against a farther wall a tall vertical mirror reflecting pale-shimmering light.)

Hurriedly I dressed. Underwear, jeans. Shirt and sweater. (It did seem as if my panties had been laundered, and had not quite dried in the dryer, the synthetic white fabric somewhat damp, at the same time somewhat warm.)

In his car driving me to my aunt's and uncle's house on Erie Street Mr. Sandman explained that, after school that day, there'd been an emergency meeting of the Math Club. As the Math Club secretary, I had had an obligation to attend.

"You understand, dear, that if you tell anyone about our friendship it will hurt you most. You will be expelled—immediately—from school. You may be sent to a facility for 'delinquent minors.' And I, too, might be shuttled to—an inferior—school . . ."

At this Mr. Sandman chuckled. As if it were so unlikely, such a possibility might occur.

Bathed me. Held me down. Licked me with his sandpaper *tongue. Until I squealed, shrieked.*

Took my hand in his and guided it between his legs where he was swollen, fattish.

Don't pretend, Vio-let Rue. Dirty girl!

The face was contorted. Of the hue of a cooked tomato, about to burst. Eyes about to burst out of their sockets. Breath in gasps. Like a bicycle pump, my brothers' bicycle pump, pumping air into a tire, that wheezing sound it makes if you are not doing it correctly, and air is escaping.

The hand gripping my hand, so that it hurts. Pushing, pressing, urgently, faster and faster, jamming my hand against his swollen flesh, my

numbed hand, as he groans, rocks from side to side, eyes roll in their sockets,
he is about to faint . . .

But no. None of this happened. For none of this was witnessed.

6.

"This endearing little blemish, Violet?—not a birthmark, I think,
but a scar?"

Mr. Sandman drew his fat thumb over the star-shaped scar at my
forehead. Involuntarily, I shivered.

"Futile to try to hide it, you know. And what caused it?"

"I—fell from a bicycle . . . When I was a little girl."

"Ah! Tragic, in a female so young."

Tragic. Mr. Sandman was joking, I supposed.

"Well, dear, if it's any consolation—you were not destined to
be a 'beauty' anyway. The scar gives you character. Other, merely
pretty girls tend to be *bland.*"

Steeled myself to feel the fat lips against my forehead, to smell
the hot meaty breath. Shut my eyes, shivering, waiting.

7.

One day, discovering Mr. Sandman's (secret) archive.

A door just beyond the bathroom. A closet, with shelves containing what appeared to be photography albums, dates neatly labeled
on their spines. Daring to pull down one of the albums, *1986–87,*
stunned to see photographs of a dark-haired girl of thirteen or
fourteen posed on Mr. Sandman's sofa, and on the four-poster bed.
In some photos the girl was fully clothed, in others partly clothed.
In others, naked inside the royal blue silk robe that was so familiar
to me.

In the marble tub deep as an Egyptian coffin, head flung back
against the rim of the tub and eyes half-shut, vacant. Beneath the
surface of blue-tinged water, the pale thin body shimmering naked.

Many photographs of this girl—*M.H.*

Abruptly then, a sequence of photographs of another girl, of
about the same age and physical type—*B.W.*

Wanly pretty (white) girls. Thin-armed, with small breasts, nar-

row torsos and hips. Captured in the throes of deep sleep. Posi-
tioned as if dead with eyes shut, hair spread out around their heads.
Lips slightly parted and hands clasped on their chests.

Turning the stiff pages, and more photos . . . More (white) girls.

Also, locks of hair. Folded-in notes fastidiously recording measurements—height, weight, circumference of skull, waist, hips,
bust.

Clumsily I shut the album, returned it to the shelf. Took down
the most recent album which was *1991–92*. But before I could open
it there came Mr. Sandman's voice from the kitchen: "Vio-let!"

Mr. Sandman was assuming that I was in the bathroom. In another minute he would come seek me. Quickly I shut the album,
returned it to its place on the crammed shelf, shut the door.

Heart thudding in my chest. Such violence, like a fist punching
my ribs.

None of the girls I'd recognized. My predecessors.

"Vio-let, dear. Come here at once."

*Already forgetting how in some of the photographs, the camera was close,
intimate. Bruised mouth, open. The silk robe had been pulled open, or tossed
away. Small pale breasts with soft nipples. The curve of a belly, a downy
patch between legs.*

*In one, a girl with opened, dilated eyes. A look of fear. A smear of blood
on her face. Hands not clasped on her chest in that attitude of exquisite
peace but uplifted as if pushing away the camera.*

But already forgetting. Forgotten. The ugliest sights.

Unless it was myself I'd seen, confused with another.

What had he done to this girl? Stared and stared.

She'd failed to fall asleep properly. She'd been stubborn, resistant.

*Or he had not drugged this girl because he had not wanted her to sleep.
He had wanted her awake, conscious.*

But why was this? Why was one girl treated differently from the others?

*You are that girl, you wish to think. Always, you are different from the
others.*

8.

Not true that all times were the same time. For there was the *last
time* in Mr. Sandman's house that would not be repeated.

Inadvertently he'd given me an overdose. A fraction of a tea-spoon of fine-ground barbiturate dissolved into sweet blueberry juice but he'd miscalculated, or he'd become complacent over the months. For so obediently the stupor came upon me, each time a mimicry of the time before, his vigilance had diminished.

And then, Mr. Sandman couldn't wake me.

Vio-let! Vio-let! Wake up, dear . . .

No memory of falling asleep. Only vaguely, something in my hand that had to be taken from my fingers to prevent its spilling.

A terrible heaviness. Sinking downward. Surface of the water far overhead, no agitation of my numbed limbs could bring me to it. Comfort in the dark cloudy water like many tongues licking together.

Violet! Open your eyes, try to sit up—the voice came from a dis-tance, alarmed.

Shaking me, and shaking me. Bruising my shoulders with his hard fingers, naked inside the silk robe. My skin still warm from the bath, not yet beginning to cool into the chill of death. Slick creamy lotion caressed into my skin, smelling of lilac. Talcum powder on all the parts of my body that would be covered by my clothes, when I was clothed again.

Except: he could not wake me.

Did not dare call 911 (Mr. Sandman would confess) for then he'd be discovered, arrested. His secret life exposed.

Yet, he did not want the girl to die.

Well, yes—(Mr. Sandman would confess)—the desperate thought came to him, he might let the girl die, he would never suc-ceed in waking the girl and so there was no alternative, he would let her die, and in that way he would be spared exposure and arrest, the outrage and loathing of the community of decent persons, he would be spared prison, how many years in prison, of which he could not bear even a few days. Yet, he did not want Violet Rue to die for (he would insist) he loved her . . .

Or this he would claim, afterward.

His solution was to dress me hurriedly, haphazardly, in the clothes he'd removed from me, and had partly laundered, and partly dried, and to wrap me in a blanket snatched from a cedar closet, and carry me out to his car, stumbling and sobbing; in the car, he drove me to the Port Oriskany hospital, to the ER which was at the side entrance of the building; half-carried, half-dragged

me inside the plate-glass doors that parted automatically, and left
me there, slumped on a chair; hurried back outside even as a hospital security guard was calling after him—"Mister! Hey mister!"
He'd left the car running. Key in the ignition. He would make a
quick getaway, was the reasoning. But so agitated, within seconds
Mr. Sandman collided with a van turning into the hospital drive as
he tried to escape.

In the telling it would become a story to provoke outrage, and
yet mirth.

For, outside the tyranny of the math teacher's classroom and
house, the math teacher was revealed as bumbling, foolish. Bringing an unconscious fourteen-year-old to the brightly lit emergency
room of a hospital, a hastily clothed and (seemingly) dying girl,
believing that he might abandon the girl there, might simply run
back out to his car idling just outside the entrance and drive away
undetected, and then, so agitated, such a fool, colliding head-on
with the first vehicle that approached him as if in his desperation
he'd failed to *see* . . .

But mostly, the story provoked outrage. Of course!

A mathematics teacher entrusted with middle-school students,
revealed to have been sexually abusing one of his ninth-grade pu-
pils over a period of seven months, routinely drugging the girl to
make her sexually compliant, at last overdosing the girl with barbi-
turates, bringing her blood pressure lethally low . . .

In the ER the girl whose heart was barely beating was revived. In
the hospital driveway the ninth-grade algebra teacher was arrested
by Port Oriskany police officers.

Taken into police custody in handcuffs, brought downtown to
police headquarters. Overnight in the county jail and in the morning denied bail by a repelled judge. Suicide watch, for the distraught man had raved and sobbed and uttered many wild things,
pleas and threats.

It would be revealed that Arnold Sandman, fifty-one, longtime
resident of Port Oriskany, faculty member since 1975 of Port
Oriskany Middle School, had been accused of "unacceptable"
behavior at previous schools, including a Catholic school in Wa-
tertown; but he'd been allowed to resign from the positions, and
school administrators at two schools had agreed to provide him
with "strong" recommendations, to get him out of their districts
without a scandal. For there was the uncertainty of several girls'

accounts—there was the uncertainty that the girls' parents would even allow them to make statements to the police, which would be revealed to the public. And Mr. Sandman denied all—everything. And Mr. Sandman did speak persuasively. And Mr. Sandman was, all conceded, a capable, if eccentric teacher whose students tended to do well on state examinations; in fact, better on the average than students taught by other math teachers. Jocosely it was said that Mr. Sandman "terrorized" students into learning math, where other, more gentle methods failed.

This time, however, Arnold Sandman would plead "no contest" to charges of protracted child endangerment, sexual molestation of a minor child, drug statute violations, abduction and false imprisonment.

The cobblestone house on Craigmont Avenue would be searched top to bottom. The incriminating archive would be discovered. Of thirty-one girls photographed by Mr. Sandman over a period of eighteen years all but six were identified; of these all but two were living in upstate New York and vicinity; the two no longer living had died "suspiciously" (suicide?) but in no ways connected with Arnold Sandman.

None of the photographed girls could remember being photographed by their ninth-grade math teacher. None could remember having been sexually abused, coerced, threatened by him but most could remember "after-school tutorials" and their math teacher being "very kind" and "patient" with them.

9.

"Violet. Please try to remember. Tell us . . ."

But I could not. My throat was shut up tight, there were no words to loosen it.

For some time I was very sick. Too weak to sit up in bed. Fluids dripped into my veins, too weak to eat or drink.

No. Can't remember. Don't make me.

Amnesia was a balm. Wept with gratitude for all that I did not remember and not for what I did remember.

The shock of it is, what was intimate becomes public. What occurred without words becomes a matter of others' words.

Sexual abuse of a minor. Abduction. False imprisonment.

In that deep sleep, in which my heart had barely continued to beat, at the very bottom of the marble coffin, I had been protected, safe. Almost I would think that Mr. Sandman's arms had embraced me.

Vio-let Rue! Vio-let Rue!

You know, I love you.

He had never uttered these words to me, I was sure. Yet often I heard them, confused with voices at a distance. Muffled laughter.

". . . what that terrible man did to you. Try to . . ."

But I did not remember. And Mr. Sandman was my friend. No one else was my friend.

Aunt Irma staring at me, disbelieving. Uncle Oscar, with repugnance.

For I would not testify against the abuser. My eyes were heavy-lidded, my voice was slow, slurred, insolent.

No. You can't make me. I've said — I don't remember.

There was a female police officer, questioning me. But I knew better than to make that mistake again.

A (female) gynecologist who would report *no vaginal or anal penetration, no (physical) evidence of sexual abuse.* A (female) therapist who would report *probable extreme trauma, dissociation.* Ms. Herne from the Children's Protective Agency.

It would be held against me that I was uncooperative with authorities trying to establish a case of repeated and sustained sexual abuse against Mr. Sandman unless it might be argued that I was a victim, mentally ill, unable to testify against the teacher who'd drugged and abused me for a period of approximately seven months.

Mr. Sandman had been careful, fastidious. My clothes had been laundered — no DNA. (Except an incriminating trace would be discovered on my sneakers.)

If you don't help to convict him he will hurt other girls, they told me. I thought — *Other girls will be hurt whether Mr. Sandman is in prison or not. That is our punishment.*

"Violet. No one is putting pressure on you . . ."

You are all putting pressure on me.

". . . but you must tell us, you must take your time and tell us, all that you can remember. When did that man first . . ."

Ms. Herne was visibly upset. For (she believed) there'd been a special understanding between us, I'd known that I could trust her. And yet, I must not have trusted Ms. Herne for the abuse had been going on for months during which she'd met with me several times and there'd been *no hint*.

Of course, there'd been a *hint*. Plenty of *hint*. Ms. Herne had failed to detect, that was all.

And now with the (ugly, relentless) publicity in the local media it hardly looked as if Dolores Herne of the Port Oriskany Children's Protective Agency had been very good at her job, one of her at-risk juvenile clients having been sexually abused, terrorized by a teacher, over a period of seven months and she had *not noticed*.

I'd thought— *Not abuse but punishment. And not the worst punishment either.*

10.

And what had happened to Arnold Sandman? He'd been in custody in the county jail. Wisely, he would not risk a trial. (The prosecutor was calling for a sentence of ninety-nine years.) Instead, Mr. Sandman would follow his attorney's advice and plead no contest, and express contrition, and repentance, and shame for his crimes; and the presiding judge would sentence him to twenty-five to thirty years in the maximum-security prison at Attica.

A death sentence. Arnold Sandman would never survive Attica.

None of this was known to me, at the time. Though if I shut my eyes and began to drift in the rapid current that was always there, inside my eyelids, far below the Lock Street bridge, amid the churning writhing snakes of the hue of eggplant, there came Mr. Sandman to stoop over me, his face no longer jocular and mocking but contorted with grief.

Violet! You know, of all the girls I loved only you.

There came a timid knocking at a door. Aunt Irma asking please, could she speak with me?

Pulled the covers over my head. So that I could see Mr. Sandman more clearly. So that I could hear him more clearly.

At last the timid knocking ceased. Whoever was outside the door had gone away and left me alone with Mr. Sandman.

BRIAN PANOWICH

A Box of Hope

FROM *One Story*

WILL SAT ON the front porch of the house, his feet tucked in
close to his body. He'd been sitting in that spot, staring out into the
yard, for at least a hundred years or so. He sat and watched both
the ghost of his father and a younger version of himself playing tag
football in the thick overgrown crabgrass. His old man purposely
leaving himself wide open and slowing his movements to let his
boy win. Will watched the figments of his imagination climb on
the monkey bars that his father had spent a full two weeks yelling
at while building piece by piece so many summers ago. The jungle
gym started out as a huge flat cardboard box that a truck from
K-Mart had dropped off in the driveway, but Will's father slowly
erected it into a steel fortress for them to climb and conquer together. Now it just looked like frail and rusted dinosaur bones—
the carcass of some ancient dead thing that had chosen his front
yard for its final resting place.

His father had died in his shop just behind the house—an aneurism in his brain. Will was fifteen and felt like he should have
had a clear idea of what an aneurism was, but he didn't, not really.
He sat on those steps looking out at his memories and trying to
ignore the fat man sitting next to him. The man's mouth had been
moving through every bit of the past hundred years Will had been
out there, but his voice had shrunk to a hum that gave the ghosts a
soundtrack of static. Will was almost thankful for it.

Almost.

He missed his father's voice. He was beginning to believe he'd already forgotten the sound of it, and he considered that maybe this fat man's words bouncing off the surface of his memories might just be saving him from breaking completely in half. He took his eyes off the ghosts and looked down at his brightly polished patent leather loafers. He traced the reflection the trees made in them with his finger. He thought about how he had never worn —or owned—a pair of shoes like this before. Why in the world would his mom spend what little money they had on these shoes, knowing full well he would never wear them again? She had been so adamant about it.

"You need to look respectful," she'd told him in the middle of J. C. Penney while she'd pulled box after box of shoes off the rack, littering the aisle with tissue paper.

"How does a pair of shoes make you look respectful?" he'd said. How does a person "look respectful" in the first place? Will felt himself slipping into his own anger. He'd lost his dad two days before and was filled with just as much grief as his mother. At least he'd thought so at the time. These shoes felt so unimportant, but as he'd tried on a third pair—the pair he was wearing now—he noticed his mother fighting back her tears. She'd been hiding her own pain behind the shopping. That's when Will loosened up and allowed her the small comfort those shoes seemed to bring her. "These are good, Mom."

"Are you sure?" she said and wiped her cheek with the back of her hand. "Walk around some and make sure they fit."

Will did and then sat back down on the little bench. He reached over to take her hand as she cleaned up the wads of tissue paper. "Mom, it's going to be okay."

She looked at him and answered him honestly for the first time without the facade of a protective mother. "No it isn't, William. No it isn't." Then she broke down crying.

This was part of Will's job now—holding his mother while she sobbed in a department store—whether he wanted to or not. But he hadn't seen her cry again since. He knew that was due to her new medicine—the little yellow pills that rattled around in her purse and sat on her nightstand. Those pills did their job too. They kept her from crying but they also seemed to keep her from feeling much of anything else. That was okay, though. Will felt enough for both of them. He wanted to cry along with her, but he knew the rules. He wasn't a kid anymore. He was the man of the house now, and men tough it out. Men keep it together. Above all, men don't cry.

Men get angry. But who was he angry at?

God, maybe.

The helplessness made him want to scream. He wanted to scream until his vocal cords strained and burst. He wanted to scream so loud it would crack the world in half, so that everything that had happened over the past few days would fall through the middle —get swallowed up by the void and be over. Even now, sitting on the porch steps, lost in his memories, he could feel that scream building up behind his tongue and teeth, swelling in his throat like a living thing. Maybe if he let it out he could stop being so angry. Maybe screaming would make him not want to take a swing at everyone in the house.

Before he'd stepped out to get some air, he'd watched as people floated around in their Sunday best, chatting about their jobs or football or the economy—whatever the hell that was. Some of them were even talking about what they had planned for later in the evening. That made Will's skin burn. *Later this evening* didn't exist for him or his mom, not in any kind of way they could have wanted. They were stuck here in this reality for a long time coming, while all these friends of the family shook hands and ate casseroles off little paper plates.

He hadn't expected to feel this way today. Angry with no one to lash out at, lonely with no one to hold on to, scared and hollow with nowhere to hide. Out of the blue, he felt the urge to punch the man sitting next to him square in his fat face. He wouldn't do it, but sitting still like this was excruciating. It was just as bad as having to listen to people he barely knew tell him over and over how "time heals all wounds." He wanted to cheat his emotions like his mother was doing with the pills. Maybe he'd sneak one from her purse later. She'd never notice. *No.* Will shook his head again. He wouldn't do that either. Dad wouldn't want him to. He just needed to suck it up and take it. He needed to follow the rules and stop being so selfish. These people in his house were only trying to help, and the truth was they probably were helping his mom just by being here. He scratched at the back of his neck and loosened the tie his mother had also bought him that day at the department store —another act of endurance he'd had to bear for her sake.

Inside the house, Will's mother had spent nearly twenty minutes spreading the creases out of a red and white checkered tablecloth before she set out all the covered dishes. A few people—Will included—had tried to help her, but she became indignant about it. She was still able-bodied, she reminded everyone. "I lost my husband," she said, "not my goddamn hands." She never cussed or took the Lord's name in vain like that, but she was angry too.

His Uncle Jack's being there didn't make it any easier.

Will didn't know much about him. He'd never even seen him before today—outside of a few family photo albums—but it was obvious that his presence at the funeral and now here at the house was upsetting his mom even more than she already was. She'd barely spoken to him at the funeral home. She'd introduced the two of them, but then she'd immediately pulled Will away to talk to one of the neighbors. Will had been so taken aback by his uncle's resemblance to his dad that he'd been dumbstruck, anyway.

The fat man sitting next to him truly had no idea that Will hadn't heard a word he'd said. It was baffling. He continued yapping until Will felt a hand touch his shoulder and a new droning sound started. Then the fat man brushed the nothing from his pants as he stood up, made a hasty sign of the cross in the air, and mumbled a few words that might as well have been a recipe for rhubarb pie. He cast a weary glance at his replacement. "Good luck," he said.

Will felt the urge to smack him again but sat still as the fat man headed inside to get in on some free potluck. The new man sat down on the steps.

Uncle Jack.

"Hey there, Will," he said. And then, after a few moments: "I hate that you had to sit out here and listen to that guy for so long. I would have come out to save you a while ago, but your mama said she wanted you to have some time with a holy man."

"A holy man?"

"That's what she said, kiddo. A preacher from one town over. I wasn't about to argue."

"Yeah, she's been a little touchy lately."

"Don't be too hard on her. She's going through a pretty rough time. If she wants to act a little touchy, then I reckon she's entitled to."

"Yeah, I guess so." Will was amazed at how quiet it got without the "holy man's" hot buzz in his ear. He turned and took in the sight of his uncle, his dad's younger brother. This close up, the resemblance was startling. Uncle Jack was so much like Will's father it made him hard to look at, so Will didn't look for very long. There were differences, of course, but those seemed—at a glance, anyway—to be matters of style. Will's father had been uptight about his appearance and manner. He always sat up straight in his chair, always kept his hair short and trim, and his shirt stayed tucked in. Will supposed his dad's twenty-five-year tenure in the Fire Service had made him that way. He always carried himself as if he were in service of someone else and ready for a business meeting. That sort of thing had been important to him, but clearly none of that mattered to Will's Uncle Jack. He was thinner, looser. His graying brown hair fell long and messy. Not long enough for a ponytail or anything, but long enough for him to have to reach up and tuck it back behind his ear every two or three minutes throughout the entire funeral, Will had noticed. He wore black Levi's and a pair of beat-up black cowboy boots that seemed to be challenging Will's own sissy shoes to a duel on the steps below them. His black button-up shirt looked expensive, but not new. Will got the feeling Jack dressed like that all the time. He hadn't just made a stop at J. C. Penney to pick up some dress-up clothes to make himself "look respectable" on the way here. He didn't wear a tie, either, but he wore a lot of silver rings and they made both of his hands sparkle in the sun. Will could see bright-colored tattoos creeping out from under his sleeves whenever he moved his wrists just the right way. Although Will thought that was cool, he knew every pair of eyes in the house behind him had washed this man down with buckets of judgment —good Christian judgment.

Uncle Jack didn't live here in McFalls County. He'd moved to Atlanta several years before Will was born and had stayed there, far away from where he'd grown up, far away from his family. From what Will could tell, that had always been fine with his parents. There was no contact that he knew of, and no one had spoken to Uncle Jack at the funeral today except for his mom—and that was only because Uncle Jack had approached *her.* He didn't get up to say anything during the service, either, which Will thought was weird. The man had lost his brother, after all. Family resemblance or not, he seemed to be a stranger.

The two of them sat in silence for a long time.

Then Uncle Jack said, "I miss him too, kid."

Those five words opened the floodgates. Will could hear this man that everyone treated as some kind of pariah start to openly cry, and Will couldn't help himself. The tears they both had been doing their best to hold back all day ran down their faces. Jack reached out and pulled his brother's son in for a hug. Damn the rules.

Once the moment turned awkward, they shifted back from each other on the step and straightened out a bit, the way men do. They sat again in silence. Jack let a misplaced chuckle slip out that reminded Will so much of his father he almost started crying again, but he didn't. He'd already gotten that out. Instead, he unintentionally mimicked Jack's chuckle, which caused them both to laugh even harder. Will supposed their sudden mood swing brought on curious stares from some of the casserole eaters behind them, but he didn't care.

"You know," Jack said, "your father was pretty proud of you. He talked about you all the time."

Will figured the drone would begin now, but he played along. "He did?"

"Of course he did. He rarely talked to me about anything else."

"No," Will said, elaborating on his point, "I mean, you two talked? I got the impression that you guys didn't talk to each other at all."

"Well, we didn't exactly have Wednesday-night chat sessions or anything, but he *was* my brother, you know. We talked. Holidays, birthdays — that kind of thing."

"Oh." Will rested his elbows on his knees. He couldn't help but wonder if what Jack had said was true or if he was lying just to make his nephew feel good.

"I'd ask him how things were going and immediately he'd get to rambling on about you."

"What was the deal with you two, anyway?" Will asked. "He never talked to me about you." He knew his words were callous. Jack didn't seem to mind. "Did y'all have a falling out or something?"

"Or something," Jack said, as if that took care of describing it. "We just led two very different lives. Your dad was always kind of a straight arrow, even when we were kids. He always did the right thing, despite what people thought of him or what it cost him. That's what made him so damn likable." Jack motioned with one shiny hand back toward the house. "It's also why his house is packed out with so many people right now."

Will rolled his eyes.

"Hey, think what you want about those people in there, but every one of them wishes they had an ounce of the stuff that made your father the man he was. I can promise you that. I know I do."

That much sounded right to Will. He let his uncle talk.

"He was the kind of guy that people just wanted to be around. The kind you wanted in your corner. Very much the opposite of me."

Jack took a deep breath and let it out slowly.

"Back in the day," he said, "me and my buddies did some dumb things — like lifting beer from Pollard's or dragging three-oh-twos up on McDowell Road. Stuff like that always had me locking horns with your father, because he never approved. He definitely had a way of making you feel his disappointment if you strayed from the righteous path."

Will felt himself nodding in agreement. He'd gotten into a fight at school once. He couldn't even remember what started it, but he could remember after he was sent home how the look on his dad's face had been far worse punishment than a whupping would have been.

"Your old man cast a long shadow, if you catch my meaning."

"Yeah, I do. He was a high-road kind of guy."

"The problems we had? That was all me. If your dad was a high-road kind of guy, then I was the low-road kind. I always found the easy way to do things and it always got me into trouble." He thought on that for a second then added, "Your dad just didn't understand. For him, being a fuck-up, and all the bad stuff that comes with it, just didn't compute."

Will felt a pinprick of joy when his uncle dropped the f-bomb. The adults he knew usually never cussed around kids. Hearing the f-bomb made him feel more grown up and less like the child everyone felt sorry for.

"When we were boys," Jack said, "I used to resent your old man for being such a tight-ass, but as we grew up I started to realize that for all of his soapboxing and straight-shooter bullshit, he never once gave up on me or backed down from someone or something I got tangled up in. And believe me when I tell you, kiddo, I brought a truckload of bad news into his life. He could've walked away from me at any time and nobody would have blamed him, but Hank didn't have it in him to walk away from anything."

Hank. That was a name reserved only for the people that truly knew Will's dad. Most everybody called him Henry, or Mr. Henry even, but never Hank. Mom called him Hank. Nana called him Hank. The name sounded strange coming from someone Will had just met, but it was also comforting, and it made the conversation sound like something warmer than it had just a couple of moments ago. It made it feel like family.

"I also realized that I was never going to change," Jack continued. "I was pretty comfortable with the way I lived my life, so I decided it was best for me to stay away. Your old man never argued with that. I was single and had no one to look out for but myself. He had a pretty wife and a kid on the way. He didn't need me around causing him any grief." Jack got quiet and a sadness swirled on the porch like a miniature twister between them. Will shooed it away in his mind. He realized he felt less lonely. The ache in his chest had dulled—not much, but some.

"Well, I'm glad you're here now," he said. "I don't really know anybody in there other than Nana and a few guys my dad worked with. I think you're maybe the only person here that isn't looking at me like I'm on suicide watch. If one more person asks me if I'm okay, I think I'm gonna scream—or puke."

Jack smiled, and it made him look more like Will's dad than ever. He put his arm around the boy again. "That's exactly what I needed to hear, because although I love your mama and all, I know she hates me and can't wait for me to get the hell out of Dodge."

"I wouldn't say she hates you."

Jack raised one eyebrow—another mannerism that echoed Will's dad. He looked back toward the front door where Will's mother had been standing for who knew how long.

"Are you okay?" she said. The question was for Will, but her blistering stare was all for Jack.

"Yeah, Mom. I'm fine."

She stood with her hands on her hips for a moment while she made that decision for herself and then finally backed away into the house. Will knew even if he couldn't see her, she'd stay within earshot of him and Jack. Jack seemed to know it too. They began to speak more softly.

"Okay, she hates you."

"Told you."

"But she's feeling no pain right now, so I think you're safe."

"Well, to be completely honest, kiddo, no disrespect, but I don't care what your mama thinks of me. I didn't come here for her. I came here for your dad—and for you."

"Why me? I don't even know you."

"And that's sort of the point," Jack said. "I know I haven't been the greatest uncle to you and you've got no reason in the world to put any stock in anything I say, but it's important to me that you understand something."

"What's that?"

"I loved your father. I did. And I didn't tell him that enough while he was alive. I never thanked him for anything he did for me or told him how much he meant to me. Now he's gone, and I can't. That's on me. I've got to live with it, and so I don't want to screw up and do the same thing twice."

Will didn't know what to say. Stupidly, he just nodded.

"William, listen. From this moment on, as cheesy as this may sound, I will never be more than a phone call away. My brother was the best man I've ever known, and my bet is that you're going to turn out to be just like him. I want to be around to see that. I need to see that. I guess I'm saying that anything you need, Will, anytime you need it, from anywhere you are, I got your six."

What felt like a full minute of silence passed. Will settled his eyes back on his shoes. "Thanks, Uncle Jack," he finally said, but it sounded thin and obligatory.

Jack took another deep breath and both of them could feel the awkwardness of why they were there creeping back in between them. "I also came here to give you something."

Will looked up. "What's that?" He assumed it was money. Money his mother wouldn't let him keep. Money his father never would've allowed him to take.

Jack smiled, but this time his smile was his own—not Will's dad's. It filled his whole face with the kind of mischief Will's father just didn't possess. "Follow me," he said, and stood up. He walked down the steps and toward a Suburban parked at the end of the driveway and fished the keys from his pocket. Will hesitated and looked over his shoulder into the laser-hot stare of his mother. He didn't know how long she'd been back in the doorway. He felt the tug of her eyes telling him to keep his butt glued to that step, but he got up anyway. He brushed at his pants the way the fat man had and defiantly followed his uncle to the truck.

Jack walked behind the Suburban, double-tapped the key fob, and stood back as the hatch opened automatically. He disappeared from sight, shuffled some things around in the back, and then emerged holding a large white rectangular cardboard box. Will waited by the front of the truck, keeping himself in clear view of the front door. He didn't want to give his mother a reason to come outside and ruin whatever this was. Jack seemed to understand. He tucked the box under his arm, tapped the key fob again, and the hatch slowly lowered back into place. He walked right past Will and returned to the porch. He set the box down on the steps and took a seat next to it. Will imagined every pair of eyes in the house joining his mother's in curiosity, but he also imagined that interest died almost immediately when Jack reached down, lifted the cardboard lid from the box, and pulled out some of its contents.

Comic books.

How old did his uncle think he was? Will had given up comic books years ago. He liked girls and cars these days. Comic books all but guaranteed he'd never get a shot at having either. His uncle was a fool if he thought he could just show up here after all this time, say a few nice things about Will's dad, and then try to buy his affection with a box of old comic books. He looked at his uncle with a mix of disappointment and confusion. It was Jack's turn to see his brother in his nephew's face.

"I know what you're thinking," he said.

"Do you?"

"Yeah, you're thinking that your loser uncle must be out of his mind lugging out a box of comic books to impress a teenager who is clearly light-years ahead of this kind of thing, right?"

"Maybe not the loser part." Will walked back over to stand next to the porch. "But I am fifteen."

"Well, Methuselah, these aren't just any comic books." Jack handled a few of the flimsy yellowed paper comics the same way Will's mother handled her nana's antique dishes. "These," Jack said, never taking his eyes off what he was holding, "are your father's comic books."

Now Will was really confused. His dad had never owned any comics. He hadn't even read regular books. It just wasn't his thing.

As far back as Will could remember, his dad had never even read a newspaper. "Are you serious?"

"As a heart attack," Jack said. "Me and your dad used to collect these together. *The X-Men, Daredevil, Green Arrow, The Flash, Tales of Suspense.*" He paused on one of the books in his hand, and Will thought his uncle might start to cry again. "And *Batman,*" he said. "Damn, your dad loved him some *Batman.*"

"You're kidding me right now, right? This is some kind of joke."

Jack looked mildly offended. "I would never kid you about something this important, Will. On my honor." He held his free hand up, palm out. "When me and your old man were boys—when we were friends—these were his prized possessions." He carefully placed the books back in the box. "Every last Wednesday of the month, if all our chores had been kept up, your nana would give us each a Susan B. Anthony dollar and we'd walk all the way down to Franklin County to the Stars and Stripes Drugstore. The only place we knew that carried all the latest issues. We'd get two books apiece with those dollars and we'd swap them back and forth all the way home. Sometimes we'd even act out the stories in the backyard."

Will still looked skeptical. "It's a little hard to picture my dad doing anything like that."

"Well, he did. In fact, he loved them even more than I did. He always said he wanted to write comics when he grew up. That was his dream."

"So what happened?" Will asked, even more bewildered. He noticed his mother had disappeared from the doorway.

"The same thing that happened to almost everything back then. I ruined it."

"How so?" Will sat back down and tried his best not to look interested in the fragile box between them.

"We got a little older. I guess I was about your age and your dad was a year ahead of me. I started becoming the asshole you see before you now and I began to treat the whole comic book ritual as 'uncool.' I started hanging out with losers and smoking cigarettes while your dad kept himself buried in these things." Jack tapped the box. "He tried to get me interested again from time to time, but I wasn't having it. I was too cool. Eventually he just gave up, and without having me or someone else to share all this with, it held less and less magic for him, I guess. Until finally he put all his books in this box, and into the attic they went. He never talked about them again — not to me, anyway. When your nana finally got sick of me always getting in trouble and kicked me out of the house for good, I stole them. I thought I could sell them to a collector or something down the road for some quick cash, but every time I tried, I could never bring myself to go through with it. After a while — when money stopped being an issue for me — they became something else."

"Like what? What something else?" There was excitement in Will's voice. Not a lot, but enough for Jack to notice.

"I know this is going to sound corny to a big fifteen-year-old kid like you, but this box of comics became a symbol of the last good thing I could remember about your father and me. It was like there wasn't just a bunch of old comics in there, but more like our childhood — our brotherhood — was still alive inside this box. I began to think the reason I could never get rid of them like I planned was because, someday, they would be the thing that brought us back together. I started to imagine that one day we would be old men on a porch somewhere — maybe this one — looking through all this stuff, and as we remembered the comic books, we'd remember each other. I don't know, I just thought if we sorted through these, we could finally sort through all our shit, too. I always thought there'd be enough time. I was wrong."

"But why get rid of them now? I mean, they still mean something to you, right? They still remind you of my dad, right?"

Jack's face stoned over. "Yeah, they do. And that's why I'm not getting rid of them. I'm giving them to you. It's like I said, I always thought they would bring me and your father back together someday, but I screwed that up like I did almost everything concerning our family over the years. Now that he's gone, I finally get it."

"Get what?"

"The real reason I held on to them for this long. It was so I could get them to the person who's now their rightful owner." He put a hand covered in silver rings on Will's bony knee. "I don't want to waste any more time. I don't want to screw this up too."

Will peered at the box, ran his fingers over the comics, and pulled out an old copy of *Swamp Thing*. He turned the fragile yellow pages carefully, like his uncle had done, and tried to see what his father saw in those faded four-color images. He tried to see his dad. He couldn't — not right then. But Jack could. He could see

Hank all over the young version of his older brother sitting next to him on the porch.

"I know you're too old for comic books, Will. Maybe you could stick them away in a closet somewhere, and maybe they're still worth something. Who knows, maybe they can pay for a few years of college down the road. I know some of these things can be pretty valuable. But whatever you decide to do with them is up to you. They're yours."

Will kept scanning the pages. "Thanks, Uncle Jack," he said for the second time. His words still sounded thin and forced, but this time Jack could hear something else. He grabbed Will and pulled him in over the box for a hug. Will laid the *Swamp Thing* comic on the porch and hugged him back. While holding him tight, Jack whispered into his ear, "*Detective Comics,* number eighty-three, page twelve, across the top of the Sea-Monkeys ad. I wrote a number. Someone will always answer that number—always. Do you hear me, son? There's an entire world out there that belongs to you—and you alone. You're my blood. There's nothing more important than that. Nothing."

Will found himself hugging his uncle back as hard as he could. He felt a hard lump of metal tucked under his uncle's arm, against his ribs. It had to be a gun, he thought. His dad hated guns. Will had never even seen one in real life. He almost pulled back and asked Jack about it, but he didn't. It was Jack who let go.

He pushed himself up off the porch, wiped at his face with both hands, and walked away from the house without saying goodbye. He looked back as he got in the car and watched his nephew pull out another tattered issue— *The Green Arrow & The Green Lantern: Hard Traveling Heroes.* It had been one of Hank's favorites. He pulled the Ruger P95 out of his holster and slipped it into the glove box before he cranked up the SUV and carefully backed it out of the drive. He knew Hank would never forgive him for exposing his son to his world, but Hank was dead, and Jack would be, too, eventually. And now the Parsons family name—and all the respect it commanded throughout the Southeast—was not going to end with him. It didn't have to. No more need for grooming one of the idiots who worked under him. Fate had provided Jack with an heir. All he needed to do now was wait for the call, and he was sure the call would come.

TONYA D. PRICE

Payback

FROM *Fiction River*

ON A WARM September morning I had gone out to pick up the
Sunday *Boston Globe* at the end of my driveway when I spotted a
big red dog racing toward me, running smack down the middle of
Pleasant Street. He gave me a quick check before twisting his an-
vil-shaped head to look back at the direction he had come. His ears
lay flat on the top of his head and his brown eyes had the wide-eyed
stare of a wild animal desperate to escape a predator.

My guess was he was either full Doberman or a mix. I called to
him but he didn't slow down, instead the sound of a human voice
seemed to panic him into picking up his pace. Looking back up the
dirt road I tried to make out what had spooked the poor thing so
bad. A powder blue Porsche raced toward me, kicking up a cloud
of dust.

People drove too fast down the narrow country road all the time
so the speed didn't spook me. The hand sticking out the passenger
window pointing a gun at the dog—that spooked me.

I froze as my mind struggled to make sense of what I saw. Two
quick gunshots jolted me out of my indecision. We had a six-foot-
high boulder at the corner of my driveway. For over five years I had
cursed that boulder every time I had to plow the snow around the
thing, now I used it for cover and blessed that rock for saving my
life.

The Porsche sped by. The guy leaning out the passenger window
fired two more rounds at the escaping dog.

People being mean to each other I could take, but I could never
abide cruelty aimed at some poor dog. Feeling helpless, and mad

as hell at the idiot behind the wheel of the Porsche, I ran out from my hiding spot and picked up a rock off my stone wall, hurling it hard at the car.

Maybe a good scare would cause them to leave the dog alone. In college I spent four years on the bench as the third-string pitcher. Couldn't find the plate to save my life. This time I nailed the Porsche with a softball-sized piece of granite, smashing the rear window just as the car slowed on the curve down our hill.

The wheels squealed on the pavement and I smelled burned rubber as the car took the curve and vanished out of sight.

My first reaction: serves the idiots right if they crashed their fancy car.

My second reaction: throwing a rock at a car could land me in jail.

A few minutes later the Porsche reappeared, backing up the street so fast the car swerved left and right as the driver struggled to keep control. This time the gun sticking out the passenger window pointed my way.

Inside our house, my husband and six-month-old baby daughter took their morning nap together in our bedroom. I started to run toward the house but stopped. If I ran inside, I might be leading these lunatics to my family.

Living out in the country, we had no neighbors close by to run to for help.

I'd left the cell phone on my nightstand. I was the one the men were after.

In an effort to lead them away from the house, I ran into the woods. Too scared to look behind me, I ran as fast as I could for as long as I could on the narrow path, taking care not to trip on the tree roots sticking up along the ground.

The men didn't call after me.

They didn't fire their gun at me.

But I was sure they were behind me.

About a half hour later, I reached Iron Mine Pond. I waded into the warm water and hid among the lily pads, waiting for the men from the Porsche to arrive.

After ten minutes of swatting flies and mosquitoes, I began to wonder if maybe the guys had come to their senses and not bothered to follow me. After another five minutes, I pulled myself out of the water, my clothes wet and my shoes waterlogged.

On the way home I kept off the path, taking care to wind my way through the wetlands, risking tick bites over being spotted by the men who had fired at the dog.

As I walked, I began to calm down. Reason replaced panic.

No doubt the men had thought better of going after me and had decided to go home rather than get into a confrontation. Shooting at a dog was probably a misdemeanor. Shooting at a person would definitely get you jail time. The worse that would come of the whole affair would be a court case over smashing the car window.

I'd never been in trouble and they pointed the gun at me. I decided I would probably not be in that much trouble after all. Maybe I could claim self-defense.

I was looking forward to a hot bath and getting dinner ready by the time I came within sight of my house.

Instead, I spotted the Porsche in my driveway, smashed rear window and all. Neither the driver nor his gun-happy passenger appeared to be inside. Where had they gone?

They weren't in the yard.

My house was a two-story colonial, cedar shingles with a big wide farmer's porch. I didn't see them on the porch.

After checking again that the men weren't lurking in the yard somewhere I edged closer to the house and saw the front door stood ajar. My husband grew up in Manhattan. He never left the door unlocked, let alone open.

More likely the men had forced their way into the house and they had left the door open, but why?

Why even go into the house? The men might have been mad at me for throwing a rock at their car but they knew I wasn't inside the house. Were they waiting for me to return?

The nearest police station was five miles away. The nearest house, three miles away. What would the men do to my family if I tried to run to get help? I doubted I could do much good in the house. My family's best bet would be for me to get help.

We had two Volvos in the garage but the Porsche blocked the driveway. Maybe I didn't need to get into my car if I could start the Porsche.

Woods lined both sides of my driveway. Using the thick pine trees for cover, I crept along the ground, staying close to the old stone fence as I inched toward the sports car.

Every few minutes, I checked the door.

With no sign of the men in the yard or on the porch, I made

my way to where a large forsythia blocked the view of the driveway. Taking care to stay out of the sightline from the house, I dashed in front of the car, then walked half-bent-over around to the driver's side.

I tried to open the door latch. The men might have left my front door open but they had locked their car.

I decided the smart thing to do would be to walk up the street in hopes of finding a car to flag down. Then I could use someone's cell to call the police. The plan seemed the best course of action even though part of me wanted to charge inside the house, but what good would that do? I might even get my family killed.

The plan made sense. I might even have followed it if I hadn't heard my baby crying.

And my husband shouting.

And the single shot.

I started to run for the house, not caring if anyone saw me or not.

There was more shouting.

Then I heard Jim's voice.

He was alive.

I needed to keep him that way.

It was the gunfire that sent me running toward the backyard gate. My husband had used a bike lock to keep the gate shut. I put both hands on the gate's top bar, jumped and pulled my legs over, landing on my feet.

The shed was new and built to look like a mini-version of our house. I didn't have the key but I decided I would smash the door down if I had to. There were tools inside. Tools I needed if I were to try to save Jim.

The double doors for driving the John Deere riding lawn mower were padlocked but we never locked the side door. I slipped inside and searched for a weapon. Something not too heavy to carry. Something that could kill.

Something I could handle.

The axe was too heavy and not terribly accurate. I went for my fishing knife. The seven-inch, serrated blade would make a nasty cut. A short bungee cord served as a belt. I pushed one end through the knife-sheaf belt loop and tied the cord around my waist. My long work shirttail just covered the knife sheaf.

I still had my old softball bat but the men might be able to get that away from me. An old can of wasp spray would be more effective. Jim and I never owned a gun—except for a cordless nail gun, heavy as hell. At least it was loaded with a tape of nails. I just prayed it still worked.

Then I went to try and save my husband and my child.

From the shed, I could see the large copper clock on our raised deck that overlooked the backyard. An hour had passed since I first saw the dog running down the street. The sun shone overhead, a harsh glare.

The large windows in our sunroom provided a clear view inside. Both the sunroom and kitchen appeared empty. Two entrances led into the house from the back: a cellar door into the basement or the deck slider. I chose the slider.

When I was halfway across the yard I heard the familiar sound of the slider opening. Caught in a no-man's-land without any cover, I charged forward, lugging the nailer. I ran to hide below the raised deck.

I dived underneath the planks, lying facedown on the stone pebble base.

A single set of footsteps on the deck above told me someone had come outside alone. There had been two men in the Porsche, but if I could get rid of one of them, then the odds might be a little better for rescuing my husband and daughter.

I needed to keep whoever was above me in the yard, separate from his buddy. I grabbed a nearby pebble and threw it into the woods on the edge of the lawn.

I heard footsteps going toward the house.

Jim's cry kept going off in my head. I had to do something and soon.

"Hey!" I stayed hidden by the side of the deck, fighting the pounding in my head and the voice screaming that I had just made a huge mistake.

Convinced surprise might be my only hope, I knelt on the ground, holding the wasp spray at my side, and set the nailer on the ground beside me.

The footsteps stopped. They changed direction, walking toward the stairs leading to the lawn rather than back toward the house.

I could hear someone on the stairs.

A teenage boy with long hair and a NY JETS cap peeked around the edge of the deck. He was a small, skinny kid. He spotted me, breaking into a wide smile that showed his braces. Up until that moment I hadn't gotten a good look at either of the guys.

Why did he have to be so damn young?

"Well, well, well . . . What are you doing out here? We've been looking for you. That Porsche you wrecked, that's Matt's daddy's car. Matt loves that car. He isn't very happy with you right now." The boy laughed. "Nope, not happy at all." He brushed a lock of long greasy brown hair out of his eyes. He didn't look cruel. He looked young. Young and stupid.

Except he was cruel, I reminded myself. He had a gun tucked in his pants' waistband. A gun he had used to shoot at the dog and me.

I had no choice but to rise to my feet. I aimed the wasp spray at him and squeezed the button. My attack came so unexpectedly I caught him full in the face. It must have hurt like hell by the sound of his screams.

Above us the slider squeaked open. "Dave? You okay, man?"

Dave wiped his eyes with his hand, then pulled out his gun. His arm swiped in every direction as if frantic to find me. In his wild swatting, he struck my arm with his free hand, then brought the gun around.

I dropped to the ground and balanced the nailer on the concrete deck footing. A bullet whizzed by my head.

There's a good chance I had my eyes closed when I pulled the trigger. I only knew I shot off three nails. When I opened my eyes I found only one of the three-inch nails had hit the boy.

Right in the middle of his forehead.

As he fell, his gun went off, breaking the window in the door to the garage.

On television, you hear stories of people who survive getting a nail in their head. I debated if I should fire again. I couldn't take a chance he might attack another time. His eyes stared at the sky. He didn't blink.

I didn't feel anything for him. All I felt was desperation to save my family.

"Shit! What did you do? What did you fucking do? Dave?" A second teenager, about the same age as the first, rounded the edge of the deck. This one looked more athletic than the other kid. He wore a muscle shirt and he had muscles to show off.

I raised the wasp spray again but nothing came out. The boy

picked up his friend's gun. Insanely, I didn't freeze this time. Instead I thought, if he shoots me I can't save Jim.

I dropped the heavy nail gun and the empty wasp-spray can. I ran as fast as I could away from him toward the far end of the house.

The fence wrapped around the entire yard. I was trapped but I ran anyway.

I had no plan.

The gun went off again. Something whished past my right ear, but I ran harder and started to zigzag my way across the yard. Once a television reporter had said running in a zigzag pattern could make you a harder target to hit.

At the edge of the house, I decided to try and leap the picket fence again. I slowed down. If I didn't clear the fence and had to hang for a moment at the top and hoist myself over, I would make an easy target.

Overthinking such things usually leads to trouble. This time proved no different. My foot struck two of the pickets. Rather than go over the fence I fell down on the lawn, landing in front of the boy with the gun.

He stood over me, his hand steady. His finger on the trigger. "Get on your feet." The order didn't sound like it came from a teenager.

This time I had no choice. He had me.

I raised my hands in defeat. "Okay."

He motioned with the gun in the direction of the deck. "We just wanted to scare you. Just hurt you a little bit for breaking the window. You didn't need to kill Dave, you bitch."

Maybe talking to him could save my family. Worth a try, anyway. "Windows can be paid for. I'll pay for the window. Shooting a dog is a minor offense. Shooting a person is murder."

"Yes, I know. You can tell that to the judge."

Then he had no plans to kill me. The little bit of hope helped. If he wasn't going to kill me, he wasn't planning on killing my family.

We went onto the deck and into the silent house. Everything in the kitchen and sunroom looked the way I had left things before I went out to do a bit of gardening.

"Where's the baby?" My daughter would be hungry by now. She should be crying but I heard nothing. "Jim?"

From the upstairs my husband called out, "Sarah?"

The boy pushed me forward. "Into the living room. "

I yelled, "Is the baby all right?"

The boy leveled the gun at me. "Shut up."

He wasn't able to stop my husband's answer. "We are both okay. Just . . . just I'm tied up."

I feared the worst as I entered the living room but the basket of white laundry I had left beside our brown leather sectional was still there. The CDs remained in place in the bookcase beside the collection of piano music my husband stored in the bookcase.

The boy walked over to my husband's grand piano. "Yours?"

"No."

He ran his index finger over the polished top of Jim's beloved Kawai. "You don't play?"

"No."

The boy didn't say anything. He just stared at me until I felt I had to offer him something. "I play the guitar."

My Martin hung from the wall. The boy smiled and walked over to admire the instrument. He took a step back, raised the gun, fired into the guitar, sending Madagascar Rosewood splinters into the air. Steel wires flew across the room like shrapnel.

"That Porsche you wrecked. That's my father's car. He's going to be plenty mad when he sees what you did to it."

So this was his game. "I told you I'll pay for the window."

"Good, you can start tonight." The boy cocked his head to one side. "Any other instruments you play?"

"No."

"Nice house you have here." He took his time walking around the room, then motioned toward the hall. "Why don't you take me on a tour?"

I led the way down the hall, stopping at the bathroom. Not much he could destroy there. "Toilet, shower."

"Let's take a look."

When I renovated the bathroom I added a handcrafted sink.

He pointed at the two oil paintings with his gun. "Tell me about the pictures."

The matched set of my niece's worthless art-camp work gave me a chance to divert attention from the sink. "They are originals. A gift from my mother who passed away last year. Please . . . don't destroy them."

"Ah, okay." With a step back into the hallway he turned and fired into the sink.

"No!" I lunged forward toward the sink, but there was no way to repair the damage.

A large chunk of porcelain cracked and fell to the tile.

The boy laughed. "Fancy sink, isn't it? Worth much more than a couple of kids' paintings." He pointed at my forehead. "Looks like you got cut."

Sure enough, a look into the vanity mirror showed a cut above my left eye. Blood had started to drip down my cheek. I wiped it with my hand, smearing it along my face.

I tried to hide my anger.

In an attempt to distract him I asked, "Why were you chasing the dog?"

He didn't seem to hear me at first. Something seemed to distract him. Then he directed his attention at me again. "What?"

"The dog you were chasing down the street. Why were you chasing it and trying to shoot it?"

The boy ran his palm over the peach fuzz on his chin. "Damn thing barked at my car when I came to a stoplight. We fired a warning shot and he just stood in the middle of the road barking his head off. Wouldn't get out of the way. I tried to run him down but he took off. What is it to you?"

"I just wondered. Maybe he thought he was protecting his territory."

"He was just a crazy dog."

"Who made you mad." I regretted the mistake as soon as I spoke.

The boy's face reddened. "Not as mad as you made me." He spoke in a calm tone, without emotion but I could hear the threat.

I had something more valuable than a sink to protect. Maybe if he destroyed enough of my possessions he would leave my family alone.

He grabbed my arm and pushed me forward. "Show me the rest of the house."

At the end of the hall, we entered my office. Here he would think he had found a gold mine of possessions to destroy.

"Nice monitor."

My thirty-four-inch Ultra Apple Monitor dominated my desk. Nabbed on eBay, I did love that monitor. Beside the monitor sat my scanner and an antique Waterford lamp with a large brass base, my first Brimfield Antique Show buy. The Hooker mahogany desk would be another alluring target. Behind the desk, placed against the wall, sat my curled cherry, hand-carved grand upright piano my mother and I had restored over a summer when I was fifteen. On the wall I had a handmade German windup clock with a big pendulum that rang a single chime with a deep, rich sound.

The boy took his time examining each piece. "Your husband has two pianos?"

"No," I admitted. "This one is mine."

He fired into the elaborately carved fern in the middle of the piano. "I knew you played. You look like a piano teacher."

"I don't play. I was saving the piano for my daughter."

The boy laughed. "Oops!" He turned and fired into the clock, severing the metal spring. Small metal disks clanged as the internal parts broke apart.

He shot into the desk, then the monitor glass, laughing each time he destroyed something. He seemed to be having such a good time. When he ran out of bullets he reached inside his jeans' pocket and pulled out a packet. He started to load the magazine without even bothering to watch me.

I might not get another chance to try to escape and I had to escape before we went upstairs in search of my best-loved possessions.

I didn't have much time. I grabbed the lamp. The thing weighed almost ten pounds but it wasn't too heavy for me to lift. Without trying to unplug it I swung the big brass base at the boy's head like a baseball bat.

I missed his head but hit the hand holding the gun and he dropped it onto the desk.

The boy ducked, covering his head with his hands as I took another swing and missed again. I picked up the empty gun and ran toward the front door. He followed.

I thought he would catch me, but as I got to the door I remembered he and his friend had left the door open.

He chased me outside. Standing on the porch he screamed, "Come back or I'll kill your family."

I knew better. To punish me, he needed me. That was my advantage. If I escaped, he would have to chase me and capture me. His game was to make me watch him destroy the things I loved. Without me to watch, he wouldn't kill my family. He had already proved that by waiting for me to return to the house.

Without the gun he had no weapon, so for the moment we were an even match. I had the gun. He had the bullets.

What I needed was a weapon.

I remembered the nail gun in the backyard. Too far away. Besides, the boy would catch me when I tried to jump the fence.

In desperation I spun around looking for something, anything I could use to try and stop the boy.

The only thing I could find was his Porsche.

Turnabout was fair, right?

I ran toward the car. "You think a smashed window was bad? You want to play smash things? Let's smash your things now."

Massachusetts has lots of rocks. Plenty of rocks. In the spring they rise out of the ground we have so many. I picked up a good five-pounder and ran toward the Porsche.

"No, get away from there. I'm warning you." I could hear the panic in his voice.

I held the rock over the car. "Get down on the ground. Put your hands over your head."

"Fuck you." The boy ran toward me.

I dropped the stone on the hood and ran down the driveway without a plan other than to escape. He was a lot faster than me, even in my prime.

I picked up another stone and waited for him. Just as he reached me I threw the stone toward his foot, hoping to break a bone so he couldn't run.

I missed.

He reached out and grabbed my left hand, then twisted my arm behind me. "So you like to throw stones, huh?"

Looking past the boy I saw the dog inching forward as if stalking prey. Ears laid flat, hair on his back standing straight up, his snarl showing teeth, the dog took a position just out of reach of the boy.

He began barking and barked and barked.

The boy turned around and kicked at the dog, "Get out of here."

The dog just barked louder. Maybe he sensed the boy's fear without the gun.

It was all the distraction I needed. With my free hand, I reached under my shirt and pulled out my fishing knife, then ran at the boy and sunk the knife in his back.

On his left side.

Where I figured his heart should be.

He sunk to the ground, moaning, then went silent. The dog inched toward the still body, barking louder than before.

I ran for the open door. Back to my family and to call for help.

I had thrown a rock to save a dog, and ended up killing two boys. Even as I rushed into the house I knew the boy had gotten what he wanted. He had destroyed something I valued almost as much as my family—that image I had of myself as a good, decent person, incapable of what I had just done.

I would never look at myself the same, but my family survived.

That was my payback.

SUZANNE PROULX

If You Say So

FROM *False Faces*

SHE'S WAY OUT of your league, a classy New York woman who would be unapproachable. Yet, remarkably, she approaches you.

In the park, early spring. You're out there with your DSLR and your tripod, concentrating on getting scenes with trees reflecting in the water, and the water reflecting the sky, so at first glance it's a puzzle. The kind of thing someone would look at, and at first wouldn't know what they were seeing. Maybe they had it upside down—then it would resolve and make sense.

It's a tricky process, and you're wrapped up in it, so you don't even sense her presence until she speaks.

"Are you taking pictures of me?"

She's the kind of woman people take pictures of. She's perfect. She's dressed probably fashionably, definitely expensively. She even smells expensive. She doesn't exactly take your breath away, but for a moment she does take your words away.

After an awkward couple of seconds you manage to answer. "Sure," you croak. "I mean, I'm not—wasn't—but I'll take your picture. If you want me to."

"Yeah," she says, and she smiles at you, a smile that makes you want to jump straight up, but you contain yourself. Then she says, "But you know what? I take better pictures when they're candid."

You stand there dumbly, as if you don't know what that word means. How are you supposed to take a candid shot of someone who'd just asked for a picture and she's standing right there?

"So I'll just wander over there," she says, indicating some trees in the opposite direction of the lake. "Do you have one of those big lenses? You look like you might have one of those big ones in your bag." The way she says this, it sounds—well, provocative. A woman like this, anything could sound that way. But those specific words . . .

Yeah, in fact you have a couple of different lenses in your bag. You have a lens the size of an elephant's trunk, but not in this bag. And while you're standing there, with your elephant's trunk in your other bag, she walks away. You grab the biggest lens you have and aim the camera at her. At her back. She seems to sense it and turns half around and holds up her hands in a way that says *stop!* Her sleeves fall back to reveal that her gloves go up at least as far as her elbows.

"Not yet," she says. "Wait till I get over there." She turns and keeps walking. The way a woman walks away from you when she knows you're watching.

She goes toward the trees and twirls around once without looking back. Click. She looks into her bag. Click. She aims her face to the sky. Click. She takes the sunglasses off, sits on a bench, crosses her legs, pulls something out of her bag, looks at it. Click, click, click. She stands, picks a piece of trash off the ground, drops it in a trash can. Everything she does, every pose, looks exactly like a picture in a magazine. And then, without even waving at you, she melts away.

There was supposed to be more. Pictures, then phone numbers, perhaps some more flirting. Instead, it's like the whole thing never happened. Like a magical interlude that took place only in your head.

But then, there are the pictures. You stick the camera in the bag and head for where you saw her last, but she's gone.

After that you can't go back to shooting landscapes. You head home, or what's passing for home this week. As you walk, you think about how, in your mind, the situation had been so full of promise. You fantasized things, simple things to be sure (getting her number), more complex things (walking into a restaurant with her, nibbling on her neck), impossible things.

Why did she pick you? Of course, it isn't immediately apparent that when you're not house-sitting, you crash at your sister's place in Queens, or that your current job, in addition to house-sitting, consists of walking people's dogs. Maybe you looked prosperous. Maybe you didn't look like a twenty-one-year-old with no niche in the world. A person who once wanted to be a tattoo artist, but then realized that would mean you'd have to get a tattoo and you didn't want one. Or maybe a wedding photographer, only you didn't think you had the temperament to put up with brides.

You don't think of yourself as the type that even normal, ordinary, girl-next-door types would approach, because they never have.

And if you thought she was flirting with you, you were dead wrong. You'll probably never see her again.

Of course you're going to keep your eyes open. Walking the dogs in the park, you're going to pass by that bench and look at it, and she won't be there. Instead there'll be an old woman, feeding the pigeons. You think you see her in a crowd, but by the time you get close enough to know for sure, either it's not her, or the person you thought was her is gone.

When you head to your sister's to check your mail, you show her the pictures, and you ask her, without going into a lot of detail, if maybe this is somebody famous, recognizable.

"I'm flattered that you think I can recognize every midlevel celebrity or fashion icon," Diane says, scrolling through the photos. "But, no." Diane shakes her head. "But she's too old for you anyway." You didn't even ask that, but she sensed it.

"I know that," you say. "Also completely, just stratospherically out of my league. Wait, she's not that old."

"She's rich," Diane says. "Did you say she was tall?"

"Shorter than me." This makes her not exceptionally tall.

"So probably not a model. And in those clothes, she's either, hmm . . . married to an old rich guy, or maybe she has rich parents, but either way . . ."

"I know. Out of my league."

"I was going to say, plenty able to pay for a photo session."

You want to protest. *But she was coming on to me.*

"Maybe she's just really good at shopping," you say. "Like, at thrift stores. Getting things for free."

"Sure," Diane says. "Maybe she's homeless. Maybe she could crash at your place. Oh wait, no. How were you supposed to get those pictures back to her anyway?"

"Yeah," you say. "Good question."

"What happens in the Forest of Arden, stays in the Forest of Arden," Diane says, as if Central Park is a magical forest and the whole episode is only your fantasy.

Still you go on, looking for her, aware that she's out there somewhere. She's changed the way you look at things. Where once you looked for architectural incongruence, or ironic juxtapositions of cityscape and nature, now you look at people. Of course, you're looking for her and not really at anyone else. Time passes, you lose hope.

And then, maybe three weeks later, you see her again. You're just done with your late-morning dog walk. It's raining buckets, cold drops finding their way under your poncho and sliding down your back. You're dodging umbrellas and ducking under and then out of canopies, trying not to get too soaked, and she's under one of the canopies.

You don't even know what made you glance up at just the right time. The first thing you register is, she has on gloves again, red ones. You stop abruptly, someone runs into you, curses, apologizes. She looks straight at you. You look back. A moment of shock. And you go on. For half a block. Then, as if she mesmerized you to do it, you go into the drugstore, buy an umbrella—a day like this, they have them right up front—walk outside, and open it before you head back.

She's waiting, as if she knew you were going to buy her an umbrella. You pass the umbrella to her under a waterfall of rain, and she takes it and gives you that smile. Which gives you courage to speak.

"I've got your pictures. How should I send them to you?"

"You have them here?"

"Not here." In fact the camera is with you, the camera bag under your poncho making you look like a hunchback, but you don't want it to get wet. "I could email them to you."

"Can you text them to me? I don't email."

"Sure," you say. "What's your number?" You pull out your phone. Don't care if it gets wet.

"Buy me a beer first."

After a bright burst of hope and happiness, you take her to a place on Eighth where you can get a free hot dog with a beer, if you want. She only wants the beer.

"Took you long enough to find me," she says, in that same tone she used when she asked if you were taking her picture.

"You just disappeared."

She moves her hands around as if shaping the air. "Well, I figured you'd find me if you were interested, and you seemed interested." She spirals her hand down and caresses her beer. You note that she hasn't taken those gloves off, which seems odd.

What else is wrong with this picture? Guys like you don't get to sit in bars with women who look like this. But you're not going to question it.

"I didn't picture you as a beer kind of girl," you say.

"Woman," she corrects.

"Sorry. I didn't picture you as—"

"Oh, so you did picture me." She gazes into your eyes. You sit up straighter and become aware of your breathing. "You thought about me."

You nod.

"But you didn't try to find me."

"I thought I saw you everywhere," you say. The words rush out. You didn't mean to say them, but they keep coming until she stops you.

"You still haven't given me your number."

"Okay," you say. "Here, it's—"

"Write it down for me," she says. "I don't write things down."

You pat your pockets, thinking you have a pen somewhere but no paper. In the end you borrow a pen from the bartender and write your number on a napkin. She takes it, stashes it somewhere, and takes a big swig of her beer. You love the way she drinks beer. It's so unlike the rest of her image.

"I'll call you," she says. As she talks she makes motions with her hands, as if she's casting a spell. Or weaving a web to catch you in. "Just for what it's worth, I am a romantic. I like it when people write poetry about me, if they're so moved."

"I—I'm a photographer."

"You said you saw me everywhere. That's the kind of thing I like to hear. It was almost a poem, the way you said that." She takes another less-than-dainty gulp of her beer.

"Okay, I—"

"Should I happen to call you, you can't call me back," she says. "I don't answer the phone. I do read texts. I don't text back, but I might read them, if they're worthy. If you sent a poem for each one of the photographs that you took." She stands, drains her beer. You stand when she does.

"Oh, finish your drink," she says. "And thank you for the umbrella." She picks it up. "Red's my favorite color. For an umbrella."

And she sweeps out. You start after her, but the bartender reminds you that you owe for the drinks.

She doesn't do email, doesn't text, doesn't write, and doesn't buy drinks, and you think, *Fair enough.*

The rain continues to fall, but at a much softer rate, as you dash out and scan the streets for the red umbrella. Oh, they're out there, red umbrellas. You pick a likely looking one and head for it. After a couple of blocks, you still haven't caught up. So many red umbrellas, you doubt you're tracking the right one. You should have bought the one with black polka dots, only it didn't seem dignified. Your phone rings.

"Are you following me?"

Definitely flirty. You stop. Again, someone runs into you. No apology this time.

"I don't think I am," you say. "But I tried."

She laughs, a beautiful melodious laugh, because of course she would have that kind of laugh. "Well now you have my number." You get the feeling that wherever she is, she can see you.

"I forgot to ask your name," you say. "I'm Asher."

"Name me," she says. "Put my name as you think it is, in one of your poems."

So you dub her Rosalind. It just comes to you.

Like anyone else you've gone through a phase of writing lousy poetry. You threw the poetry away of course, on pain of anyone ever seeing it. You sit there—in Casey Feinman's place in Murray Hill this week, an actor with three very spoiled cats—and look at the pictures. Scroll past those first ones, the landscapes, which in truth don't quite give the illusion you were after, but they're not bad. Some of them you legit can't tell what they are. They look more like some kind of Rorschach test than what you had in mind, but they might still work.

But forget that, focus on the woman. Write the best poem possible and send the best shot.

The end result is reminiscent of something you read, or heard, possibly some rock lyric. Maybe "Uptown Girl." Well, apologies to Billy Joel, and off it goes, along with the picture, your favorite. The one where she was just sitting on the bench with her legs crossed and looking anywhere but at you. You send it off, go through the nightly cat-feeding ritual, and fall asleep on Casey Feinman's lumpy couch.

You wake up and see, on the coffee table, your wallet spread open. Your cards, all of them—ID, credit card, library card, gym-membership card that was expired anyway—have been replaced with black valentines. The valentines have messages scrawled on them in metallic Sharpie, the usual messages in a girlish script. "Miss You!" "Kiss Me Quick!" "Bye-Bye!" Then you wake up for real.

Just a dream. A cautionary dream. Because even as you were writing the lousy poetry, part of your brain was thinking other thoughts. She's too good to be true, therefore she is not true. She's after something. She's crazy. She's a spy. She's married. She's actually a man.

No. You would know that. She's not a man. Not with those hands. Maybe she's crazy. You can't refute that. You've heard the phrase *don't stick your dick in the crazy,* and yet that's just what you're aching to do.

Married? Probably not. It's not like you could see a ring with those gloves on, but if she's married, why is she asking for romantic texts? So nope on that one.

Maybe she's a spy. You can't refute that either. Spying on . . . what? You? She's just a very compelling woman, and you should probably text her all those photos and forget about her because then she'll have what she wants and you'll never see her again.

When you're giving four dogs their afternoon walk, your phone rings and you give a little skip because it has to be her, nobody else ever calls you. And it's your sister, saying you've got some mail that looks like a check. So at least some things are looking up.

You write one last poem, saying that you would like to replace all her credit cards with valentines from you, and you send her the rest of the pictures. Immediately you wonder why the hell you did that. Then you realize. It's like you couldn't take the suspense of wondering if she'd call, so you made sure she wouldn't. No worthy poem, no more suspense.

You're done with her. End of story. Period. Instead of anticipation of seeing her, or getting her phone calls, you feel relaxed, relieved. You can look at it dispassionately. You did all the giving, she did all the taking, and you got nothing. But you didn't lose much either.

Not two hours after you've sent this off, your phone rings. A blocked number, so you don't answer, but even if it was her, you wouldn't answer, because what's the point? You grit your teeth and tell yourself you don't need this. Chick wouldn't even tell you her real name. You had to make one up. You don't need her, she's playing with you. Any connection would have been only temporary anyway, for immediate gratification of base desires. Replace those valentines with, say, a poker deck. Or Cards Against Humanity.

Then your phone beeps, once every three minutes or so, reminding you that you've got a new voicemail. An annoying chirp, like an electronic drip. So of course eventually you have to listen to it or delete it.

When you hear her breathless honey voice saying she *loves* the poem, you start thinking that maybe she, too, wants only immediate gratification of base desires, so yeah, this could work. As long as she knows you're not after her trust fund, or whatever, and you know she's not after — what? You can't even think what she might get out of you, other than free photos, which she already got, and it's not like that cost you anything. As long as you're both completely honest about who you are and what you expect, what could go wrong?

Various things, as it turns out. First there is the dancing around of whether you're going on a date, and what constitutes a date, what you would both like to do on a date, and all that. You end up going to another bar, having beers and bar food, and then heading out on the street and holding her hand.

Which is still gloved. Kinda weird. Again you think: What is she covering up? Bad tattoos? Pus-oozing eczema? Slash marks? It's like you're getting a fetish about them. Or not about them, about seeing her hands.

So. "How come you always wear gloves? It's not that cold."

"Oh," she says. "I'm a hand model. I really have to do everything to protect my hands. I even wear them indoors." Then she puts her hands up to your face and holds it while she stares into your eyes. "Does it bother you? Do you mind?" Then she kisses you. Or at any rate that's what you remember. And the next thing you remember is her asking to go to your place. Or, technically, Casey Feinman's place. You begin taking steps in that direction, and so does she.

"And you don't have like a roommate or something?"

"Just three cats," you say.

She stops dead. "Oh, that won't work. I'm deathly allergic to cats."

You stop, too. "How about your place?"

"That won't work either," she says. "You have to get rid of them."

For one wild moment you think about it. You wouldn't get rid of them permanently, of course. Put them in the carrier, put the carrier somewhere outside the apartment. Your head clears a little. Realistically, if she's that allergic, that won't do it. You'd have to vacuum the place for hours. But for a minute there, Casey's cats were in jeopardy.

Probably you wouldn't have done anything to them. You have less than a week left there, and then you'll be at Sid Elam's place. Sid has an aquarium.

But it's a dicey moment. If you say things are moving too fast, that sounds like you have some long-term relationship in mind, rather than something quick and dirty, and—you don't. You just can't see it.

"Give me a week," you say. "To get the place aired out and vac-uumed and all. Not even a week. Six days." It's a test. If she's gone in a week, if you never see her again, well, you tried, and you will come back in the night and sneak in and kill those cats. Just kid-ding.

She pouts a bit, predictably, then says she can't wait, and you make out a little more and then reluctantly tear yourselves away from each other. And you're floating. Bouncing around, literally hitting your head, as you go up Casey's stairs, on a plank you've never hit your head on before. Six days.

Five days. You're still floating, but you've sent her a couple of texts with no response. You defy her instructions and call her, which gets you nothing but a nice recording of her voice that somehow causes you to float again and makes you want to call the number about a hundred times.

Four days. She leaves you a voicemail. Curious how she manages that since the phone is always on your person, always on, and you'd answer any call on the off chance it might be her. Still, a voicemail telling you she will be coming out of a photo shoot at approxi-mately three o'clock today. So if you want to see her, you should text her at two forty-five if you think you'll be there. You do, and you're there, and you don't see her. You're not floating quite as

high. You text back that you missed her, where was she? You hear
nothing. You text again. Nothing again.

Three days. A black mood descends. Why is she playing these
games?

Your phone rings, and it's her.

"Sorry," she says. "Things took a little longer than I thought, and
I guess you didn't wait?"

You pull out of your black mood. "How long was I supposed to
wait, anyway? I hung around for like an hour."

"I looked out the window when I took a break and I didn't see
you," she says. "I've got another one tomorrow. Earlier, at nine.
Text me if you want to see me then, and—"

"Why text you? Why can't I tell you right now that I want to see
you then?"

She's silent.

"Okay," you say. "You mean you'll be coming out at nine or going there at nine?"

"Going there," she says. "It should take about an hour." She gives
you an address in the warehouse district, then adds, "Text me when
you get there."

"If you say so." But a bit of annoyance creeps into your previ-
ously buoyant mood.

And then it turns out you can't make it because, of all things,
you have a job interview, something your sister set up at her colleague's husband's law firm. So you text that to her: *I have a job
interview at nine, other side of the city. Don't know how long it's going to
take. Will text you when I know.*

You come out of your job interview, turn on your phone, and
there's a voicemail. "Oh, dear," the voicemail says. "That is not the
kind of text I want to get. I want to get texts that say how much you
want to see me, not that you don't want to see me at all. What is
your problem anyway? Do you want to make this happen, or what?"

You do want to make this happen. Obediently, you text her right
away: you really, really want to see her, and you're sorry you missed
her. And your phone rings moments later. You answer it with a little
shudder of anticipation.

"That's better," she says. "Okay. I was very lonely when I came
out of my photo shoot, but I'm better now, and I'm hungry."

"Come over now," you say, being ensconced in your new cat-free establishment. "I'll make you lunch. I'll cook." Sid has a great kitchen with all the stuff. Stuff you don't even know what it does.

"Just give me the address," she says. "I'll be there in about an hour."

You half-believe she won't show up. You race around getting items for a simple kind of lunch you think she'll like. Heirloom tomatoes, French bread, mozzarella cheese, fresh basil. You're almost in a frenzy.

Of course she's late, but she does appear at the door, dolled up as usual. "I already ate," she says (and what did you expect?). "But here," she adds, "you can undress me."

The shock nearly stops your heart. She doesn't want to eat, but she wants you to undress her?

"I don't really use my hands," she says. "Because of my job, you know?"

You wonder who dressed her, then. Because buttons that are being undone—and yes, you're doing it—had to first be done. So who did that? Then you don't think of that, you're removing all of her clothes, except the gloves, and all of yours as well. And you're making love to her, and she's lovely, soft in all the right places, creamy, fragrant, noisy, perfect. She doesn't use her hands much, mainly just to position your head where she wants it, but it doesn't matter. She uses everything else.

Afterward you lie there thinking that you still don't know her name. You think of how strippers always take the gloves off first, not that you know this firsthand. You've seen damn few strip shows and none that featured gloves.

In afterglow, you wonder if it would be this good if she hadn't played all those games. Then she tells you that she's now hungry again. You have the first semblance of normalcy as you make the best tomato mozzarella sandwich in the history of the world while she talks to you, telling you about her job. And while she manages to get her clothes back on while wearing those gloves.

When she tastes what you made, she tells you you ought to be a chef.

Then she apologizes for not being able to help clean up and asks to borrow your phone. She doesn't make any calls though, just presses some buttons. You see her, out of the corner of your eye, as you wash the dishes (you were going to wait until she was gone, but then you think it might be good if she sees how expert you are at keeping a kitchen clean; she might want to keep you around). And then she's gone.

After the spell wears off you still feel pretty lighthearted. Okay, you've just had sex with a woman whose real name you don't know, and whose hands you've never seen, and now you're thinking, wondering if you can straighten it out. Learn her name, tell her who you really are and that this sleek, modern apartment is Sid's, not yours. Maybe make something out of this after all. After more sexual encounters, obviously.

You text her right away saying that she's wonderful, and you had a really good time, an understatement, and you hope she did too, and you can't wait to see her again.

And from her? Nothing. Nothing for hours. Nothing for a whole day.

You send her a couple more texts, the kind she likes, about how you are dreaming of her creamy skin, and longing to see her, and in fact looking for her everywhere again.

Nothing.

You call her phone and get her voicemail, as she said you would, because she never answers the phone, but listening to her voice is enough. You leave a couple of tender messages. You try to make them full of innuendo and subtext without being actually dirty. Or sometimes you just listen to her voice.

Nothing from her. Nothing for two days.

You can feel your body language showing defeat as you walk through the city accompanied by four dogs. Your shoulders slump. You try to pump yourself up. You remember everything she said. None of it tells you why she isn't calling you back.

And then, after two days of despair, she does call. It's 11:32 on Saturday morning just as you're dropping dog number four off with his doorman. She sounds slightly breathless, but warm. "So, hi there."

You realize you ought to play it cool but there's no way. "Hello!"

You can almost hear the smile in her voice (she knows she's got you).

"Yeah, hello, you! Listen, sorry I've been so out of touch. I did get your messages."

Before you can answer she goes on.

"I'm reciprocating, that is, can you come over for lunch? I know it's short notice. My place. Well, actually, my parents' place. They're out of town this weekend."

You're shot in the head with glee. "Sure," you say. Anything she wants, at this point, and she knows it.

She gives you an address on Riverside Drive and tells you to come right now, and text when you're like a block away and she'll leave the door open.

Riverside Drive and she doesn't have a doorman? You ask about this.

"No, no, it's a townhome," she says. "A row house. Just come on in, when you get here, I mean, after you've texted me. I'll be busy in the kitchen but I'll come open the door, when you text."

Hey, you're on your way. With a couple of questions.

She said she didn't cook, didn't clean, didn't type, didn't text, and now she's making lunch?

It's not her place but her parents'?

But whatever. You get to her block. You're impressed. You knew she was out of your league. This whole part of town is out of your league. You take a deep breath and text, *I'm a block away, see you soon.* Your heart hammers. She could probably hear it from where she is, if she opened the door. This is some expensive real estate. Sure, row houses, but these are practically historic landmarks. In fact some of them *are* historic landmarks. Narrow but tall. Another deep breath as you stand outside. Do you look presentable? The stairs look endless. The door is open a few inches, as she said it would be, and from your vantage point you can see part of a large entryway, with a chandelier.

You hear a scream. Definitely coming from inside.

You bolt up the stairs, following the scream, as another scream rends the air. You don't have time to admire the entry, the oak staircase, the stained glass, because you're following the sound of her voice. You burst into a room off the hallway and there she is, kneeling on the floor beside an old man who's sprawled out flat. Old enough to be her father.

You recognize him immediately. Almost anyone would. He's a rich and influential old man, prominent, socially and politically connected. Another minute and you'll think of his name, or maybe not. Blood streams out of him, and his face is pale. His lips move. Her father?

Rosalind turns from him to you. Almost as if she just saw you. Almost as if she's surprised. Beside her is a gun.

"Someone shot him," she says clearly. "A man came in with a gun, and shot my husband! Did you see him? He left right before you got here. I'll bet you can catch him. Help me! Go catch him! Take this! Then run!"

Everything moves very slowly. With an easy movement (she's still wearing gloves) she swoops up the gun and tosses it your way in a slow, gentle arc.

And reflexively—

(At the same time things are moving very fast in your head, as it suddenly resolves, every incident with Rosalind playing like a movie on fast rewind. Your texts to her, your phone calls, her borrowing your phone, your encounters, more texts, strange requests, photos of her fairly close, hands up, telling you not to take her picture, more pictures of her taken at a distance, doing ordinary things. The Rorschach has been made very clear. You had been looking at it one way, but you had it upside down. It was all there but you didn't make sense of it in time. It's a different picture now. You don't know everything, but you know exactly how screwed you are.)

—you catch it.

Neighbors

FROM *Epoch*

THEY CAME AT dawn, ground crackling beneath the trample of hooves, amid it the sound of chickens flapping and squawking. Then voices, one among them shouting to dismount. The corn shucks rasped as Rebecca rose, quickly tugging her wool overcoat tight against her gown. She waked the children who shared the bed. As they rubbed questioning eyes, Rebecca whispered for them to get under the bed and be absolutely still. Hannah's chin quivered but she nodded. Ezra, three years older, took his sister's hand as they raised themselves off the mattress. He helped Hannah under the bed and followed.

A pounding on the door began as Rebecca gathered the salt pouch from the larder, the box of matches off the fireboard. She considered lifting the loose plank beneath the table and placing what filled her hands in the firkin, but the pounding was so fierce now that the latch looked ready to splinter. Rebecca shoved what she'd gathered under the bed too, whispered a last plea for the children to be quiet. She waited a few moments, some wisp of hope that the men might simply take the chickens and the ham in the barn and leave. But the man at the door shouted that they'd burn out those inside if the door didn't open.

Rebecca knew they would, that these men had done worse things in Shelton Laurel. Just months ago, they'd whipped Sallie Moore until blood soaked her back, roped Martha White to a tree and beat her. Barns had been burned, wells fouled with killed animals. *There's nary a meanness left for them Seccests to do to us,* Ginny Lunsford had claimed, but she'd been proved wrong when eleven men and a thirteen-year-old boy were rounded up, marched west a mile on the Knoxville pike, put in a line, and shot.

Rebecca lifted the latch. As she pushed the door open, boot steps clattered off the porch. A low swirling fog made the horses mere gray shapes, those mounted upon them adrift from the earth, like revenants. Rebecca stepped far enough onto the porch to show her empty hands. A rein shook and a horse moved forward, its rider a man whose age lay hidden behind a thick brown beard. He alone wore an actual uniform, though his butternut jacket lacked two buttons, his officer's hat stained and slouched. He raised a hand but before tipping his hat he caught himself, set the hand on the saddle pommel. The man asked if anyone else was inside.

Rebecca hesitated.

"I'm Colonel Allen, of the North Carolina Sixty-Fourth Regiment," he said. "You've heard of us, of me."

"Yes."

"Then you know you'll rue any lie you tell me."

"My chaps," Rebecca said. "They're but seven and four."

"Anyone else?"

"No."

"Bring them out here," Colonel Allen said, and turned to a tall man behind him. "Go in with them, Sergeant."

Rebecca went inside, kneeled by the bed and helped the children to their feet. Hannah was whimpering, Ezra's eyes widened with fear.

"Will they kill us, Mother?" Ezra asked.

"No," Rebecca answered, her hands huddling them onto the porch. "But we must do what is asked."

They stood beside the cord of wood Brice Fothergill had cut for them in October, charging nothing for his labor. Rebecca took off the overcoat and covered the children. After all of the men had tethered their horses, Colonel Allen and the sergeant stood in front of the porch as the others gathered behind them. The chickens had calmed and several clucked and pecked nearby.

"Come a little closer, chickees," one of the soldiers said, "and I'll give ye neck a nice stretch."

Hannah started to cry. Rebecca stroked the child's flaxen hair as she whispered for her to hush.

"Them young ones look stout for their ages," the sergeant said. "Must be eating well."

"A nit makes a louse," a soldier wearing a black eye patch said, and another man loudly agreed.

Allen raised a hand and the men grew quiet.

"Your man," he asked, "where is he?"

"Likely hiding up on the ridge," the sergeant said, "waiting to take a shot at us once we're headed back. That's their way up here, ain't it?"

"Yes, Sergeant," Allen said, staring at Rebecca as he spoke. "They'll not face us like men. They leave their women and children behind to do that."

"I've got no man," Rebecca said.

"What about them children," the sergeant scoffed. "They just sprout out of the ground like turnips?"

"My husband's dead."

"Dead," Allen said skeptically. "How long's he been dead?"

"She's lying," the sergeant said when she hesitated. "Him and some of his bluebelly neighbors is probably beading us right now."

"Aaron's been dead two years," Rebecca said.

The sun had climbed the ridge now, and yellow light settled on the yard and cabin. The fog began unknitting into loose gray strands and all could be seen—the outhouse and spring, the barn where a ham wrapped in cheesecloth hung from a rafter, stored above it hay for the calf her closest neighbor, Ira Wilkey, would bring once it was weaned. Unlike many in Shelton Laurel, Ira had enough land to hide his livestock, so offered the calf for a quilt Rebecca made from what clothing Aaron left behind. We'll not make it through these times if we don't look after each other, Ira answered when she protested the trade was unfair to him.

The sergeant stepped to the side of the cabin, his eyes sweeping the clearing.

"I don't see no grave."

"He ain't buried here," Rebecca said.

"No?" Allen said. "Where, then?"

"In Asheville."

"Which cemetery in Asheville?" the sergeant asked.

"I can't remember its name," Rebecca said.

"I told you what we do to liars," Allen said.

"I argue he's close by, sir," the sergeant said. "He could be hiding in the barn."

Allen turned to a man.

"Take two men and go look, Corporal," Allen said to the man with the eye patch.

"Where's your pa, boy?" the sergeant asked.

Behind them now, Rebecca pulled the overcoat tighter around the children.

"All he knows is his daddy's dead."

"That right, son?" Allen asked. "Your pa's dead?"

"Tell him your daddy's dead," Rebecca said.

"Yes sir," Ezra said softly.

"Where's he buried, boy?" the sergeant asked.

"He don't know none of that," Rebecca said.

"That right, son?" Allen asked.

"Yes sir."

"Yes sir, what? You know or you don't know."

Ezra looked at the ground.

"I don't know," he whispered.

"I can likely guess some places," Allen said to his sergeant. "Can't you?"

"Antietam or Gettysburg maybe."

"I'd say more likely Tennessee, since they head west to join. Shiloh or Stones River, there or maybe Donaldson."

At the last word Rebecca's right hand clutched Hannah's shoulder so hard the child gave a sharp cry.

"So it was Donaldson," the sergeant said.

Rebecca didn't respond.

"My first cousin was killed at Donaldson," Allen said. "A good man with children no older than those you got your hands on."

"I had a friend killed there," the sergeant added. "Grapeshot ripped his legs off."

The two men said nothing more, appearing to expect some response. The corporal and the two men came out of the barn.

"Ain't no one hiding in there," the corporal said, "but there's a ham curing and it's enough to give some bully soldiers a full feeding."

One of the men whooped and slapped a palm twice against his belly.

"What else is in the barn?" Allen asked.

"No livestock," the corporal said, "but enough hay to make a pretty fire."

For a few moments the only sound was the snort of a horse as

Rebecca and the men waited for Colonel Allen to give his orders. *Soldiers.* That was what the corporal claimed them to be, but they looked nothing like the soldiers sketched in the newspapers her father-in-law had brought with Aaron's letters in the war's first months. Those soldiers wore plumed hats and buttoned jackets, sabers and sashes strapped on their waists. They looked heroic and Rebecca knew that many, like Aaron, had been. Some of these men before her were surely heroic at one time too, but now their ill-matched clothing offered no sign of allegiance except to their own thievery.

"Bost," Allen said to a man who wore a frock coat Rebecca recognized, "you and Murdock and Etheridge gather what chickens you can."

Several men shouted encouragement as Bost dove for the closest chicken. White feathers slapped his face until he pinned the bird firmly to the ground.

"Kill it now?" Bost panted, his scratched face looking up at the colonel.

"No, we'll take them with us."

A second man retrieved a burlap tote sack and the squawking chicken was shoved inside. The second soldier knotted the sack and tied it to a saddle as the other two men began their own chases.

"Take a man and get that ham, Corporal," Allen said. "Sergeant, take two men and go inside. Look around good. You know how they hide things."

"Nothing inside is worth your while," Rebecca said. "There's a root cellar behind the barn. It's partial hid by old board planks. Near all what food we have is there." She met Allen's eyes, saw that, like Aaron's had been, there were gold flecks within the brown. "These chaps are cold. Just let me and them go inside, and you take everything else."

"She must be hiding something real good," the sergeant said. "It's yankee money or clothes that boy there can't fill. Maybe the son-of-a-bitch himself is hiding under the bed."

"Take a man and see, Sergeant," Allen said, and turned to Rebecca. "You and your children come on out here."

"Let me get their shoes first," Rebecca said, but Allen shook his head.

Rebecca helped the children down the porch's one step and into the yard. Frost crunched beneath their feet. As Allen gave more orders, Rebecca glanced furtively toward the ridge, looking for a bright wink of sun on metal, then farther down the valley. Smoke yet rose from Ike Wilkey's farm and, beyond it, Brice and Anna Feathergill's home, which meant the Confederates had come in the night unseen. Hannah began whimpering again but Ezra stood silent, his hands balled into fists. *Don't*, she whispered, and used her hand to open his.

She should have burned the letters, as she had done with the newspapers her father-in-law had brought. But there were only five because Aaron died early in the war, so early her father-in-law had been able to travel the eighteen miles from Asheville in broad daylight, this before bushwackers as well as Colonel Allen and his men made any stranger in Shelton Laurel a suspected spy or thief, thus shot on sight. *I will return with a wagon to take you and the chaps back to live with me.* That was her father-in-law's promise when he'd brought the last letter, which contained a brass button taken from Aaron's field jacket. *My hope is that this button might offer some remembrance,* the commander had written.

But her father-in-law had not come again, with or without a wagon, and Rebecca had wondered if it was suspicion of her allegiance, not fear, that had kept him away.

"Put a match to the barn?" the corporal asked when he'd returned with the ham.

"We'll feed the horses first," Allen said as men returned with potatoes and apples from the root cellar, what chickens had been caught.

The two privates came out of the cabin, one holding the salt tin and matches. The sergeant followed, in his hands the firkin.

"It's near all letters, except for this," the sergeant said. He cradled the container with his elbow as he reached inside and removed a button with CSA stamped into the brass.

He handed it to Allen, who examined it a moment before putting it in his jacket pocket.

"You know it was took off one of our own, probably killed up here by some coward sniping from behind a tree."

"What do the letters say?" Allen asked.

"You know I never had any school learning, Colonel."

Rebecca glanced toward the ridge, then the closer woods before she spoke.

"They're just personal letters," she said softly.

Colonel Allen took the firkin and sat on the porch step. He lifted the lid, took out a letter, and began to read. As he did so, Rebecca remembered the night Aaron had filled the travel trunk with not just clothing but his briar pipe, pocket watch, and pen knife, the tintype taken on their wedding day. She thought of the two shirts and pair of breeches she'd cut up for Ira's quilt, and how her fingers lingered on those cloth squares, sometimes pressing one against her cheek.

After he'd read the first letter, Allen read quicker, then merely scanned. Coming to the last, which, unlike the others, had been written on rag paper, he read slowly again, then raised his eyes.

"Why didn't you tell us?" he asked, his voice as perplexed as his eyes.

When Rebecca didn't respond, he refolded the letter carefully and set it back in the container. Colonel Allen placed the lid back on and stood.

"Tell the men to put everything back, Sergeant Reeves."

"Sir?" the sergeant said.

"Free those chickens, and put that ham back too," he said, addressing the corporal as well. When the sergeant didn't respond, he added, "That's a direct order."

"Yes sir," the sergeant said, not alone in watching hungrily as the ham was returned to the barn.

"Mrs. Penland, it is too cold for you and your children to be out here," Allen said. "You must go inside."

He took off his hat and followed them. Colonel Allen set the firkin on the fireboard and went out to the porch, first for kindling, then one of the hearth logs Brice Fothergill had cut. Allen took a tin of matches from his pocket and lit the kindling, waved his hat to coax the fire into being.

"You children," he said as he stood. "Come closer and get warm. You too, ma'am."

Rebecca did as he said, placing the children before her. The flames thickened and Hannah and Ezra ceased to shiver. Rebecca took a quilt from the bed and laid it before the fire.

"Lay down there," she told them.

"Their real ages?" Allen asked.

"Seven and ten."

"Yes," he said, looking at them. "I guessed about that. Had my son and daughter lived, they would have been only a couple of years younger."

Rebecca hesitated, then spoke.

"I know," she said, "about their dying I mean. It's said you blame men here for it."

"They are to blame, they terrorized my family."

The sergeant knocked and opened the door.

"Your orders have been carried out."

Colonel Allen nodded and the door closed.

"The commendation from General Buckner," he said, nodding at the fireboard. "It speaks well of him as a soldier, and the letters speak equally well of him as husband and father. I regret that I had to peruse them, but it was necessary. I ask your forgiveness for that and for what has occurred today. I, we, will attempt recompense. We have sugar, and if you need more wood cut . . ."

"No," Rebecca said. "I want nothing from you but what you and your men came here to do."

"Your anger at our ill-treatment I understand, Mrs. Penland, but had you simply told us what we now know."

"And after you've left Shelton Laurel, what do you think will happen if you and your men leave this farm as if you'd never come?"

Colonel Allen's mouth tightened into a grimace. The only sound was the fire's hiss and crackle. Rebecca looked down and saw that Hannah's eyes were already closed. Ezra's too were beginning to droop, though his mouth remained in a defiant pout.

"What would you have us do, then?"

"What you came here to do, as I've said," Rebecca answered, "that and not tell what's in the letters, not even to your men."

He nodded and stepped to the doorway.

"Corporal, go get the ham."

"But sir, you said . . ."

"I know what I said. Get the men to catch three chickens, no more. You can kill them. We'll eat them when we're out of this godforsaken valley."

"That won't be enough," Rebecca said.

Allen turned.

"Yes, it will."

"No," Rebecca said. "It won't be."

"What more, then, would you have me do? You have no well to foul."

"The barn, you must burn it."

"I will not do that, Mrs. Penland. Your husband died for our cause. It would be a dishonor to him. The ham and chickens will be enough. Tell your neighbors we were here only minutes. Say we set the barn afire but did not stay to ensure if it fully caught. But those letters, they *should* be burned. If one of your neighbors were to come upon them. . . ."

Colonel Allen stepped out of the door and gave orders to mount.

The clatter of the men and horses leaving did not wake the children. Rebecca went outside, not looking toward the way fare the soldiers had come on or looking up at the ridge. She looked down the valley and saw that smoke still hovered above the two farms. A thin skein of smoke, nothing like the billowing plumes that rose a year ago at Brice and Anna's place, last June at Ira's. Everyone in Shelton Laurel would soon know the soldiers had come. They would hear or see them passing on the pike that led back to Marshall. Some of the men might have time to fire a few shots. Then they would come and see if Rebecca and the children were safe.

But they would not arrive for a little while, so Rebecca went inside the cabin. Not wanting to waste a match, she pulled a half-burned piece of kindling from the fire and walked to the barn. Nine years, Rebecca thought, remembering how Ezra was already kicking in her belly when she and Aaron had arrived from Buncombe County. The cabin had been here but not the barn. Ira had come first to help build it, then others bringing axes and oxen. In a week the barn had been built. She remembered Aaron's warning the night before he left for Asheville — *Always say Union.*

A thick matting of straw lay in an empty stall. Rebecca dropped the kindling and soon flames spilled into the adjoining stalls before laddering up gate posts and beams. Only when flame blossomed in the loft did Rebecca leave. Frost still limned the ground and that was a blessing. It would keep the fire from spreading.

When she returned to the cabin, Rebecca opened the firkin and saw Colonel Allen had not put the button back. It could have been placed inside a mud chink where it would have been impossible to find. *Not even his button, not even that,* she thought as she took out the letters and held them before the flames. Foolish not to have done it before, Rebecca knew, and told herself to open her hand and let them go.

But she couldn't, so Rebecca put them in the firkin and placed it back in the cubbyhole. She went back outside and saw that the barn had crumpled except for the locust beams. The thick smoke that had clouded the sky minutes before was now no more, signaling that the Seccesh were now gone.

By the time Ira and Brice arrived, the fire would be no more than a smolder. The two men would kick the ashes, hoping to find a locust beam with only its surface charred. They'd douse the beam with water from the spring and drag it from the rubble. The Ledford and Hampton men would arrive next and soon after whole families. The Galloways and Smiths, then the Moores and the Sheltons. The remaining chickens would have to be saved for their eggs, so there would be no meat come winter, but the women would bring peas and potatoes enough to get the three of them through the winter. Men would bring axes as well as muskets and rifles. The surrounding woods would sound like a battlefield as the cold metal struck in the early November air. All day the women would cook and tend fires. Children would gather kindling and scuff among ashes for the iron nails that had secured the shingles. Everyone would work until dusk, then return the next day to help more. Ira Wilkey might or might not say *We will get through this together* but that was understood. They were neighbors.

AMANDA REA

Faint of Heart

FROM *One Story*

I. June, 1969

THAT MORNING, NORA Stevens left a sink full of breakfast dishes and walked outside to investigate the barking of her father's dog. It was an old dog, one that hadn't mellowed with age, and many nights it had kept them awake barking at a strip of tin flapping against the barn, or coyotes singing in the distance, their voices carried on the wind. It was a terrible summer for wind, even for southern Colorado. It wailed down the river bottom and blew grit into everybody's eyes. It made hairdos impossible. Many women Nora's age still wore bouffants, and she planned to wear one herself at her wedding to Ron Whitehead in the fall—a voluminous updo half-hidden by a shoulder-length veil. She'd planned it down to the last detail. Having reached the age of twenty-six unclaimed and having grown up without a mother to instruct her in beauty and manners, she felt a certain duty to prove herself as a bride, to show Ron's family she was as sweet and ordinary as any other girl he might've wed. In this campaign the wind had begun to feel like a sentient foe. It would rip the veil right out of her hair. It would howl around the church like wolves.

At her approach, the dog didn't calm down. In fact, it got louder, interrupting one bark with another until she swatted its head with her open hand.

"Quiet, Rascal!" she said. Her father's dogs were always named Rascal—a long line of them going all the way back to his boyhood. This one was barking at its own doghouse.

Sighing, she bent to look through the little arched doorway. She didn't expect to find anything inside, really—a cornered skunk at the very worst. But there in the darkness she discerned the form of a huddled child.

She stood, cinching her housecoat around her. There was no reason for a child to be on the property, much less in the dog-house. There weren't any neighbors nearby, nobody but old Tobias in his shack at the bottom of the hill, decrepitly tending his long-haired goats. The nearest school was a twenty-minute drive and it was summer besides.

She hunched down, hoping her eyes had played a trick on her. But there they were again: a pair of muddied knees encircled by plump child-arms, and below that, two small pale feet.

Nora's heart was thundering. For a moment, she thought it might not be a child at all but some deformed and naked night-thing, an unearthly being she didn't even believe existed and yet suddenly feared. The dog nosed at her elbow.

"Hello?" she managed. "Who's in there?"

The child began to cry—a soft, pitiful sound. The dog began barking again, with such alarm that Nora finally took hold of its scruff and dragged it into the house. There she buttered a slice of bread with a shaking hand and as an afterthought, sprinkled it with sugar.

Back outside, she knelt a few feet from the doghouse.

"Are you hungry? I've brought some bread. There's water in the house—do you want me to get some water?"

She waited, but no answer came. She heard shuffling from within the doghouse, and a set of palms appeared on the plywood.

It was a girl—three or four years old, if Nora had to guess, potbellied and chubby-cheeked, naked except for a pair of dingy white underwear. Her hair was tangled, and on her knees there were streaks of something brown that Nora later would recognize as dried blood. The child crouched just outside the doghouse, rub-bing one eye with a dirty fist.

Slowly, Nora extended the bread.

The child's eyes were big and turned down at the edges in a way that might've looked merry when she smiled but now gave her an appearance of sad wisdom. She glanced left and right, presumably in search of the dog, and seeing it gone she bolted straight across the dry patch of ground, right through the outstretched bread and into the warm center of Nora's body.

Nora gasped. She tried to hold her at arm's length, and to remind her of the bread, which was now smashed between them, butter on the girl's neck and in her hair. "Now, now," Nora said, "stop that—let's not—you mustn't—" But the child clung with fierce hands, gripping and pinching and climbing until her legs were wrapped tight around Nora's waist. It was all Nora could do to regain her feet.

"My God," she said, hoisting the child with her forearms. "My God in heaven."

She hurried toward the field, where her father's tractor was making its way along the east fence. He saw her coming and shut the engine off. For once there was no wind.

Anita Dewey was the girl's name. She lived two miles south, on a rambling property covered in scrub oak. Her family didn't farm—her father was a welder, and their acreage was strewn with car parts and metal structures that stuck up out of the weeds like dinosaur bones. You couldn't see their house from the county road unless you knew just where to look.

Anita had gone missing, along with her brother Gerald, from a summer barbecue the day before. It was somebody's birthday and people had gathered to celebrate in the Dewey family's backyard. Smoke drifted from a charcoal grill fashioned by Mr. Dewey himself. Men in flannel shirts hunkered around a card game, drinking beer, while women shuttled food to a large and shrieking group of children. They were climbing up and rolling down a hill at the edge of the yard, dry grass clinging to their hair. Country music blared from the house—loud when the door opened, muffled when it slammed.

It was late afternoon when Mrs. Dewey noticed her kids were gone. She stood in the middle of the yard looking all around. She wasn't worried yet—they were at their own house, after all, and there were plenty of older cousins to look after the little ones. Surely they were around here somewhere.

That's when a little girl tugged her arm. She said she'd seen Anita and Gerald leaving with an older boy.

"What older boy?"

A big one, she said. Carrying a green bag over his shoulder. She pointed in the direction he'd gone, down a trail through the tall weeds and over a big log that bridged the creek. He'd had Gerald on one hip, while Anita had walked alongside him, holding his hand.

As it turned out, the mother of the older boy was sitting nearby. Her name was Linda LeDivic, and when she heard that her son — who owned an army rucksack, and had it with him that day — had gone off with the Dewey children, she stood so abruptly she overturned her plate. Her soda fizzed away into the grass. She was a shy woman with a soft voice people often strained to hear, but that day she spoke up loud so there could be no mistake.

"We'd better find them quick," she said.

All this, Nora learned later.

She learned the children's names from the postmistress and heard the rucksack described by the man who helped her father with the farm equipment. She found out about Mrs. LeDivic from a teacher at the school where she worked that summer as a substitute. And she was told the contents of the rucksack (a crushed pack of Pall Malls, a notebook filled with strange drawings, and a noose made from thick rope) from her fiancé, Ron, who'd been called not long after the children disappeared to join the search party. It took the sheriff more than an hour to get there, and by that time half the men in the county had gone vigilante.

In pairs and groups of three, they fanned out from the Dewey place, shouting the children's names. But after an hour or two they settled into a grim silence, each man fearing what he might find. Meanwhile, the LeDivic boy's mother was collapsed on the Dewey's couch in a fit of hysteria, with a couple of neighbor women trying to help her breathe — behavior that comforted nobody.

They found the boy's shirt first, about half a mile from the Dewey's backyard: small and blue, hanging in the high weeds. The boy was lying a short distance away. Naked in the yellow evening light, he looked so much like a corpse that Mr. Dewey dropped to his knees like he'd been shot. The noose was still thick around the child's neck, and scattered nearby were bits of bark and splintered wood from the limb that had snapped above him by the grace of God. He was bruised and cold, but he was alive, and there was a great bustle of activity to get him home to his mother, and then on to the hospital in town.

But as darkness gathered, Anita was still missing. Her father and the other men walked the fields and forests, calling her name. The police were also searching by then, but Mr. Dewey kept apart from them, running ahead, unable to bear their stern and pitying faces, which seemed to say already how it would end, how it always ended. He wanted to be the one to find her, to cover her up, to shield her from their eyes.

"I still don't know why you didn't call me that night," Nora complained to Ron, a week after she found the girl. "There was a missing child, not to mention a madman on the loose, and you couldn't be bothered to pick up the telephone?"

Ron shrugged. They were in the backseat of his old Plymouth, Nora lying with her head in his lap while he sipped from a bottle of bourbon. He had one elbow out the window, which let in the cool evening air, and there were crickets singing in the weeds along the edge of the road.

"Aren't too many telephones out behind the Dewey place," he said. "And like I said, I didn't get home till half past two."

"Well, you could've called anyway. You might've saved me a lot of worry."

"That I doubt."

Nora sighed. "I just keep thinking of what a long night it must've been for that little girl. I can't even bring myself to imagine it."

But in fact she couldn't stop imagining it. She thought about the child wandering the dark countryside, stumbling over rocks and through skunkbrush. She heard the crack of the branch that saved the boy from hanging, and the dull thudding of the little girl's feet as she made her escape. She wondered whether LeDivic had spoken to the children while he tried to hang them, and what he might've said, and whether the children had cried for their mother or gone mute with shock. All week, thoughts like these had driven her to distraction. She'd burned herself on the stove and left the front door standing open. She'd pricked her fingers while tailoring her mother's old wedding dress. Maybe it was the surprise she couldn't shake—the fact that something so terrible could happen on an average day, like a curtain lifting to reveal some grim

other world rubbing up against this one, then falling shut before
she could fully apprehend it. She couldn't forget how the child had
clung to her while they waited for the sheriff to arrive, or the way
she'd smelled—like creek water and musty earth.

Now, when she felt Ron fumbling with the buttons of her
shirt, she pushed his hand away. She was thinking about the way
Mr. Dewey had wept when he came to retrieve the girl, how he'd
grabbed her out of Nora's arms so abruptly you'd have thought
Nora was the kidnapper. She wanted to talk about this—about all
of it—but she'd already told Ron everything at least twice.

"Maybe we could forget that deal for tonight," Ron said. "Give
yourself a break."

But how could she forget? How could she be expected to return to normal life, to fooling around in the backseat of Ron's car,
as though nothing extraordinary had happened? If finding a kidnapped child in a doghouse didn't give a person pause, whatever
would?

Not to mention how often people asked about it. Given her role,
she was expected to have some insight. "How are you holding up?"
the women asked, reaching out to give her arm a gentle squeeze.
"You must've had quite the scare!" Men were more irreverent,
though no less nosy. "Well, if it isn't the big hero!" Or, "How's life
in the limelight?"

Nora understood they weren't really asking after *her*. What they
wanted was the grim particulars. They wanted to hear about the
child's terrible shivering, which started right after Nora and her
father got her inside and could not be stopped by blankets or sips
of warm broth. They wanted to hear about her underwear stiff with
urine and her ankle swelled with cactus needles. They wanted to
know what exactly LeDivic had done. What exactly the child had
told her.

The inconvenient fact was this: the child had revealed nothing.
Aside from asking for her brother once, she hadn't spoken at all,
and by the time the police arrived she was just staring out the window at the shapes of the trees. The sheriff and his deputy were no
more forthcoming, and in the end Nora and her father were left to
piece things together from the newspaper, just like everybody else.

Local Teen Abducts Two Children, Tries to Hang One.
Hanged Boy Recovering from Injuries.
Trial Begins in Abduction and Hanging Case.

Alongside every story, the newspaper ran the same grainy photo of Clay LeDivic. At first glance he looked just like any other young man, smiling for what must have been a school photographer. His forehead was wide and smooth, partially covered by a swoop of sandy hair, but his eyebrows were so blond they looked more like blank places where eyebrows had been peeled away. This gave him a startled appearance and drew attention to his eyes, which were small and dark, like buttons. He was only fifteen, but if Nora stared at him long enough she saw a quiet, adult menace.

Woman Who Found Escaped Child Speaks Out.

Of all the articles, this one saw the most wear. Nora cut it out and saved it along with the other clippings in a kitchen drawer, reading it so many times the paper went soft and pliant. It was exhilarating to see her own words in print, and to read them as though she were someone else, an average person picking up the paper, drawn in by her account. *I knew there was something wrong from the moment I heard the dog barking. I could just feel it. And when I saw that child, there was no doubt in my mind she'd been running for her very life.*

In the accompanying photo, Nora sat on the porch steps, hands folded in her lap, hair pulled over one shoulder. She wore a skirt she now regretted, but her expression was appropriately resolute, and the black-and-white gave her a kind of gravity, as though she knew all the world's tricks and wasn't about to be taken in by them.

It was hard to say what Ron Whitehead had seen in her. But whatever it was, he'd seen it right away. They were at a Grange Hall dance, Nora with her girlfriend Marjorie, who was homely to the point of painful but always scheming after this or that bachelor, and Ron playing chaperone to one of his big-boned sisters. He was passing Nora's table, and then suddenly he wasn't — he stood there gaping at her, so that the first thing Nora noticed about him, rather than his sunburned nose or his thick farmboy's hands, was his interest.

Next to her, Marjorie squealed. Then she commenced whispering wetly into her ear what Nora already knew: that Ron was the eldest son of the Whitehead family, which was large and well-regarded. In fact, they were everywhere you looked, volunteering at church, parading their livestock around the county fair — broad-chested, rosy-cheeked, loud-laughing Whiteheads. Nora had never attended football games in high school, but according to Marjorie,

Ron had been something to see on the field. He'd also dated the prettiest girls. His disinclination to marry any of them after graduation had made him all the more popular, and now that so many boys had gone off to Vietnam, he was the most eligible bachelor left.

It wasn't long before Nora caught him looking at her again— this time from across the room, with a hopeful expression. Already she wished he'd develop a bit more cunning, but she supposed it might be useful to have a man whose every thought appeared right on his face. He had a ruddy sort of charm, and everybody knew and liked him, which was more than could be said for Nora, who was sallow and shy and bookish, with big gray eyes that tended to water. As a girl, she'd been prone to headaches that kept her confined while other children celebrated Halloween and rode horses and performed in Christmas pageants, and perhaps it was these early absences that had pushed her to the margins. There was something off-putting about her, she knew, some seriousness or intensity that made people's smiles lose their warmth. At school and at family gatherings she had a sense of being tolerated but not particularly enjoyed, and she often wondered if this was typical of only children, or of motherless daughters, or of women who felt strongly about certain things: tidiness, timeliness, simplicity, composure. She'd learned by now to keep these opinions to herself, but it seemed people could still sense them there on her tongue, as though she carried with her some inextricable air of censure.

She and Ron made an odd fit. But he was proud to have her on his arm, and he beamed when he introduced her to people at dances and at the feed store. He was impressed by what he considered her great intelligence, and he also found her funny, which nobody else ever had done. He had a great big laugh that expanded his already sizable chest and further reddened his wind-chapped face. He had a tendency to grab her up and spin her around. His hugs were warm and sudden and crushing.

They went to dinner and spent time with friends, but what Nora remembered most were those hours alone in his Plymouth, after the public part of their dates was over. Then, they haunted the backroads and darkened oil field sites, lounging in the dashboard lights, listening to Ron's eight-tracks. They paid to park at the drive-in movie but saw very little of the screen. Often they didn't even hang the speaker in the window, and John Wayne's head would materialize silently in front of them, filling up the windshield like a storm cloud, and Nora would feel his look of disgust aimed at her. It was thrilling to defy him and allow Ron's hands in her hair and under her clothes. Passion came to her slowly, and at first she didn't quite know what to do with it, aside from narrate the experience to Ron, telling him how warm his body felt and how much she liked his shoulders, and asking him questions about his previous sexual experience—until he suggested she shut up and enjoy herself for once. They grappled for hours in that old car, fogging up the windows, inadvertently honking the horn, forgetting all possibility that someone might see them. He was a different Ron then—not the grinning man who shook hands with everyone they met, but serious and single-minded, growling with desire. His back was so broad Nora could barely get her arms around it, and she felt crushed beneath him, erased, subsumed. She made noises it embarrassed her to remember later. When at last she stumbled out of his car in front of her house, she could not have told you what day it was, or named a single constellation in the sky.

When they announced to his family their engagement, Nora had the sensation of being surrounded by a herd of curious cows: parents, aunts, uncles, and sisters all crowded around, looking at her, chewing on their impressions. Finally, they smiled and clapped Ron on the back. His mother, a sentimental woman with ponderous hips, alternated between crying and squeezing Nora's hands, looking down at them beseechingly, as if an agreement might be forged within her grasp.

Nora's father only said, "It's about time, at the rate you two have been going." He pretended to be indifferent, but she knew he was relieved. A widower who had yet to live alone, he'd long ago given up hope that anybody would ever take this sad, strange daughter off his hands.

Even in a small town, news doesn't stay fresh for long. People move on. And that summer, the LeDivic kidnapping was only one of several alarming events. On the same day as the Dewey boy was released from the hospital, a disagreement over communism spilled out of the dancehall and somebody was stabbed, staining the cement with blood. Elsewhere in the country, college students took over campus buildings, shouting about civil rights and the war. They stomped and chanted until their anger was heard in the smallest backwaters, and by the least involved citizens, including Nora's father, who'd never paid much attention to anything save for his crops. Now he spent evenings listening to the radio with his chin on his fist. Society itself seemed ready to blow apart, but it was hard to pinpoint the danger—whether it was the Viet Cong or the black radicals or the women tearing off their bras. And in the midst of it all, an astronaut stuck an American flag into the moon. The event was broadcast on every television across the country, into every hushed living room. Nora didn't understand why anybody would want to go to the moon in the first place, and seeing two puffy men meander over the surface clarified nothing at all. Her father would accept no part of it. "It's a damned fake," he said, and would continue saying for years. "It said 'simulated' right there on the screen. Am I the only person in this goddamned country who can read?"

In the newspaper, Nora learned of a pregnant starlet who'd been killed in California. Her murder was described as "ritualistic," and Nora shuddered to think of LeDivic, with his notebook of bizarre drawings and his carefully tied noose. Was LeDivic a sadist, like the hippie they suspected in the Tate murder? And how many sadists were there in any given town, driving down any given road? For every missing person there was someone who knew where they could be found, in flesh or in bones, and it bothered Nora to think the culprits walked around with this dark knowledge, hiding it, possibly even treasuring it. As a girl, she'd seen a boy disembowel a toad that had been lured onto the playground by spring rain, and perhaps what was most disturbing—she explained to Ron as they sat eating in a local diner—was the boy's glee, his obvious enjoyment of the toad's suffering.

"Woman," Ron said. "You sure know how to throw a man off his feed." He wiped his mouth and dropped his napkin onto his plate.

"I think everybody is capable of cruelty, don't you?" she went on. "Given the right circumstances, anybody could be. But it's different when people enjoy it. That's the part I don't like to think about, whether Clay LeDivic enjoyed what he did to those kids."

"So quit thinking about it."

"That's easy for you to say. None of it happened to you."

Ron made a noise in his throat. "None of it happened to you either, Nora. You've made too much of it. I think *you're* the one who's enjoying it, if you want to know the truth."

This stung so badly that she stood up from the table and stared at him through brimming eyes, unable to speak. Then she fled the diner for the parking lot, where she roamed for a while but ultimately had nowhere to go but Ron's Plymouth, since home was too far to get to on foot. She sat fuming in the passenger seat for a chilly half hour, and when Ron still didn't emerge, she had no choice but to go back inside the diner to get him.

She hadn't even reached the door when she saw he wasn't alone. Through its big rectangular window she could see two girls sharing his booth. One she recognized—a cheerful Italian girl who went to Grange Hall dances. But the other was unfamiliar. She had a head of springy blond curls, and she was sitting so close to Ron their shoulders touched. Rather than coming out to find her, he was telling a story or a joke, gesturing with his hands, regarding the girls with a serious, confidential expression. When he finished, the blonde laughed wildly, throwing her head back so that the overhead lamp made her throat look smooth and white as marble. Ron seemed pleased with himself, and while Nora watched from the darkness, he leaned in to plant a kiss on the strange girl's neck.

Woman—that's what he'd taken to calling her in the months leading up to the incident in the diner, as though they were the only two humans on earth. Don't sass me, woman. Or, woman, don't give me any more of your lip. He was making fun of a certain type of man, she realized, but that didn't mean he wasn't also making fun of *her.* He sometimes called her Neither Nora, and Nora Noreen. And he had a habit of twisting the lyrics of songs that came on the radio, making them dirty and about her and belting them out the truck window. He had a strikingly good voice, and it was a shame he wouldn't just sing the songs as they were meant to be sung. Sometimes, when she cooked Sunday supper, he tried to lure her into dancing by the stove.

"I'm cooking," she'd protest.

"Ah, well. It doesn't look too complicated."

"It's Beef Wellington!"

"I'll beef your Wellington."

This he'd say loudly enough for her father to hear, if he was in the next room. He'd take her hands and shuffle her around the creaky old floor. Rarely could Nora bring herself to enjoy it. She was busy with the details of the recipe, or thinking about the book she was currently reading, or some scrap of gossip she'd overheard, or just nothing, a comforting blankness.

Of course, these were differences they might've worked out between them in the course of forty or fifty years. Married, they might have grown toward each other, she becoming looser and softer, Ron growing quieter, more contemplative, losing some of his boyish imprudence. They might've had children that combined their natures, a smiling daughter and a tall, gray-eyed son.

But she never spoke to Ron Whitehead again. Not during the long drive home from the diner, or any day after. He wrote letters, but she didn't read them. He showed up at her house, but she wouldn't come downstairs. His mother came by with a homemade lemon cake and tried to say what a misunderstanding it had all been, how sorry Ron was, how miserable he was without her, all the weight he'd lost. She said the two of them would look back on this as a minor bump in the road if they could only get past it.

Nora barely heard her over the roar of her own blood. What a fool she'd been to make herself vulnerable in the first place, and to such a ridiculous man! How vain she'd been to believe the things he said, how weak! Her fury formed a barrier around her, and deep in the middle of it Nora felt an icy calm, a pain so deep it was almost gratifying. She sent a handwritten card to everyone they'd invited: *We regret to inform you that the Stevens-Whitehead wedding will not take place as planned.* She stuffed her mother's wedding dress down into the garbage barrel in the backyard and stood back from it while it burned.

In December, everybody was glued again to the television, this time to watch the first draft lottery for Vietnam. It was all anybody talked about for a while, those dates. Any mother who had borne a son on April 24th had to promptly send him off to war; any mother who'd held off until April 25th could keep her boy at home.

Ron's was the third birthdate drawn.

"See?" she told her father over dinner. "He'd have left me regardless."

II. August, 1987

For ten years, she taught the fourth-and-fifth-grade combo class as there weren't enough students to make a whole class of each.

Governing a classroom suited her, and the children found her a strict but reassuring presence. But then her father got sick and she stayed home to nurse him. He needed care around the clock, and the days stretched into years, eight of them before he died frail and indignant in his bed. Now that the old farmhouse was hers alone, Nora opened the windows for a week to let the stale air out. She got rid of all the furniture and bought new. Big floral sofas. The kitchen wallpapered in a pattern of ducks.

Saturdays she went into town for groceries. If the weather was nice, she made a day of it, buying the local paper to read on the bench in front of the store. Framingham was a growing town but largely peaceful, so there wasn't much to read about aside from the odd spectacular car accident, mostly caused by drunks. There were funnies in the back of the paper, and she read these too, wondering if anybody really found them funny, and if so, what they were smoking.

Mostly, she watched the other shoppers come and go. She looked for people she recognized, taking particular note of who was getting fat and who was getting old, though she supposed the latter wasn't entirely their fault. Her sharpest attention was reserved for the young ladies, who'd taken to ratting their bangs and wearing boxy unflattering clothes and looked every bit as frightful as the hippies, only more self-consciously so. She looked for Anita Dewey among them, wondering if she'd recognize her crescent eyes, even under some tumbleweed of hair. She would be a young woman now, and Nora often wondered where she lived and what she did and what she remembered about her night in the wilderness. It aggrieved her that she'd been prevented from knowing the girl. Twice she'd tried to bring food to Mrs. Dewey—a meatloaf, a casserole—only to be stopped at the door. "We appreciate your interest, Ms. Stevens, but we're trying to put that whole thing behind us." And later, when the children were in Bible study and she saw them getting out of their car in front of the church, she'd rushed over to say hello, perhaps a bit more breathlessly than she'd meant to, and was met with "Ms. Stevens, please."

Now the little boy would be a junior in high school. Nora knew from one of the teachers that he'd fallen behind a grade or two, and that he struggled with his schoolwork, his head drooping and eyes fluttering like a narcoleptic. Brain damage of some kind, apparently. People said he was lucky to be alive, and Nora agreed, though she thought luck was a strange thing to ascribe to a person kidnapped, stripped naked, and hung—all before the age of four.

She folded the newspaper on the bench beside her. All around, the parking lot had begun to fill with cars—doors slamming, engines starting, shopping carts rattling over asphalt—and she had to admit that some small, stupid part of her lingered in the vain hope of seeing Ron. She'd heard from Marjorie (married now, and a mother of three) that Ron had made it home from Vietnam in one piece and had moved to a suburb of Phoenix, more than four hundred miles away. Still, he came back every summer to visit his sisters, accompanied by his Asian wife, whose named sounded to Nora like someone spitting—Pa-tooey or Hi-yuck. They had several children themselves—oriental-looking, like their mother—so Nora figured if they ever stopped in for groceries they'd be hard to miss.

But today the parking lot was full of tourists from Texas and California, lumpen people in khaki pants. They came to see the mountains, and to ride a coughing old train, and sometimes you could see them wading around in the river downstream from the old uranium mine, where the water was radioactive. That very morning she'd seen someone fishing, and she was thinking about this when a gust of wind lifted a page from her newspaper and tumbled it down the sidewalk.

A passerby caught it with a quick stride. He was a young man with broad shoulders and baggy Hawaiian shorts. He had two children with him, girls preoccupied with lollipops.

"Oh, thank you," Nora said. "This wind! Can you believe it?"

The man didn't answer. He went on, one hand on each of the girl's heads, steering them toward the store. There was a briskness in his movements, a kind of mustered pluck, and Nora felt the same compassion she always felt when she saw a man tasked with childcare. "Samantha," she heard him say as they approached the automatic doors. "No running off. You hear me? I want you right here by me the whole time, both of you." He straightened his shoulders and Nora saw that he was older than he'd looked at first, probably in his mid-thirties, with a potbelly pushing against his T-shirt. His blond hair was cut short as a soldier's, and he had a tattoo on one of his calves, a large compass in black ink.

It was only after the automatic doors swooshed shut, and the three of them disappeared inside, that Nora realized who it was. *LeDivic*. The name rose in her throat like bile.

How could he be walking around, completely free? A regular man, with errands to run? With children?

She gathered her purse and stood, breathing hard, watching the doors through which he'd passed. She didn't know what to do but had a sudden, strong conviction that she should keep an eye on him, at least, so she took a cart with a wobbly front wheel and followed him inside.

The store smelled like fried chicken, and Nora was aware of the drippy saxophone music being piped in from overhead. Her cart thumped and squealed past the pharmacy and the movie-rental kiosk. At last she found him in the dairy aisle, chewing a thumbnail, contemplating the cheese. One of the girls sat in his shopping cart, posing what sounded like questions, while the older one had wandered a few yards away, stepping heel-to-toe, following the pattern of the floor tiles. She wore a bright yellow sundress, and her hair had not been combed.

Nora turned to examine some premium charcoal briquettes. Why they were sold in the dairy aisle she couldn't imagine, but she lifted the bag into her cart and pushed it closer to LeDivic.

"You like watermelon flavor," he was telling the child in the cart. "You liked it last week."

"But, Daddy, my head grew, and so did my tongue, and now my taste buds don't like watermelon anymore."

"Well, I'm not getting you another sucker. You'll have to live with the one you've got."

The child let out a shriek of protest and threw something over her shoulder. Nora flinched; she didn't know what had caused the sting of pain until she reached up and felt the lollipop hanging from her hair. She could smell it too. Sickly sweet and tart, nothing like real watermelon.

LeDivic gasped.

"Oh, Jesus. I'm sorry." He turned the child around by the shoulders. "Jenny, look what you did! Apologize to this lady. Tell her you're sorry for throwing your sucker."

The little girl scowled, refusing to speak. But Nora didn't care. She was too shocked by LeDivic's nearness, by his casual demeanor, by the deep timbre of his voice. It felt as though a silent marching band was parading through her head, the way she sometimes felt when she drank too much coffee and went out to weed the garden in the heat. She looked at the hairs on his forearms and the brown bag of potatoes in his cart. Slowly, she reached up and pulled the lollipop from her hair.

"Here, let me help you." LeDivic took the lollipop from her. Then he pulled a napkin from his pocket and, before Nora could stop him, dabbed her hair where the lollipop had been. She felt his touch just above her ear, two quick movements before he made a hopeless noise.

"It's one of those gum-pops," he said. "There's a little goo left, but it'll wash right out."

He laughed nervously and scratched the back of his head, looking dismayed by her lack of reaction, and by the fact that she was still standing there, blocking the aisle, one hand gripping the handle of her cart.

"I'm Nora Stevens," she said in a thin voice. "I live off County Road 219."

LeDivic looked at her. "So?"

"So I know what you did to those little country children."

She wasn't sure why she'd called them this; she'd never used the phrase before, and it sounded strange as soon as it left her lips. But LeDivic heard it loud and clear. He lifted the little girl out of the cart and told her sister to help her pick out a cookie from the bakery case. Then he moved closer to Nora. She noticed again the width of his shoulders and the muscles in his arms, which were tanned and scratched from outdoor work.

"Listen, lady. You need to mind your own business."

"This is my business. I'm the one who rescued that little girl you tried to hurt!"

"Keep your voice down." He stepped so close she could smell his deodorant or shaving cream or the soap he used in the shower. "Now you listen to me," he said in a fierce, panicked-sounding whisper. "I'm an American citizen. I'm a Marine, a decorated serviceman. That thing you're talking about was a long time ago. I was fifteen years old, and I got treatment for it. Every kind of treatment they could dream up. They drugged me and scanned me and electrocuted me and shoved shit up my nose into my brain, you understand? So don't come meddling in my life, following me through stores, insulting me. And don't you so much as look at my kids. They aren't any part of this."

LeDivic's eyes held hers; they were flat and brown and unwavering. At either end of the aisle, people were coming and going. The music burbled overhead.

"That little boy still has fits because of you!" Nora hissed.

"No shit," LeDivic said. "You think I don't know that? You think I don't know my own cousin? And for your information, he's not so little anymore. He's six-foot-three and he plays on the football team. We go down to the field and watch his home games."

Nora stared, unable to hide her shock. She couldn't recall having heard anything about the families being related, not in her news clippings, or in all the talk she'd heard.

"And the girl? I suppose she's your cousin too?"

LeDivic flashed a brief, incredulous smile. "Yeah. That's how it works. Now is there anything else I can help you with?"

Nora gripped the cart, which was cold and sturdy before her. She looked down the aisle, at the people floating past the doughnut case, and at LeDivic's girls, who were coming toward them now, eating cookies as they walked.

"Is she all right? Can you at least tell me that?"

"Who? Anita?" LeDivic's shoulders loosened a bit, and he spoke in a measured voice. "Sure. She's fine. In college back East somewhere. Fancy place, I forget the name. She got a scholarship. Made her mother proud. She's just about the pride of the family, I think."

He glanced over his shoulder at his daughters, who'd stopped to take some unauthorized item off the shelf.

"Unlike me," he said. "I'm pretty much at the other end of the spectrum. Now, are we done here?"

When Nora didn't speak, LeDivic clapped his hands, a sound like gunfire.

"Girls! Let's go. Hurry up. Sam, put that back. Let's get going."

Nora hurried in the other direction. She abandoned her cart and didn't get any groceries and had to come back in the middle of the week when she ran out of coffee. It was a month before she'd find the sticky napkin with a strand of her own dark hair in the pocket of her jacket.

At home that night, she watched television. First the news and then *The Cosby Show*. During a commercial, she got up and went to the kitchen drawer where she kept the old news clippings. Without looking at them, she threw them into the trash.

The next morning there was a chill in the air. Fall was coming, and she watched the deer make their daily pilgrimage to the apple orchard behind the house, pausing as they did to graze on the fescue that overgrew her father's fields. She hadn't replaced the last Rascal, so the deer strode fearlessly into the yard. They got so close to the windows that Nora could see the wetness of their eyes and the tufts of black hair around their ears. She watched as they stood on their hind legs to get the last stubborn apples from the trees, and she spoke to them from behind the glass, teasing them, giving them names.

She ate peanut butter cookies for dinner sometimes, because there were no more men around requiring meat, and in the evenings she read her father's collection of Louis L'Amour novels, wherein rugged men fell in love with tender women, and the villains died quickly and without complaint.

On those rare occasions when the phone rang, she made her way into the kitchen, shuffling in warm socks. Sometimes the line was dead when she got there. Other times she thought she heard someone hang up. Once or twice it rang in the middle of the night, and she held it to her ear, listening to the tone. Alone in a big house, it was hard to keep her mind from blooming with dark thoughts. She saw movements in the shadows, slinking forms. She heard boots on the stairs and what might've been a knock at the front door, the soft rapping of knuckles. Imagined, no doubt, but paralyzing.

When morning came, as it always did, she pulled the curtains aside and looked out at the yard. Leaves were drifting down from the apple trees. Deer had slept there in the night and left impressions of their bodies in the grass. The sky was blanching. Another winter was coming. There was everything and nothing to be afraid of.

DUANE SWIERCZYNSKI

Lush

FROM *Blood Work*

Shots

I WAS DOING shots of cold Żołądkowa Gorzka and snacking on
herring in a small zakaskas when the torture squad came for me.

The scout was a familiar face, which tipped me off straight-
away. Petite, dark-haired, top-heavy. Same lipstick, same dark hair
brushed over the ears, same straining buttons on her eggshell-blue
blouse. Had a first name that sounded like it should have been a
last, but damned if I could remember it at that moment. We'd used
her on various missions over the past sixteen months. Her appearance was no doubt meant to lull me into a false sense of security, or
lull me directly into her bosom. But I knew better. There were four
vodka shots lined up in front of me, and if I was going to be killed,
I wanted to go out completely blotto.

I had been ordering the shots in fours just to be safe. The place
was by no means crowded, as it was just after ten a.m., a good hour
before most Poles ventured in for their first fix of the day. But the
bartender could get to talking, or decide he had to visit the facili-
ties for an extended period of time and forget to refill my glasses as
often as I'd like. It was important to have reinforcements at hand.

Polish zakaskas are perfect if you didn't want to bother with the
rigors of a cocktail menu. That's because there is only one cocktail
on the menu: a cold shot of Żołądkowa Gorzka. Perfect Grizzly efficiency: You will drink *this*, and you *will* get drunk. After endless
months of tiki joints and dark oak saloons and steak houses and
cocktail lounges and dives and airport bars, it was strangely nice

to be deprived of choice. Żołądkowa Gorzka, which means "bitter vodka for the stomach," was a rather new brand that followed traditional Polish methods of blending herbs and dried fruit. Despite the name, it was more sweet than bitter. There was some wormwood, gentian root, and galangal tossed in as well. Not that I cared about the taste. The spirit did the fifty-meter-dash across my tongue on its way to my bloodstream. It was amber in color, which could fool people into thinking you were shooting some good old-fashioned Kentucky bourbon in the middle of Warsaw. I liked it more with every shot.

The menu in a zakaska is just as simple. Aside from the ubiquitous herring (which provided all the protein I required), you had your choice of six inches of smoked kielbasa, some *pierogi,* or maybe even some steak tartare, if the zakaska was fancy enough. This wasn't one of those zakaskas. I went with the herring, which was difficult to ruin. I needed the protein.

As I raised the next shot glass to my lips the scout raised her own glass and said, "Na zdrowie."

I held the glass in place, muttered a quick "Na zdrowie" in return, then downed the shot. Some part of my brain knew that I was reaching my limit, the redline, but other parts of my brain told that annoying part to shut up. We'd paid good zlotys for those three remaining shots, and goddamnit we were going to do them, death squad or not.

Oh, if only the pretty little scout hadn't offered the Polish cheer. That meant the gunmen and butchers were nearby, closing in fast. I needed to down these shots now. They might be my last for a while. I just wanted to linger here and watch the street scene, let my brain go pleasantly fuzzy for a while.

I was in Warsaw for a simple snatch, dupe, replace, and grab of a potentially incriminating and embarrassing set of cables. This was my job: cleaning up mistakes or documents or communiqués. Sometimes I was tasked with producing a pseudo doc, for misinformation purposes. Sometimes not. Almost always they had me destroy the real doc, but this time they wanted it back for some reason. So I hid it in a place only I knew about, then came here to the Pijalnia Wodki for extraction.

The presence of the ample-chested scout, however, meant there would be no extraction. My transport man had no doubt been captured or killed, this petite girl sent in his place, and the Grizzlies would soon force their way into this dingy place, and they wouldn't care how many shots of vodka I had lined up in front of me. They would simply take me. And then—

I didn't want to think about *then*.

I'd spent all night working on the dupe and switch and had been sipping steadily at an oversized steel flask of Canadian Club, as well as some bottles of port wine I'd found in a wooden cabinet. Sitting here, our pre-arranged meeting point, I decided to go with the local tipple. Someone had named this joint Pijalnia Wodki—"Drinking Room for Vodka." You had to admire the straightforwardness. The walls were badly chipped, and the fixtures and furniture were scavenged from at least four different ruined hotels. Why bother repainting the walls if they're chipped? The people weren't here for the walls. They're here for the vodka and ennui. Maybe a plate of herring on the side.

"We have a car outside," the scout said in Polish, though it took a few moments to translate the words in my mind. "Are you ready to leave?"

"That's nice," I replied, in English. "But, uh, who are you?"

She slid off her chair and moved close to me, pushing her breasts into my upper arm, smiling at me a little.

"You know me." Again in Polish. Translation approximate.

"You're pretty. Let's have some vodka together."

Eyes narrowed. Suspicious, but willing to play along. In English she said, "Sure."

I signaled the bartender. As he retrieved the bottle from under the bar I downed my second, barely feeling the cold-warm burn, and then the third shot, turning the glasses upside down and slamming them on the bar top after each. By the time bowtie was pouring four more shots into fresh glasses, I knocked back the final vodka. The scout watched me with vague disbelief in her eyes. Which is exactly what I wanted her to do, because she didn't notice me dose one of the new shots as I slid it toward her across the scratched wooden bar top.

So much of this came down to simple sleight-of-hand. The human mind can only focus on one thing at a time. While the scout was watching my hand raise the fourth shot of vodka to my lips, she was physically incapable of seeing my thumb and middle finger pinch open a hush puppy directly above the shot glass I was sliding in her direction.

She drank the vodka. I downed another and smiled. Goodnight, honey. In under a minute you're going to be facedown on the bar top. Which at home might get us ejected from the premises, but not here. Passing out is part of the whole experience.

Double

Sixty seconds later she was not asleep. She was bright-eyed, amused. Showing me her perfect teeth, which were on the lupine side. Maybe she was an Eastern European werewolf and totally immune to the Agency's finest knockout drops. She certainly looked feral.

I thought to myself, damnit, what if she'd switched shot glasses on me, and *I* was the one digesting the knockout serum?

I'm not proud of it, but I had no choice. In the desperation of a given moment, you do things you may regret later. And what I did was this: I took a leisurely mouthful and hooked my shoes under the rungs of her stool. Then I spat the vodka into her eyes, point-blank range, and simultaneously jerked my feet back, sending her tumbling from her seat at the same time. Then I ran.

Poor kid. The sting would be in her eyes most of the morning, and her tush might be sore. But it was nothing compared to what they would do to her later when her new employees decided to punish her. The alcohol in her eyes would be a memory of heaven. Hell, she might not even have realized she was working for the Grizzlies. She might have thought it was us all along.

But I had my own problems to sort out. I knew my chances of escape were nil. If the Grizzlies were smart enough to switch out my transport man for one of our own scouts then they would have all possible exits covered. Didn't mean I shouldn't try.

My legs were wobblier than I thought, which made for an interesting and somewhat amusing exit from the zakaska. My internal compass was a little off. I had been here in Warsaw less than fifteen hours and still had the afterimages of the last city I'd visited (Krakow) burned into my brain.

There was an amusing chase interlude on the relatively quiet streets. The Grizzlies had sent multiple agents to intercept me. There were dodges, fakeouts, some backwards walking. All the usual. It might have worked on one of them, but not the baseball team they'd sent after me. At this desperate juncture I made a heroic attempt at a subterranean escape, diving into an open sewer, but thick hands grabbed me by my HST suit and yanked me back into the daylight. I suggested we all get a drink together, discuss this like men. While my Polish was good, I don't think my words carried the amount of bonhomie I'd been attempting. A rank-smelling hood was slipped over my head and something sharp pinched the crook of my arm.

Bell

Chained naked to a metal bed frame in a stark white room, I couldn't help but think about the various Soviet torture techniques I'd heard about over the years.

There would certainly be sleep deprivation. Pained cries from fellow prisoners. Real or otherwise. Beatings with leather gloves. Noise assault—there are even stories about the Grizzlies using a subcontrabass tuba at point-blank range to blow out an eardrum.

But it appeared that I was in for something special. My clothes had been completely removed, which indicated they were going to maul sensitive parts of my body. Maybe even remove some parts of my body that I was never meant to see. Hold it up to the light, insult it, as if I were made of defective parts, then place it inside a steel tray and go in for more exploration. Sorry gentlemen, you're not going to find it hidden up there.

For now, though, they were content to let me freeze in quiet contemplation. I'd heard the Soviets were fond of using the cold room as a kind of torture icebreaker, as it were. For all I knew, we did the same thing. The removal of clothing was an especially nice touch. You never feel quite as vulnerable and weak and inadequate as you do when your legs are spread and your testicles have retreated to a hiding spot somewhere below your liver.

I didn't want to wait. Better they torture me with the vodka still running through my veins. It wouldn't make it hurt less, but perhaps I wouldn't mind as much.

"I'd like a vodka martini, please," I said. "One toothpick skewering the following garnishes: one anchovy-stuffed olive, one cherry tomato, one pickled pearl onion. Served as cold as this room."

Predictably, there was no reply.

Some men in my situation would revert to name, rank, and serial number. I preferred to order a cocktail. In the case of a torture room, I believe a martini is entirely appropriate. Mencken said the martini was "the only American invention as perfect as the sonnet" and I'm inclined to agree. The shape of the glass. The crisp bite and warm afterglow. There is nothing more pure. The very thought of a martini comforted me, even though I knew it would most likely be a long time before my next. If there was to be a next.

I had been tempted to request a vodka Gibson. Typically Gibsons require gin, but I had so much vodka running through my system I thought it ill-advised to change horses now. There are many origin stories of the Gibson, but my favorite is of the alleged American diplomat (no such man has ever been identified) who frequently traveled to Europe during the dark days of Prohibition. While his colleagues indulged, this diplomat named "Gibson" (in this version) felt it was important to stick to the spirit of homeland law. So he would order a martini glass filled with cold water and garnished with a single pickled pearl onion, so that he would be able to distinguish it from the sea of other cocktail glasses at various dinners and receptions. Admirable. Going without, while those around you sipped and gulped and grew increasingly blotto.

I was feeling Gibson's exquisite pain now. The blood in my alcohol system was waging civil war, attempting to reclaim its native territories. Dreadful clarity began to return. The colors around me seemed suddenly faded and dull. There had been a song playing in my head for the past few years, a song I had barely noticed, but now the record was over and the needle scratched into blank vinyl. As the hours passed, and even more hours passed, I began to understand my captors' strategy. They knew they had apprehended a souse. Torture would hurt me, but nowhere near as badly as if I were stone sober. They were drying me out.

This was a very, very bad idea.

Fix

If you're reading this, I'm going to assume you have the proper clearance. So it doesn't matter if I reveal classified secrets, does it? That, or you are one extremely bewildered barkeep and about to enjoy the story of your life.

Which is to say, the story of *my* life.

Some years ago I was a student at Stanford University who needed book money. Textbooks for my classes, but also novels for my own entertainment. At that time in my life I didn't have much of anything else. No women, no booze, no life of intrigue, no expense account. I was a bookworm. A classified advertisement in the campus newspaper brought me to a basement office a few blocks away from campus, and within a few days I was beginning my slow transformation into an unstoppable living weapon.

They didn't advertise that, of course. They billed the program as "answering psychological quizzes." Research for graduate studies. Military war games, strategy scenarios, codebreaking, that sort of thing. Once you answer the first multiple-choice question, however, you're already in way too deep. Months blurred by before I realized that I was being transformed into . . . well, something other than a mild-mannered college student.

Along with the quizzes and strategy games they enrolled me in martial arts classes and weapons training. They told me it went along with the experiment; one fueled the other. I have to admit, it was fun. I was never particularly athletic, nor had I ever held a gun in my life. But within a few months I knew how to break a man's wrist and could field-strip a rifle blindfolded. They clapped me on the back, told me I showed great aptitude for this sort of thing. They brought me on as a full-time trainee.

Not long after that they began hypnosis sessions, just to clear my head they told me. It was around this time that I began to suffer from memory loss and the sensation of missing time.

The deeper I tumbled into the experiments, the more lost I felt. I also had the unshakable feeling that the experiment was not turning out the way they were expecting, and sadly, my project was only one of 129 under the same secretive umbrella. I wasn't abandoned so much as ignored as they followed other more promising ventures — poisons, telekinesis, astral projection, and the like. I was tumbling out of control and there were few people to notice.

Until the rampage.

Now this I truly shouldn't discuss, even here. God knows I don't want to discuss it. Suffice to say that my project handlers realized their efforts to turn me into a living weapon had worked all too well. Only the weapon inside me was not activated with a code phrase, as intended. It had bubbled up out of my mind spontaneously, and at an extremely inopportune moment.

Instead of prosecution they gave me a new identity, and someone else went to the electric chair. From what I understand, the poor bastard deserved it anyway. After months of experimentation there were no easy solutions. I was more or less a violent psychopath twenty-four hours a day, seven days a week. No solutions, that is, until I broke the collarbone of a PhD then sneaked off for a cocktail. Which was the only thing, it turned out, that would keep the weapon inside me in check.

Tight

Sometime later I regained my senses. I was still naked, but now with a busted left wing and blood all over me, much of it not my own, and with a crippling hangover. Heart racing. Internal organs like jelly. Skull five sizes too large for the skin and scalp that tried to contain it. Extremities cold and trembling. Iron crab firmly locked in place inside my chest.

I was still in the torture dungeon but I couldn't remember what I had done; the memories were like movie clips minus a coherent narrative. The snapping of an arm bone (my own). The gouging of eyes, the crushing of throats (not my own). The Grizzlies truly had no chance, no matter their number. If only they'd taken my drink order.

I found my clothes neatly folded in a cardboard box, along with my wallet, fake passport, watch, even my flask. Which was empty. Bastards either drank it or dumped it and that was a filthy crime either way. I could feel my adrenaline reserves building back up and that was bad. I twisted open the flask and breathed in some faint Canadian Club fumes but that only made it worse. I was Tantalus, alternately stopping down and reaching up.

I had no choice but to quickly shower the blood off my body in a stall most likely reserved for interrogation sessions. The tiles were chipped and scummed over with what seemed like decades of mildew and splattered blood. The cold water was like razors against my flesh and I somehow felt dirtier after the shower than before it. But at least I had the appearance of a regular citizen again. It hurt to button my shirt and I found myself incoherently angry at the buttons themselves, who I decided in that moment had no right to exist. It took a superhuman effort not to pluck them from my shirt and snap them in half.

On the way out I had a glimpse of what I had done.

Boy did I need a drink.

Bent

As it turned out, I ended up at the same zakaska where they'd fingered me. If their colleagues were looking for me, this would be the last place they'd look. Plus, it was only a few blocks away from the site of my would-be torture. When in doubt, go with what you know.

My plan was to have just one. One cold nourishing shot of that sweet amber fluid, just to keep the living weapon quiet. The bow-tied bartender looked at me with faint surprise when I held up a trembling index finger. That finger, half a second later, was joined by a middle, ring, and pinkie.

"Your sweetheart was badly injured," he said in Polish as he tilted the bottle of Żołądkowa Gorzka four times in rapid succession. "Her tailbone. She had to go to the hospital."

"She was not my sweetheart," I said. "If she said so, then she was telling filthy whore lies."

The bartender's reaction was one of astonishment. Had I not translated "filthy whore lies" correctly? Either way he left me to my shots, which I downed with Soviet efficiency.

I thought that four shots would be enough. There were things to do, a border to cross, and a handler to reach. I could find more drinks along the way. Mom and Dad would be wondering about me. I wasn't sure how long I'd been gone in that torture room. Not too long, apparently, if the bartender was talking about my sweetheart's tailbone as though the memory was still fresh. Maybe a day, or two? I wondered how long ago I'd killed my captors. I should have checked their bodies. Sometimes in the aftermath, when my adrenaline was depleted, I would just sit there in a fugue state for hours. Again, another downside to the whole living weapon idea.

I should be going, but something compelled me to order another four shots. And then four to join that. Pretty soon I was feeling like myself again and feeling optimistic about the future. I even ordered some herring.

But as day turned to night, and I pushed the needle up past the redzone, my mood darkened considerably. I wanted out. Out of all of this filth and blood and pain and violence and tears and lies and headaches and rage. To think: at some point, this had just been about book money.

Hatch

I was sitting in the Vienna International Airport cocktail lounge having a Manhattan rocks, idly munching on peanuts, waiting for the phone call. The girl had promised she'd fetch me when it came. I tipped her well and ordered another Manhattan, as well as a beer chaser. I wanted to be all sorted out for the plane. Of course, I wasn't going anywhere until the call came.

You may be wondering why the Agency would employ a full-time lush who was just a few short hours away from a crazy murder jag at any given moment. I've wondered the same thing myself.

From an operational standpoint it makes a certain amount of sense. Plenty of Agency men drink, but none of them go at it with quite the same can-do spirit. To the outside observer I drank way too much to be a professional anything, let alone an Agency professional. Nor did I look the part. Later I had learned that I'd been selected for the big top-secret 129 flavors project because of my physical appearance. Tweedy, featherweight, four-eyed. If you're going to have anyone be a living weapon, might as well be someone who looks as if he'd have a hard time lifting the swatter, let alone working up the courage to swing it. And looks as though he might even shed a few tears for the fly.

There's an expression I've heard. High-functioning alcoholics. Well I was a *higher*-functioning alcoholic.

What else was I going to do with my life? Certainly couldn't go home. The folks, friends, whoever . . . they wouldn't recognize me. I'd burned away most of my former self in those lab trials. And good riddance. You wouldn't have liked him much anyway.

By the time I had four cherries lined up on the paper napkin at my elbow, the girl came for me. The receiver in the phone booth across the way was on top of the box. I picked up my drink and ordered another two. This time, I told her, forget the cherries. I stepped into the phone booth, nudged the door closed with my knee, and sat down. Some of my drink sloshed out over the edge of the glass, baptizing my knuckles.

"Hello, Mom," I said.

"What in the blue blazes happened?"

Oh. This was Dad, which was a surprise. I thought I'd be receiving instructions from Mom. Dad was more to the point, but Mom was more fun.

"Oh, nothing," I said. "I just barely escaped a torture room with my life and managed to scramble out from under the Iron Curtain. I've been sitting here waiting for your call. I'm very bored. The lounge here doesn't have real maraschinos. Just those nuclear-neon things you find in a supermarket. What's the point of that?"

"You slaughtered your extraction team," Dad said.

I waited a beat before replying: "You know, I'm fairly sure I didn't."

"Only the girl lived. She told us you went crazy."

"If that was the extraction team, why did they decide it was a good idea to give me an orchiectomy?"

"You're not making any sense."

"They were a torture squad, Dad. They took out my transport man, put the girl in his place. You need to find her. She'll be able to tell you everything."

Dad was quiet for a few moments. "Dannemora says you assaulted her then fled the pickup."

"She has her version, I have mine."

That left Dad utterly exasperated. He had no idea how to respond, and I had no idea how to follow up. I drained the rest of my Manhattan then rattled the ice in the highball glass.

"Did you make the drop?"

"Of course."

"Tell me where."

"I can only tell Mom. You know that."

"Mom is unavailable."

"Then it can wait."

Another long, awkward pause.

"Go somewhere," he finally said. "I want you to be out of sight for a while until I sort this out. Can you do that?"

"I can do that. I'll send word the usual way. Oh, and when you speak to the girl, send her my apologies, and I do hope her tailbone is feeling better."

Dad clicked off somewhere during that last sentence. I hung up and walked back to my table where two fresh Manhattans, no cherries, were waiting for me, along with a full glass of beer. Nat King Cole's "Those Lazy, Hazy Crazy Days of Summer" was playing through the hall.

Dad had ordered them for me. Like I said: to the point.

So I've been sitting here, sipping my drinks and recording these memories on a series of napkins, which are really too small for this kind of undertaking. But, you make do with what you've got. Like these Manhattans, for instance. Something about the rye is *off* to my palate; leave it to Dad to ask for a rail brand. However, it is getting the job done all the sam

[End of a manuscript discovered on a series of napkins at Vienna International Airport]

ROBB T. WHITE

Inside Man

FROM *Down & Out*

HE TOLD HIS cellie and other cons in his pod he believed in the
redistribution of wealth and that was why he'd always stolen for a
living. Though it was a medium-security institution, he had earned
some respect because of his stories of the many scores in his past.
His age gave him an air and a gravitas the younger men couldn't
touch. He'd taken his lawyer's advice and accepted the Alford plea
they offered for the jewelry store heist in Sheboygan, the legal
thing that let him plead guilty without admitting he'd done the
crime. Shit like that drove him crazy but it added to the stories he
could tell, just like the one about how he should have gotten away,
but his partner on the job traded him in for less time. His partner's
treachery didn't bother him anymore. He would have done the
same thing. Most criminals would shove their own grandmother off
a dime if she was standing on it.

He had always thought of himself as special, not an ordinary
criminal, until a young black guy confronted him in the chow line.
All the mean-mugging he'd seen in his jail life, he knew there were
better actors in prisons than in Hollywood. But this guy wasn't buying into his status and he chest-bumped and cursed him before
turning back to the serving line. A small thing but he'd backed
down and it was seen and word in any Graybar Hotel got around
fast. A few weeks later, his own cellie took over some space on the
table they used to share.

At forty-one, he thought, *I've become the toothless wolf in the pack.* That
night he woke with a nightmare: he had stolen a Ryder van full of
gold and silver bars. A laughing circle of young gangbangers tore

the metal door loose and stole every bar inside while he pleaded with them to leave him a few. Pathetic. His scars and stories meant nothing now.

Tommy called from Minneapolis when he got out. A huge score lined up at MoA, he said, the Mall of America. He told Tommy he was out of his fucking mind. They had security up the ass what with all this crazy terrorist shit and brainless gangbangers gunpointing shoppers.

"So what?" Tom said. "I've got Bob."

Who the fuck was Bob?

"Give me a disgruntled employee over the best cutting torch on the market." Tom laughed.

He used to steal in the summer, play in the winter—another of his prison mottos the young cons used to lap up. His last lawyer had taken the cash a sister in Coeur d'Alene was holding for him. Minneapolis in October might not be Duluth, but it's cold enough to coat the lawns and cars with frost most mornings. Tommy's score, if it panned out, meant Key West—maybe even retirement. It had to come sometime. Back before ATM machines, when banks kept real cash on the premises, he would have booked for the Maldives by now. It's easier than ever to get the cash in the drawers from the tellers—they're ordered to give it up—but banks in small towns don't keep much around. He hadn't seen a major haul in years. The FBI had a long memory too, and that was another reason to go for it now.

He had developed ulcerated colitis three years ago, and he was told he had to be careful what he ate. He once spent three days holed up in a Motel 6 in Casper, Wyoming, instead of casing a bank because of his goddamned irritated bowels. On the road, he was forced to watch how much coffee and junk food he consumed. Sometimes he had no choice. All of it was adding up to one word in blinking, neon green: *Retirement.*

He had met Tom in a bar.

"Ain't you drinking, bro?" Tom asked.

"I got a fuckin' beer in front of me, don't I?"

"Have a real drink, chickenshit."

"I'll stick with the beer."

Hard liquor on his stomach was the same as gulping from a can of Drano. He turned to Tommy, who looked no different from the last time he'd seen him, maybe more bulked, leaner in the belly.

"Tell me about your guy," he said.

It always seemed to start in a bar, the way a lot of good and bad things did in his life. His parents were alcoholics and he learned early on what booze could do. Still, they tried to instill the values of their faith in their kids even if they didn't have much luck. His sister in Idaho was the only one of his siblings who escaped unscathed. One brother was a suicide, another doing life in Walla Walla. Two other sisters were alcohol and opioid addicts. Their parents had died young, the father of bleeding ulcers. He still remembered the grim trail of rust-brown feces that leaked from him down the carpet stairs as the paramedics came for him the very last time.

The Triangle was Tom's kind of bar, a shitkicker dive, your basic country-western with way too much steel guitar; whiny notes poured from the speakers, the same raggedy-assed-looking crowd packed tight on the same stools. Some tattooed trailer-trash taking a break from popping out babies with violent boyfriends gyrated in an orange bikini onstage and gave hump-sex to a shiny pole slimed with sweat and even more bacteria. His eyes boxed the room. Tom sat at the bar a distance from two rednecks in greasy ball caps chattering about their trucks and some pussy they'd just made up.

He shared a cell in Brushy Mountain with Tom years ago, and they kept in contact the way cons do. Tom said his inside contact worked for the Mall of America. The guy would get them inside where the money bags were loaded into the armored cars.

Then "Big Tom" Youtsey got himself violated on a domestic abuse charge before he could introduce him to the inside man. Tommy was in county, but he had no way of contacting him what with all calls being recorded. The only thing he remembered was Tom telling him his man drank nights at this shitty rathole.

For three straight nights from six in the evening until midnight, he nursed a beer, scanned the crowd, and kept the bartender happy with a couple drinks on him. But no one jumped out. He had no idea what the guy looked like. Plenty of truckers, some cheating spouses, he guessed, mostly guys; a bunch of working-class yahoos and a few singles, bikers drifting in from the road like windblown tumbleweeds. But nobody showed up wearing a security guard's uniform or looked to him like a county clerk wanting to take a walk on the wild side. He tipped the bartender a ten on the third night for allowing him space all week on the bar stool.

Heading for his car across the stone parking lot, his thoughts were grim, mainly about spending the coming winter pinching pennies in some squalid trailer park with a bunch of inbred white trash and their squalling brats.

A voice called out from somewhere: "You the guy?"

He was too far from the streetlights or the bar's neon to see who it was. He swiveled his head around until he spotted the glowing tip of a cigarette trace an arc in the blackness. He followed it to the source.

"You Tom's man?" he asked.

"I don't know a Tom," he said.

"My mistake."

He took a few slow steps.

"Wait up," called the voice.

He turned around. He still couldn't see him well. The man looked average-sized, clean-shaved, wore a windbreaker. Nothing too redneck about him. An ordinary Joe.

"I might be, at that," he said.

Another step and he'd be close enough to chest-bump, like back in the yard when you wanted to see if a guy had the balls to fight.

"Prove it," he said.

He did it with three words: "Mall of America."

Bob turned out to be one of those kinds of men the FBI profilers liked to call "angry loners" on their wanted posters. He hated his job, he hated his ex-wife, he hated his neighbor's dog for barking when he had to work the swing shift, and he hated anybody who couldn't see he wasn't just some nobody like everybody else.

After a couple days of going over the plan, Bob grew to dislike Steve Pine, the name given by the man from the parking lot. Bob thought of him much like he did his ex.

Bob was no criminal, the man calling himself Steve Pine thought, that much was clear. What he had going for him was a grudge against the world the size of Australia. *Maybe,* he thought, *that'll be good enough this time.* Pulling into Bob's driveway at dawn and there he was, waiting in his car at the curb.

"Fuck me, you. I knew you'd be here early," Bob complained. "Look, I'm dead tired, man. They had us doing inventory and emergency drills all night long."

Too much whining as they headed to his front door. Bob walked like an old man with bent shoulders as he pawed at his pants pockets for his house key. There was booze on Bob's breath.

"I don't think your neighbors across the street caught all of that," Pine said to Bob, steadying his arm. "Why don't you repeat it a little louder?"

"You're real hilarious, Pine," Bob said. He was still fumble-fucking with keys on a ring trying to unlock his front door. "That ain't even your real name, I'll bet."

"Don't bet," Pine said to him and gripped his upper arm tighter. "You'll lose."

As soon as they were inside, Pine punched him—once, very hard, in the gut. Bob dropped to the floor as if somebody had handed him a basketball-sized lump of uranium. He gagged and started bucking sideways. The solar plexus was a quick way to get someone's attention. Pack wolves held a misbehaving pup's snout into the dirt; cons used their fists in their cells to settle friendly differences.

He waited for Bob to recover. A foul reek filled the tiny foyer where he stood looking down. A ropy string of yellow bile had come up last.

"Stupid motherfucker," he said quietly. "We're two days from something that's either going to make us wealthy men or put us in prison for twenty years and you're dicking around."

Bob said nothing, didn't even try to stand up. He lay on the floor and whimpered. He was tempted to double him up again with a kick to the same place.

A jolt for aggravated first-degree armed robbery in Minnesota was twenty years. That was what Bob faced. He faced LWOP, life without parole. He surprised himself when he realized his fist was still balled and cocked.

He brought Bob a glass of water and helped him drink; then he raised him to his feet, gently, like a mother with a just-walking child.

"Let's go over it again, Bob."

Bob slapped the glass out of his hand. It flew across the room and landed unbroken in his La-Z-Boy, the one article of furniture in Bob's living room besides the hi-def TV.

"Feeling better?"

"Fuck you, Pine."

He watched him stomp off to his room and slam the door. Robbing was like playing poker, Tom used to say. You don't play the cards as much as the people sitting across from you. But with partners, it was more like pinochle, and he wasn't sure Bob could go through with it. Bob swiped copies of paperwork from the place, loading schedules, and staff shifts. He xeroxed them when he was alone. He said the supervisor left them lying around on her desk.

"Lazy bitch leaves her door wide open," Bob bragged, sounding like a TV bad guy.

He didn't mention to Bob the copier was counting every duplicate while he was on closed-circuit TV no matter where he was in that vast complex of stores. Tom had called Bob Captain Obvious when he first mentioned his inside man to him.

Bob was a gold-star employee of five years, ten years, and then fifteen years. His "dedicated service" certificates were computer-signed by the company's CEO, who had probably never heard of his dedicated employee. They were lined up on the wall encased in glass photo frames. He found the letter denying Bob's application for promotion shoved in a drawer, ripped in two, and then taped together. Bob heaped abuse on the female supervisor every chance he got, calling her "a stupid hatchet wound," and accusing her of "sucking her way to the top." The whole thing nearly came crashing down during a final rehearsal when Bob decided to surprise him with a dozen photos he'd taken with his cell phone. "So you'll know your way around better," he said.

"I didn't . . . tell you . . . to do that," he said. The words were fishbones in his throat; he could barely suppress the rage pounding in his veins. *You stupid, stupid fuck,* he thought.

"Relax, Pine. Nobody saw me take them," Bob said.

He had to go into the bathroom, shut the door, and douse himself with water before he felt it safe to come out again.

It was too late to back out, though. The following night would either be payday or doomsday. He let Bob drink himself shit-faced that night. He'd kept him away from the Triangle for fear he'd say something stupid. Prisons were jammed with braggarts from bars. It was always in the back of his mind that he'd already talked in that bar anyway. How many guys had he drunkenly approached before he met the real deal in Tom? In the joint, they loved those crime shows where one spouse murders the other and the narrator reveals how many barflies and snitches they'd buttonholed looking for a hit man. The killer never had a chance.

It didn't surprise him that Bob never once tumbled to his final role as the tethered goat. The tiger would spring once he was gone with the swag and all the arrows of guilt were pointing straight at dumbfuck Bob. Without a second man, there wouldn't be four hands stuffing cash into garbage bags, only his two. Half the take, but if Bob's numbers were accurate, there would still be plenty to retire on even after allowing for Tom's cut. That was understood, too, once Tom had got himself jammed up. Don't trust anybody not to sell you down the river. Better to keep everyone happy. Except for the dumbasses, the clueless assholes that couldn't hurt you.

The next day was another fall day with leaves in bright colors, gold and red all over town, not the soggy, all-day drizzle Blooming-ton of the past week. Bob's sour mood was abetted by the hangover.

"Just be yourself," he had told Bob all day long. "Act your part. Everybody will be on the floor with you when I come into the room. Look scared."

"I am scared," Bob said.

Bob never understood that it was too risky to meet up right away to split the cash. He grudgingly accepted his explanation, but Pine didn't want to shine too bright a light into Bob's dim-bulb of a brain. He needed some time before the company figured with certainty the robbery had been an inside job. Bob had to be prepared for an FBI interrogation, he reminded him.

"I don't know If I can go in tonight," Bob moaned. "My stomach is all messed up. Maybe tomorrow is better—"

"Just pre-fight jitters, Bob," Pine told him soothingly.

They were dressed in matching security guard uniforms sitting at the Formica kitchen table. Bob's one foot was rabbit-thumping the floor, beating a nonstop tattoo of fear.

"Those patches you made," Bob erupted suddenly, "they look like shit. They look like fuckin' Frankenstein stitches."

"Nobody's going to study them up close, Bob," he replied. "My jacket will cover the shirt."

Bob nodded his head; his eyes were bugged, and his face was greasy with perspiration.

"Remember, I might need you to vouch for me as a new-hire in case your district supervisor makes a surprise appearance—"

"Oh fuck you, Pine! I told you a dozen times by now he ain't coming. We always get a tip ahead of time when that prick's about to show up."

"Bob, take a drink. Just one. Then rinse your mouth out."

Bob looked at him as if Pine had just asked him to tango.

"You want me to drink?"

"It'll calm you," he said.

"I've got to go to the bathroom . . . right now!"

Bob bolted from the table. A few seconds later he heard Bob's bowels evacuating in a noisy torrent. A few minutes later, it was followed by the sound of vomiting.

Bob returned, his face ashen.

"Calling the Irishman?"

"Huh? What Irishman? What the fuck—"

Pine imitated a vomiting sound as he pronounced the name O'Rourke.

"You're so fucking funny, you ought to do one of those comedy acts," Bob said. But he was calmer, his color better.

"Sit down, Bob." The smell of the bathroom had followed Bob back to the tiny kitchen. He'd done so much jail time, with its shit smells and body odor of unwashed men, that it was nothing. Bob had talked all day long as the hours got closer. Just nerve-shot chattering before a job by a rookie. "Monkey mouth," they called it in the joint. He finally quieted down.

"Time to go, Bob," he said.

"I just can't . . ."

He hoisted Bob to his feet and shoved him ahead out the door. He tucked black garbage bags and the fish billy under one armpit. It alarmed Bob when he first noticed it. "What's that for?"

"Oh, you know," Pine told him, "for those everyday occasions when you need to tap someone to sleep."

The sawed-off Remington twelve-gauge was secured in a sling sewn into the jacket under the other armpit. Bob didn't know about the Glock in Pine's ankle holster.

"What's that?" Bob asked before getting inside his car.

"It's my lucky saint's medal," Pine said. He stopped to put it around his neck. He had worn it since his fourth-grade confirmation ceremony back in Providence. He thought that when he spoke the words "renouncing the devil" he would be entering a new, better life and that the sordid catastrophe of his home would be cleansed when he returned. He kept the medal anyway.

"Drive the speed limit," he told him. Bob's eyes through the window were moist. He guessed Bob had been sneaking in a few nips.

Pine took his own car and stayed on Bob's tail from the 77 turn-off to East Broadway all the way to the turn at the 28th Street lot where the armored company's depot was located. The MoA was the busiest hub station in Minnesota and was linked to Minneapolis by both bus and rail. The lower level of the eastern parking lot was patrolled by security to keep commuters from parking there and connecting to the St. Paul International Airport or Target Field where the Twins played.

They joined a cluster of uniformed guards chatting to one another as they headed for the single entrance. Several of them greeted Bob and gave him a curt once-over. His jacket covered the wad of nylon zip cuffs tucked into the back of his belt.

They took the long walk down the drug tunnel, their name for the single unfinished corridor lit in patches by overhead fluorescent lighting. This led to the first security door. Management's heightened concerns over acts of lone-wolf terrorism had relaxed security at the main depot because new policy dictated more staff had to be shifted from collection points.

An older, white-haired guard was checking badges ahead. Pine and Bob were last in line and waited until the others were out of sight when they approached. Bob held his badge up just as he reached the turnstile and accidentally brushed the guard's arm in passing. When the old man turned back to check Pine's badge—a fake like everything else—he hit him on the top of the head with the fish billy. The old guard sank to the floor like he'd stepped into a pit full of quicksand.

"What the fuck," Bob hissed. "You weren't s'posed to hit him!"

"Keep watch," Pine ordered.

He had the old man hoisted up under the arms and was dragging him to the utility closet. He opened it with one hand and put the old man face-first on the floor. He had the nylon cuffs on him and a strip of duct tape across his mouth in seconds.

"Pine, what are you doing?"

"Shut up. Just a tiny variation in the plan."

He couldn't take a chance on Bob's terrified, shining face giving everything away right up front. He'd decided earlier that he was going to put the old man on the floor rather than try to fool him with his half-assed ID.

He knew exactly where they were going thanks to the cartoon-like sketches Bob had scratched out with his box of Crayolas. There would be four people to deal with, including the supervisor. Shift change should allow for a window of opportunity large enough for Pine to remain undisturbed in the deposit room before the real guards came trooping in with their collection bags.

The canvas sacks were stored in rows on metal shelves inside a big steel cage. Bob preceded Pine through the door again. The motion of his shotgun and the shouted command to "Hit the floor!" worked the first time. No heroes here. Nylon zip ties secured hands behind backs; he left feet untied. Pine had practiced on a prone and squirming Bob in his living room so many times by then he could have done it in his sleep. He let the cold metal barrel of the shotgun rest against the nape of each one's neck to make his point about not resisting. The sole woman guard lay between the two men. Bob, acting his part, was the first one to hit the floor, already cuffed en route; he twisted his head to look up at him. He took the woman's key ring and let himself inside the locked metal cage. Once inside he began shoveling the canvas money bags into the garbage bags.

He was thinking how much more there was still on the shelves but weight considerations—and Pine's own age—made leaving it necessary. Sprinting a couple hundred yards across a parking lot with fifty pounds of money in each hand was all he reckoned he could accomplish in the time allotted.

A sixth sense, the kind most cons develop if they do enough time, alerted him to something out of the corner of his eye. He was reaching down for a better grip on the second garbage bag when he saw a gun barrel coming around the corner of the supervisor's office.

In one even movement, Pine scooped the shotgun off the shelf and fired from the open cage door just as she squeezed off a round at him. Her slug made a ferocious ricocheting sound off the metal walls, missing him, but his blast blew her head into a red mist. That was how his mind recorded it. He went practically deaf from the boom.

She must have been behind the door when he passed leading

Bob as his hostage. The woman on the floor was not the supervisor; he had failed to read the desperate look in Bob's eyes on the floor.

His hearing came back. The men on the floor were thrashing around like fish on a deck and begging for mercy or help. He drew his Glock and stepped behind the first guard and put a slug into his head. The second guard, the same, the woman last. He wasn't sure why he did the men first. She raised herself up, like a supplicant before a throne, made a hunching movement like a caterpillar crawling, when the round tore through the top of her head and gouged a chunk of concrete from the floor. Bob's neck craned to follow him as he stepped calmly behind him. A string of popping noises, loud farts, and then a hideous banshee wail from Bob as the strip of tape across his mouth came loose. The bullet churned through the back of his head, pulped his brain, and bounced around in his skull. No exit.

The smoke, blood, and smell of shit was overpowering. He gripped the bags and hustled in a fast scissor-walk back the way he had come. The long corridor seemed to stretch out in front of him like in that nightmare he'd had with the wolves. He made it outside. He was sweating, his knuckles turned white gripping the heavy garbage bags. He heaved one, then the other into the trunk, tore off his jacket and shirt, and replaced his outerwear with a Vikings jersey and ball cap. A chorus of sirens erupted from the nearby interstate. His timing was nearly perfect.

He didn't count the money until he had put three states between himself and Minnesota. It was less than he had hoped—$184,000 —but a good haul nonetheless.

Lying on a bed in a Valdosta motel that night, he wondered about himself and the distance he had come since childhood. Why had he never used his spatial gift to make something of himself—say, as an architect or a designer? Why crime? He had never killed anyone on a job before this. Murder was unforgivable, it provoked God's wrath. An act of contrition on his deathbed could still save him from damnation. He just wanted out, to be safe now from SWAT crashing through his door at dawn. The money would give him that. He felt calmer than he had since he'd left Minnesota. His only worry was Tom expecting too big a share now that he was national news.

His reverie broke just as a movie came on. The screen flashed a warning for parents: "Intense Sequences of Violence, Gore, a Scene of Sexuality, and Cigarette Smoking." Sounded like his house when he was a boy.

His fate was linked to his saint's medal in some serpentine way he did not fully understand. They had cheated him too. St. Christopher had been booted out of the community of sainthood. It wasn't for his early years of dissipation, drinking and brawling in taverns, it was because church investigators had recently deemed his miracles had not been true ones—at least, they said they could not be verified by modern methods. The Vatican had revoked his canonization and knocked him down a peg to the "blessed" category where he would remain for the rest of eternity.

He felt tired and his skin itched. Just nerves, Pine thought. His stomach roiled with acid. He knew he would be on the six o'clock news and he wanted to wait for the update. He needed to see how close they were.

Maybe I can still turn it around, he thought. *Maybe I don't have to stay a criminal.*

I never wanted to be this way.

I never chose it.

This whole life . . . it just . . . happened to me.

They say the devil knows his own.

The man whose real name was Christopher but who had recently called himself Steve Pine lay on his bed and meditated, his mind doing its own riff through his past—those early failures followed by the successful robberies where the money was good but never lasted. Those bodies on the floor back in Minnesota intruded. It would have been unthinkable when he started down this path—to take a life so easily. Bob was an easy one, a pragmatic decision. That wasn't even Pine's doing because Bob wrote that part for himself. He felt nothing inside for him or any of them. Suicide, they told him, was the only irredeemable sin. He took off his St. Christopher medal and laid it gently on the pillow beside him. He took the Glock out of his ankle holster, brought the barrel to his mouth, and applied a pound of pressure just to see what it felt like to pull the trigger. Except for the taste of bluing in the metal, he had no other sensation, no fear of ending his life in an abject squalor of brain and blood on a headboard in a highway motel. The money in the trunk of his car had all the meaning that mattered now.

*

He trusted his instincts. Key West was too risky—too many snow-birds from up North came down and he'd stand out to local cops and bar owners. He'd save it for later like a good middle-class cit-izen deferring pleasure until circumstances were more in hand. First things first: a place to stay, nothing flashy like those deluxe resorts at the tip of Little Torch Key. A small trailer park on the leeward side of Dolphin Marina fit the bill; a decrepit sign stuck between a couple of palm trees declared lots, trailers, and rent-als available, inquire with the manager. He introduced himself as "Keith Reynolds," financial-services consultant, out of Chicago.

The park manager was a Vietnam vet with tobacco-stained teeth and shoulder-length gray hair. He said a retiree named Jefferson had just brought his double-wide down from South Dakota and "then, by God, dropped deader than Julius Caesar from a massive coronary" after only a week down here. He looked inside, nodded, asked the manager about the price and was told it could be his at a huge discount because "the old boy's family, they don't want to pay a big-ass fee to have it hauled back home."

He agreed to the price, asked to pay cash—he planned to open up an account at a bank in the Lower Keys tomorrow.

"I'm sure the family will let you have all his stuff at a good price," he said.

"No thanks," he replied.

The manager said, "No problem, man," and then said he'd ar-range with some moving people to have the furniture carted away to a storage facility.

He thought of his St. Christopher medal back in Valdosta, now most likely the property of a motel maid. He wasn't free of all su-perstition, but he didn't want anything a dead man had touched hanging over his new life.

He thought he felt his luck changing. He began to breathe more easily and stopped looking over his shoulder so often. The sun-shine, the ocean breezes, the postcard sunsets were everything he dreamed of back when he was languishing in his prison bunk. He drove his car close to the back of his trailer and threw a blue plastic tarp over it in case somebody glimpsed the out-of-state plate and got curious. One night was spent counting and sorting his money. He decided it was safe inside the trunk for a couple more days until he could dispose of the car. Just to be sure, he let the air out of the tires.

His first goal was to find a bank to begin depositing small amounts of money. Banks were required to report deposits of $10,000 or more; he suspected they reported amounts much lower, so he planned to stagger his deposits in odd amounts. The park manager suggested the bank on Islamorada Key, and he made plans to go there the following day. He'd box up $50,000 for his sister in Iowa and ask her to mail Tom a few bucks, have her get the message to him he'd catch up on old times with him soon.

He wore the suit and new shoes he'd picked up at a mall in Homestead on his way down to the Keys. He practiced the story he intended to roll out of an eccentric aunt who died suddenly and left him cash. He practiced it in the rearview mirror until it sounded natural.

The assistant manager told him he himself had been called by an elderly woman just the other day who wanted to know if she could cash "a gold bar" at the bank. He laughed along with the man, playing an amiable nitwit, joking like a squarejohn with a man he'd have snarled at and put a gun in his face not so long ago.

"She was a dear soul but very much belonged to a different time," he told him, assuming the role of an amiable nephew.

When he returned that afternoon, his bone-white shirt was damp behind the collar and his silk was folded up in his pocket, its job completed.

The manager was raking lava rocks around the palm trees out front.

He stopped raking when he saw him exit the Uber car.

"The two moving men was here while you was gone. They got your place cleaned out," he said. "Refrigerator and everything."

"That's fine."

He had no further interest in the man or the topic and headed down to his trailer.

Inside, he found a carton of lukewarm beer that had been re-moved from the fridge before the moving men took it. The place was empty, all blond wood, polished. No dead man smell anywhere. He popped the tab on one can and took a long swallow. He thought of engaging a charter for some deep-sea fishing off Islamorada the next morning. He'd take his time filling up the trailer with his own furniture. No rush, no rush at all . . .

He was raising the can to his lips for another sip of beer when a thought struck him like ice in the belly. *No, not that.* He rushed to the back window and flipped the curtain aside. The blue tarp was gone, as well as the car beneath it.

He unscrewed the vent in the bedroom and removed his gun. He slipped it into his belt and raced to the park manager's trailer. He banged on the door.

A smell of marijuana drifted out when it opened. The manager's pale chest and pot belly clashed with the skinny, sunburned arms; his nipples peeked from behind an unbuttoned shirt like a pair of mismatched rosettes.

He drew an imaginary line bisecting them and imagined the bullet going in there punching everything to mush before it exited his spine.

"My car . . ." he choked out, "my car is . . . gone."

"Them boys asked me if they should take everything, like you told me, and I said, yeah, it's all got to go. I let 'em use the phone to call for a tow truck."

He bent low, sick to his stomach, and punched himself in the forehead with his fist. No act of self-abasement; he had to dispel the tsunami of rage and panic. Killing this idiot standing in front of him was not going to get his money back.

Calmer now, his hands shaking, he asked him where the stuff had been taken.

The manager handed him a card.

"I forgot to give you this when we was talking out front just now."

It had the name of a storage facility: Bonefish Self-Storage. Marathon, FL. Someone had written in block letters the word *UNITS* and two numbers: 149, 150.

"Nothing closer?" he asked, some of his spit flecking the manager's bony chest.

"All's I know is they say they got a contract from the owner."

His hand swung around to his belt and stopped.

No, not him. It might not be too late. Think, think—

"Give me your car keys," he said.

"Hunh?"

"Give me your fucking car keys, asshole, and a bolt cutter. *Right now!*"

He drove and wept, big sobs erupting unbidden from his throat. Mile markers on the Overseas Highway were a blur, the sunlight dazzled him, but he stared dully through the windshield. The glint off the windshields of opposing traffic heading north created a mirage of dazzling light and flashing chrome, a snake unwinding beside him, its belly full of happy tourists whose faces appeared in his peripheral vision. He blanked out all thought as if he were on a caper. No thought but one now: *find the car, get the money, ignore the world.*

He took in at a glance that the facility in Marathon was surrounded by a cyclone fence and closed-circuit cameras mounted on poles.

The lock snapped. The metal folding door rattled on its castors. The car was backed into unit 149. The first thing he noticed was that both doors were left wide open and the trunk lid was up, like a giant metallic insect unable to take flight. He forced himself to look inside.

He snapped the lock of the next unit and saw the dead man's items neatly arranged. They'd done the unloading first; the trunk was popped merely to see if there was anything of value that could be taken and not be missed, such as a tire lever, maybe the whole jack set, asserting the scavenging rights of the unskilled laboring class.

He had only the money in his wallet he'd taken with him that morning. Not enough to track the thieves, certainly, and more pressing, not enough to sustain him for more than a few days in his empty trailer.

He expected to find the police waiting for him back at the trailer park. Instead, the manager—shirt undone as before, but high on weed from the odor wafting toward him—snatched his keys back, grumbled something derisive and obscene, and then slammed the door in his face.

He couldn't bear walking back to the trailer. He headed mindlessly in the direction of the marina and soon found himself on a sandy path that cut through saw grass down to the shoreline. Sand fleas hovered around his shoes with every step; dust took away the mirror polish as he trudged along.

He waded into the water up to his knees, uncertain. He should make the Grand Gesture: curse God and die.

He took out the Glock, thinking *This is as good a place as any—*

He placed the barrel at his temple. He looked down at the refracted image of his legs, his dress shoes submerged in muck. The warm air and salt-scented tang of the open sea was a balm, a belated gift after the torment of those last several hours. The gun seemed to lower itself of its own weight. He stuck it back inside his belt and stared again over the flat sheen of the gray-green waters of the Gulf of Mexico. Sandwiched between two oceans—the Atlantic just on the other side of the key—he felt small and insignificant. God wouldn't care. His suicide might make the paper in Key West, but not in Miami. That is, if his body didn't go out with the tide and get nibbled to a skeleton by fish.

He heard a noise behind him and turned around. A small white-tailed deer stood there calmly staring back at him.

He laughed. *Bob, sending me a fuck-you message . . .*

"If you came to see me off, you're in for a disappointment," he told the deer.

The tiny creature bolted as soon as he began plowing back to shore and disappeared into the thicket. His heart was a lump of ice despite the heat. He could survive. The country had other disgruntled employees, plenty of inside men. Meanwhile, he was going to have a long talk with the park manager. He may know more about that tow truck operation than he had volunteered.

The island wasn't all that big, and they had to expect someone would come looking before too long. He wondered if they'd expect it would be someone like him.

TED WHITE

Burning Down the House

FROM *Welcome to Dystopia*

THEY BURNED DOWN my block today.

I saw them. They had flamethrowers, big tanks on their backs like backpacks, and black nozzles that spurted flame. I was across the street, just coming home, when I saw them.

They were big men, more than a dozen of them, dressed in black. They'd kick in a door and then torch the place. They were efficient, systematic. In less than ten minutes, that whole side of the street was burning.

I ducked into an alleyway on my side of the street. No sense letting them see me. I saw what they did to the people who ran out of the burning buildings or dropped from windows to the street. They shot them. They do that every time they burn a block.

It was all going up in flames—my little hideaway, with my cache of paper books, so very flammable, tucked away in the center of the block. My home.

Suddenly a grimy arm locked around my neck from behind and I felt myself being yanked backwards and nearly off my feet.

I thought I recognized the arm—and the smell that enveloped me. It was the smell of primroses.

He pulled me into a narrow doorway and whirled around to close the door with his butt, flinging me loose to stumble toward a dilapidated armchair. I almost sat in it before deciding it probably had bugs.

"Well, missy, there it all goes!" he said, gesturing in the direction of the street. "How long till they do this block, huh?"

Rudolph was a deceptively stringy-looking man, shambling in

appearance, but very strong. He could probably pick me up with one arm. He dowsed himself with cheap fragrances because he never bathed.

His little hole was no bigger than mine had been, a roofed-in and closed-off space between two older buildings. It's illegal to do that, but pretty common. I hadn't built mine; I found it. Someone had died there and it had been abandoned and mostly forgotten. I'm not sentimental and I'm not squeamish, so I moved in. Now I'd have to find a new place. But not Rudolph's. Among other reasons, it was too close. Odds were it would be burned next.

Rudolph was giving me the eye.

"Yer a scrawny kid," he told me, "but yer female, and I could use me one."

"In your poppy dreams," I said. A knife appeared in my hand. It had a long blade and I kept it sharp.

"Hey, now," he said, backing away from me. There wasn't much room. "A simple no would do it."

"You got it," I said. "No." I looked around the dimly lit room. Boxes had been piled, on their sides, against all the walls, creating uneven shelves, filled with objects that looked like and probably were scraps, stolen from dumpsters in the affluent areas — broken appliances, plastic tubs filled with mismatched nuts and bolts, and stuff I couldn't identify. A battered sofa took up one end of the room. I could see it wasn't the kind that opened up. I couldn't imagine sharing it with Rudolph. "You'd have to sleep in the chair," I said.

"Why don't you just get the hell on out, then," he said. "Take your chances with the fire troopers, huh?"

"I think I will," I said, moving to the door. I could see it was made of planks bolted to crosspieces. I recognized the carriage-bolt heads when I opened the door and saw its outer side.

"It's yer mistake, missy," he said as I pulled the door shut.

The alley doglegged just beyond Rudolph's door, and I moved around the corner quickly. The air was full of smoke, which was a bad sign. The wind could blow embers across the street. This block might be next, and sooner than Rudolph thought. So many old, wooden buildings with tar roofs, crammed together, a tinderbox just waiting for a match. I had to keep going, cross another street, hope for the best.

Dusk was coming. That was both good and bad for me. Good,

because I'm stealthy and I can get around without being noticed. Bad, because there's a whole different crew out on the streets after dark, and my chances wouldn't be great if I encountered the wrong people. Normally I'm home, holed up, after dark. Now where would I go?

I decided to head for Hooker Street. That's its real name—I think there was once a General Hooker—but it's now also a good description. I cut through the alleys that snaked through the blocks. I grew up here. I know them all.

I found Jonny. Or maybe he found me. That prosthetic eye of his has some kind of built-in radar, I think.

"Hey, Shivvy," he said from somewhere close behind me. That's his nickname for me, because I'm good with a knife. I didn't jump. I recognized his voice. "Change ya mind?"

I turned to face him. He's a kid, like me—but not very much. Jonny got put through the mill when he was twelve and had to be rebuilt. I used to wonder who paid for it. But I figured the reason he started running girls was to pay it off. He looks almost normal, until you realize that all his uninked skin is fake—and that's his right arm and the right side of his face. Fake skin won't take tats.

"I been looking for you," I said. "They burned my block down. I need a new place."

He grinned at me. "I can fix ya up," he said. "But wha'choo gonna do fer me?"

"I won't cut you," I told him. "How's that?" I smiled back. Two big guys pushed between us as if neither of us were there, heading for the door of a juice house. Jonny in turn ignored them.

"Choo'know," he said, "when ya get ridda that scowl, ya don't look so bad."

"I'm not gonna work for you, Jonny. You know that."

"It won't be work. It'll be fun." He laughed, saw my reaction, and held up his hand. "I'm not asking'choo ta work for me."

"Yeah?"

"Nah. I wan'choo to live with me. Now, hear me out." His face got serious. "I got respect for ya, li'l Shiv. Ya someone I trust wit' my back, you know what I'm saying?" He grasped my arm with his left hand, the real one, and pulled me into a barred doorway. I think we both felt exposed on the street.

"I been thinking about'choo. This fire thing just pushed it together. Ya need a place to stay, and I need ya. Win-win, right?"

"Uh-uh," I said, shaking my head. "Not if you want to sex me."

"Aw, come *on* now," he said, his voice getting all soft and husky, his pimp-voice.

"Not ever," I said. "No. I'm not one of your girls."

"Choo breakin' my heart, girl."

"You got a crib you're not using?" I asked. "Some place I can use for a few days?"

"Then what?"

"Then whatever. I'll move on, quick as I can."

"Choo don't wanna crib," Jonny said, shaking his head. "They trade 'em off, hot beds. One after another. Never empty long." He squeezed his eyes shut to show me he was thinking. "An'choo not willing to get in my bed, so . . ." He brightened. "How about a rich man?"

I wasn't going to tell Jonny that I'd never let any man get my clothes off, nor any woman either. I never had and I could think of no reason why I ever would. But a rich man . . . that offered new possibilities.

There are two kinds of people in the world: the rich and the rest of us. I think there's been a genetic drift. I don't think the rich are quite human anymore. I think they're a new race.

They think so too. I can read, and I read a lot. Mostly I read books, which I always picked up wherever I found any, but I'll read anything—even the newscreen captions I spy through windows. And sometimes I sneak into the Closed Zone, where there's free stuff I catch on my tab. I shouldn't have had a tab, of course, and now I don't. It must have been destroyed in the fire. But I had found one somebody lost. They're useless outside the CeeZee except for what you put in the memory, and basically you can't access anything to put in the memory unless you're *in* the CeeZee, so I used to sneak back in for new ebooks when I got bored with the ones I had. Delete a few, add a few—and then make a quick exit before I was noticed by the cybercops.

But I know what the privileged people think. I eavesdrop on them electronically when I can, and I read all I can. Most of what I read is written by them, for them.

They believe they are superior. They talk about breeding a super race. Past tense. Like they're already more highly evolved. So "uber."

Now some of them have decided to get rid of the rest of us. They regard us as vermin, wallowing in filth. They're exterminating us. They're burning us out. But there are a lot of us. It's going to take time.

"They see us as disease-ridden," old Nellie once told me. "Like we ain't healthier than them. But we got immunities. So that's why they use fire and don't let nobody escape. Disease control."

"They shouldn't worry so much about us," I said. "They should worry about the mosquitoes."

"The mosquitoes?"

"They're what carry disease," I told her. "Like, you know, all those viruses. Zika, dengue fever."

"Wassat?"

"Tropical diseases. Now that it's warmer, we got tropical diseases."

"Yeah? You sure know a lot from them books you reading," she said, shaking her head. "But that old-times stuff, that won't do you no good now, here. You gotta get your head outta them books, you want to live to grow up."

She was shot, out on the avenue, by a block cop who was aiming at somebody else, a few months ago. I hadn't thought about her since then. But having your block burned down sharpens the memory, I think.

Jonny's "rich man" was, he said, an infrequent customer, a man who descended from his no-doubt high-rise place in the CeeZee to go slumming in the badlands for some hot sex. I tried to figure out how I could turn him to my advantage.

Actual sex was out, of course, but maybe the *lure* of sex? Unfortunately, I don't look much like a street girl. It's not just that I don't dress like them. I'm kind of skinny, narrow-hipped and flat-chested for my age. I'm not pretty. And I wear my hair and clothes so that from any distance you'd take me for a boy. Jonny tells me he thinks that's sexy, but it keeps most of the male predators at bay. Jonny has his own problems.

But Jonny tells me his rich man isn't looking to sex me. He wants to meet me because Jonny told him I read a lot.

"What is he, some kind of kinky?" I asked.

"He's smart. And he reads too."

And, when I met him, he was nothing like what I expected.

We met in an eatery tucked behind a fight club, Jonny introducing us. I was impressed with Jonny, being able to get in touch so quickly with his rich man, and setting things up right away. It was possible I might have a place to sleep tonight. Well, there's always *somewhere* to sleep, but I sleep better when there are no rats sniffing around me. But I should have considered the implications of this speedy meeting.

"Don'choo let her looks fool ya, Doc," Jonny said.

What I wondered was how the looks of this rich guy—Dr. Jones, if you can believe that—would affect me. He was about six and a half tall, somewhere north of his youth, but still very fit, very toned. He looked like a Greek god, or maybe a media star. He had curly blond hair and penetrating blue eyes. I thought he was gorgeous and wondered if that made him a real threat.

We got soy burgers. Jones only had one bite of his, so I finished it off after I'd wolfed mine. I hadn't eaten since morning.

He said he'd been looking forward to meeting me, ever since Jonny had mentioned me—he didn't say how or why my name had come up. "I'm really delighted," he said to me across the tiny table.

"Why?" I asked. "What am I to you?"

"Well, you're literate, for one thing—you read."

"Plenty of people read," I said.

"How many people do you know," he asked me, "who actually read for pleasure, who *enjoy* reading?"

I glanced at Jonny. He looked uncomfortable. "Not many," I admitted. "But how many do *you* know?"

Jones grinned. "Touché," he said. "I think it's a dying art—writing, especially. Literature. Do you write?"

"Me?" I'd never thought of it. I shrugged. "What would I write about?"

"Your life?" he responded. "Anything you know. Anything you care about."

"I cared about my home," I said. "They burned it down today."

A look that might have been real concern passed briefly over his face. "I'm sorry about that," he said. "Maybe I can help you there."

I folded my arms and pulled them close, and I think that told him something, so he changed the subject.

"The reason I wanted to meet you—I'd like to give you some tests."

"Why? What kinda tests?"

"Well, let's just say that I've been in a dispute with some of my colleagues and I think you can help me prove my point." He picked up a slim case from near his feet. He opened it and removed a large e-tablet. "Just a few basic tests—IQ, aptitude . . ."

"You want me to take these tests *here*?"

He looked up and took in his surroundings, maybe for the first time. He shrugged and smiled thinly. "Maybe not," he said. He turned to Jonny. "You got some place that's quieter, a little more private?"

Jonny shook his head. "Not less ya wanna try a juice house, hope nobody's got bad juice, havin' a fit."

I frowned and Jones said, "I guess not. Okay, let's go uptown." He packed his tab and stood up. He towered over us. Jonny's not much taller than me.

"Uptown," I said, "where uptown? How?"

Jones gave me a very boyish grin. "You ask a lot of questions, don't you? I've got a car that'll pick us up. We'll go to my place."

"In the CeeZee?"

"Of course."

"You don't need me," Jonny said. I figured he'd collect his payment later, if it hadn't been up front. He pushed his chair back, one leg catching on the rough-planked floor, and stood. "I'll see ya, l'il —" he broke off, maybe not wanting to use his pet name for me in front of Jones. "See ya 'round, Nik," he said, and left me with Jones.

It didn't bother me. I didn't need Jonny for protection. I knew I could handle Jones. He still hadn't told me why he wanted to test me.

When we got out to the street, there was a black car waiting, all polished and gleaming in the scattered lights, the windows mirrored. Nobody was near it, which struck me as odd, until I saw a juicehead wobble up to it and start to lean against it. There was a visible spark and a yelp and the juicehead staggered quickly away from the car.

Jones said, "The car's protected," and worked his remote, springing the doors open. "Get in," he said, gesturing. "It won't bite."

As I got into the car he went around to the other side and got in next to me. He touched a button on the dash and the doors closed. The car pulled out from the curb, executed a neat U-turn, and headed for an avenue uptown.

No one could see in, but we could see out. Not easily, though.

From the inside the windows looked tinted, darkened, so that only bright lights could really be seen—and there weren't many of them left on the avenue. Most had been vandalized years ago, the remaining streetlights bunched together along short stretches in "good" neighborhoods. There were few other lights. Shop owners and residents alike were stingy with their electricity.

Fortunately, the car didn't need light to go where it was programmed to go.

"This is pretty neat," I said. "I never been in one of these."

"Really? It's just a car."

"To you, maybe."

He gave me a searching look in the car's dim interior light, like he couldn't figure me out. That was all right. I hadn't figured him out either.

Jones leaned toward me. "Why do you always wear that fierce look? Do you ever smile?"

"What do I have to smile about?" I pressed my back against the door.

He shrugged. "I don't know, but life has many little pleasures. Riding in this car, perhaps?"

"Okay." I let my face relax into a small smile. "How's that? For your car."

"Much better," he said. "Makes you look cuter."

"I don't want to look cuter."

"No? You're a girl. You *need* to look cuter, be attractive. It's going to be your stock in trade, when you're grown up."

I lost the smile. What kind of advice was that—from a *doctor*?

He changed the subject. "How old do you think I am?"

"I don't know. Older than me. What? Forty maybe?" That seemed like a safe and maybe flattering guess. Younger men like to be taken for five to ten years older. But I was wrong.

Jones chuckled. "In a sense, you're right. That's the target age for my treatments. Actually, I'm eighty-six. You couldn't guess, could you?"

"Is this another test?"

He laughed. "I've got the body and, um, the stamina of a forty-year-old man." He seemed to smile and laugh a lot. "And the wisdom and experience of an older man."

I wondered what he was selling, and hoped it wasn't what I thought.

"What kind of a name is Jones? Is that your real name?"

"Why do you ask? Do you think it isn't?"

"Jones—Smith—" I said. "Bogus names, scam artist names. Meet Mister Smith, wink-wink." What I didn't say was that half of Jonny's customers were Smith or Jones. I'd made a natural assumption.

"Well, it's the name I was born with. And there are lots of real Smiths and Joneses, you know. Common names, really."

"Okay, so what's your first—"

I was interrupted. Somebody shot at us in one of the unlit patches. I heard a bell-like sound from the left front fender, and a moment later another bullet hit the window next to Jones's head with a thwack. The window didn't break. It just grew a scar. "Don't worry," Jones told me. "The car's armored—bulletproof." I didn't relax until we got to the next stretch of lights.

That was my mistake, and I was caught off guard when the car suddenly leapt into the air and came down on my side, skidding to a quick stop, dumping Jones on me, half-crushing me, my ears still ringing from the explosion. It had to have been right under the car when it went off. I wondered if it had been in the street or attached to the underside of the car.

Jones stepped on me with a muttered apology as he attempted to stand up. He threw himself, shoulder first, against what had been the floor in front of his seat. I had no idea what he was doing until the car teetered on its rounded side and fell back onto its wheels, rocking on its springs. I fell back into my seat and Jones caught himself before he fell on his face into his.

He seated himself and we exchanged looks. "You okay?" he asked.

"Sure. You?"

"A little battered. Nothing serious."

I looked out my window. "Company," I said. A group of four or five men were converging from the darkness. They were carrying big pry-bars, the kind you can use to bash someone's head in. They looked purposeful. Not random sightseers, curious about the explosion.

"Let's see if this thing still works," Jones said, and punched a button on the dash. The nearest man swung his pry-bar at my window, but it bounced off, leaving no mark, and the car didn't give him a second chance. Tires chirping, it scooted us up the avenue.

"This is a rough area," Jones said, looking back at the frustrated attackers as they disappeared from sight, abandoning the road as quickly as they'd appeared in it.

"They're *all* rough areas, until you're in the CeeZee," I told him. "What did you expect?" I retracted its blade and put my knife away.

"I'm not usually down here after dark," he said. He hadn't noticed the knife.

"No kidding," I said.

We came to another burning block. The car plowed through the smoke without slowing. "Why do your people do that?" I asked. "Set fires."

"My people? I don't know what you're talking about. Those fires are caused by the deplorable conditions in which some people live. I'm amazed they haven't burned the whole city down by now. I guess we have the firefighters to thank for that."

I stared at him, incredulous. "Firefighters?" I said. "You see any firefighters back there? You see anybody trying to put out that fire?"

"It was too smoky to see anything back there," he said, turning around to peer out the back window too late.

"Let me tell you something," I said. "I watched the fires being set on my block. Big men, in black uniforms, with flamethrowers. And you know what they did when people tried to get out, escape the fire?"

"What?"

"They shot them. Killed them, those who weren't killed by the fire. Who do you think they were working for?"

"I don't know," Jones said, shaking his head. "It certainly wasn't me."

Twice the car turned off the avenue to take side streets to a parallel avenue. Jones said some kind of problems forced the detours. "It's all automatic. The car knows. I don't."

"So, okay," I said after the second detour, "why do you want to give me those tests? What're you trying to prove?"

"Well," he said, "I don't know what you know about the One Percent, but we are not monolithic. We don't all think alike. We have disagreements, even controversies."

I shrugged. "Like everyone else, huh?"

"Pretty much."

"But you guys don't think you're like everyone else though, do you?"

"What do *you* know about that?" His tone became sharp.

"I *read,* you know," I said, folding my arms again.

"Right. Well, I've gotten into a disagreement with several of my colleagues. It's about human intelligence."

"Which side are you on? Race-based intelligence quotients, or—"

His mouth fell open.

"It's not a new argument," I told him. "Goes back centuries."

He closed his mouth and then opened it again to say, "You're quite right. But our argument isn't over racial variations in IQ—an old and pretty dead issue, really. Our argument is different and concerns the growing genetic gap between the One Percent and the, um, others—between me and you." He gestured at each of us in turn.

"A genetic gap? Can we still crossbreed?" I let a trace of sarcasm creep into my voice.

Color rose in his face. "It's—not that great a gap," he said. "Not yet."

"So—?"

"So I think you're as intelligent as most of us—in the One Percent, I mean. I want to prove it."

"You must know you'll lose," I told him. "You think I'm an idiot."

He stared at me, his mouth working, no words coming out.

"You know one high-scoring IQ from my side of the fence means nothing. You know it's statistically worthless—no matter how high I tested it wouldn't win your argument for you. You know that. And I know that. Maybe I'd ace your tests, but so what? You know I like to read, so you think I must be smart? How smart does that make *you*?" I felt my voice rising, and I stopped. I shouldn't have said a single word. I realized that, too late to take any of them back. So I leaned back against my side of the car and glared at him.

"What do you *really* want from me?" I asked, finally breaking the silence.

The car's interior was only lit with little glowing lights on the dash, so it was hard to make out Jones's expression when he said, "I'll explain it to you upstairs. We're here."

I hadn't been paying attention. We'd entered the CeeZee without my noticing the brighter lights and cleaner streets. Now the car pulled into a building entrance, a portico just off the street. Jones did something and both doors swung open. Warily, I climbed out.

He took my arm gently and led me through the big, bank-vault doors, through an air-lock-like vestibule, and into the building's lobby.

As we went through the first doors I glanced back at the car. My side was scraped up and dented. "What about your car?" I asked.

He laughed. "It's not my car. It's a public car."

I didn't know what that meant. "Won't somebody get mad about the damage?"

"No, it's pretty much expected now—when they're taken out of this zone."

The lobby surprised me. I'd expected better. It was all chrome or maybe stainless steel and glass and it probably looked really good fifty or a hundred years ago. Now, like its faded carpet, it looked almost shabby and it smelled musty.

Jones hurried me through the lobby to a bank of elevators. The door to one of them opened as we approached. We entered, the door closed, and we started up. I've been in elevators before and I looked without success for the floor buttons, or even a floor indicator. Nothing. Just smooth paneled walls and a glowing ceiling.

Jones saw me turning around, scanning the elevator's blank interior, and chuckled. "It knows me automatically and it knows where to take us."

"What if you wanted to visit someone else?" I asked.

"I have a remote," he said, as if that answered everything. Maybe it did. But I felt a stab of fear, the kind a trapped animal feels.

The elevator stopped and the door opened onto a clean undecorated corridor. Jones led me down the plain but well-lit hallway to one of the unmarked doors we were passing, and when he stepped up to it, it opened.

"How'd you know which door was yours?"

"I've lived here a long time. And of course only this door opens for me."

Inside his apartment things were very different. In a curious way I was reminded of Rudolph's place. Both were full of stuff and dimly lit. Jones's stuff was undoubtedly better and on nice built-in shelves, but it still amounted to clutter. And instead of Rudolph's cheap fragrances, this place had a cinnamon-incense odor—pleasant, but odd.

I turned slowly around as I took in the big room, finally coming to the shelves on the wall that had been behind me as I'd walked in.

Books! Lots of books! More than I'd ever seen in one place, a whole wall of books, floor to ceiling, the shelves even running over the door, and the ceiling more than nine feet high. I saw a funny-looking ladder, its top resting on wheels that ran in a track along an upper shelf. Handy. It was hard to read any of the books' spines in the dim light, so I couldn't tell what they were about—but there were so many! For that moment I completely forgot Jones.

A stab of adrenaline brought me back to reality. All those books were great, but I had walked into a chrome-and-glass trap, with no way to get out on my own. I shouldn't let myself be distracted. I slipped my hand into my pants and fingered my knife for reassurance.

It was a big, irregular room, with alcoves, heavily draped windows, and doors to other rooms, and filled with things. There was a lot of furniture—upholstered easy chairs and lounge-recliners, a big L-shaped couch that could seat half a dozen and little tables scattered between the chairs. Standing on pedestals were an ancient suit of armor that looked like it might have been worn by somebody my size, and a bigger space suit, probably a replica, but maybe real. It was white, but looked grimy, the face plate fogged.

Then I saw her. She was standing in an alcove, shadowed, and looking directly at me. She didn't move. She was dressed as I was, her hair short and uneven, a small cowlick falling over her forehead, a sullen look on her narrow face.

I turned and stared at Jones. "That's me."

He grinned at me. "A hologram. I shot it when we came in."

"Why? What're you doing with it?"

"I don't know. I haven't thought about it."

"Is that why you brought me here?"

"Of course not. It's just a memento, something to remember you by."

"I think it's creepy."

I walked over to it. It continued to stare coldly at me. I reached out to touch it, but my hand passed right through the image, like it was a ghost. Maybe it was. Maybe it was my ghost.

Jones opened a refrigerated cabinet and removed two glass bottles. "Something to drink?"

"What is it?" I asked. I couldn't make out the labels on the bottles.

"Just water," he said, twisting off their caps and pouring one with each hand into two tall glasses.

"It's green," I pointed out. "And fizzy."

"Vitamin water," he said. "A little flavor, a little color, and some carbon dioxide for the bubbles." He set down the empty bottles and handed me a glass. "Cheers," he said, and took a sip from his glass.

It was cold and didn't have much flavor. I'd once had something called club soda, which was just carbonated water, and this wasn't very different. I was thirsty, so I drank the glassful in several swallows, and burped.

Jones had gotten out his tab again, and I could see the first page of the IQ test on it—multiple choice, five choices per question, just touch the correct answer.

"I'm tired," I said. "I don't want to do that." And I realized that I really *was* tired. I couldn't smother a major yawn.

"I'm sorry," Jones said. "It *is* pretty late. Sometimes I forget the time when I get into a project." He gestured at the test. "This can wait for morning. Let me show you a room where you can sleep."

Vague alarm spread through me, but I felt foggy with fatigue. I couldn't stop yawning. I followed him through several doors to a small room with a single bed. He didn't turn on any lights in the room, but I could see the bed in the light from the doorway, and I went straight for it and collapsed on it, facedown.

Sunlight on my face woke me up. I was lying on my back, under covers, in a girl's bedroom. I knew immediately it had to be. Everything was in bright cheerful colors, and stuffed animals sat in a small easy chair across from the bed. My clothes were tossed over them. I did not remember taking them off.

The bedroom door was closed. I scrambled out of the bed and then stopped, transfixed by the sight of the sheet I'd been lying on. It was blood-smeared in one area, in the middle of the bed.

I looked and found a little dried blood on my upper inner left thigh.

I knew exactly what that meant.

I started for the door and then stopped and turned back to my clothes. I needed to get dressed first. I ached in a new place as I pulled my clothes on. They smelled, but they were all I had now.

I couldn't help looking out the window. It faced east and the early sun. I was high up and I could look out great distances, but I couldn't see much—just the vast city extending into the haze, the horizon indistinct. There were other tall towers nearby, and I could tell that they defined the area of the CeeZee.

The bedroom door wasn't locked. I opened it and ventured out, not sure which way to go. But I found the next door I came to was to a bathroom, which I realized I needed. I went in and locked the door behind me.

It was spare but had all the necessities. I showered thoroughly, after which putting my clothes back on again felt disgusting. I examined myself while I sat on the toilet, but learned nothing new. Finally I wiped the steam off the mirror and stared at myself. Did I look different now? The hologram's twin stared back at me. If I did, it wasn't obvious.

When I opened the bathroom door I found myself face to face with Jones.

"Hi. Sleep well? Ready for breakfast?"

I just stared at him. He looked unchanged, still the Greek god, his hair a little tousled, morning-fresh, a dimpled smile for me.

"You drugged me," I said. Start small and work up, I decided.

"Just a mildly opiated relaxant, same as I had," he said.

"Why lie about it? We both know what you did."

I waited for him to deny it, but he just smiled, as if dismissing my accusation, and said, "Come on. Let's eat. Let's get some food in you. The way you ate those burgers, I'll bet you don't eat well. You need to put a little flesh on your bones." He turned and casually walked down the hall, almost sauntering, like he hadn't a care in the world, leaving me to follow.

Put a little flesh on my bones, huh? He'd seen my scrawny body naked and didn't care that I knew it. *He exposed his back to me,* I thought. *He's a fool.*

Unwillingly, I followed him into his dining room. It was a relatively small room—but bigger than the bedroom I'd used—dominated by a large table in the middle. A chandelier hung over the table and cast a warm light. There were chairs along the walls and one already pulled up to the table.

He swung out another, placing it next to his, but I ignored the gesture and went to the other side of the table, opposite him, and pulled up a chair. We both sat, facing each other, Jones with a shrug and a disarmingly rueful smile.

"What would you like for breakfast?" he asked.

"Whatever you're having," I said.

"Okay," he said. He reached into his pocket and pulled out a slim black object, putting it on the table. While he held it in place with his left hand, he jabbed his middle right-hand finger at it repeatedly, then stopped. He looked up at me. "On the way," he said genially. He put the black thing back in his pocket.

A discreet chime sounded. Jones rose and went to a cabinet on the wall behind him. When he opened it I could see two plates of food sitting there. A mouthwatering aroma wafted out with the steam. I realized how hungry I was.

Jones set one plate in front of me and one at his place and turned back to get two cups of what smelled like first-rate coffee. I stood up and reached across the table to swap our plates.

He saw me doing it and laughed heartily. I was starting to truly hate his laughter. "They're exactly the same," he said, still laughing at me. "I don't care which one I have." And to prove it, he picked up a fork and took his first bite of his eggs.

A large omelet, slices of toast, sausages, coffee—it was a decent breakfast and I ate all of it. I also drank all my coffee, after switching cups while Jones watched, grinning. I drank it black because Jones did.

When I put down my fork on my empty plate he asked me, "Feeling better now? How about a smile?"

"I'm no longer hungry," I said, "but I don't feel like smiling at you."

"You did last night," he said with a twinkle in his eye.

"What are you talking about?"

"Last night. I made you happy then."

I pushed to my feet, the chair catching on the rug and falling over. I didn't care. "You miserable smug bastard!" I glared at him. "You raped me. You *raped* me!"

"I didn't," he said, shaking his head but still smiling. "You loved it. I had trouble keeping *up* with you. *So* demanding!"

I stared at him. I couldn't believe his gall, his calm denial.

"What's the matter? Didn't I measure up to your usual lovers? You told me I was better than Jonny." The words seemed to ooze out of him.

"You lie," I told him. "You drugged me and you raped me. You are the first man to ever sex me."

His mouth dropped open, the phony smile gone at last.

"Your first?" A sly look spread across his face. "You were a virgin? Delightful! Well, good thing that's behind you now. You should thank me. You *will* thank me."

I sighed. A total disconnect. I picked up the chair and returned it to its spot at the wall.

"I started to ask you last night—in the car," I said. "What's your first name?"

"My first name? Euclid. Euclid Jones." He mock-bowed. "At your service. And yours is Nicole, isn't it?"

He seemed happy with the change of subject. Like what he had done to me the night before had no consequences, no real meaning. And like my moving on to something totally different was the most natural thing in the world. I felt cold inside.

"No. Jonny told you, but you got it wrong. It's Nikola. Do you —did you have a daughter?"

"Why do you ask?"

"That room, that was a girl's room."

He gave me a lazy smile. "It *is* a girl's room."

"Whose?"

"It could be yours. Think about it. You said you needed a place." He gave me a considering look. "We'll have to get rid of that body hair—your underarms, your legs . . ."

I didn't want to go there. "How many of those books have you read?" I gestured through the doorway to his big front room.

"Most. Well, some. I inherited them with the apartment." Another smile. "I'll call you Nicky."

"Show me. I love books." Nobody calls me Nicky.

He led the way to the front room and the books. "What would you like to see?"

I looked around and noticed his tab where he'd left it the night before. The display screen was blank. No more IQ test. No longer needed, I guessed.

"What's up there?" I gestured at the upper shelves, which held fat volumes that looked like sets of books, uniformly bound.

"Let's see," he said, sliding the ladder over to the area I'd pointed out, and mounting it with lithe grace, totally confident of himself.

I waited until he was reaching to his right to pull free a book, complaining that these books were wedged in and hard to pull out, leaning over the edge of the ladder. Then I yanked the ladder hard to his left.

As I'd hoped, he lost his balance, dropping the book to the floor, flailing with his arms and falling. What I hadn't expected was that his left leg got entangled with the ladder, between the rungs, causing him to hit the floor headfirst with a solid thud.

I approached him with my knife out. His leg was still hooked in the ladder, his head and shoulders on the floor. His head seemed to be at an awkward angle.

His eyes followed me, but the rest of him didn't move.

I nudged his body with my foot. No resistance, limp.

"I think you broke your neck. What do you think?"

He blinked at me, rapidly. Then a tear formed at the corner of his left eye. His lips seemed to quiver, but no words came out. He was breathing shallowly.

"I can't leave you like this," I told him.

He blinked slowly.

I gestured with my knife. "I'm gonna have to kill you," I said. "That was my intention anyway."

His lips opened, formed an O.

"Why? You're wondering why I want to kill you?" I laughed, a short humorless bark. The first and last time he would hear me laugh.

"I want to kill you because you're such a clueless arrogant fool."

He blinked several times.

"I want to kill you because you're the enemy—an enabler of the fire troopers, a user of girls."

I wanted him to argue with me, to defend himself, to justify himself, but he said nothing. Not even his lips moved now. But he was looking directly at me, giving me his full attention.

"But most of all I want to kill you because you stole from me the only thing I had left that I valued. *You raped me.* And you didn't even care." I wanted to work myself up into a rage, but instead I felt a cold knot forming within me.

He closed his eyes—in resignation? In defeat?

"Open your eyes, damn you!"

His lips compressed and his eyes stayed shut. Denying me to the end.

I slit his throat and watched his blood and his last breaths gurgle out and then stop.

It was strangely unsatisfying. I knew I had done what I had to do, but I didn't feel triumphant. I felt defeated.

I sat down in one of the big chairs and cried. That didn't make me feel much better, but gave me the necessary resolve to finish what I'd started.

I went through his pockets until I found his remote, that black object. It felt oddly comfortable in my hand, like it had been molded to fit it, and I guess it had.

I looked over at the alcove. My hologram was still there, still watching me.

"One of us is damned," I said. I looked at Jones's remote. There were a variety of buttons of different sizes, shapes, and colors. Some had letters or numbers. Some had pictograms. One showed a dotted stick figure. I touched it. The hologram disappeared. Satisfied, I stowed the remote in my pants.

Then I started pulling the books off the shelves, dumping them in a growing pile on the floor, fallen open, any which way. This felt sacrilegious to me until I realized that none of these books called out to be read. They were dusty and old, with fine print and dull titles. None seemed to be fiction. I doubted Jones had looked at even one. The book he'd pulled out was titled *Greek Rural Postmen and Their Cancellation Numbers*. Another was about "stray shopping carts," whatever they might be. I grabbed them with a growing frenzy. They made a huge pile on the floor before I'd pulled half of them off the shelves.

I stopped then, my heart pounding. I was feeling a touch of hysteria. I needed to calm myself. I had to act deliberately, think things through—although I'd made my plans hours earlier and I knew what I had to do.

All those books! My breath caught in my throat as I considered my plan for them. The air was full of dust now. I'd never thought of myself as a book burner.

I went to the front door. When I was only two steps away, it silently unlatched and stood ajar a few inches. Okay. I'd needed to know that, be sure of that. I couldn't allow myself to be trapped in Jones's apartment. As I'd hoped, his remote worked automatically for doors, and, I assumed, the elevator.

I went back to the pile of books. Some of them had fallen on and around Jones. That gave me an idea, and I stacked more of them on him. "Because you really loved books," I muttered at him. Was there anything he *hadn't* lied about?

I used my lighter to start the fire, near the base of the books. It would be his funeral pyre, I figured.

I waited until the fire was well established and it was getting smoky, making me cough and my eyes tear up. I wanted to stay longer and see the fire grow, but I knew I shouldn't.

A drop of water hit me on my head. Startled, I looked up. In the center of the high ceiling was some kind of a knob. Water was dripping from it. I suddenly realized what it was—a sprinkler, activated by the fire. But water wasn't spraying out. It was dribbling. More drops fell on me and I caught one in my hand. It was dark-colored, and when I let it run off my hand it left behind tiny flakes of rust. The sprinkler head must have been clogged up. It served Jones right, I thought, for living in such an old building.

I couldn't wait any longer. I went out into the hallway and pulled the door shut. I could still smell the smoke when I got to the elevators, but then the elevator door opened and I escaped that floor.

The remote got me back to the lobby and out the doors without incident. I saw two women in the lobby, coming in. One of them gave me an odd look, but they continued past me. I looked like some street kid, but I was leaving. I was no threat.

Out on the street, I crossed the avenue and looked back and up. I was facing west and the late-morning sun gleamed brightly in reflections from the building's glass outer walls, which seemed to ripple. The building was over a hundred floors tall. I had no idea where to look, but just then I heard a faint explosion and then the much closer sounds of glass hitting the pavement and high up I saw a thin plume of black smoke which got bigger as I watched. I didn't watch long.

I still had unfinished business.

Big Lou was lounging in Jonny's place when he let me in. She took one look at me and got up and left.

"Hey, girl," Jonny said when I came in. "How'd it go? Ya do good?"

"I'm here, aren't I?"

"That Doc is somethin' else, ain't he?"

"He is now," I said.

"I knew'choo comin' back to me," Jonny said, purring. "That Doc, he showed ya the error of ya ways, now he broke ya in, made'choo a woman."

"That what you wanted, Jonny? For him to—how'd you put it? —break me in?"

He grinned, full of himself. "I knew, once ya broke yer cherry, ya'd get over being like that. I got big plans for ya. This yer new home, li'l Shiv."

"I'd like that," I said, cuddling up to him. I reached into my pocket and pulled out the remote. "Of course, I could live uptown."

Jonny's eyes narrowed. "Wassat? Where ya get it?"

"This?" I gave Jonny one of my rare smiles. "Oh, this is just a little thing I picked up. Jones called it his remote. You ever see one before?"

"A remote? Sure. But the Doc? Don't he need it—?"

I watched the expressions chase themselves across his face as I said, "Not anymore, he doesn't."

His expression settled into anguish. "You didn't—"

"What did you think I'd do? The bastard raped me. Drugged and raped me. No man does that."

"You did him?"

"And set his place on fire. Poetic justice. Burned him out."

"Gawd," Jonny said. "I never thought—"

I interrupted him. I slid the blade of my knife—which I'd taken out while distracting him with the remote—into his side, just under his rib cage. He didn't have his protective vest on, relaxed in his own place. The knife is very sharp and I don't think he even felt it at first. Then I twisted it viciously, rotating it and scrambling his insides.

Jonny gave me a look of disbelief and great disappointment, opened his mouth and coughed out blood. He tried to pull away from me, but he didn't hit me or try to attack me.

I told him I was sorry, and I really was. We'd shared a lot together, grown up together. "I knew you got money from Jones for me, for connecting us up. But you shouldn't have sold me out, Jonny. You knew what he was going to do. You *wanted* him to. You betrayed me."

I'm not sure he heard that last. His eyes got a glassy look and he folded over on himself, clutching his gut, doubled up.

He didn't make much of a mess. I got it cleaned up. Then I thoroughly searched his place and found his money stash. I used very little of it to pay two juiceheads to take his body out and dump it in an alleyway. I knew it would be found first by the locals, and what it would tell them.

I've taken over his place. I live there now. It's better than my old place — there's electricity for one thing — but he had no books. I'm going to have to start a new collection.

He did have a newscreen. I turned it on and watched a report on the fire and murder uptown. Tiny surveillance holos of me with Jones in the big lobby, and me by myself leaving. I looked like a boy, and that's who they think it was. Apparently Jones had brought boys up to his apartment before. Both boys and girls. I was far from his first victim, but I didn't find that news reassuring.

I'm running Jonny's girls now. Big Lou has been a real help. It's not the life I wanted for myself, but you take what you can get and I need to survive.

I guess I'm really grown up now. Next week I turn fifteen.

Contributors' Notes

Robert Hinderliter's short stories have appeared in *Columbia Journal, Sycamore Review, New Ohio Review, Fugue,* and other places. He grew up in Haviland, Kansas (population 600), and now lives in Gwangju, South Korea, where he teaches English literature at Chosun University.

• "Coach O" is one of many stories I've written set in Haskerville, Kansas, a fictionalized version of my hometown, Haviland. Haskerville is like Haviland in many respects, although home to slightly more weirdos, degenerates, and unfathomable mysteries.

The idea for "Coach O" came when my wife and I were having drinks and brainstorming story ideas. I wanted to write about a football coach in the biggest game of his life, but my wife suggested a more unique angle: a sports story in which no actual sporting occurs. So the setting switched from the game to the pep rally, and I started to think of all the ways Coach Oberman's life could be unraveling, and how it might all come to a head. One aspect of small-town life that interests me is the impossibility of keeping secrets. The answer to the question "Who knows what?" is usually: "Everyone, everything." In a half-square-mile town with six hundred people, there's nowhere to hide. So I wanted Oberman to feel that all his secrets and failures would soon be on public display. He's surrounded, boxed in, and therefore increasingly desperate.

Sharon Hunt's first published mystery story was in *Ellery Queen Mystery Magazine*. "The Water Was Rising" was nominated for the Arthur Ellis and International Thriller Writers' awards. Additionally, her stories have appeared in *Alfred Hitchcock Mystery Magazine*, on the mystery site Over My Dead Body, and are forthcoming in other publications. She has also written a lot about food and the memories it evokes. A novel she is reworking was nominated for a Crime Writer's Association Debut Dagger Award. "The

Keepers of All Sins" is her first story selected for inclusion in *The Best American Mystery Stories* anthology. She lives and writes in Ontario, Canada.

• An image usually prods me into writing a story and it was no different with "The Keepers of All Sins." For that story, the image was of a young woman on a ferry, growing more and more dehydrated. In reality, that young woman was two, my sister and me. Touring Europe, we had an afternoon to kill in Geneva and decided to take a boat tour. Somehow we ended up on a ferry instead and for seven hours were stuck on deck with little shelter from the sun and no water, because we assumed there would be a canteen onboard. I had experienced severe dehydration before and knew the signs—"feeling dried out like a prune" as my Newfoundland grandmother would say, the fuzziness that blankets your brain and how your limbs eventually take forever to do the most basic things. People boarded and debarked, but no one noticed our growing distress. When finally we stumbled back onto land and into our train, we were distraught, not about taking the wrong boat but because we were so ill prepared. For the rest of the trip, I was obsessed with water, which became central to this story.

Also central is the man from Hamburg whom the young couple meets. He was fashioned after a man from that same city we met on a train on that European trip. Our man, nameless but not forgotten, was aggressive and slimy although no doubt thought himself charming and we two naïve enough to fall for his lines. I could hear my grandmother's warning: "Stay away from men who watch you too closely."

This man did. He was a photographer, he said, and invited us to stay at his place in the red-light district for as long as we wanted. He was at our command. Other girls "not as lovely as you" who stayed with him had an unforgettable experience and we would too.

The train was full and we couldn't change seats so did our best to ignore him.

Realizing he wasn't getting anywhere with us, he grew sullen and before disappearing into the night, bent close to me. "This city can be dangerous for stupid girls."

"Then it's good we're not stupid," I remember saying, but not being stupid doesn't always save you from harm, as my main character sadly discovered.

Reed Johnson is a fiction writer, translator, and scholar who holds an MA/PhD in Slavic languages and literatures along with an MFA in creative writing from the University of Virginia, and currently works as a preceptor in the Harvard writing program. His fiction and nonfiction have appeared in journals like *New England Review* and online at *The New Yorker,* and he is writing a mystery novel set in Russia, where he spent nearly a decade of his life.

• When I was growing up, our family didn't have much money, and we were often on the lookout for things to do that didn't cost anything. One such free weekend activity was the open house. No doubt many of us have been to an open house with no intention of buying, and so we understand that there might be nothing real about this sort of real estate: the open house is a space for the imagination to roam, a place to picture alternate selves and alternate lives spent living there. At the same time, it's rare that these houses turn out to be completely blank rooms on which we can project these imagined selves. The open house almost always contains the remainders and reminders of another set of lives—the lives, that is, of the current inhabitants. And in turn, these traces suggest other sets of dreams (or, as is sometimes the case with families moving out, failed dreams) that might collide with one's own, creating interesting echoes and patterns of interference. In this sense, the open house is a lot like the story: a structured space that both constrains and spurs the imagination, an armature that gives shape to thoughts about how our lives might otherwise unfold.

Arthur Klepchukov found words between Black Seas, Virginian beaches, and San Franciscan waves. He adores trains, swing sets, and music that tears him outta time. Art contributes to Writer Unboxed and has hosted Shut Up & Write(!) meetups since 2013. His literary fiction appears in journals like _The Common, Necessary Fiction,_ and _KYSO Flash._ His crime fiction debuted in _Down & Out._

• A few years ago, I reached out to my oldest friend, Kyle Stout, about catching up in San Francisco. He didn't want to come to the city when it was about to rain. _But it's a damn fine town in the rain._ I jotted down what could be a phrase or a title. After Kyle and I made a short film in an Oakland coffee shop, we were inspired to find other limited settings for our stories. BART, the Bay Area's subway system, somehow felt appropriately grungy and fitting. With a setting in mind, "A Damn Fine Town" took shape at The Lemon Tree House Residency in Tuscany. The irony of writing abroad about traveling without traveling seeped into my character's attitudes. I'd still love to make a short film version. So on your next train to the airport, keep an eye out for Mr. Suitcase or Kid Cape. And keep an eye on your luggage.

Harley Jane Kozak was born in Pennsylvania, grew up in Nebraska, completed NYU School of the Arts Graduate Acting Program, and migrated to Los Angeles. She starred in a few dozen films (_Parenthood, Arachnophobia, The Favor,_ etc.), three soaps (_Texas, Guiding Light, Santa Barbara_), countless plays, and a lotta TV before taking a fifteen-year maternity leave and turning to crime fiction. Her first (of five) novels, _Dating Dead Men,_ won the Agatha, Anthony, and Macavity awards. Her short prose has appeared in *Ms. Magazine, The Sun, Santa Monica Review,* and eight anthologies, including *The Best American Mystery Stories of 2019.*

• When Les Klinger and Laurie R. King invited me to contribute a story to their Sherlockian anthology series, I jumped at the chance, although not without trepidation. Fans of Watson and Holmes are a rabid bunch, rivaling those of *Star Trek, Star Wars,* and Shakespeare, and a writer ventures into those territories at her own risk. Probably that's why I had a hard time coming up with a premise, plot, character—any doorway into a story. One night, a voice woke me from a dead sleep with the words "This is the first line of your Sherlockian short story." I grabbed a pen and paper and wrote down what the dream voice dictated. The next morning, I stared blankly at the scrawled words. *It's not every day you walk into your apartment to find your cat has turned into a dog.* My big nocturnal "aha!" by daylight had all the literary weight of a grocery list. However, it's not like I had any competing ideas, and also, I don't like to argue with the voices in my head, so I started typing. The result was "The Walk-In."

Preston Lang is a native New Yorker and a product of its public schools. He's published four crime novels so far.

• This story was written specifically for an anthology to honor the terrific journalist and crime writer William E. Wallace, so it seemed appropriate to focus on a struggling reporter getting into trouble. I realize now that in the first sentence, I boldly called out the hitman subgenre as unrealistic but then went on to write something much less believable than the average assassin story. It was fun to write.

Jared Lipof's short fiction appears in *The Los Angeles Review, The Emerson Review,* and *Salamander.* He lives in Asheville, North Carolina, where he's at work on a novel.

• Rendering an actual human being in fictional form can be tricky. Even more so when it's family. Relatives will read your work and say the events in the fiction did not occur *exactly* as described. They'll remind you how it really went down, as if that was even the point. But when you use your recently deceased father as a template for a character, whatever pressure is relieved by his inability to give you notes is offset by the fact that you really wish he could read it. At which point you realize you were just trying to perform a magic trick. "He's not dead if he's in the story," you tell yourself. And even though you're wrong, it was worth a try. Special thanks to Jennifer Barber at *Salamander,* whose editorial instincts brought out the best possible version of this story.

Anne Therese Macdonald is the author of the novel *A Short Time in Luxembourg.* Her short stories have been published in various journals and anthologies, including *Blue Earth Review, Belletriste, Dublin Quarterly, Matter: A Journal of Art and Literature, Words on the Waves,* and most recently the Rocky Mountain Fiction Writers' anthology *False Faces: Twenty-Six Stories About the Masks We Wear.*

• "That Donnelly Crowd" evolved from a culmination of several events in my life, especially the years I hitchhiked through Ireland during the Troubles and my return during the Celtic Tiger. In the story, a young American woman is attracted to Joe Donnelly, a man caught between these two eras. He is from a family of terrorists but claims that he's in Ireland to build a modern factory. Against this, I explore the tendency of Americans to cling to the fantasy of an ancestral Ireland over the reality of today's modern country. Colleen, the American woman, is a troubled soul. Like so many of us, she succumbs to her own fantasy. She sees in Joe Donnelly what she wants to see, unencumbered by the reality before her, ignoring the little signs that tell her to run the other way.

Mark Mayer has an MFA from the Iowa Writers' Workshop. From 2012 to 2014 he lived at Cornell College's Center for the Literary Arts as the Robert P. Dana Emerging Writer. His first book, *Aerialists,* won the Michener-Copernicus Prize. He lives in Paris with his wife and two rabbits.

• I wrote "The Clown" immediately after Trump was elected president. Many new stories justifying the Trump voter were suddenly in circulation, and I was feeling fretful about how fiction writers are told to create empathy for ill-doing characters by presenting their inner lives and stories — by making the evils they commit products of situation and circumstance. I was asking myself whether literary fiction always absolves its criminals and whether there was a limiting case. The story is part of my collection *Aerialists* (2019), in which every story reimagines and reinvents one of the acts or characters of the circus.

Rebecca McKanna is the recipient of *Third Coast*'s 2018 Fiction Prize. Her writing has appeared in *Colorado Review, Michigan Quarterly Review, Joyland,* and other journals and was published as one of *Narrative*'s Stories of the Week. She is an assistant professor of English at the University of Indianapolis. She lives in Indiana, where she is finishing her debut novel about a young woman uncovering the dark truth about her mother's childhood. Visit her at rebeccamckanna.com.

• When I grew up in Iowa, Grant Wood's *American Gothic* was everywhere. Despite or maybe because of its ubiquity, it wasn't until my mid-twenties when I started thinking about what the painting said about midwestern life. Around this time, I was writing a series of stories about different women who had been impacted by the same serial killer. When I was back in Iowa visiting my parents for Christmas that year, my mother and I drove to Eldon to see the American Gothic House and Center. I was startled by how small the iconic house seemed in person. As we walked through the museum, I imagined an employee receiving a letter from the serial killer, and the story took shape from there.

I'm indebted to the editors at *Colorado Review* for originally publishing this story, especially Stephanie G'Schwind and Steven Schwartz. Thank you to Otto Penzler and Jonathan Lethem for giving it a home here.

Jennifer McMahon is the *New York Times* best-selling author of nine suspense novels, including *Promise Not to Tell*, *The Winter People*, and *The Invited*. She lives in Vermont with her partner, Drea, and their daughter, Zella.

• I was on vacation with my family a couple of years ago, doing lovely touristy things during the day. But one night I had a terrible, vivid dream.

I dreamt that I was a twelve-year-old girl, an outsider, the one others teased, and they were playing a wicked sort of trick on me. A whole series of tricks that ended in fire and death. I was wearing an absurd costume they'd dressed me in. I was Hannah-beast.

But then, the dream shifted—I wasn't the victim, I was one of the girls playing the trick, laughing at poor, stupid Hannah, thrilling at how clever my friends and I were. Knowing it was wrong, but going along for the ride anyway, telling myself it was just a joke.

The dream stuck with me throughout our pleasant family vacation, and it was obvious why—in real life, hadn't I been both girls at one time or another?

I'm a big believer in ghosts but sometimes what I find most frightening are the ghosts of my own past. The things that haunt me most are the choices I've made. Like Amanda, they're the things that have me looking over my shoulder, jumping at shadows, sure I hear some long-ago voice taunting, teasing:

Say boo.

Joyce Carol Oates has long been fascinated by the phenomenon of "mystery"—in art, as in life. She is the author of a number of works of psychological suspense fiction including the novels *Beasts*, *A Fair Maiden*, *Jack of Spades*, and *Rape: A Love Story* (recently adapted for the screen as *Vengeance: A Love Story*, starring Nicolas Cage, arguably the worst film adaptation ever made in the history of American cinema, though film aficionados might wish to quarrel with this), and the story collections *The Female of the Species*, *The Doll Master*, *Dis Mem Ber*, and *Night-Gaunts*. In 2018 she was awarded the LA Times Book Prize in the Mystery/Thriller category for her novel *A Book of American Martyrs* and in 2019 she was awarded the Jerusalem Prize for her lifetime achievement in literature. She has been a member, since 1978, of the American Academy of Arts and Letters and in 2018 was inducted into the American Philosophical Society.

• "The Archivist" is an adaptation of a section of my novel *My Life as a Rat,* which had its genesis in a short story titled "Curly Red," originally published in *Harper's,* in a very different form. In the short story, I was exploring the commingled guilt and hurt of a young woman who had been exiled from her family, for having (reluctantly) informed upon her older brothers, who'd participated in a hate crime; in the novel, I am exploring the psychology of exile, the assimilation of guilt by the victim who, if she is victimized again, as in the story "The Archivist," will not defend herself but accept further punishment as deserved, and will not inform upon her abuser. It is often wondered why victims of sexual abuse don't report their abusers, and in "The Archivist" it is clear to us that the teenage girl-victim identifies more definitively with her abuser than with those adults who might wish to help her—because she considers herself guilty, deserving of punishment. But "The Archivist" is also an exploration of the culture that averts its eyes from abuse, in this case shielding a flagrant bully/abuser who happens to be a high school math teacher of quasi-popular status.

Brian Panowich feels a bit strange writing about himself in the third person but he will do his best. Brian started out as a firefighter who wrote stories and morphed into a writer who fights fire. He has written three novels, a boatload of short stories, and maintains a monthly column called "Scattered & Covered" for *Augusta Magazine.* He lives in East Georgia with four children who are more beautiful and more talented than anyone else's. He also might be biased. Brian's first novel, *Bull Mountain,* topped the 2015 best thriller list on Apple iBooks, placed in the top twenty best books on Amazon, and went on to win the International Thriller Writers Award for Best First Novel, as well as the Southern Book Prize for Best Mystery. The book was also nominated for the Barry Award, the Anthony Award, Georgia's Townsend Prize, and was a finalist for the LA Times Book Prize. *Bull Mountain* was also selected for the coveted "Books All Georgians Should Read" list by the Georgia Center of the Book, and has been the recipient of several foreign press awards. Daniel Woodrell and C. J. Box really like his latest novel, *Like Lions,* so Brian is pretty happy.

• I remember when my wife and I bought our first home. It was a three-bedroom townhouse that was immediately too small the month after we bought it because she got pregnant with our son, Wyatt—the youngest of our four kids. I was a full-time firefighter at the time and I only worked ten twenty-four-hour shifts a month. I enjoyed my time off. Our first summer in the townhouse I bought a big yellow inflatable pool for the backyard and read a lot of books in a lawn chair while the kids got bigger and bigger right before my eyes. One of those books was a collection of stories by various masters called *Best American Mystery Stories of the Century.* I don't have a clue where I got it from, but it was an old faithful read, and I discovered a lot of authors I'd come to idolize. Tom Franklin's "Poachers" was in that book and it quite literally changed my life—but that's a different matter altogether. The point is, I remember as if it were minutes ago, thinking to myself how amazing it must feel to be included among the writers in that book. I also thought about how far out of reach and impossible it would be for a forty-year-old Elmore Leonard–loving fireman to ever see his name tagged on that wall.

Hey, y'all. Not impossible.

Because here I am, holding the can of spray paint.

Huge bearhug to Patrick Ryan, my editor on "A Box of Hope."

The story was written for my father. I cry every time I read it. I hope he's pleased.

Waiter, more wine, please.

Tonya D. Price publishes both fiction and nonfiction. Her short stories have appeared in *Pocket Book* and *Fiction River* anthologies. She draws on her MBA, high-tech business career, and time overseas at the World Health Organization to write international thrillers. She designed her nonfiction series, *Business Books for Writers,* to help authors who are not business-savvy navigate the serious business of writing. She is currently working on the fourth book in the series. In her most recent novel, a World War II young-adult historical, an American teenager struggles to retain his birthright identity while held as an enemy alien behind the barbed wire of the Crystal City Family Internment Camp. You can find Tonya online at www.tonyadprice.com or on Twitter @BusBooks4Writer.

• When I needed to write a fast-paced story for an anthology submission, I remembered a spring day as I walked to my mailbox at the end of our long driveway. I spotted a large dog running toward me down the middle of our country street. I worried he might get hit, as the street is on a hill with a large blind curve. A blue sportscar raced past me, windows down. Two teenage boys screamed what my grandma would call "bad words" at the dog. I tried to distract them by picking up a softball-size rock from my stone wall. I tossed the stone at them while yelling "Slow down!" The rock landed harmlessly behind the car as it rounded the curve, brakes screeching. My first thought was that the car had hit the dog. A few minutes later I was relieved to see the dog unharmed and hiding in the pines beside our house. When I sat down to write the story, I asked myself, "What would have happened if the rock had hit that car?" I had great fun answering that question, but I have never looked at my house in quite the same way.

Suzanne Proulx is one of countless authors to have published a book entitled *Bad Blood.* In her case that book was the first of a series featuring hospital risk manager Vicky Lucci, which has been translated into several languages. She is a longtime member of Mystery Writers of America, has been a reader for MWA's Edgar Allan Poe Awards, and is the editor of *Deadlines,* the newsletter of the Rocky Mountain MWA chapter.

• I envisioned "If You Say So" as a Valentine's Day story, but kind of a grim one. He has his scenario—who he thinks he is, how he thinks other people perceive him, how he wants her to see him—and of course she has her scenario, and nobody is quite who the other thinks they are. Not at the beginning, and in this case, definitely not at the end.

I had written the first draft when I saw the call for entries from Rocky Mountain Fiction Writers for the *False Faces* anthology. I thought "If You Say So" would be a good fit, and was really excited when Angie Hodapp and Warren Hammond, the editors, agreed.

Ron Rash is the author of the 2009 PEN/Faulkner finalist and *New York Times* bestseller *Serena,* in addition to six other novels; four collections of poems; and six collections of stories, among them *Burning Bright,* which won the 2010 Frank O'Connor International Short Story Award, and *Chemistry and Other Stories,* which was a finalist for the 2007 PEN/Faulkner Award. Twice the recipient of the O. Henry Prize, he teaches at Western Carolina University.

• During the Civil War, Madison County, North Carolina, like most parts of southern Appalachia, had strong Unionist sympathies. When Secession was proposed in 1861, the county voted solidly against it. Once the war began, the county became known as Bloody Madison. In the most notorious incident, Confederate troops massacred thirteen men and boys in the Unionist stronghold of Shelton Laurel, the place where the story is set. But the impetus for "Neighbors" was contemporary events, and those who are caught between allegiance and denial of community.

Amanda Rea lives in Colorado with her husband and daughter. She is the recipient of a Rona Jaffe Foundation Writers' Award, a Pushcart Prize, and the William Peden Prize. Her stories and essays have appeared in *Harper's, One Story, American Short Fiction, Freeman's, The Missouri Review, Kenyon Review, The Sun, Electric Literature*'s Recommended Reading, *Indiana Review,* and elsewhere.

• When my brother and I were children we were told a story about a distant relative who tried to hang us. According to family lore, the young man led us away from our backyard and into the forest, where he was later caught trying to hoist us into a handmade noose. Neither of us were hurt or remember the incident; it remains, for me, just outside the realm of believable. But I have always been intrigued by what the hangman's mother reportedly said when she learned two small children were alone with her son: *We'd better find them quick.* When I started writing "Faint of Heart" there was something about this line, the mystery of it, that felt like an entryway. Still, the story took an appalling number of drafts (and, incidentally, years) to finish, and I'm grateful to Patrick Ryan of *One Story* for giving it a chance, and to Otto Penzler and Jonathan Lethem for showcasing it here.

Duane Swierczynski is the two-time Edgar-nominated author of ten novels including *Revolver, Canary,* and the Shamus Award–winning Charlie Hardie series, many of which are in development for film/TV. Duane has also written over 250 comic books featuring The Punisher, Deadpool, Judge Dredd, and Godzilla (among other notable literary figures). His original graphic novel, *Breakneck*, with artwork by Simone Guglielmini and Raffaele Semeraro, was published in 2019. A native Philadelphian, he now lives in Los Angeles with his family.

• "Lush" was partly inspired by an article I read years ago where a liver specialist tried to estimate exactly how much James Bond drank and came up with something like forty-five drinks per week. (The results were published in the *British Medical Journal.*) It was kind of a miracle that Mr. Bond could tie his shoes, let alone engage in fistfights, daring escapes, and endless sexual dalliances. So I got to thinking: what if a spy *had* to drink? I wrote the story, but couldn't think of anyone who would want it.

Enter Rick Ollerman, who years later asked if I might contribute to his anthology honoring beloved bookseller Gary Schulze, who died from leukemia in April 2016. The only rules: the story had to mention a book, bookstore, or tuba. Of course I said yes (I'm never one to shrink from a challenge, especially when it involves a large brass instrument), and I thought about "Lush."

Blood Work appeared in August 2018, right when my fifteen-year-old daughter Evie was enduring a second round of chemo in her own battle against leukemia. (She would lose that battle on October 30.) I think Evie would have enjoyed this loving Bond parody—we watched quite a few of the Daniel Craig movies together, even though she probably wasn't old enough. Every December my wife and I host a book drive in Evie's honor, something Gary Schulze no doubt would have appreciated. I just haven't found a way to work in a tuba. Yet.

Robb T. White was born, raised, and still lives in Northeast Ohio. He made it to China once but has been content to remain in his backyard with garden and hammock. He has published several crime, noir, and hardboiled novels and three collections of short stories. He's been nominated for a Derringer, and many of his stories have appeared in crime zines or magazines including *Yellow Mama, Black Cat Mystery Magazine,*

Switchblade, and *Down & Out.* His new hardboiled series features private eye Raimo Jarvi (*Northtown Eclipse,* 2018). *Murder, Mayhem and More* cited *When You Run with Wolves* as a finalist for the Top Ten International Crime Books of 2018.

  • "Inside Man" was a different writing experience for two reasons: first, *Down & Out* editor Rick Ollerman, who accepted the story "conditionally," worked me over in the details, grammar, and word choice until he was satisfied, and we're talking weeks, not days. I don't think the Dead Sea Scrolls received as much critical attention, and for his keen eye, and that story's place in this prestigious anthology, I'm very grateful.

The other reason is that my narrator fits a niche I've tried before to squeeze my other narrating criminals into—and not always successfully. Cold-bloodedness doesn't always work well with the jocular. If it does work here (I defer to the reader), then my ex-con's heist borders on a kind of hopeless, disciplined lunacy that will affect the reader as I intended. Mindful of those readers who like to peruse a writer's notes before taking up the story, I'll say no more about it here.

I suppose, as a crime-fiction writer who turned late in life to writing fiction, I was never tempted by elaborate plots or clever characters. The thrill has always been in a character's self-revelation through a brutally honest introspection in that neutral zone between writer and reader. This also speaks to my natural antipathy to avoid anything remotely "cozy" in my fiction. I made it to page 25 of my one and only Agatha Christie novel (title forgotten over the decades since) before that paperback went flying into the garden, where it did more good as compost than if I'd forced myself to finish it—not finishing a book begun being a lifetime taboo, not easily violated then or now. I think it was Browning who was chided by his wife in a letter for his lack of spirituality, or something similar, and he responded with a line I've regrettably forgotten and won't try to paraphrase. The gist was that we all need an "appreciation" for evil. For that, an unblinking gaze is required. Stories serve as a prism for that. Hard to do in any era but in our time where everything is psychoanalyzed and nuanced, dissected and filtered through a collective and increasingly more delicate sensibility, it's almost impossible to do. Let the shrinks and behaviorists scoff. I deplore academe's desire to eradicate the word *evil* from our consciousness.

Genre fiction also gives us something besides entertainment and is worth the effort Rick Ollerman and every good editor or publisher demands. Besides, unless I'm wrong about anthropology's origins, the more violent chimpanzees came out of the trees first, not the gentler bonobos, those sexualized apes from the simian tree. I place my hope in the future of humankind there—in the heavens, the Milky Way, to be precise. If there really are a hundred billion stars swirling about the black hole in the center, then about half should be surrounded by planets, as the astronomers tell us. That increases the odds mightily that there might really be intelligent, civilized life in the universe. It's just not down here very often.

Ted White began his writing career as a jazz critic, writing for *Metronome* magazine in 1960. Since then he has been a science fiction writer (more than a dozen novels, many short stories) an editor (assistant editor of *The Magazine of Fantasy and Science Fiction* for five years; editor of *Amazing Science Fiction* and *Fantastic Stories* for ten years; editor of *Heavy Metal* for one year; editorial director of *Stardate* for one year), an agent (at the Scott Meredith Literary Agency, then solo), an FM radio deejay, and a musician (winds and keys) still currently in a band, Conduit. He has lectured at the Smithsonian Institution. He is currently the copy editor of the *Falls Church News-Press*, a local weekly.

• This is one of my favorites among the stories I've written recently. I was most active as a writer in the 1960s and 1970s, but returned to short stories in 2013, essentially in retirement from the mundane jobs I'd held for the previous two decades. Nikola is a character with whom I fell in love when I wrote this story. I admire her literacy and her guts. She lives alone in a grim world, but she's a survivor.

Other Distinguished Mystery Stories of 2018

ALLYN, DOUG
  Big Blue Marble, *Ellery Queen Mystery Magazine*, May/June
BOURELLE, ANDREW
  Gentleman's Exit, *Pulp Adventures*, Issue 29
BRACKEN, MICHAEL
  Itsy Bitsy Spider, *Tough*, April
BUTLER, ROBERT OLEN
  The Hemingway Valise, *Bibliomysteries*, The Mysterious Bookshop
CEBULA, MICHAEL
  The Gunfighters, *Mystery Weekly Magazine*, April
DEAVER, JEFFERY
  The Christmas Party, The Mysterious Bookshop
DEVERELL, DIANA
  Payback Is a Bitch, *Fiction River Pulse Pounders: Countdown*, ed. by Kevin J. Anderson, WMG Publishing
EARDLEY, B. J.
  Not a Mother, *False Faces: Twenty Stories About the Masks We Wear*, ed. by Warren Hammond and Angie Hodapp, RMFW Press
FORTUNATO, CHRIS
  The Boot Scraper, *Literary Yard*, June
GATES, DAVID EDGERLEY
  A Multitude of Sins, *Alfred Hitchcock Mystery Magazine*, January/February
KAIDER, DILLON
  It Follows Until It Leads, *Santa Cruz Noir*, ed. by Susie Bright, Akashic Books
KENNEDY, TRAVIS
  Priceless, *Landfall: Best New England Crime Stories*, ed. by Verena Rose, Harriette Sackler, Shawn Reilly Simmons, and Angel Trapp, Level Best Books
KOLAKOWSKI, NICK
  Amanda: A Confession, *Unloaded, Vol. II*, ed. by Eric Beetner and E. A. Aymer, Down & Out Books

THE BEST AMERICAN SERIES®

FIRST, BEST, AND BEST-SELLING

The Best American Comics

The Best American Essays

The Best American Food Writing

The Best American Mystery Stories

The Best American Nonrequired Reading

The Best American Science and Nature Writing

The Best American Science Fiction and Fantasy

The Best American Short Stories

The Best American Sports Writing

The Best American Travel Writing

Available in print and e-book wherever books are sold.

Visit our website: hmhbooks.com/series/best-american